THE RAT KING

JENNIFER M. WALDROP

The Rat King

Cover Design: JV ARTS *(*justventurearts.com*)*

Editing: Casey Harris-Parks, heart full of ink (heartfullofink.com)

Proofreading: Belle Manuel

www.jennifermwaldrop.com

July House Publishing | Your story, your way

www.julyhousepublishing.com

For all the powerless witches out there,
trying to break the curse.

PART I

CHAPTER 1

AVERY

"You're sure he's a king?" I asked, swallowing the knot in my throat.

Naturally, I was skeptical. Who could blame me? Real kings didn't exist anymore. Only figureheads, relics of human history like the Queen of England. As far as I was concerned, the concept of a monarchy was a thing of the past. An oligarchy, sure. The patriarchy, yes, obviously. But in South Beach, a king wasn't a thing unless you counted the Tarpon Kings or Michael Jackson, the King of Pop.

Aunt Esmerelda raised two dark eyebrows as she eyed my reflection in the mirror hanging over the black bathroom vanity we sat before. Her brows resembled little half-moons arching over her deep umber eyes in an almost cartoonish way. She nudged her round reading glasses which were adorned with little silver stars at her temples back into position further up her nose as she spun my stool so I faced her. A little chain that had metal suns and moons every few inches hung down from either side framing her face. That, her signature black lacquered nails, and her belted black dress gave her a classic witchy vibe.

She even had a cool witchy name unlike me. But I wasn't a real witch, so I guessed I didn't deserve one. The magic gene had activated in her and my mother. Mine lay dormant as it occasionally did throughout the matriarchal lineages. I was still an honorary member of the coven, however, and had their protection. I was also subject to their laws, which superseded those of our government, not that they knew anything about the witches, our laws, or traditions. They didn't even know we resided amongst them shaping our lives according to our own priorities,

3

magically bound agreements, and guiding principles, one of which was coven first.

That's how I found myself promised, according to an eighteen-year-old coven agreement with the realm of the warlocks, to wed a king from a plane most ordinary humans didn't know existed.

Aunt Esmerelda flicked a wayward strand of her bottle-red hair out of her face. The rest of her bright locks cascaded in waves down her back as she leaned over the worn marble surface to fish out an eyeshadow compact from my makeup pouch.

"Yes, baby, a real king. We've been over this—"

"A million times, yes, yes. I know." It was true, we had, but it was still hard to believe, and the doubt rose to a crescendo the closer it came to becoming my reality.

I studied my aunt. Something about her usually cool countenance was off. A fine sheen of perspiration appeared over her deep golden brown skin her mixed heritage gave her. She said she and my mother were *melting pot witches* and had a little of many races from around the globe in their heritage, but mainly Afro-Latina. My father was an Irish Catholic man from Michigan with an unruly shock of red hair and unusual amber eyes. All of which resulted in my medium gold coloring and the amber flecks enlivening my muddy brown irises, a trait I played up with cosmetics.

When I called Dad to tell him my plan to leave this plane and marry a king, he murmured, "*That's great honey,*" then something about needing to take my half-sister Kelsey to soccer practice. He gave me an absent, "*Love you,*" and hung up. I wasn't sure he'd even been listening, but it didn't matter. I was used to it.

My mother died when I was barely a year old. Dad fell into a deep depression, and Aunt Esmerelda took over raising me. I saw him occasionally, but he eventually found a new wife, had children with her, and that became his family. I was a reminder of his loss.

Being raised by my aunt, who was a full-blown powerful witch, kind of made up for not having either parent around. She never missed an opportunity to *guide me*, as she'd call her lessons. So, while I didn't have magic, I had a number of other skills. One being an uncanny ability to read people. Or maybe I got that skill from the four years I spent bartending at one of the busiest nightclubs off the beach.

Either way, my aunt's wan skin alerted me to her anxiety level about this hand-off. The spell which would take us to this hidden land took quite a bit of power, but I knew Aunt Esmerelda could do it. And soon six other witches would come who would bind their energy to hers, so they could draw her back to this side of the plane once her work was done.

She noticed me watching her, my gold-flecked amber eyes meeting hers in the mirror. "Don't be nervous, baby. The king will love you." She ran a hand through my ashy locks, twirling a section around one of her ringed fingers. When she dropped the piece, she'd tamed it into a loose beach wave that fell with the other strands to the middle of my back.

"Should I pack a curling iron?" I asked her. "Or will they have those?"

Her thin lips pressed into a frown. "Darling, you will have people to help you with your hair, dressing you, and taking care of your every need. You know this. I don't think a curling iron will be necessary."

"Okay…" I said. "What about my makeup? You said they don't have a Sephora there, and I cannot live without my mascara." To my surprise, the knowledge of our counterparts wasn't much. The planes had been separated as long as anyone could remember, and information rarely passed between them. I supposed our limited knowledge was to be expected.

A warm smile spread across her face, making the apples of her cheeks into tight balls of joy. "I got you a present." Aunt Esmerelda shuffled away, then came back with an elaborately wrapped gift box. She set it on the vanity and motioned for me to open it.

My eyes widened as I opened the package. "Wow." It was as if the Mac counter exploded into the purple quilted travel pouch, which was inside the gift box. Except everything had been taken out of its box or the sealed plastic, which was handy because those little perforations on sticks of eyeliner never came off as easy as the manufacturer intended, but it all appeared new. "This is amazing. Thank you!"

"It gets better," she said. I leaned forward, ready to accept whatever better would be. "Me and some of the other witches have spelled these cosmetics, so they will never expire or need to be replaced."

"Wait, what?" I stammered. "You mean to tell me you could have given me never ending mascara this whole time?"

My aunt chuckled, spinning the little stool I sat upon, so it was facing her once again. She picked up one of my old eyeshadow pallets and nudged my chin lifting my head. I dutifully shut my eyes. Normally, I preferred to do my own makeup, but this would probably be the last time I saw my aunt for a long while, and I knew she wanted to do this for me, so I obliged.

The soft bristles of the crease brush glided over my lid. When they stopped, I peeked to see her go in for another dip into a color called *Sunset Stroll*.

"You know we don't waste our power on such trivial things. But now, with this sacrifice you are so graciously prepared to embark upon for your people, you deserve this gift. To feel like the beautiful and fierce woman that you are. A queen. Look at me dear." I obeyed. Her eyes misted over as she finished and assessed me, decided she was satisfied with her work, and spun me back to the mirror so I could see myself.

I looked good, and I knew exactly what she meant. I'd been groomed over the last three months for this task. As it turned out, queens did more than sit around eating cake and holding little dogs. My coven educated me on history, politics, public speaking, charitable leadership, and, of course, anything and everything that was known about the parallel plane the warlocks ruled, including the mages themselves. Which, sadly, wasn't much.

My brain was filled to the point of bursting. While trepidation was ever-present since our matron came to me with the proposition to complete this transaction for my people, I'd become resigned to it. And besides, didn't every Disney movie watching girl dream of discovering they were a secret Anne Hathaway style princess?

I was going to shoot straight past princess to queen. So, not knowing my future husband, bad. Becoming a queen, hell yeah.

And I would do all of that with a bad ass make-up kit. Maybe women in the world where I was going wore a rainbow of colors on their faces, and I'd finally get to put my stage makeup classes into action from that theater degree at the University of Miami I never completed.

6

I sighed. "It is just a little hard to believe that in a few days, I'll be in a land that not even the most sophisticated military technology can locate, married to a warlock king. He's the warlock, correct?"

"I believe it is the brother who's the powerful warlock king, but he was exiled, from what I understand. King Xavier Helicanus, the warlock's brother, is like you, dear."

I frowned. King Helicanus was like me... without magic. It was impressive that in a land full of mages, this man who would be my husband was able to maintain such a powerful position. A fact which intrigued me.

A light rapt sounded at the door. "Come in," Aunt Esmerelda said.

"Is our virgin sacrifice ready?" Vivian, a quick-witted blonde witch about my age asked, giving me a devilish wink in the mirror to which I rolled my eyes. Sometimes the things that came out of Viv's mouth had me shaking my head.

"I'm not a virgin and this isn't that great of a sacrifice, Viv," I said. And it wasn't, all things considered. The needs of the many outweigh the needs of the few or whatever. I would go, and the coven and all the witches around the world would be safe for another set period. Blah, blah. The thing was, I was looking forward to the adventure, as unbelievable as that sounded. I rolled my shoulders.

"It's not like I'll never see you all again, and I'm happy to do it," I said, as Cara, a tall, true redhead, and the matron of the bunch who I was guessing my aunt had modeled herself after walked into the room. Matilda, a raven haired, olive-skinned witch was a step behind her, followed by the final three. Jade, the youngest of the three, was of African descent. As in her parents were from and still lived in Kenya. Hazel, who, you guessed it, had hazel eyes and mousy medium brown hair, and a quiet disposition. And then there was Tabitha, who had a black pixie cut and a tiny flat nose that literally reminded me of a cat, no joke.

"We're ready," Esmerelda said, ushering me to my feet. The little cottage sat at the edge of the botanical gardens where the witches carved out and spelled this particular clearing for their rituals. It was a short drive from Miami and its major international airport and had convenient parking. Under the thick canopy of the towering tropical forest, the

7

humid, near steamy air and numerous ponds gave it an eerie vibe. Perfect for a modern-day witch's needs.

The cottage itself appeared to the outside world as a gargantuan Sweetbay Magnolia. To us it was something that looked like a home Hansel and Gretel would live in, but with air conditioning. The exterior door curved at the top and had a circular window. Every time I came here, I got the strange urge to order one of those gingerbread house kits and put it together, then promptly eat it, of course.

"Do you think it is going to be more like *An American in Paris* or *Barefoot in the Park*?" I asked as we walked out into the clearing where the moonlight streamed down into it framed by the towering bald cypress trees hovering around its edges.

"More like *Blood Wedding*," Vivian said, and snorted. Esmerelda whacked her arm, and I caught the other woman's smirk out of the corner of my eye.

I tried to ignore the comment, but the twenty-five percent of my mind that was filled with trepidation latched onto it. The play *Blood Wedding* was a tragedy about an arranged marriage and a third character who was the bride's true love from what I could remember. I was quite sure either one or both of the lovers die at the end.

"That is incredibly rude, Viv," I said. "Especially considering the momentous sacrifice I'm making to keep you and all of those children you keep popping out safe." I gave her my own smirk and shot a glance at her swollen belly. "I told you, I expect you to name this one after me."

"But what if it's a boy?" Jade asked, blinking her innocent, dark eyes between us.

"Avery, it is. Either way, Viv. That was the deal," I said.

"Viv wasn't pregnant for like ten minutes and you managed to get her to agree to name her next child after you?" Tabitha asked.

"That's what I heard." Hazel's voice was nearly a whisper.

Esmerelda, Matilda, and Cara shared a look, then Cara pointed a finger toward the sky. The moon had reached its apex, and it was time.

I turned toward my friends. "I expect you to put a hex on Viv if that baby comes out and she names it Frank or something."

We fell into a fit of giggles, even as the older witches urged us into the circle with me and Esmerelda at the center.

"Any final words?" Vivian asked.

I shook my head, latching onto my aunt's arm with one hand. My other tugged at my oversized backpack straps again to make sure it was still there. "Umm, catch you on the flip side?" I hoped it sounded as cool when I said it as that movie I saw.

"Don't ever lose that fire, Avery." Cara began chanting. The other witches joined her, followed last by my aunt.

I wasn't sure if it was the sensation of moving between planes, or the ominous knowing look in Cara's eye that caused my stomach to drop.

CHAPTER 2

AVERY

The weightless sensation ebbed as my feet gained purchase on the pine-needle covered ground. My flats flickered like evaporating static on an old black and white TV set, and I assessed the rest of my form flashing into reality. My world tilted as my equilibrium settled and Esmerelda's hand shot out, wrapping around my arm.

"Steady," she said, before releasing me when she was certain I wouldn't topple over. Metal creaked and my head snapped up to follow the sound.

A tall, *very tall*, brown-haired man stepped out of a maroon carriage which sat on a dirt road, partially obscured by a large copse of spindly pine trees. Long legs carried him over to us, the power he exuded seeming to part the trees as he passed. We'd landed a little off the road, and as he approached, he ran his calculating, green-flecked hazel eyes up and down my frame, frowning.

"She doesn't have magic," he said, observing correctly. He ran his fingers through his shoulder-length dusty brown hair.

Was this my soon-to-be husband? If so, I could work with that. Though his charcoal cloak hung off him like a blanket, the glimpses I caught of the body beneath was powerful as he'd prowled toward us. Muscled, but not too bulky. Strong features, and a displeasure which seeped into his guarded posture. For a man who lacked magic himself, his disapproval seemed rude. Who was I kidding? The dude was hot if you could ignore the judgemental look on his face.

"No," Esmerelda replied. "But the gene is latent in her and will be passed on to her and His Majesty's heirs." She shrugged. "Avery was selected because of that fact, and we agreed the witch we would send was to be of our choosing. The deal was sealed in blood."

I whipped my head toward my aunt. "Blood?" I asked. That was new. And apparently this man was not the king.

She ran her hands up and down my arms, from my shoulder to my elbow. "King Xavier Helicanus is a kind man. He will treat you well," my aunt said, breezing past my question.

Her features were impassive, resolved. A shiver tracked up the length of my spine. I got the distinct feeling there was something she wasn't telling me.

"If you're not him, then who are you?" I asked the man, lowering the heavy pack from my shoulders to the forest floor. Dew gathered on the carpet of pine needles, and I started to lift my bag so the worn black leather wouldn't soak up the moisture when it disappeared in a flash. "My things," I cried, raising my hand to cover my gaping mouth.

"I'm Nighval Helicanus, warlock at your service. Your bag is there." He nodded to the back of the carriage, and a self-satisfied smile split his face at my slack-jawed expression. I'd seen magic my whole life, but not used so casually. "Welcome to Ras alhague," he said, his words dripping with superiority and something else. Agitation? Doubt? Regardless, he clearly thought my aunt and I were beneath him.

Long live the patriarchy. Apparently, it was alive and well in this plane. I didn't even try to stop my nose from wrinkling at the man. But I was to be his ruler, so I shoved down the undignified responses that were bubbling up and extended my hand.

"Pleased to meet you. I'm Avery Plath, like the poet." Nighval's brow wrinkled like he had no idea what I was speaking of.

"Umm..." Aunt Esmerelda hesitated. "They may not have heard of her, dear. Remember, some things are different here than in our plane. Like, for example, warlocks like to flaunt their pow—"

"I think it would be best if you let me explain the ways of our world to Ms. Plath. Don't you think, Esmerelda?"

My aunt gave the warlock a mock-innocent smile. "Of course. Oh..." she said, trailing off. "They are drawing me back home. I must go, my dearest Avery. Raising you has been my greatest honor." She pulled me into her arms. "I know if anyone can save us, darling, it is you." When she pulled away, my eyes widened, and hers filled with tears.

"Wait, I thought *coming here* would save you," I said, as Aunt Esmerelda's form flickered.

"Let your heart be your guide." Her voice trembled in a hopeful, yet decidedly melancholy way.

Hold on. I was fairly certain that line was from a Disney movie. Or maybe it was, let your *conscience* be your guide. Either way, what did my heart have anything to do with it? "Aunt, please. I have questions. Can't you hold them off for a few more minutes?" My stomach turned queasy. I shifted on my feet as I reached for my retreating aunt. Her form flickered again.

She said, sniffling, "I love you, dear," and was gone. Gone.

I was panting as a mild panic gripped me. My aunt was gone, and I was in this sparse forest with this weird warlock man named Nighval, who I could feel waiting impatiently at my back. I scanned my periphery, instinctively mapping out an escape route. But I knew there was no way she'd have left me here with this man if there was any chance he'd hurt me, so I took a deep breath attempting to be rational.

Not a single building in sight. Only the two tracks of well-traveled dirt road running through the forest in either direction, which looked more like what I envisioned the Oregon trail to be than an actual road. The forest itself seemed to be a repeat of the same five pines and the occasional cedar, over and over. The tree species and brisk temperature told me while the plane may be parallel, they weren't overlapping. A shiver shuddered through me, and I hugged myself trying to still my racing heart.

Say I changed my mind... I would totally be screwed. I could follow the road, but who knew how long it would take to reach the nearest city and there appeared to be no other way out. I'd be lost in the forest. I had to rely on the annoyed man stalking back to the carriage. That dependance alone made my skin crawl. Perhaps I hadn't thought this through sufficiently. I sighed. Too late to turn back now. Best to keep my eye on the prize.

As if sensing my tumultuous thoughts, Nighval asked, "Did they not prepare you?"

I turned toward where he was casually leaning against the carriage, which I only now noticed had no horses attached to its front. I guess initially I hadn't noticed since cars didn't have horses, but this thing didn't appear to have an engine compartment either. Warlock magic. Show offs indeed.

"I am completely prepared," I said, feigning confidence I didn't feel. The carriage was suspended between four large rubber wheels, and in the center, there was an open leather bench with a burgundy convertible top-like umbrella arching up over it from behind. The vehicle appeared to be some combination of a vintage horse-drawn buggy and a Ford Model T. In the back, just in front of the two largest wheels, sat my backpack and what looked to be a picnic basket.

He saw me eyeing it, then gave me another assessing look like he was trying to determine how much fuel a woman my size required. "Hungry?" he asked.

I scowled. I was taller than average, had T&A, as we called it in my witchy plane, and I could rock a sequin catsuit like no other. I knew this because a black one was a part of my sexy cat Halloween costume last year, and I raked in more numbers than any of my girlfriends by a long shot.

"I'm not hungry, thank you." When he didn't reply, I said, "Don't you have a king to be escorting me to?" I crossed my arms over my chest and lifted my chin, trying to seem queenly.

A subtle smile played at the edges of his lips as if he sensed queenly was the furthest possibility of how I actually felt. The expression dissolved as quickly as it appeared. He pushed off the carriage, holding out a hand to me, which I begrudgingly took. I tried to hoist myself into it using his hand and the railing, but the damn thing was really high, and unless I hiked up the dress in a very unladylike way, I was going to need more help. Nighval released my hand, gripping my waist with his long fingers and practically shoved me up into the carriage. Momentum tipped me forward, and I stumbled onto the bench, quickly righting myself. How embarrassing. Queens were supposed to be graceful, but I wasn't off to a great start.

Nighval chuckled as he easily stepped up and seated himself beside me. "You have a waist under all that fabric after all." He eyed my cream

linen shift dress. The eyelet design around the neckline and hem, and the delicate ruffle at the sleeve made it understated in a demure way. Elegant and comfortable—that's what I was going for. Perhaps, along with exciting makeup choices, the women here also wore wild outfits.

"What is under my clothing is of no concern to you, warlock." I threaded my fingers on my lap, then turned my head away from him in as haughty a motion as I could muster.

When I glanced back at my escort, his eyes were distant and his hands were moving in a set of tight gestures which reminded me of American Sign Language, but within a more restricted space about the size of a basketball.

He placed his hands in his lap as the carriage lurched forward. Then the trees were zipping past so quickly my head spun, and I had to grip the bench to keep ahold of my bearings.

"How?" I asked.

"Magic." He looked down at me from his side of the bench before flicking his gaze toward the sky.

"Going this fast doesn't exhaust your power?" I was genuinely curious. If my aunt used as much power as I imagined it took to make this carriage go this quick, she'd need days if not weeks to recover.

He kept his eyes forward. "The witch who cursed us was able to keep us from our power with the exception of a few hours during the full moon, so I have plenty."

"And the rest of the time?" I asked, urging him to continue.

He shrugged. "You'll soon see. When we don't have our power, things are *different*."

"How different?" A foreboding tug pulled at my thoughts.

"It's best if you see for yourself."

"At least, tell me something. You told my aunt it was best if I learned it from you."

Nighval sighed, resigned. "The witches molded seamlessly into the modern world from what I understand. Your people's power differs from a warlock's. It comes from the earth, the moon, and external forces. Warlocks' power comes from within, gifted to us by the Goddess, so it is more dependent on the strength of the man and his connection to the higher planes. Warlocks used that strength, before the curse, to run our world."

"And since the curse?"

"As I said, things are different. There hasn't been enough time to advance our society on this side of the plane so you may find things here..." Nighval searched for the word.

"Antiquated," I supplied, which was the wrong thing to say, and I was graced with a sneer.

"They would not be *antiquated* as you say had one of your kind not shut us off from our magic." Nighval's words were seething, and he was clearly pissed at whoever had cursed his people.

I'd never had magic, but based on how the witches in my coven who did loved their power, like it was one of their children, I knew it must be painful to be blocked from it. "So, about this witch curse. Are you going to tell me more about that, or shall I just let my imagination run wild?"

He chuckled, exposing a row of gleaming white teeth which brightened his face considerably. "Let's just say you've been caught up in some family drama."

"Is it bad?" I asked, knowing the answer to the question before he answered.

Nighval gave a dark chuckle. "It's not good, but we have you now and Xavier is determined to give it a try this time. Who knows—maybe he'll have beginner's luck."

I swallowed. "You're not making me feel any better about this." A lot worse, actually.

"Are you sure the witches prepared you, Ms. Plath? Because you don't seem very knowledgeable about why you are here and the task you're up against." There was an antagonistic glint to his eye as he stared at me.

I did not like the condescending tone of his voice. I did not like the way he was looking at me like I was a lost little lamb, even if I was kind of coming across like one, a fact I'd stew on along with the reason later. And I certainly didn't like him implying I wouldn't be able to handle whatever I was about to encounter. Technically, I was a witch, even though the gene was latent, I wasn't afraid of a witch's curse.

"I assure you, warlock, I am perfectly prepared and capable of—" I waved my hand through the air. "—besting any challenge that comes my way. So don't worry. I'll be fine and if I'm meant to break this curse, it will only be a matter of time. All you need to do is sit back and watch."

I gave him a smug smile, wondering about the details of this curse which restricted the magic from this plane to one night every moon cycle. And how somehow breaking this curse would save my people. No problem. I'd kiss the frog or outsmart a sea witch. I was a theater major and knew all the classic tales. Maybe there would be a few bumps along the way, but I had this.

Warm energy from Nighval's gaze bore into me, and I glanced up at him to find him watching me intently, like he could read my thoughts. Warlocks couldn't read your thoughts, right? I narrowed my eyes at him. His gaze skimmed over my face, leaving a trail of heat in their wake. He appeared no more enlightened, so I guessed that answered that.

"You're strong," he said.

"I am," I replied, struck by his observation. His unexpected vote of confidence sent a nervous flutter through me. I was strong, it was true. But still, something about the way he said it made me want to live up to the proclamation.

"That's good because you're going to need to be," he said, and the carriage jolted, slowing.

It came to a stop in front of a massive white castle I took to be Ravsted based on the description the witches had given me. Like the fairytale *Sleeping Beauty*, it was a German countryside castle with spires reaching to the clouds and faded blue roof tiles covering their conical roofs. Larger rectangular shaped buildings sat in the center of the spires and long windows with pointed tops ran along their lengths. Stained glass in varying shades of blue rested inside each one, but some panels were busted or missing.

At the top of a great flight of stairs, two massive wooden doors opened outward. Deep gouges crisscrossed the wood planks like Beast had gotten angry and clawed them in an attempt to escape. Two large gargoyle-like sculptures of mythical creatures stacked on top of each other were positioned on either side. Several of the creatures were missing their stone body parts and rubble was littering the ground. The castle would have been beautiful once, but had fallen into disrepair.

My heart thundered, but I got ahold of it. One, a curse. Two, a crumbling castle. Bad things always came in threes. How did the witches not warn me about this? With each realization the word betrayal flashed through my mind. My own aunt—she couldn't have known. It was inconceivable.

My stomach sank as a soft male voice drew my attention. "You're late."

Both Nighval and I turned in the direction of the voice. A man wearing a deep navy cloak and knee-high black boots was standing on my side of the carriage with an arm lifted up to me. I couldn't see what he wore under the draping piece of fabric, but more importantly, the man was wearing a crown, a gleaming silver band with huge sapphires embedded in the metal. My breathing hitched as I took the king's hand.

The man wasn't bad looking. His flat sandy brown hair was tied back neatly at the nape of his neck, and his light brown eyes glittered with intrigue as he took me in. He wet his smooth-looking cherry-colored lips as his gaze made its way to my face. He was tall, broad shouldered, but his hand felt soft in my hand, unlike Nighval's calloused one. He wasn't as handsome as Nighval either, but I wasn't repulsed by him. Nighval's face held all hard angles and smooth planes, but this man was softer, more rounded and a little ruddy at the tip of his nose and his cheeks.

His smile was kind, as my aunt suggested. He looked like the type of guy you'd meet at a frat party and immediately friend-zone. Pleasant looking, but not hot. As he stared up at me, I decided the king was not number three. I remembered the portraits I'd seen of Henry VIII and counted my blessings. I'd been willing to do this on behalf of my coven regardless of what the king looked like and upon first glance, I could have done much worse. As I savored the relief that washed over me, a church bell gonged once, twice, a third time. The sound was still vibrating through the courtyard where we'd parked the carriage, and I stepped down with the king's help. As I turned to fetch my backpack from the back of the carriage, I came face to face with Nighval.

Stumbling back into the king's chest, my hand flew to my mouth. Nighval wasn't the warlock who'd picked me up from the clearing any longer. He was... he was... *a rat*. Or more specifically, a rat-man. His nose had flattened into his face and the tip was pinkish. Whiskers poked out from either side over smooth cheeks lightly dusted with a fine black-brown fur which made his already angular face even more so. The green in his eyes was gone. They were now more of a burned caramel with the whites no longer visible. His forehead sloped at a deeper angle than it had moments earlier, softening his heavy brow. And his eyebrows were nearly blended into his fur. His medium brown hair was now a flat brown and somewhere between a rats and a man's. The ears which poked out were also a strange combination of the two, human-ish, but more rounded and lined with cream fur similar to peach fuzz. I glanced behind him to see if anything poked out underneath this cloak. No tail, thank God.

He was still recognizable as the man from before, but now I could understand why he told me to wait and see. Had he explained this, I might have thrown myself out of the carriage to spare myself from seeing him cursed like this. At least my future husband was still human—the thought caught in my mind. Bad thing three still loomed before me.

Nighval cleared his throat and held my backpack out to me in a clawed hand. Literally clawed. It was also human like, but instead of five digits, there were four. A tiny pinkie, a thumb and one larger one, like the two middle fingers, were fused together, then a pointer finger. Each was tipped with wicked claws. I didn't take the pack. I could hardly move as a sense of foreboding took root in my chest.

Instead, I looked up at his face again to find his beady eyes drilling into mine. His lips twitched before a grin split them, exposing his teeth, but the front two on the top and the two on the bottom were oversized. It was horrible. And he was watching me take him in—savoring my reaction as if he were enjoying watching my panic rise.

I tore at the top of my dress, the high neckline restricting my airflow. I needed more oxygen, or I was going to pass out. Focus on the facts. *You're going to be a queen... married to a normal human king.* Right? Oh God, I hadn't envisioned my emotional state capable of dwindling quite so rapidly. But there was no way my aunt, my friends, my coven would have sent me here had they known what I would be faced with.

My swirling gut told me the curse affected my future husband, too, but I couldn't bring myself to rip my eyes away from the monster before me to confirm it. I didn't need to. I knew. My mouth dropped open, and I panted as a hot wave of nausea scorched through me, doubling me over. The strong woman I knew myself to be had apparently skipped town, and I was at the mercy of my body's fight or flight response. Another wave of panic hit, and my world tilted. I dropped to my knees, hyperventilating.

Oh, God. No, no, no, no. This wasn't happening. This wasn't how my fairytale began.

"Avery, you're safe," the king said, kneeling in front of me.

Surely, he wasn't cursed, too. My gut had to be wrong. I tilted my head up toward him and screamed.

CHAPTER 3

AVERY

I woke in a large four-poster bed covered with a plush and heavy blanket. Light streamed in through a floor-to-ceiling multi-paned window to my left, and I could see particles dancing in the rays of light. Long green curtains hung from a gold rod that was set across the windows and dust collected on the folds as if no one had bothered to pull them closed in a long while.

I squinted, taking in my surroundings as my memories of the night before flooded back to me. After I'd fainted—that's right, *fainted*—someone deposited me in this room. The bed was soft, and it was in decent repair compared to what I saw of Ravsted from the outside.

Taking a few calming breaths, I tried to make sense of the situation I found myself in. These people were under a witch's curse, apparently some family drama, according to Nighval, that took away their power and turned at least him and his brother, my future husband, into rat-men.

Presumably, once the curse was broken, they'd become human again, and I'd be able to go on about my life as queen as planned with a reasonably attractive husband and a kingdom to rule. And all of that would somehow save my people. From what, I did not know.

Right as I eased into my resolve, welcoming my strong inner goddess back, two rat-women strolled into the room in a very routine fashion, like they'd done this before. The one who appeared to be older, stepped up to the side of the bed and said, "I'm April. That is Alice. We are charged with taking care of you, so if you need anything, please let us know. We're running a bath and will help you get your things in order and get ready for the day. Do you have questions?"

I sat up, blinking, and shook my head, willing my face into a neutral expression. April had a long tuft of hair at the top of her head, which was pulled back behind her ears in a no-nonsense bun. Her jowls sagged and her general appearance was tired. She had a medium build and wore a gray frock with a white apron cinched at the waist. The female she called Alice was younger, quite thin, and wore the same uniform. Her brown hair was in a long braid down her back and she stood behind the other woman, waiting. Their features were so rat-like, it was hard to pick out the distinct human traits that made them unique, and I wondered what they looked like in human form.

The thing that was most notable about them was the scars. They crisscrossed their faces, necks, and exposed arms, presumably from the sharp points at their fingertips.

Alice saw me eyeing them and said in a gentle voice, "Most of them happened soon after the curse while we were still learning to live with our new bodies."

"Oh," I said, not really knowing what to say to that. "Hang on, I do have a question now that you've brought it up. Can you tell me about the curse? I can see what it does, but I want to know what it takes to break it and what that has to do with saving my people. Nighval wouldn't tell me anything." By now, I had ahold of my emotions and planned to force determination into the leading role. I shot them a friendly, open smile.

Alice avoided my eyes escaping into the bathroom and a moment later I heard water running. April winced, but walked over to my backpack, moving it from the floor to a chair which sat in front of a wood desk. She unlatched the leather closures and began emptying it, sorting my things into piles on top of the desk as I watched her from the bed. "She shouldn't have said anything, Miss."

Frustration bubbled to the surface, and I reminded myself to exercise patience. My situation wasn't their fault, but I hated being in the dark. I really wanted to ring the information out of the woman. She looked like, with a little bit of pressure, she would give in. Yet, as I watched her scarred hands work, I knew I couldn't do that to her, when my anger should be directed at a coven of women a plane away or the warlocks who, it seemed, kept this vital piece of information from them.

Even if I was to be queen, that didn't change who I was inherently. I had been someone in the service industry. Someone wealthy men snapped at whenever I took too long to make their drinks. Literally would put their pointer finger and thumb together and snap at me. Occasionally, they would whistle to get my attention and, more often than not, they wouldn't even say hello or make eye contact as they rattled off their orders. We were all but objects to them, and I would not treat these women that way or any of the other castle staff. If that's how things were in this world, that shit was going to change with me as their monarch.

"Okay, April. I will ask His Majesty about it when I see him. Can you tell me how long this curse has been in place?" I asked, because that would at least give me a better sense about the gravity of the situation.

"Hmm," she said. Her chin lifted, tilting to the side slightly. I imagined she was trying to calculate precisely how long it had been, which meant it had been a while. She finally answered, "Sixteen years."

"No, seventeen," Alice corrected, walking back into the room. "She's the seventeenth one. I counted."

April's face knotted up while her eyes moved absently, like she was doing some math in her head. "You're right. I always forget about Madeline."

"Who's Madeline?" I blurted, as alarm bells went off in my mind. She was the seventeenth what? Witch sent here? It couldn't be. And why was I just now hearing about this? The thought made me more than a little anxious.

The women's heads snapped toward each other, and their eyes wide as if they said too much. "We really shouldn't say, Miss. It's not our place."

"Well, you can't exactly give me a teaser like that and then leave me hanging, can you? It's cruel," I said, knowing that I was pushing the limit on what I felt was acceptable considering my position. But after what I saw last night and what I'd just heard, I really had to know. I just had to.

"Madeline wasn't here long. She couldn't handle it, him, really. None of them could," April supplied.

"Who?" I demanded.

"The warlock, but you really need to ask His Majesty about this, Miss. He is a gentle man and very tolerant. But I don't think that he will take kindly to us sharing any of this with you. In fact, I believe we have already said too much." April's insistent tone shut down the follow-up questions her explanation aroused. Namely, what was so wrong with the warlock I'd met that seventeen witches had called it quits? Had I been one witch earlier, I'd have gotten stuck with the man and probably found out the answer firsthand. But somehow I'd gotten lucky and was betrothed to Xavier. The knowledge should have filled me with relief, but that's the furthest thing I felt.

"She's right," Alice said, worrying her lip, exposing her two rat front teeth. It was a horrible visual, but I would not look at them and wince. I would save that for their king. My future husband. Alice continued, "Please don't say anything." Her dark eyes met mine, and I could see the plea in them.

I huffed, throwing off the covers. "Fine, but you owe me," I said, not thinking anything of it. It was something I would say to a girlfriend whenever I played the wing-woman and struck up a conversation with the ugly friend so she could get the attention of the cute one she'd set her sights on. The way the two rat-women tensed indicated to me those words carried a lot more weight on this plane.

I waved my hand through the air as I sauntered into the bathing chamber. It was a modest space with an old timey looking porcelain tub, a toilet closet, and a small sink. I had a feeling I should be grateful for modern plumbing. The women followed me into the steamy room.

The witches warned me that this world would be different, and I was prepared to adjust my expectations. In my plane I had my creature comforts, my little luxuries. Here I had attendants. Two who were currently waiting to attend me. Fortunately, I wasn't particularly modest. Between dancing around in leotards my whole life, string bikinis, and the copious amount of money I spent at the spa on the ground floor of my building, I was used to being nearly naked around strangers. I was determined to let this be something I enjoyed. Aside from the people helping me looking like mutants, this should be normal-ish. I would imagine them as if they were costumed characters like the performers in *Cats* and consider their help a live in spa experience.

A dozen bottles and jars were lined up on a bench awaiting me. They laid fluffy white towels and an even fluffier white robe out along with an adorable pair of slippers with a pair of embroidered eyes, and a nose and little tufted mouse ears sewn onto the top. They probably thought it was cute, but I thought it was sadistically ironic.

"Don't worry. You don't actually owe me. I won't say anything. That's just a phrase that we say where I'm from. Like whenever we do somebody a favor and we're trying to guilt them about it," I explained, raising my arms so Alice could pull my white shift dress off, her fur brushing against my skin. *Don't react*, I scolded myself as I felt my features begin to twist uncomfortably. I redirected my attention to the dress realizing whoever had delivered me to my bed hadn't bothered to remove it. This I was grateful for. The thing was a rumpled mess now, and the linen would need to be cleaned and ironed. That was fine because I noticed there was a whole wardrobe full of brightly colored clothing I was dying to get my hands on.

An hour later, they'd scrubbed, dried, and dressed me in a happy yellow, a-line dress that complimented my warm skin tone. April stood behind me taming my waves into a feminine low ponytail. As her furry fingers brushed against my temples when she smoothed out my flyaways, I didn't flinch. Proud of my fortitude, I grinned at her reflection in the mirror, earning a grin in return. I shifted my head back and forth and praised, "It looks great, April. Thank you both."

The women shared a wary glance as if my compliment was unusual, before curtsying and leaving me at the vanity to tidy the bathroom. Whatever. They'd get used to me and my ways. None of us had a choice. At this point, that was about the only thing I was certain of.

I finished getting ready by applying a minimal amount of makeup. Standing up I gave myself a once-over. My insides might be a jumbled mess, but outside I looked like a ray of sunshine, ready for whatever the day was going to throw at me. Fake it till you make it. I would not scream again, and I would not faint. And I would not give into my festering anger. I knew this wasn't going to be a cakewalk, and I'd almost convinced myself my coven hadn't known the extent of what I'd be facing. That they'd prepared me as best as they could. Anything else was unfathomable. I was ready to be queen. I would rinse and repeat that mantra.

A knock sounded at the door. Alice scurried over to it, and she let a mid-height, narrow rat-man inside. His dark fur was slicked back away from his forehead with some type of gel, and he wore a boxy coffee-colored three-piece suit. The thick white pinstripe and the watch chain draping across his vest made me think we could have been on the set of *The Great Gatsby*. The rat-man gave me a once over, studying me in return.

"Ah, good to see you are ready for the day. I am sorry you experienced quite a shock upon your arrival. Nighval can be," he scrunched his face in disapproval, "abrupt. My apologies. I trust the witches have prepared you, and you are ready to see your future kingdom."

"I am," I said, straightening my spine. I wasn't sure who this man was, but he seemed to hold some authority, and I offered him the respect of meeting his gaze, keeping my expression blank.

"I'm Leviticus, advisor to His Majesty King Xavier Helicanus, and your humble servant. If you need anything, all you need to do is ask." A wry smile tilted Leviticus's rat-lips, and he held his partially human, clawed hand out, gesturing in the direction of the hallway.

"Actually, there is one thing I need," I stated.

"Yes?" he asked.

"I understand there's been a curse placed upon the kingdom which is why I'm here. Is there somewhere I could find more information on that?" When his eyes narrowed, I threw in for good measure, "See, in my plane, we have cell phones and the internet where we can look things up. I mean, you could tell me about it, or point me in the right direction." I gave the advisor my best winning smile. Rat lips curved down into a frown, and I realized Leviticus would not be the one to tell me about the curse.

"Come, Miss Plath," he said, outright ignoring my request.

That really pissed me off. It was one thing to deny it, but to fail to verbally acknowledge what I'd said was incredibly rude. "Really?" I asked, my temper getting the better of me. "At least you could respond out of courtesy."

Leviticus drew in a deep breath and let out a sigh. I could only imagine this wasn't the first conversation he'd had like this over the years, so on one hand, I understood. On the other hand, rude. "I'll recommend His Majesty introduce you to the library, as much information is contained there. You may, of course, speak with him about the current state of affairs of our kingdom, and he may divulge as he wishes." He gave me a reluctant smile that was more of a grimace and gestured toward the hallway once again.

"Thank you," I said, only borderline pleased with his intentionally vague answer. In the few short minutes of knowing him, I was getting the impression he'd make a great politician in my plane.

Still, it was better than a no and if I couldn't get Xavier to tell me about the curse, which seemed to be the trend thus far with everyone I'd met, maybe I could discover what I needed to know in the library. It had been going on for long enough there ought to be some sort of record about it and where else would that be kept than a royal library? It made perfect sense to me. Knowing that by the end of the day I might be able to discover it and at least know what I was dealing with lightened my heart and my steps as I headed for the door.

I gave a quick once over to my room, which I had a feeling was going to become my safe space and followed Leviticus out into the hallway leaving April and Alice to finish their work. Exposed cords draped down the stone wall and every so often a light bulb in a little metal cage illuminated the corridor. It was like they had gotten the technology, but hadn't taken the time to run the electrical wiring through the old building, or try to disguise it like I had seen in some of the old castles I'd visited during my study abroad course a few summers ago.

Leviticus ushered me into the first open room. Like my suite, it was on the exterior wall and had huge windows, some of which were cracked open to let the breeze come through. There was a fireplace twice the size of mine with soot and a few extinguished black coals in it. It looked like it hadn't been used in some time.

"This sitting room is available for you to use whenever you like. Just notify your attendants and they will order a fire to be readied for you. Go on, look around," he said, nudging the small of my back so I had to take a step forward into the room.

Mirroring my rising dread, raindrops pattered on the thin glass. I noticed there was a guard shadowing us and neither he nor Leviticus bothered to close the windows. Water droplets ran inside them and pooled on the wooden planked floor below, which was already stained dark from previous rains. If Leviticus noticed me staring, he didn't let on.

I made my way around the room, running my fingers across the wing back chairs which sat in front of the fire, their upholstery worn at the edges and much of the hunter green brocade rubbed away.

The red and cream handwoven rug at my feet also had dark stains, burgundy in color, and places that looked like they had been stomped with muddy boots and only haphazardly cleaned. I made my way across the room to the wall, which had full floor to ceiling cabinets and shelves. A thick layer of dust coated everything on the shelves, including the shelves themselves.

The objects which sat upon them were interesting, however. A clock which no longer ticked and had two big arms coming out from either side of it that held half melted candles, a ceramic figure of a red-eyed bull looking creature which seemed like something out of a Roman myth, a glass vase dotted with all the colors of the rainbow that started out fat at its base and came to a delicate point at its opening. In it was a single dried hydrangea stem, its large flowering head dwarfed its container.

It was like after the curse they'd given up and that made my heart ache. Turning to Leviticus, who was waiting patiently at the doorway, I said, "Where to next?"

He gave me a pleased smile. I decided if I was going to live in this castle, the first thing I was going to do would be to see this room getting a thorough cleaning, even if I had to do it myself. Maybe I'd even get some new furniture. I was queen, after all, and from what the witches had told me, the crown wasn't lacking in funds.

As we moved through different rooms, the rain increased, and I could hear it pounding down onto the roof of this sagging building. I caught glimpses of the gardens outside through the windows. They were another thing in this castle that was unkempt, but they seemed unruly in their beauty, and I was dying to get out amongst the blooming flowers. I never had much of a green thumb, but considering I had to give up my cell phone coming here, I needed a new hobby. Surely somebody here knew how to keep a garden and could teach me.

Leviticus ushered me in through another room. "You will take breakfast in your apartments, but your other meals will be had here." My eyes widened, and he seemed pleased by my reaction. The room was enormous. Ridiculously enormous for a dining room for me alone or even me and the king. At least it was clean. It was probably the cleanest room we'd been to so far.

A long table sat in the center, and a heavy red tablecloth ran down the middle. At the far end there were two place settings and a knot of dread cinched tighter in my stomach. A doorway stood open behind it and when I allowed my eyes to rest upon it, he was there. Xavier Helicanus, the rat king.

My feet had a mind of their own as they took a step backwards. Then another. I bumped into the hard chest of my guide. His hands caught my shoulders, and he urged me forward. "I will leave you with His Majesty. If you should need anything, please do not hesitate to ask." He paused, frown returning as he turned toward his king. "I promised Miss Plath to recommend she be introduced to the library. She wishes to learn about our plane." Leviticus gave Xavier a pointed look, then bowed before exiting the room, leaving me alone with the man I was meant to marry.

CHAPTER 4

AVERY

S eeing Xavier for the first time in the daylight I was able to get a good look at him in this form. His fur, including the hair at the top of his head was a medium brown-grey and pulled into the same man-pony he wore the night before. Without the heavy cloak, I saw he was softer than I perceived initially. He didn't wear a suit like Xavier. Instead, he wore slacks that sat low on his hips and a thin grey sweater that clung to his wide shoulders and concave chest.

His expression, like it was last night, was bright as he took me in. "Very well. I will make it my first order of business once we've finished lunch. I see you've recovered from your shock last night. How are you feeling?" He leaned forward clasping his hands in front of his chest putting his eagerness on full display as he made his way from the doorway to the table.

"Hello, Your Majesty. I'm fine, thank you." My voice cracked feebly. My strong inner goddess was fleeing again, damn the bitch, so I grabbed her by the hair and demanded her participation before she could fully make it out the door.

He gestured to the place setting at his right at the head of the table. "It's only Xavier between us, my bride. Join me," he said.

I forced my legs to move though the word *bride* was currently clogging my thoughts. I wanted this, I reminded myself. Not exactly this, but still it had been a dice roll regardless. I forced a grin and sat in the chair he held out for me. An uncomfortable silence blanketed the room until attendants brought out dishes laden with decent smelling food, dishing out multiple heaping servings onto our plates. As I sat with the unfortunate reality of my situation twisting my stomach, I wasn't sure I'd be able to eat. Normally I wouldn't turn down a meal, but I hadn't geared myself up for eating with this rat creature in my periphery so soon. And I was doing so well up until this point.

Xavier cleared his throat, pushing up the sleeves of his sweater as if he were preparing to dig in. "I want to apologize about my brother. It was cruel of him to expose you to our curse like that. I hoped he would deliver you from the meeting point sooner so I could have prepared you before the reprieve ended." He shook his head as he picked up the knife and fork which sat on either side of his overfilled plate.

"It was our fault. We were running late because I wanted to make a good impression. I took too long to get ready. What is the reprieve?" I unfolded my napkin, placing it in my lap. I supposed I needed to force myself to at least attempt to eat.

Xavier seemed to get lost in his thoughts for a moment. "The hours of the full moon where everything goes back to normal. The warlocks get their power back and we become human again. I look forward to our time together on those nights, and I assure you, I'll treasure the memory of the first time I saw you stepping down from that carriage." He hesitated, and a guilty expression sprouted across his rat-human features. "The truth is my brother could have used his power to deliver you to me directly. He had no need of the enchanted carriage to get you to Ravsted."

My attention snagged. "Oh?"

"He can be rather *challenging*. Brutal really. I only keep him around because he's... useful," Xavier explained, carefully selecting his words.

"But he's your brother," I said.

Xavier frowned. "I was seventeen the first time I saw Nighval slit someone's throat. Eighteen when he used his power to exercise his *justice*. When our father died and he took the throne, the power went to his head." He leaned toward me conspiratorially. "I cautioned him to rule with a gentler hand, but he was so bloodthirsty, no one could control him."

"If he is so dangerous, why did you send him to collect me?" I asked, narrowing my eyes at him. Based on what he said it was a terrible judgement call.

"I'll admit that was my mistake. And I didn't mean to worry you. I assure you that you are perfectly safe here. He wouldn't dare hurt you. Now, why don't we enjoy our lunch and move on to lighter topics?" he asked. "Have you thought much about our wedding?"

I didn't know what to think. My future husband had permitted me to ride alone through a dark forest with a maniac capable of Goddess knew what only to call it a mistake and brush it under the rug. A chill of what might have happened swept over me, and I had to suppress a shiver. Now he expected me to talk about our wedding as if I shouldn't be rattled by what I heard seconds ago.

Xavier however seemed nonplussed as he dug into his plate. With each bite, he plucked it from his fork with his two enlarged front teeth, then sucked it back into his mouth, closing his lips around it. The strange tick seemed to consume all his attention and it took him a few moments to notice that I hadn't picked up my fork. His eyebrows wrinkled as he regarded me.

"If this isn't to your liking, I can easily have something else prepared for you. I want you to be comfortable here. And I want you to know that pleasing you is my number one goal." He gave me a soft smile like he pleased himself with the words, and I gulped down the knot in my throat.

Picking up my fork, I stabbed a few pieces of boiled potatoes, putting them into my mouth. With the amount of green herbs on them, they probably tasted delicious, but only stale sawdust played across my tongue. My stomach lurched as I swallowed. Why did he have to eat like that? Just the sound alone... I needed to get it together. I was being incredibly rude, and I knew it. It probably wasn't his fault they were cursed. I gritted my teeth as my eyes closed, and I took a deep breath. I opened them with resolve, stabbed another bite of the potatoes, and forced myself to eat it.

Eventually, the food's flavor returned and while it wasn't the greatest thing I had ever eaten, it wasn't bad. It was food that I would typically imagine in my plane as fit for a holiday dinner, but I guessed this was lunch here. As Xavier said, I could work on that. If I wanted something lighter, like greens or a chicken salad, they probably had the ingredients to make it. I just needed to tell them what I wanted.

I glanced up to find Xavier watching me. Reaching for my goblet, I took a sip of the water. "How do you find it?" he asked.

"It's good," I replied. "Honestly, it's a little heavy for what I would typically eat for lunch, but the flavor is nice." I gave him a halfhearted smile, and he seemed pleased with that, too. Something about his demeanor, the smug set of his jaw, annoyed me.

"I will have Leviticus arrange for you to meet with the cooks, and you can instruct them on what you would prefer to eat for lunch. And, of course, any other meal you prefer," he said. "I'm not picky."

His hand moved in the direction of mine, which gripped my discarded napkin on top of the table to the side of my plate. My breath caught. He wanted to touch me and that was the last thing I was prepared for. Just the idea of the soft pink pads of his fingertips grazing against my skin sent a revolting shiver down my spine. Releasing the napkin, I slid my hand into my lap where it clasped the other.

"I need to ask you something," I blurted, trying to divert the attention away from his intended action and before he could bring up the wedding which he seemed to have forgotten again.

His lips pressed into a line, but he nodded. "I figured you'd have questions."

"I hope this doesn't come across as insensitive, but I recognize a curse whenever I see it," I said, letting him assume I'd neither discussed it with Nighval or my attendants. "The blood of witches runs in my veins, and I spent my life around them. What has happened to you?" I tried to make my tone sympathetic, but I feared the bitter edge of my disgust shown through. How did Belle do it? I could hardly make it through our first lunch without my discomfort rearing its ugly head.

Like he was expecting it, he gave me a grim smile. "Ah, yes. Your assessment is correct. Many years ago, we were cursed, but that isn't something I want you to worry about. I will give you time to adjust and to get to know me before we say our vows. Speaking of," he said, and I tensed. I'd been sitting here, bracing for when he decided to bring up the wedding again. "I've been giving a lot of thought to our ceremony. I envisioned it to happen the full moon after your arrival, but now I'm thinking you might require a little more time to adjust."

It felt as if someone opened a window. "Yes, that would be great. You are so kind to offer that. I..." I stammered, before collecting myself. I needed time to get used to the idea of the reality of my situation, and I couldn't let this opportunity pass me by. "I wish to get to know you, of course, before we say our vows." I fluttered my lashes sweetly at him, hoping he'd buy it.

He studied my face for a painfully extended moment. "Then I will look forward to each full moon when you are able to see the man that I am instead of this cursed thing. We can settle on a date later."

Like he didn't want the conversation to continue, he rose, helping me from my seat. "Come. Let me show you the library. Do you enjoy reading?" This time I couldn't avoid the hand he wrapped around my wrist. His fingers were gentle as he placed my hand in the crook of his elbow waiting for my response.

"Yes, I do. That would be lovely," I said, resisting the visceral urge to snatch my hand away. Resigned, I held on and followed him out.

As Xavier guided me through the castle, he pointed out paintings of his ancestors, historical artifacts that lined the walls, and various rooms Leviticus hadn't gotten to show me earlier. And this was only a small portion of the sprawling complex that was Ravsted. A few hallways later, we arrived at the library, and he released me, ushering me into the room with his hand on my shoulder. Like everything else here, the lack of upkeep gave the place a dank and dismal quality.

"Where's the librarian?" I asked, running the tip of my finger along the nearest shelf. My nose wrinkled as I wiped the thick layer of dust on my dress. Had the curse somehow caused these people to forget how to clean? I mean, becoming a cursed being was awful, but that was no excuse for the state of the castle in my mind. Someone needed to do something. Fortunately, I was never one to shy away from a little work.

"Well, I don't know, Avery. There hasn't been a librarian here in years." He scanned the room as if he were trying to see what I saw.

Xavier looked like he was about to say more, but I stopped him, saying, "Actually, it's no problem. Only curious." Yep, that furthered my resolve. First, the library, then the sitting room. Then I'd see about the rest of this place.

My hopeful features must have been giving away my newfound mission because Xavier said, "I see this pleases you."

Not exactly, but I had to start somewhere. "Sure."

"Good. With that, I'll leave you to enjoy the library until dinner." In a swift motion, he raised my hand to his lips and brushed a kiss onto the back of my hand that had dread unfurling in my stomach. The door clicked shut behind him as Xavier departed. I slumped against the end of the nearest bookshelf and drew in a few deep breaths. What about him was causing such a strong repugnant reaction? If I was going to be married to the man, I had to figure it out because despite everything, I was determined to go through with the wedding.

A dark chuckle sounded from the end of the row like the man emanating it was once again reading my thoughts. I spun to find Nighval leaning a shoulder against the end of a perpendicular shelf, partially shrouded in shadows. He turned a burgundy leather bound volume over in his hands as he observed me. The warlock was such a contrast to Xavier. Where the king turned my stomach, something about Nighval in his rat form terrified me. It must be my base instinct reading him and considering the guarded conversation with my attendants earlier, it wasn't far off. Then there was Leviticus's comment. *"Nighval can be... abrupt."* I got the sense that he had more to say on the topic of the exiled king, but was refraining.

I pushed off the shelf and turned toward him. "What do you find so humorous, warlock?"

"You and my brother," he said, not missing a beat. "He seems excited about you."

The words themselves were encouraging, but I sensed their mocking edge. "It's none of your business."

I kept my chin high as he stalked out of the shadows, running the tips of his claws, which appeared to be encased with pewter colored metal caps, down the row of books. Each thump between volumes made my heart jump, so when he finally passed me, my heart was in my throat.

I tried to keep my expression passive as he paused, eyed me over his shoulder and said, "You won't find the answers you're looking for here."

The man was a solid head taller than me, maybe more. Intimidating was an understatement. I swallowed a lump and asked, "How do you know what I'm looking for?"

A grin spread across his face, exposing the elongated sets of teeth, and I felt my skin pale. "Wild guess." He winked before turning and sauntering toward the door.

"Where will I find answers, then?" I shouted after him.

He didn't turn around again, but said, "I'd start with your betrothed. Don't you think he owes you that much?"

"I tried to ask him, but he won't tell me. Can't you just tell me?"

"And why would I do that?" When I couldn't come up with an answer, he continued, "Pressure him enough and he'll break. He does so very much want to please you." Something about his sly tone gave me the impression that he would enjoy knowing I was pestering his brother for answers he made clear he had no intention of giving me.

"Thanks," I said, muttering the word under my breath. I knew it. I had to get Xavier to talk. And why was the exiled former king roaming about the castle freely? Especially if he was supposedly a dangerous man. I lifted my hand from the table I'd leaned on to steady myself. Dust coated my palm, and I let out a frustrated breath. One thing at a time.

CHAPTER 5

AVERY

A week later, and I'd made it through half of the library. The space was deceptively large like the rest of the castle and easy to get lost in, as I'd done in the enumerable hallways a few times since my tour the first day. At least the library seemed to have some organizational plan which governed it. I'd been tackling one stack at a time, taking care to pull every volume and wipe it down before replacing it.

Footsteps clipped across the stone floor as Alice hefted in a fresh mop bucket. April followed behind her with some clean rags and set the bundle on the table I'd cleared in the center of the room. The table beside it held piles of books that had been shelved in the wrong location I planned to deal with later. I found ledgers next to spellbooks and fiction in the non-fiction section. I doubted they had the Dewey Decimal system here, and I wasn't a librarian by any stretch, but that would not do.

"Did you see about getting a ladder?" I asked her, getting to my feet. I'd just reshelved the books on the bottom row of the stack I was working on when they came in.

"Leviticus said he'd ask His Majesty for approval first. I don't think he liked the idea of you getting on a ladder," April said.

"Then how else am I going to clean the windows?" I asked, putting my hands on my hips.

As if summoned, Xavier stomped into the room. "What's the meaning of this? And why does Leviticus tell me you require a ladder?"

A grinning Nighval and another very large light-furred rat-man with the same dark eyes they all had in this form were on his heels and stopped to hover over the king's shoulders. Voyeurs, no doubt, and I wondered if the second man was a Warlock, too.

I'd been asking about the curse at each meal I shared with my intended since Nighval had given me the thought, but Xavier hadn't budged. The new rat-man leaned over and whispered something in Nighval's ear that had them both chuckling and Xavier tapping his foot as he stared me down.

I glared at all three of them. "I'm cleaning, obviously." I waved my hands around the sparkling half of the library.

"But you are to be my wife, the queen. Cleaning is beneath you, and I won't have it," Xavier said.

"Excuse me?" I replied.

Xavier, seeming to recognize he'd overstepped, stilled his foot. "What I meant to say is I have people who can do this for you. If you wish for a task to be done, all you need to do is mention it. There is no need to trouble yourself. It is my desire to take care of you, my bride."

My teeth clenched at the pet name he'd taken to calling me. The lighter furred rat-man rolled his eyes, mirroring my sentiment. "Since no one cares to divulge what's going on here with the curse and what exactly needs to happen to break it, this gives me something to do, something I can control. Unless someone feels like sharing?" I squared my shoulders showing him I wasn't budging.

The tip of Xavier's rat-nose and the insides of his furry ears reddened as he said, "May I please have a moment alone with my intended?"

April and Alice didn't hesitate before scurrying from the room. Nighval and his friend turned to leave the room, but as they did, Nighval clapped a hand on Xavier's shoulder and said something in a hushed tone that sounded like, "Don't lose control, brother. An entire kingdom is counting on you."

I repressed a groan. The last thing I needed was Xavier feeling any more pressure than was already placed on him, namely because that might hasten our nuptials, and I was still getting used to the idea of being wedded to one of these creatures. We hadn't discussed a wedding date yet, and that was fine by me. Especially since no one would tell me how I could help turn them back human again.

Xavier pulled out a chair and beckoned me to sit. As I did, he dragged a chair beside it and sat so we were facing each other. He held upturned hands out to me, and I reluctantly placed mine in his. The moist, pink pads of his thumbs brushed over my knuckles which were dry and cracking from a week of scouring years' worth of grime away.

He frowned as he studied them, before meeting my eye. "There is no need for you to suffer like this. I was under the impression you were spending time in here reading. Imagine my surprise when Leviticus informed me my bride was performing manual labor."

"But truly, Xavier, I don't mind getting my hands dirty. I enjoy workin—"

"If you need to occupy your time, you can see about making the final arrangements for our ceremony. Then there is, of course, the management of the castle staff. I didn't want to overwhelm you when you first arrived. You were quite shocked, but now I see that you are ready to take on more. I'll have the senior housemaid arrange a meeting."

I shifted uncomfortably in my chair trying to recall the list of castle staff I learned and where precisely in the pecking order a housemaid would fall. "If I'm to be in charge of running the Ravsted, shouldn't I be meeting with the steward, or is there not one?"

Xavier placed my hand on top of the other still cradled in his and gave mine what I took to be a condescending pat. "Leviticus manages the steward."

"Then I'll deal directly with Leviticus."

An exasperated sigh escaped my future husband. "That won't be necessary. Please, Avery. Try to enjoy the life I'm offering you. You're safe here and anything you request is at your fingertips, including my heart." I gasped at his confession, and he chuckled. "It's true, my bride. I'm already beginning to care deeply for you."

Oh my. On the surface level, one might interpret the words as sweet, but his tone was decidedly self-indulgent. Like he was proud of how smooth he believed himself to be. Yuck.

"Okay," I said, edging back in my chair until I could twist to get my hands out from between his clammy palms. I hopped to my feet. "Thank you?" I should be happy the man was developing feelings, but it had only been a week. No, that wasn't it. There was just something off-putting about Xavier Helicanus. At this point, none of the other rat-people seemed to weird me out like he did, so that wasn't it. It was something else.

"Listen," I said. "You're right. I'm still a little overwhelmed. I think I'm going to head back to my room and take a nap. Definitely send the head maid, though." I gave him a weak smile and rushed from the room. The man sent my thoughts scrambling and not in a good way. Despite that, I knew one thing to be true. I wasn't the type to sit around and be waited on, and I certainly wasn't going to let this man stop me from fulfilling this role exactly how I intended to. He'd figure that out soon enough, then we'd see about his feelings.

I'd gotten myself lost again as I escaped Xavier and his feelings in the library. It flabbergasted me that he thought his approach might be effective, but that was typical with overconfident men.

How long had I been wondering around this time in this expansive building? At least half an hour. I came to an intersection of two dimly lit hallways I didn't remember having come across previously. The one to the right was empty save for a few flickering lights haphazardly strung down the length of the ceiling. A rat-woman in a high waisted pea-green colored gown was locking a door in the other hallway to the left. I stepped toward her and she started.

As I crossed the distance between us, she fingered an auburn tuft of hair as if my presence made her uncomfortable though I had no idea why that would be the case. Unless she were doing something she shouldn't be. I ignored her body language, pressing ahead. "Hi. I'm Avery."

I didn't think I'd seen her around Ravsted before, granted most everyone I saw were either advisors or castle workers. By her elegant clothing and the lifted way she held her chin, I didn't take her to be either of those. Perhaps she was some type of Lady. Maybe an advisor's daughter. She was young enough, but that didn't explain why she had a key to a room in the castle.

"I know who you are." Her eyes narrowed, skipping to the hallway behind me. "I'm Olive," she finally supplied. "I was just leaving—"

"Do you live here?" I asked, not releasing her. That had to be it. Maybe she was a lover of Nighval's and had followed him here from his exile.

Her lips twitched like she was trying to force them into a smile, but they wouldn't cooperate. "I'm staying here now."

Her ambiguous answer aggravated me. Had she met and been like this with any of the witches who'd come before me? Would she tell me? I clearly didn't have enough to do because I was actively grasping, spinning stories to keep myself occupied.

Footsteps sounded behind me. I turned to see the warlock in question saunter past giving me and Olive a curious, somewhat unpleasant look before continuing on. Had his posture stiffened? Perhaps she wasn't his lover then.

I turned around to see her eyes had gone almost comically wide. She feared him.

"What is it? Do you know about him?" I assumed she, like everyone else, knew about the exiled warlock former king. But maybe if she felt enticed to gossip, she'd let something about the curse slip. Then I could get her to tell me about it.

She hesitated for a moment, then stole a glance down the hallway as if she was checking to make sure no one was within earshot. "I try to avoid him. I'd do the same if I were you."

"Why?" I pressed.

A faraway expression crossed her features as she dipped into a memory. "He's lethal. During the reprieve, his power goes unchecked. He could do anything. That's what we fear now that His Majesty has taken the throne. That the warlock will snap and do something awful." She took a deep breath and seemed to gain her composure as something calculating drifted across her features. Then her gaze locked on mine as if she wanted to impress upon me what she was about to say. I leaned forward, welcoming it.

Seeing that she had my full attention, she whispered, "I heard he slaughtered an entire cult a few years ago because they didn't follow the Goddess. He killed over thirty people in cold blood. I'm surprised he hasn't tried to steal you away to get back at his brother. You should be careful." She held the key between two clawed digits, slapping it into the palm of the other hand. My heart seemed to catch its nervous rhythm.

I wanted to know more. I *needed* to know more, but she was bouncing on the balls of her feet now seeming eager to get away from me. "Perhaps we could have tea sometime? I feel like I could learn a lot about this plane from you." If I flattered her enough, maybe I could get her to talk. Olive, however, looked horrified at the suggestion of tea.

A light set of footsteps approached. I glanced over my shoulder to see April swishing towards us down the hallway. "Ah, there you are. His Majesty sent me after you."

"Yes, I got lost." Damn it. I felt like I was finally getting somewhere only to be interrupted. When I turned back, a relieved looking Olive was dropping into a curtsey. "Good day." As she left, I could have sworn I heard her mutter, "*As if you'll last.*"

CHAPTER 6

NIGHVAL

Link and I stepped into Xavier's office to find him sitting at his desk with his neck craned over a document. A week passed since he charged into the library ready to reprimand his future queen. I had fully expected the vein in his forehead to burst when Leviticus informed him of what she was up to. Whatever transpired between them after he sent us away considerably lightened his mood. He tapped his pen on the desk as he glanced up toward us, grinning.

"What are you doing?" I asked, my eyebrows arching in curiosity. The man never approached his actual duties with such interest.

"I'm working on my wedding vows," he said.

I stifled a groan.

"Would that explain why Sir Richard Musson is still detained?" Link asked. "I was supposed to bring him back to Belfield during the reprieve."

Link was right. Using his power during the reprieve to return Musson to his wife and two sons on the estate on the opposite side of the kingdom made sense. He was disloyal, edging on treasonous in recent months and the sentiment seemed to seep off him. The last thing we needed was him to take a cross-kingdom trip sprinkling it as he went. I should have dealt with him sooner. But if it didn't directly affect Xavier directly, he didn't care. And by his disgruntled expression, my brother looked like he wanted to reprimand Link for his tone. Fortunately, he'd quickly learned to strike a balance with the Council of Warlocks. Link, our other friend Eshan Moltentide, and I had grown up together, and Xavier would forever be the annoying little brother to us.

"Richard can wait, what I'm doing is far more important than flexing my power, Nighval. I have a curse to break, and since my bride has learned of it, she's made quite the effort to get to know her future husband." Xavier grinned as he reclined back in his burgundy leather chair as if the words alone were enough to prove his point.

They were enough to get on my nerves. This was how nearly every conversation with him went. I'd point out something that needed to be dealt with, but he'd find some way to spin the conversation and let me know he disapproved of my ways. It was ridiculous. I never flexed my power without reason, and I'd been a far better king in all aspects but the one.

The fact that he did seem to be making progress with the witch grated on me more than any snide remark ever could because her defiant tone that day in the library gave me the impression that what he said was true. She seemed like the type of woman who'd put her best effort into a task, despite the futility of it, just to say she'd given it her all.

"Just let me execute him and be done with it. The man is incapable of reform. It's come to my attention his law-flaunting sentiment is leaching out from Belfield and affecting his neighbors," I said, letting my tone speak for itself.

Musson was a problem. He'd always been, but now that my brother was in charge, he'd grown bolder. I'd reviewed the ledgers. The last time he paid his taxes was when I was still king. Two of his neighbors were now delinquent and the rumor was he was finding other more barbaric ways to flaunt the law. Best to eliminate him. But Xavier failed to learn, and problems were already beginning to arise due to his lackadaisical leadership style.

My dislike for my brother rose to new heights as the click of heals pacing into the room drew my attention. I stepped aside so the witch could approach Xavier, who casually flipped over the paper containing his vows.

"Good afternoon, Your Majesty, Nighval." Her wide-eyed expression told me she'd just heard my call for the man's death and my willingness to do it. *Murderer*, her glare said.

That's right sweetheart. I'm just as big and bad as they've told you. "Have something to say?" I snarled.

"I just don't think capital punishment is appropriate. Ever." She lifted her delicate chin. "It seems His Majesty is in agreement and prefers to deal with criminals in a more civilized way."

I opened my mouth to rebuttal, but she angled her body away from me effectively cutting off and turned to Link. "I'm Avery." She shoved a hand in his direction.

He took it, obliging with a shake. "Link Coldcloud. A pleasure." The asshole shot me a knowing smirk, and I considered murdering him for it just to make a point.

Seemingly finished with the formalities, the witch turned to my brother. "The senior housemaid has only been able to spare two maids for my projects. I've told her repeatedly it wasn't enough, but she insists they're understaffed. Did you know there are only six maids in this entire castle? It's no wonder there's an inch of grime on everything."

I shifted uncomfortably as hot streaks of shame rose up my neck. While I agreed with her, she hadn't been here for the last eighteen years and dealt with what we had. Coming to terms with being a cursed being, grappling with the changes to our bodies and senses changed things. As time went on, another year, another failure, things were forgotten about. A staff member would quit, and we didn't take the time to replace them. We became used to the disrepair.

Now this energetic witch had inserted herself into our world and seemed determined to change things for the better. Not one of the women before her had been so bold. The metal caps fitted to the ends of my claws dug into my palms as a wave of jealousy swirled through me.

"I'll go deal with Musson. Come on, Link," I said, turning to flee from the unwanted thoughts being in this room with my brother and his bride-to-be caused.

"You are not dismissed and you'll leave Musson to me," Xavier said and pointed to a spot on the ground where he apparently expected me to stand. The bastard wouldn't flex his power in front of our subjects, but he seemed to have no difficulty trying it with me to impress the witch.

I walked to the opposite side of the room and leaned against the wall beside the open window. Sunlight streamed in harshly, leaving enough of a shadow beside the bunched curtain I could retreat into. Xavier's lips pressed into a firm line, but he didn't attempt to redirect me again.

The witch, privy to our power struggle coughed. "Umm, hi, Xavier," she said, drawing his attention back to her. "How am I supposed to whip this place into shape with such little staff? Can't we afford more?"

"Of course. As I said before, anything you wish." He grabbed a fresh piece of paper and began writing on it. When he'd signed his name, he handed it to her. "Just give this to Leviticus next time you see him, and he'll arrange for it."

She reluctantly took the paper and scanned the contents. "I don't need Leviticus for this. I'll hire them myself."

Xavier gave her what I took to be a condescending frown. She apparently took it the same, as her arms crossed firmly over her chest. Perhaps my brother wasn't making the progress he believed himself to be.

Before I could stop myself, I said, "If the witch wishes to oversee the hiring of additional maid staff, I don't see what the harm is, Your Majesty." I'd rather hear cats howling than call my brother that, but the effect was worth it because Xavier understood my mocking intent.

The witch's eyebrows raised hopefully, and she passed a glance between me and my brother.

"Avery, my bride, we've discussed this. How are the final arrangements for the ceremony coming? I know that must be keeping you busy."

Her frown deepened. "Everything was already taken care of when I got here." The paper wrinkled in her hand as her fist balled around it.

Xavier's eyes were trained on it as he said, "Oh, I know what will help."

"Telling me about the curse?" she suggested. Beside me, Link choked. She smirked in his direction before turning back to my brother. As the witch's frustration bubbled to the surface, I savored the angry edge it gave her delightful voice.

"No," he said, opening a drawer to pull out a notebook. Flipping a few pages, he held it out then shifted his gaze between Link and me as if he wanted to make sure we were paying attention. "Avery, my dear, I've written you a few poems. I'll read you my latest."

Her features went slack, and she took a subtle step back which I couldn't help but relish.

"I think you'll like this one," he said, eyes roving over her reddening cheeks. An uncomfortable static charged the room as Xavier, seemingly unaware, cleared his throat and began.

"My bride's smile is like the sun, her eyes sparkling copper coins,
When they land upon me, they fill my heart's coffer,
The graceful sweep of her neck causes swans to weep,
The full curves of her hips cause—"

"Actually, maybe you can read it to me later? After you tell me about the curse, of course. I'll go find Leviticus." She bounced twice on her toes before turning to dash from the room, not making eye contact with any of us as she left.

The blushing woman couldn't have been more embarrassed, and I was dying to know what animal Xavier thought wise to compare his bride's hips to. Oh, yes, brother. You're now coming to understand wooing one of these other plane witches isn't as easy as you imagined. A dark chuckle sprang unbidden from my chest. "Well played, brother."

Link, who'd been quietly observing the exchange, joined my laughter. "Send word when you've dealt with Musson. Otherwise, I'll be back for the reprieve."

"I'll be at the ready if you need me," I said and followed Link out the door, feeling happier than I had in weeks.

CHAPTER 7

AVERY

Tonight was the reprieve. The first night the full moon would grant me a few hours to spend time with Xavier not in rat-man form. That meant, I'd officially been here a month. Every day since I arrived, I had lunch and dinner with the king. And every day his *feelings* toward me would evolve and grow so now they seemed to be a living thing, like a Venus flytrap, ready to swallow me whole. The poems he read me a few days ago in the privacy of my own room had brought the ick to another level. In my plane, we'd call him a love-bomber. It was a lot and while he continually professed to give me my heart's desire, he refused to give me the one thing I wanted more than anything else. Information.

Though I asked him at some point in every single interaction, he hadn't yet budged about the curse, and my patience was thinning. So much so that I refused to leave my room when I awoke this morning in protest. I still could hardly bear to look at the man who was destined to be my husband.

On the bright side, as I'd cleaned the library, I discovered a plethora of spell books. It was a trove that I knew Esmerelda and Cara would sell one of their kidneys to get their hands on. I brought various tomes I found promising to my room and had been combing through them. If Xavier wouldn't tell me about the curse, maybe I could discover something about it in these books.

The hour for lunch ticked past. Midway through the next, I looked up from the volume I was reading and noticed Xavier standing in my doorway with an enormous bouquet of red and pink roses. He walked to the foot of the bed where I was bundled in the covers and extended them to me. When I didn't immediately jump up and take them, he asked, "Are you well?"

"I am getting tired of asking you about this curse and you giving me nothing, so no, I am not well. And I will not be well until you tell me about it. Would you like to tell me about it today?" I asked, setting down the spellbook and crossing my arms over my chest.

His lips dipped into a frown, and he put his hands on his hips. "Avery, we've been through this. The curse is not something that you need to worry about. The rain has stopped. Would you like to take a walk through the gardens?" He lifted the bouquet again as if the flowers would somehow sway me.

"If I take a walk in the gardens, will you tell me about the curse?" I asked, training my eyes on him.

"No," he said, not expounding.

The finality of how he said it made my brow twitch and the space behind my right eye throb. I was on the verge of a rage headache. It was time for me to expel some of my frustration and the rat-man attempting to put his foot down seemed like the perfect candidate to receive it.

"Tell me now," I hissed.

"No," he said. "Get dressed. I'll take you to the gard—"

"Tell me about the curse," I yelled. Goddess above I was so angry I was going to strangle the man. How could he expect me to be totally fine living in the dark like this? Especially when everyone else in the Ravsted seemed to be in on the secret, or at least have an idea.

"Avery, calm down," he said as he paced in front of my bed.

I shot him a seething glare. "I will not calm down. And for the record, where I'm from, it is frowned upon to tell a woman to calm down, often having the opposite effect." I gritted my teeth and thrust a finger toward the doorway. He would not win today. "Out."

"Avery," he cautioned as my hysterics rose.

But Cara had cautioned me not to lose my fiery spirit, and I was only now beginning to suspect she may have been the only one of the witches who truly knew the rat's nest, pun intended, they were throwing me into. And if she knew, and I was the eighteenth witch, what did that mean for me if I failed? Self-preservation caused my urgency to spiral into a sharp peak.

"I swear to all that is holy, if you don't tell me, I will not walk down that aisle with you." I forced myself to stare him down. The longer things went on without me knowing anything, the more out of control I felt, and I was done.

He sighed and slumped down into a chair opposite the bed, so he was facing me. I was sick of this battle and the set of his shoulders told me I was close to wearing him down. I'd never seen him so resigned, so perhaps this was the day he would break.

"You'll willingly walk down the aisle with me if I will tell you?" he asked, his dark eyes lifting to find mine.

My breath caught. "Do I have a choice?" Coming here had been a choice, but I thought the marriage was a done deal.

He ran his hands across his rat hair. "What do you want me to say, Avery? Do you think I want to force you to be my wife?"

My brow wrinkled. "I don't know. Apparently, me and seventeen other witches were brought here because of an almost twenty-year-old blood deal that I know nothing about. Whose blood, by the way?"

"Not mine. Nighval's and my father. And it wasn't a blood deal exactly. The witch responsible for all this harnessed the power in his blood as he died to enact the curse. Together with the power she'd been saving and stealing, what ran in his veins was the only way she was strong enough to do what she did," Xavier said, flinching as if the memory were too painful to speak of. "Never mind. Here we are, and we have a chance to affect the lives of a lot of people who have had a curse placed upon them by a madwoman." He gave me what I interpreted as an earnest, pleading expression.

I bristled at him calling one of my fellow witches, who I knew spelled the curse, a madwoman. "And how do we do that?" I asked, ignoring the slight. Better to find out now so we could do it and get the curse over with. Then at least I wouldn't be stuck married to a half-rat-half-human. Or better yet, maybe I could go home, and this could all be over. I usually wasn't the type to give up so easily, but this castle sucked. This king sucked. And the rainy seaside air sucked, though apparently it was warmer before the curse. Screw being queen. At least back home I felt like I had some control over my life. Becoming queen, in theory, should have given me more, not less.

"Do we have a deal? Next full moon you'll willingly become my wife?" he asked, burying his face in his hands.

"Yes," I said, a little too eagerly. It was what I'd already planned to do, so why not let him think he was winning something, too. The next full moon was a month away. Surely by then Xavier would grow on me. Knowing that the information I'd been seeking was moments away had an immensely calming effect. Perhaps I'd been a little overzealous in my frustration ready to throw this all away. I could still be queen, but now that my thoughts were flowing more freely, it occurred to me I should have included a few more conditions. Namely, that Xavier gave me his blessing to be the type of queen I wanted to be and not the sheltered dove I was getting the impression he had hoped for. Oh well, he'd come to terms with who I was eventually.

"Okay, Avery." He closed his eyes for a long moment before opening them to land their heavy weight upon me. "My people expect our marriage, but that isn't what it will take to end the curse," he said, and I leaned forward. "It's only a step." Xavier in rat-man form was horrible to look at, but I could hold his gaze without visibly cringing now.

My anticipation had me wringing my hands in the blankets. Were we supposed to produce an heir? A shiver raced down my spine. That was about the worst thing I could think of, but I had been willing to come here and marry the man to save my people from the warlock's wrath. I just hadn't understood fully what that entailed. The thought that the matron of my coven knew and had kept it from me and my aunt made bitterness take root in my mind.

And there were ways to get pregnant without having to bed the man. Surely, they had those here. If not, I could close my eyes and he could wear mitts or something. Horrible, awful, disgusting, but if that is what it took, I would do it. No, that couldn't be it. The conflicted expression on his face had my curiosity rising. "If I'm going to marry you, I want to know all of it."

Xavier nodded and spoke. "Our father was a latent warlock, but he didn't know it. Have you heard the name Samara Wrede?" I shook my head, and he continued. "She is an immensely powerful witch who can cross both planes. Like my brother, one of the few who can. Samara came to ours, searching for a man just like our father, who was ignorant of the blood he carried. She seduced him, married him, and had two sons, which, as you know, is highly unusual for a witch to bear. It was the impact of my father's blood mingling with hers. They discovered soon after his birth, their first son, Nighval, was a warlock."

"It devastated our father when Samara confessed the secrets she'd been keeping from him. See, she'd fallen in love with our father and he her, but when he discovered the betrayal, it changed everything. He saw her as a monster for what she'd done, how she'd used and manipulated him. By then they learned she was carrying me. Eventually, after I was born, and Nighval and I were growing up in his care, he found a willing warlock, and they tried to banish her back to your plane, but it backfired, and she was cursed to stay here in ours."

"Is she still here?" I asked, reeling. I knew a ton of witches, and I couldn't imagine one of them doing such a thing. Coming to this plane to trick a latent warlock into having children with her. I was unfathomable.

"She is, but she hardly ever leaves the home she's built for herself. When she learned what our father had done, she confronted him. Our father spent years convincing us of what an abomination our mother was, so we refused to see her. We were young boys then, but we chose to live with him, to love him and shun her. She'd lost everything." Xavier paused for a moment, like he was reliving a memory. "I was fifteen when she finally snapped. She showed up to Ravsted on a dreary day and murdered our father right in front of our eyes with a bolt of lightning she tore down from the sky. It was like she'd been storing up the power for years, meditating his murder and how she'd use the power she stole from his blood for what came next. While my father's flesh singed at our feet, she gave Nighval and me a choice. Reconcile with her or she would make us as unlovable as we believed her to be."

"What did you do?" I asked.

Xavier chuckled. "You see us. Not only did she curse Nighval and me, but she cursed our people. See, my father had been king of this land, Ras alhague."

"Goddess," I said. "That's how he was able to raise you and keep you away from her."

"Yes, that and the Council of Warlocks all the kings keep," he said.

"And what breaks her curse?" I asked as a sickening foreboding feeling sucked me deeper in the bed. I shook my head as my suspicions rose. "No."

Xavier nodded. "A woman, more specifically a witch, must find it in herself to fall in love with either Nighval or I. And you've met Nighval. He was king for years after my father died, but none of the women the witches sent us lasted. The first one came exactly a year later, the day he turned twenty."

Geez, that meant his father had been killed on his nineteenth birthday. "What happened to them?" I asked, the name Madeline bouncing around in my mind. I ran through the women of my coven and the name wasn't familiar. The witches must have come from different covens from around the globe considering this was the first I'd heard of this. Somehow ours had been the last in line for the job which now fell upon my shoulders.

"A few never recovered from the initial shock of what we are now, and we still take care of them in a village not far from here. One woman ended her life, more went missing, ran away and are living somewhere in this plane still, likely aided by our mother. There was no way for them to return home. She wouldn't allow it and no warlocks were willing to offer any of their power to send a failed curse breaker to another plane, including my brother who's become bitter from years of rejection. It all circles back to us. If we'd only accepted her, but we were young and our father had poisoned our minds against her. Eventually, the people tired of Nighval's failed attempts, and it became my turn. They made me king and now, Avery, you're our last chance."

"No way," I stuttered. On one hand it was almost romantic, but on the other... An image of Nighval the first moment I'd seen him appeared in my mind, but I shoved it away as quickly as it'd come. Xavier was my intended, soft hands and all. "What happens if I can't fall in love with you?"

"Then you will be queen of a permanent race of rat people, and I will rule by your side as king," he said, eyebrows knitting together. The same gravity I imagined he felt came to rest on my shoulders as well. Perhaps we could bond over that. "Now do you see why I didn't want to tell you?"

"Yes," I admitted. Suddenly everything seemed so dire. As I studied Xavier trying to absorb what he'd told me, he seemed to focus on everything in the room except me. He was hiding something still. "What is it you're not telling me?"

His beady rat-eyes narrowed in a pained way, then he shook his head burying it in his hands. His breath was muffled when he said, "Nighval made a vow to destroy the witches if the curse became permanent."

My mouth became dry, and I swallowed. "What?"

"I'm sorry Avery. The warlocks' dealings can be very private, but what I know is he went to your realm and threatened the covens. Whatever he did is why they started sending witches. Now you're the last one."

Shit, that was a lot of pressure. But that was all the more motivation to figure this out. There had to be some way to fix this without the warlocks hurting anyone I cared about or these people getting stuck this way.

It was true I was getting used to them, but to spend the rest of my life as the only human amongst a race of cursed rat beings made my stomach clench. I could totally see why seventeen women couldn't deal and bailed. This was like some sort of parallel fun house gone wrong and the monsters around every corner were these cursed rat beings. Transformed creatures who were hard to even look at without cringing, much less having to wed one or touch their furry skin. Prickles erupted across my skin at the thought, and I had to hold back a shiver. And everything came down to me and my ability to find love with one of them. No pressure or anything. "But why am I the last chance?"

"She gave us a full nineteen years." He rolled his eyes. "You know how the witches are with the moon. To her I supposed it meant something, or maybe she needed it for the spell to work, but as far as I'm concerned, it's arbitrary."

I didn't like his tone and how he seemed to belittle the rituals of my heritage. Of course, *I* understood the significance. There was a reason they did things at certain positions of the planets and the moon.

"Sounds like a Metonic cycle." When his brow wrinkled as if he didn't have a clue what I was talking about, I said, "It lasts for two hundred thirty-five lunations before it repeats, and the moon cycle returns to the same place once again to repeat the pattern. She would have used the lunar reset to harness more power." Enough power to curse an entire plane?

I shivered as my mind speared off in a different direction. "When was Nighval born?" I asked. "You said he was nineteen when your father was killed, and she enacted the curse?"

"That's not important," he said, but a seed lodged in my mind. He went on. "What is important is knowing that I am willing to take care of you in any way I can to soften your heart to me. If you could learn to love me, see me as the man I am." Xavier stood, stepping toward the bed, and I edged back until I bumped into the headboard.

Before I could shut the faucet of my mouth off, I blurted, "I could never love—" and caught myself before I said more.

Xavier stopped short, his features going taut. "A monster like me," he finished for me, but that wasn't what I'd been about to say. Hurt flashed across his eyes, and he stared at me for a long while before he spun and stormed from the room. I flew out of bed and chased him out into the hallway.

"I'm sorry, Xavier. I didn't mean to," I called to his fleeing back. "You don't understand. It's not the rat thing..." And he didn't understand. I'd agreed to the marriage, and I'd hoped for the fairytale, but no one had ever said anything about love. My heart ached because no matter how hard I tried, I didn't think I could force myself to fall into love with *him*. If it was a different man in this form, maybe I could get past the rat thing over time, but the spark wasn't there. In fact, my romantic feelings toward him were quite the opposite.

He stopped before he turned the corner, throwing a grimace over his shoulder. "I understand, Avery. More than you know."

CHAPTER 8

NIGHVAL

I caught sight of the witch illuminated by the light from the full moon streaming in through the open window as she rounded the end of the bookshelf I was now perusing. I needed to find a certain spell book I recalled from training as a boy, but this was a welcome distraction. Had my ridiculous brother made any progress since he'd read her that laughable poem?

"What are you up to?" I asked.

She was in another shapeless dress like the white one she'd had on the day I retrieved her from Esmerelda. That witch was one of the few witches privy to the gravity of their predicament and willing to bet the future of their kind on her own niece. An unwelcome pang of pity hit me square in the chest. It was too bad. This one had been amusing to talk to on the ride to Ravsted. Watching her fight my brother had my curiosity in full bloom. I'd not noticed a single speck of dust as I pilfered through the ancient tomes, a credit to the woman's attention to detail and tenacity. I chuckled inwardly. The fact that she defied my brother and returned to finish cleaning the library elevated my opinion of her greatly.

The witch flinched at my voice, but lifted her chin and said, "I guess the word exile means something different in this plane." She eyed me like she posed a question.

Begrudgingly, I would go to their wedding, which was why I was here and not on the other side of the kingdom, but I didn't wish to speak of that with her. Xavier had given her time to warm up to our world. It should have been tonight—this first full moon—according to his grand

59

plan, but he'd softened upon meeting her. Now I was stuck here another month.

Honestly, I was shocked he'd been able to pull it off, but this woman seemed to have a little more grit than the women the other witches had sent for me. Latent witches who were soft and sweet, pretty, and fine. Gentle-hearted women who I'd been half convinced were sent to thwart my attempts to break the curse. Neoma hadn't even been able to speak the common tongue, English, I'd learned. Others were nominally fluent, speaking bits and pieces of many different languages in their plane. Finally, they'd sent a woman who might be able to survive the pairing and thrive in our world, and I'd given in. The pressure to step away and allow my brother a chance to woo the next and final witch finally got the better of me. I didn't even fight the exile when it came. It was practically my idea. I was so defeated. I narrowed my eyes at the witch, who trembled, but moved toward me still.

I smirked, looking down at her. "It's a loose exile. My brother tends to over exaggerate his power over me and he's aware of the necessity to stay on my good side. I'm in the library because I needed a certain book, but I didn't expect to find you here. Don't you have a fiancé to be attending to?"

I thumbed a title and pulled it out. She did the same, mirroring my motion. Interesting that we had ventured down the same aisle.

She scanned my face, snagging on each scar, her scrutiny making me wish I'd taken a few seconds to glamor myself when I caught sight of her. It didn't matter, though. She wasn't mine, a knowledge that annoyed me more than it should have.

"You were right. Your brother told me about the curse," she blurted.

I whipped my head in her direction. Of course, Xavier had told her. *Idiot.* When I suggested she pester him about it, I'd only meant to annoy him. I hadn't expected he'd actually tell. The man had a weaker constitution than I anticipated. This ought to be interesting. "And?" I asked.

"He told me that the warlocks, led by you, will seek revenge on the covens if I don't fall for him. I think it's grotesque to threaten and punish every witch because of the actions of one."

"I hold the witches responsible for what one of you did to us. They didn't even respond to our pleas for help when it first happened, so I was forced to resort to threats. And don't think for a second that your people wouldn't do the same to us warlocks if one of us had found a way to spell their world, blocking them from their precious power." I stepped toward her letting her see the dangerous glint I knew my eyes held.

"Your mother," she whispered.

"Yes, my mother. I offered your Council of Matrons eighteen years' worth of chances, witch, and not one of you had enough of a heart to break the curse. Time is up."

"What happens if I can't figure out how to fall in love with Xavier?" she asked, studying me.

"My mother stored up power for over a decade to be strong enough for that curse. Can you imagine how powerful I am not being able to use my power but once a full moon for a scant few hours?" A shiver wracked through the witch, and I stepped even closer. She retreated a step until her back hit the rows of books and her chest was rising and falling in quick succession. I put my arms on either side of her head and stared down at her wide eyes. "So, you're smart enough to understand what will happen if you do not break this curse?"

"Can't you talk to her, since she's still here? Surely after all these years you could get her to lift it?" Her voice trembled as she made the suggestion as if in seventeen years I hadn't tried.

"This curse doesn't work like that. The magic she used as binding. Permanent," I said, practically snarling as I caged her in. Little did she know my mother wasn't the only one who'd delivered an unbreakable curse and it seemed Xavier had left that part out.

She lifted a hand and for a second I thought she was going to press it to my chest, but she held it in the air shivering between us. "You don't have to do this. I'll try to fall for your brother, if you promise to leave the witches alone. Please, Nighval." My lips curled back as she pleaded my name. "*Please.*"

A guttural laugh escaped my throat. "Even if I wanted to void my vow to end the witches, I couldn't. What has been set in motion cannot be undone. Like my mother, I made a binding blood oath with the Goddess. And I did not just offer her my blood, witch. Every warlock on this plane is bound to the oath." She blinked up at me, horror glazing her eyes. "The Council of Matrons knows what's coming if you fail, so I suggest you find a place in your heart for my brother"

Her lips parted, and my eyes locked on them. "But," she stammered. "But love doesn't work like that."

"What?" I said, my voice taking a rough edge, as she ducked under my arms and walked down the row, away from me. Her shoulders were square and stiff, but she stopped at the end of the row, clutching the volume she'd selected to her chest.

Looking over her shoulder at me, she said, "Love is a mystery, Nighval. I can't just make myself fall into it. Marrying him, providing him a child, or even growing to love him over time, I could do with greater ease. But to fall in love... Your mother knew what she was doing when she set up this nearly impossible task."

The witch stepped out of sight, and I stood there for a long moment, her words digging their claws into my mind. She didn't believe she could fall in love with Xavier and my brother was considered by all to be a good man. A gentle and kind man. I wanted to chase the witch and shake her, try to make her see that getting saddled with my brother should have made things easier for her, and she had to do it. Otherwise, I'd bring every warlock in this plane to theirs and take my vengeance on the witches. The power draw might kill us all, but the witches would suffer, too.

I raised an unsteady hand to the shelf. There was an opening right where the volume I'd come for should be. I stormed off toward the witch's rooms, fully aware of the tingle of anticipation at the thought of more time in her presence. That wasn't ideal.

I couldn't imagine she was going to hand the book over willingly. Taking it from her was another thing I was looking forward to. Again, not ideal. As I paced down the hallway after her, I got the strangest sensation of familiarity, almost like I'd chased after her before. Or perhaps it was that I would do it again.

62

CHAPTER 9

AVERY

J esus, Nighval was huge, and really, really scary. And he hadn't softened his features or removed his scars with his magic like when he'd picked me up. In the library, in the moonlight streaming through the broken windows, I saw the warlock in all his terrifying glory and completely understood how none of the witches sent to him ever even made it past go. His hair was darker, the same length as before, and tucked behind his ears, making his cheekbones poke out so they were almost gaunt. His nose was a hard line, like a squared off pyramid, but longer. Dark heavy brows protruded over nearly black eyes. And his lips, well I still never had seen them in any shape, but a thin angry line, even when he spoke.

All of this sounded intense, and it was exactly that. Especially with the scars. The largest one ran over the bridge of his nose and across his cheek. A smaller one sliced through his eyebrow and ran to his hairline. Another was about an inch long near the corner of his mouth and ran in a straight line down his chin. There were a few smaller ones, and given the circumstances, they seemed to have healed as well as possible in this weird throwback plane.

His presence was ominous, male, and possibly hot if you were into the scarred grim reaper dark mage sort of thing, which I wasn't. I saw the appeal of softer magic'd Nighval from the first night, but real Nighval was something else entirely. And it wasn't just this plane. If Nighval had walked up to the bar where I worked and ordered a drink, he would have frightened me then, too. He just had that kind of presence.

When he'd boxed me in, no doubt trying to intimidate me, my heart had seized, and I didn't think I breathed for a whole minute.

Squeezing the book to my chest, I raced down the hall in the direction of my suite. I sent Xavier away when he came to my room at the start of the reprieve with that look in his eye and another poem gripped in his clammy hand. He was all human and barely contained excitement, seeming to have gotten over the fact that I practically told him I didn't think I could fall in love with him. Since he told me about the curse this afternoon and we set a date for the wedding, it was like he doubled down on his seduction technique giving me silly grins, personally delivering me a late lunch, and asking me questions about my likes and dislikes. And then he lingered like he expected some sort of reward for his efforts in the form of kisses. I told him I wanted to wait until our wedding night to try to be physical. We chatted for a bit, he confessed more feelings, and he left dejected.

I should try harder, because thank God I got Xavier and not Nighval like so many of my sisters had. But the way Xavier chewed—it was disturbing. And his eyes, the way they moved across my skin, so eager, like a puppy. No woman wanted to sleep with, much less fall for, a puppy. Unless it was an actual puppy and the sleeping with would be puppy cuddles.

So, I went to the library, determined to find some loophole or spell that might reverse the curse myself. I would discover it and get a message back to my aunt and they'd find a way to use it to free these people of the curse. Sure, I figured Nighval and the other warlocks of this plane had already sifted through every piece of available material, but I was a witch. Without power, but still. I'd grown up around powerful witches, watching them do their spells, reading their works in case I ever needed to teach my daughter our craft. Maybe I could discover something they hadn't.

I got to my room and set the book on the desk. Flipping on the lamp, I opened its thick leather cover. I made it through the first passage, trying to make sense of what I was reading, when the door opened with a creak. Jumping, I turned to see Nighval standing in the doorway. He glanced from me to the book and stalked in my direction. My heart hitched and sputtered at an erratic pace, and I closed the volume.

64

His focus narrowed in on it, and I pulled it toward me protectively. "Get out," I said, my words clipped and loud enough, but he ignored them. Stopping in front of the desk, Nighval braced his hands on the edges and leaned down to get eye level with me.

"What do you think you're doing with that?" He nodded at the book, still possessively clutched in my grip.

I scooted back in the chair, but made myself hold eye contact. I was prepared to be here, to hold my own, I reminded myself, and I would not cower before this man. I would be queen in a month, which would make him my subject.

"I said, get out," I growled. Yep, I employed the tone described in every romance book ever when the brooding hero had something really important to say. Unfortunately, I think it backfired because a wide, toothy grin spread across Nighval's face, exposing two rows of perfect teeth.

I wrinkled my brow as I stared at them. "How do you keep them so—" I started to ask when he cut me off.

"Answer me, witch." His grin had a dangerous edge to it and my breath caught.

I unclenched my jaw. "I have been going through your spell books—"

"Why?" he demanded.

"I thought maybe I could find—"

"You thought you could find a spell that could break the curse?" His scarred face tensed, and he gave me a pitying look I really didn't like.

"If you would shut up for one second, I would answer you." I crossed my arms, book tightly nestled inside and raised my brows at him as I sat there, waiting.

He didn't speak, but regarded me.

I gave him an agitated huff. "You aren't a witch, therefore you don't think like one. And yes, I thought it was possible that you might have missed something that could be helpful. And if I figure it out and end your mother's curse, I figure it will void the one you made on my people."

"I doubt—"

"You doubt that?" I asked, this time cutting *him* off. I blinked at him in mock sweetness. "I'm sure you do. Considering you've had seventeen chances to make a witch warm to you, I'm gathering your abilities are somewhat lacking, warlock."

His face twisted into a scowl that made me want to retreat, but I didn't. He did not like being confronted at all. Good. I kept going.

"And because of that, your people no longer thought you a suitable king." He flinched. "People talk, warlock." Technically, I was bending the truth, but it was effective, and I'd put it together from what I had heard.

The warlock's eyes flickered, and he stormed around the desk toward me, and I jumped to my feet. His large, calloused hand wrapped around my wrist, and he tugged. My forearm muscles burned as I tried to stop him from pulling the book out of my grip, but I failed.

Book in hand, Nighval turned toward the door. It wasn't the book—it was preventing him from taking it that motivated me. I latched my fingers into the crook of his elbow, tugging so he was facing me. Intrigue danced in his eyes as he turned toward me. I'd worked at a bar long enough to know that look on a man.

With my other hand, I wrapped it around the leather spine and stared up into Nighval's dark, amused eyes. "You think you're tough, witch? That you're not scared of me any longer?"

"My name is Avery, warlock," I spat.

Rustling in the hallway caught my attention, but I didn't disconnect my gaze from Nighval's. Xavier burst into the room, stopping short. Finally, we both turned to him to see his mouth dropping as he took in me and his brother engaging in some sort of epic stare-down.

I started as the church bell gonged. As the bell cried out a second time, the air around Nighval shimmered. He jerked the book I still gripped, and my gaze found its way back to his. He held my stare as his features changed. I drew in a sharp inhale. I held my breath as I watched whiskers sprout around his scar and the definition of his nose flatten. My other hand was still gripping his arm, and he used it to pull me closer.

Opening his mouth, his teeth lengthened, and I drew in quick panicked breaths as he said, "Witch." The second I unclenched my hands from the book and his arm, he disappeared. Like gone, with no *poof* or anything. I hadn't seen his hands working like they'd done in the carriage, but they must have been, but I was so focused on his face I hadn't noticed. The bell gonged its third time, and I was alone with a fully transformed Xavier.

My hand went to my throat, because apparently, I was a pearl clutcher, to add to the list with fainting, and Xavier in rat-man form rushed over to me. He quickly slipped the metal tips onto the points of his claws and grabbed my shoulders, turning me to face him.

"What's the meaning of this?"

"Wh-what?" I stuttered, trying to free myself from the king's grip. "I just need a second." When they transformed before, I hadn't seen it, but watching Nighval's masculine face melt into that creature hurt to watch. My heart actually ached so badly I wanted to curl myself into a ball.

"Why was my brother in your room, Avery, and why were you two looking at each other like that?" he asked. Xavier's barely there rat brows knitted together, and his eyes took on a darker shade than normal. Even his disgusting rat teeth were visible as his lip tried to peel back.

"That book," I said, a little stunned that his anger was directed toward me. Still, my chest constricted as I took him in. I was only now beginning to understand their plight.

"Book?" Xavier asked, shaking his head.

"Yes, I ran into him in the library, and I guess I took a spell book he'd been looking for, so he charged in here to take it," I explained.

"That doesn't explain what I walked into."

I turned my head away, trying to make sense of whatever Xavier was accusing me of. "I don't know what you're talking about. He challenged me, and I didn't like it. What he said—he made me want to put him in his place."

Xavier searched my face and then his expression, softened like understanding dawned. "Okay, Avery. He scares you, but he is my brother. He can be a little intimidating—actually, I think he gets off on it, but he means you no harm. I promise you are safe with him."

"But," I stammered. "How am I supposed to believe that when I can see the tension between the two of you?"

Xavier angled his body like he meant to step forward. I retreated a step, and he stilled, letting his shoulders drop ever so slightly, but I caught it. "We have a long history. It's not important. What is important is you're with me now, and we're getting married. I know you have your doubts, but I promise the feelings will come. You just need to give us time. I can't wait to see you in your wedding dress. You will make a stunning bride." He gave me a weak smile before he grabbed the doorknob. I wished I felt as optimistic as his words conveyed. "Oh, and I would try to avoid spending more time with him than necessary. It never seems to go well for your kind."

He nodded and left me with the ominous warning hanging in the air.

I slumped into the chair at my desk, trying to make sense of what happened when a folded scrap of paper that hadn't been there when I'd come back from the library caught my attention. I picked it up, about to stuff it into a drawer assuming it was another one of Xavier's poems he'd accidentally dropped, when a heavenly male scent drifted up from it.

My heart skipped a beat as I unfolded the paper.

In particularly neat penmanship were the words, *The fourth floor of the main residence could use your attention. –N*

I brought the paper to my nose and inhaled. Thunderstorms and firewood permeated my senses, and I dropped the paper like it was a hot coal. Across from the bed, the fireplace flickered. For a moment I considered pitching the delightful smelling note into it. No, I'd better keep it in case I forgot which floor the warlock suggested I peruse.

With that I fished my little key out of its hiding spot, unlocked the bottom drawer of my desk and set it inside. As I changed and crawled into bed, my thoughts couldn't help but drift to the note. The words, obviously. Not the scent.

CHAPTER 10

AVERY

"Does Xavier know you're up here?" a smooth voice said from behind me. I spun to find Link in rat-man form behind me. His faded brows arched over his sloped forehead as his eyes made an assessing sweep over me and the door handle I was fidgeting with. It had only taken me a few days to muster up the courage to sneak away and venture up to the fourth floor.

"No, and you're not going to tell him either."

At my words, he grinned. "And why is that, Miss Plath?"

"Call me Avery, and because your buddy Nighval was the one who suggested I explore the fourth floor." I pulled a bobby pin from my hair and stuffed it into the keyhole. I had no idea what I was doing, but I'd seen people do this in movies. Considering this was the only locked room on this floor, it had to be the one Nighval was steering me toward.

"Nighval told you to try to break into locked rooms in the castle?" He quirked his lips to the side as he eyed me. When I didn't respond, he said, "I knew following you up here was a good idea. I can always tell when there's mischief afoot."

A mechanism in the lock budged, so I wrenched the pin a little further. A pop sounded and the thin piece of metal snapped in half leaving one end jammed in the lock. Pinching the end, I tried to pull it free, but my fingers slipped. Shit.

Ignoring Link, because he very well knew that wasn't precisely the message I'd received, I walked down the hallway to the next open door.

"What are you doing now?" he asked as he paced along behind me.

"There was a balcony in this room, I think. If they're close enough, I could climb between them—"

"Oh no you won't. Did it ever occur to you the room was locked for a reason? Besides, Xavier will have my head if he found out I was privy to your plan and didn't stop you." Link attempted to grab my arm as he chased me into the room, but I jerked it out of his reach. I got to the windows and as I tugged on the moth-eaten curtain his huge hand wrapped around the fabric above mine and as we tugged in opposite directions the fabric shredded.

I let out an exaggerated sigh as I glared up at him. "You're on the Council of Warlocks, right?"

"Yes, why?" he asked.

"Well, Link, I'm going to be your queen, and Xavier and I will preside over the council, correct?" I raised a brow, thinking I had a checkmate.

"Something like that," he said, and I got the impression that he was curious enough that he was going to play along.

"Well, then I insist that you let me do as I wish." I put my hands on my hips as I waited for his reply.

"What do you think is in that room that you're so insistent upon seeing?" he asked.

"I don't know. Skeletons, mummies. Or maybe it's where the king has imprisoned the witch who cursed you," I said, giggling. But the wariness that eclipsed the warlock's expression suggested that it hadn't been an outlandish guess after all. I gave him a toothy grin. "I'm warm, aren't I? See, that is exactly why I'm getting into that room."

I poked my finger into his chest until he took a step back. I pulled the shredded curtains back enough that I could unlatch the window, push it open and slip out onto the balcony. Link followed and came up behind me as I surveyed the distance between the adjacent balcony leading to the room next door.

"It's too far—"

"Exactly," he said.

"I was going to say, it's too far for me. You could make it." I raised a challenging brow as I gestured for him to give it a go. When he only crossed his arms over his chest, I said, "Fine. I guess I'll have to try." I put my hands on the ledge nearest the building as if I would actually do it.

Right as I was about to hoist myself onto the ledge, Link stormed off, saying, "Come on. I'll pick the lock."

I clapped my hands in front of my chest and skipped after him. Acting classes paid off again.

Link squatted down by the lock so he could slip a cap-free claw inside and leaned his ear forward to listen. After a few tries, the pin I'd wedged in there popped out and a sharp ping sounded. He reached up, yanked on the handle and it turned. Eureka!

I rushed into the dim room stopping short when it occurred to me that wasn't such a great idea. Who knew why the room was locked? And by the thick layer of dust covering the luxurious furniture, it had been that way for a long time.

I stilled to listen for a moment. Only silence greeted me and the sound of wind whistling through a gap in the windows in the adjacent room which lay ahead. Link flipped the light on, and I scanned the space. We were in a large sitting area with grand shelves that were built into the wall on either side of a massive fireplace. A still life of peonies hung above it and several pieces of spindly furniture were scattered around. The suite appeared to have belonged to a woman with very particular taste at some point in Ravsted's history.

Wow. Did this room belong to who I thought it did? I grabbed Link's arm, noting the thick muscle under my hand. The large man was equally as struck as I was. "Link, do you know who this room belonged to?"

His eyes met mine and he nodded.

"It was hers, wasn't it?" I asked. I approached an ornate desk which might have been cream under the coating of grey dust and tried the first drawer. It opened easily. Inside was a stack of old letters bound with a simple leather tie. The swirling script was a little difficult to read, but I got enough that I understood I held the romantic correspondence between Xavier and Nighval's parents.

I replaced them and closed the drawer, moving onto the next which held bobbles, dried up pens, chalk and blank notepads. Moving on, I studied the objects on the shelves. Nothing worth breaking into this room for, so I went toward the bedroom. Heavy footfalls sounded behind me as I left Link searching the sitting room and for a moment I wondered if he'd found something interesting. Then as I heard the door click shut, the lights went out. Oh well. I didn't need his help now that I'd got the door open, but he didn't have to turn off the light on me. This place was creepy enough as it was.

I stepped through the French doors to see the gold curtains were pulled open and a sliver of sunlight warmed the center of the room. Reaching over I flipped a switch on the wall and the light from the top of the bed flickered to life. The painting it highlighted above the headboard immediately struck me. A chestnut-haired woman was depicted in a John Singer Sargent style which highlighted her glowing pale skin. That one feature made her look so much like Nighval had in the moonlight that night in the library it was uncanny. Her features were refined and delicate, and her clear blue eyes stared directly at the viewer.

"Don't let her beauty deceive you," Nighval said, and I jumped.

I turned to see him flick the light back off before tucking himself into the shadow of a large armoire adjacent to the door. "Where did Link go?"

"He left when I came in," he said.

Okay... that much was obvious. Let me try a different angle. "This is your mother, isn't it?" It had to be. The woman was beautiful in an austere sort of way like a praying mantis or the king cobra, much like her son who stood before me.

"Yes," he said and when he didn't elaborate, agitation gurgled to the surface.

Surely this painting wasn't the reason he led me here. Could no one here shoot me straight without me having to wrestle the information out of them? "Why am I here, Nighval?"

He tapped her armoire three times and my breathing picked up. He didn't move as I made my way over to it and pulled the knob simultaneously nervous and excited about what I'd find.

"Oh my god. Are these her spellbooks?" I asked, slapping my hand over my mouth. At least a dozen leatherbound journals were neatly lined up on the bottom shelf beneath a hanging row of gaudy clothing, and I bent down to pick one up.

A key in the locked entry door rattled. My heart lodged itself in my throat. I could only imagine Xavier and Nighval had keys and my instinct told me I didn't want the former to catch me in here, much less catch me alone again with his brother. I pushed the armoire door shut and clutched the book to my chest as Nighval's hands shot out and he tugged me to him as if he had the same thought.

"My brother. Shh..." he whispered as he gripped my hips, pulling me into the shadows with him. His hands slid up to my waist to hold me in place, and I could feel the heat of him as we stood there barely breathing. If it weren't for my arm wrapped around the spellbook which was pressed into his firm stomach between us, the length of my body would be squished against his. Having his metal-capped fingers searing into my sides was nerve-wracking enough. I didn't dare look up.

In the sitting room, the sound of wood scraping against wood suggested Xavier was in the desk I'd opened minutes earlier. He carried on in the other room for what felt like an eternity. With each second that ticked on, a guilty niggle bit at my conscience. I shouldn't be hiding in here like this with my husband's brother. But we hadn't been doing anything improper, so I didn't know why it felt so wrong. The wood scraped again, closing, then footsteps retreated, and the door clicked shut.

When I was sure we were alone once again, I pushed on Nighval's chest with my free hand. His fingers dragged against the fabric of my dress as his grip loosened. "Nighval," I warned under my breath.

His fingers sprang open to release me like he surprised himself by holding on too long. I stepped back, sucking in a deep breath as I did. The same scent from his note crashed into my senses, and I almost stumbled back. Whoa. I took a few more steps back into the sunlight streaming in through the window.

My mouth opened and closed as I struggled for something to say. Since I'd gotten to this plane, my reactions were on tilt, hitting me so strong and out of nowhere.

"What?" he asked, frowning as I gathered my composure. The way his dark eyes took me in made me think he had his own thoughts about our proximity. He probably hated my kind and projected his resentment of past witches onto me which totally wasn't fair.

"You know it would have been a lot simpler for you to bring me here instead of sending me on a wild goose chase," I said, opening the armoire again and moving a stack of spellbooks onto the bed.

"I wanted to see how curious you actually are. And to answer your earlier question, I thought about what you'd said before. You're right. I've been through these volumes over a dozen times, and I can't put anything useful together related to the curse. Now that you know about it, it wouldn't hurt for you to take a look from your perspective."

I kept my attention trained on the volume I'd flipped open to hide my grin. The warlock heard what I said and wanted to give me a chance to solve this. Right as pride began to swell in my chest, he said, "Not that I think you'll discover anything."

Deflated, I turned to him. He had to be taunting me. Otherwise, why would he have suggested I come here? Sure enough, the corner of his mouth lifted which I could barely make out as he stood in a shadowed corner. That must be his thing—shadows. He probably thought they made him seem more intimidating as Xavier suggested he got off on. The smirk seemed to be a permanent fixture on his face now.

Fine. I'd taunt him back. "And why are you always lurking in the shadows, Nighval?" I asked.

"Why do you care?" he said, not budging.

I rolled my eyes. "Never mind. Are you going to help me carry these spellbooks down to my room, or are you just going to stand there, all ominous like?"

"What if Xavier sees them in your room? Then he'll know you've been naughty and are trying to find a way to get out of the curse without falling for him." He tapped his lips. "What do you think he was doing at that desk?"

"Good question," I said. "I looked there first. All that's in there is stacks of letters between your parents." No way. I left the book I'd been studying and rushed to the desk. I yanked the drawer open and pulled out the bound stack of papers. They weren't the ones I'd thumbed through earlier.

"Oh my god, he's been getting the poems from your parent's letters." I leaned against the desk as I flipped through them recognizing the words. A giggle burst from my lips as I scanned another page. Then I was full-on laughing. When I finally contained myself, I noticed Nighval had stepped out of the shadows and was leaning against the doorframe between the rooms to watch me. His arms were crossed over his chest, and the scar which ran through the fur at the corner of his mouth seemed to deepen as he repressed a grin.

"Your father was a terrible poet. But I guess it worked on your mother."

"I should remind you that she is more than a little unhinged," he said.

This time when our eyes met, warmth and humor was exchanged, and my stomach did a weird dropping thing. What was wrong with me? Like he sensed it, his features glazed over and any hint of connection was gone, almost making me think I'd imagined it. But, of course, I had. This was the scared rat-man who'd run seventeen women off. He was incapable of warmth and connection. I should know better than to try to be friendly with him.

"I think I'll just stash these in the room next door in case Xavier comes back for more poems, and he locks it behind him. You can go," I said, my tone coming off colder than I intended. Why did that realization sting so much? I didn't care about that disgruntled man any more than I cared about anyone else here. Well, maybe my girls, Alice and April. We'd become friendly as we'd worked alongside each other, and they were no longer exchanging confused glances.

I didn't turn around as footsteps retreated and the outer door snapped shut.

CHAPTER 11

NIGHVAL

After my encounter with the witch in my mother's old rooms, I hadn't left Ravsted and a series of monotonous weeks came and went. Of course, I wanted to retreat back to the Lieden Palace on the other side of the kingdom, but I promised Xavier I'd stay until after the wedding. I felt duty bound to do it, and I only had one week to go, so here I was, slinking through the halls, trying to avoid her. Trying to avoid that feeling I got when I thought of seeing her again. Trying to avoid another dismissal.

That angry mouth and the fire in her eyes, her openly shared playfulness, and the way her words clipped back at me without restraint. No one spoke to me like that. Not even my brother. And I'd only ever laughed with the small handful of friends I kept close, Link, Eshan, and Jetta. But there was something about this witch that I refused to ponder. Just feeling her waist beneath my fingertips was too much. She was the last thing that ought to be on my mind. I should be doing everything in my power to help my brother get this woman to fall for him. If he failed, then I'd be stuck in this form forever. We all would.

This time of year, it rained more than it didn't, and it had been gloomy for the last several weeks. Finally, the clouds cleared and the sun was coming through. Being here, back in the castle, usually didn't bother me, but something about this stay was getting under my skin. No, not something. Someone.

Xavier suggested I should join them for lunch, but the last thing I needed was to be in the company of a beautiful woman who I could not have. Who would look at me with disgust as she took in my horrible appearance. Who mocked me for clinging to the shadows, the thing protecting her from this awful creature I was. And I'd forced her to watch me become the monster. Even as I'd done it, I knew showing her the transformation made me an asshole, but I was angry, and I didn't even know why.

The last seventeen years hadn't been easy, but at least my brother, as much as I despised him, had enough grace not to throw it in my face. The witch, on the other hand, didn't seem to have a problem goading me.

I had done everything Xavier had asked of me, and I needed some fresh air. To enjoy the sun for a few hours before it started raining again. I grabbed the novel I was reading off of the table in the sitting room I occupied and strode out the door, down the hall, and into the garden.

All of the rain turned the foliage bright green, and flowers were blooming on nearly every plant. Xavier was lucky to have his wedding this time of year because they would be able to harvest the flowers from the garden and the castle might be transformed if only for a moment, into a shadow of its former self.

I walked deeper into the garden, nearing the little hut that sat at the center. It was white stone, like the rest of Ravsted, and had a peaked roof with a swallow shaped wind dial atop it. There was a bench on the opposite side of it that would be in full sun now and was where I was headed.

Melodic laughter filled the air, and I stopped short. The witch had taken my spot. My one place of solace in this Goddess forsaken castle, and she was now occupying it. That was fine. There was a smaller garden on the opposite side of Ravsted. I would go there. As I went to move away, I stepped onto the path and loose gravel crunched below my feet.

"Hello?" she called. I didn't respond, so she called, "Hello?" again.

A book snapped shut and before she could rise, I said, "It's me," like she would know who *me* was. "Nighval."

"Oh," she said in a tone laced with overt disappointment.

Had she been hoping it was Xavier? "You don't have to sound so dismayed about it," I said, stepping closer, drawn forward like the glutton I am.

"Sorry. The sun is out, and I thought I could be spared a few hours without a thundercloud around. Apparently, I was wrong," she said. Her voice had shifted to something more like amusement. Like she enjoyed sending her little jabs in my direction.

I could play back. "You're in my spot. First you take my book, then you dismiss me after I do you a favor, and now you take my spot? What else do you plan to take from me, witch?"

She chuffed. "If you want your spot, warlock, then come and get it."

"You know very well you couldn't handle me." I had never wished it had been a full moon more than this very moment, so I could see if there was something to that split second of playfulness she'd given me a glimpse of as she'd realized my brother's forgery. I wished I didn't look like this monster, that I could charge around the corner to challenge her and see how brave she really was. But now I was bluffing because the truth was, I did not want her to see me like this. That's why I clung to the shadows in her presence.

"Well, I'm waiting. What will the big, bad warlock do?" she said, the tease digging its claws into me.

When I didn't respond, I heard the rustling of fabric. "Stop," I said. "Stay put."

"What, why? You seem so eager to get your spot back," she said, and I edged closer to the corner of the building.

"Would you believe me if I told you I didn't want you to see me like this?" I asked, unsure what came over me. My chest felt raw and flayed open as I'd uttered the shameful admission. Why I'd given her this truth when I knew she'd use it against me, eventually, I couldn't say. My heart beat wildly as I awaited her response.

The sting didn't come as the witch sucked in a breath. "Xavier doesn't mind me seeing him in that form."

"Xavier's a fool," I said. Something so fine, so fucking flawless wasn't meant for my idiot brother. "Where is he, by the way? I thought you two were having lunch."

"April said he was called away last minute to deal with something," she said, pausing, and I could tell she wanted to say more. "I have his portion here if you're hungry."

"I don't see how—" Gravel moved under her feet, causing my breath to hitch. I didn't think she was cruel enough to ignore my wishes, so I stood in place, waiting. She set something down and then a basket poked out from around the corner.

"I'm finished eating," she said. "The rest is yours."

When I heard her settle back onto the bench, I stepped forward and retrieved the basket. With it, I sat down and leaned against the wall, crossing my legs at the ankle. I fished inside and pulled out what looked to be diced up chicken in a creamy sauce wrapped in some sort of flatbread. Probably something from her plane she had the cooks make. There was also a half-eaten bowl of fruit and a glass bottle of water that was untouched. I moved the paper off of the sandwich-like thing and took a bite. The creamy dressing, the walnuts, and the avocado made a delicious combination.

"This is good," I said.

"Kind of a strange way to have a picnic when you're eating on the other side of a building from someone, isn't it?" she asked.

I huffed a laugh and continued chewing. When I swallowed, I asked, "What are you reading that made you laugh? I assume since you haven't come running to me with the solution to the curse, you've moved on to some lighter material?"

I could almost feel her grin whenever she said, "Wouldn't you like to know?"

"I would. That's why I asked you," I said.

"Well, you're right. I haven't found some grand solution and currently I'm biding my time reading something I pulled off the romance shelf called *Secrets of Scoundrels*. And I would call to attention that your library has a very weak selection of fun books."

"Fun books?" I asked.

"Yeah. Most everything in there is history, ledgers, or spells. There's hardly any fiction. You brought a book with you out here too?" she asked, her voice lifting hopefully.

"I did," I said, glancing down at the title I was about halfway through.

"Are you going to tell me what it is?"

"Wouldn't you like to know?" I asked, letting my voice take on a rare, teasing edge. She groaned, but didn't take the bait, so I said, "It's a thriller called *The Reaper's Kiss*, about a serial killer called The Reaper and the team of warlocks who hunt him down."

"Sounds morbid," she said, and I could hear the rustling of pages. "Happy reading, warlock."

"Happy reading, witch," I replied. After that she said nothing else, and I picked up my book flipping to where I had stopped last. As we sat reading around the corner from each other, I couldn't help but notice the quiet was welcome, peaceful. Birds chirped, and the wind rustled through the leaves, but the charge of the air wasn't uncomfortable. Did she sense it too?

We sat like that for a long time. Long enough that gray clouds eventually covered the sky and thunder cracked overhead. The witch cried out as the first droplets fell. Instantly, I was on my feet, pulling off my cloak. I held it around the corner for her. "Here, take this," I said. "I'll clean up. Get inside before you get soaked."

She didn't hesitate, taking it out of my hand. A moment later, she had it wrapped around her head, covering her face, and she was darting past me toward the castle. An unbidden smile formed on my lips as I tracked her. Something about seeing her in my garment, watching her flee, called to my blood. But instead of chasing after her, I stood there and let the rain wash away any dangerous illusions I might have before they took hold.

CHAPTER 12

AVERY

D ipping my mascara wand, I pulled it out and swiped a few more passes on my lashes. Tonight marked the two-month anniversary of arriving in this plane, and I was to be married. This was by far the most makeup I'd worn since I'd arrived here, and I kept going with the one thing I usually took comfort in because my nerves were zipping around in a really nerve-wracking way.

This wasn't at all how I'd imagined my wedding day to be. I thought I'd have surely made some friends by now. We should be sitting around, giggling, and sipping champagne. Them reminding me of wild stories from my single days. I knew I wouldn't have that coming here, but I thought I'd at least have something. A few friends to share it with.

I mean I had April and Alice, but it didn't really count since they were paid to work for me. And while I had awkwardly bumped into Olive a few times since our initial encounter in the hallways, she was adept at avoiding the tea I'd suggested or any further conversation. Even the handful of visiting Ladies who had come through the Ravsted had been standoffish of me. As if they, like everyone else, had been through this before and weren't willing to make the time commitment. That was fine though. It felt weird being the only one in human form around a bunch of rat-women, because my eyes wouldn't behave, and they seemed to be a pack I wasn't a part of.

Outside of those few encounters, Xavier was saving all of our public functions until after the wedding, so there were few other opportunities to meet anyone. I'd been spending most of my time, since I'd finished cleaning the library, my suite, and the study, assessing, and putting together a plan of action for the rest of the castle which included much needed redecorating. Leviticus had gotten me two additional maids so far and they were making decent progress with my projects. While I still didn't feel like I had free reign to do whatever I wanted, Xavier had permitted most of my ideas, and I was feeling decent about my time here.

My head snapped toward the creaking door to find Nighval stepping through. "What are you doing here?" I asked. The warlock was the last person I expected to see walk through my bedroom door tonight. I hadn't seen him since our little picnic, and admittedly, him arriving was a welcome distraction from the nerves that were zapping through my gut.

"Xavier asked that I deliver you to the ceremony. In case you decide to change your mind at the last minute, or perhaps he is gloating," he said, leaning against a wall, crossing those long legs at the ankle. "Not going to run, are you, witch?"

He said it like he almost wanted me to. Like he wanted his brother to fail. But I would not fail at this. I made a promise, and I would keep it. And besides, pretty much all royal marriages were arranged things. Tons of women over the centuries had been in my position and made the best of it. And who knew? Ten months was a long time and maybe something magical would happen, and Xavier and I would fall in love. Stranger things and all.

Nighval's dark gaze met mine in the mirror as he walked by. "Back in your true form and back to being a dickhead, I see. Oh, that's right. I recall you could never get one of us to marry you." I made a show of looking him up and down and said, "It totally makes sense."

He flinched as my jab landed. Not only was it a full moon, it was the reprieve which meant the man Nighval faced me and he wasn't bothering to soften his appearance on my behalf. While I wouldn't say I was getting used to it, since those first shocking moments, I didn't find him nearly as frightening as in our last handful of encounters. Maybe I was settling into my soon-to-be role as queen and the authority of the position was coming naturally because *I was prepared.*

Nighval sneered as he stepped up behind me. "I still don't understand why my brother told you. Honestly, it never occurred to me to tell a woman she was meant to break a curse in order to get her to fall in love with me. But good for him. You two will make quite the couple. I imagine you are eager for your wedding night."

I sneered back at him. "I can see there is no love lost between the two of you. What's that about?" I didn't think asking him would be any harm. After all, between the two brothers, he'd been the most forthcoming.

Sighing, Nighval strode over to me, gripped the back of the stool I was sitting on applying the perfecting touches of makeup, and spun it around so I was facing him. As he lowered his scarred face to mine, I decided I was still totally terrified of him. "Sibling rivalry, jealousy. Power struggle. General personality conflict. You know the usual."

I had a feeling there was more to the story. "There seems to be a lot of animosity between you. More than sibling rivalry would warrant."

"What scent are you wearing?" he asked, ignoring my inquiry. He closed his eyes, then leaned forward. I thought he was going to kiss me for a brief second before his head moved to the side of mine. He inhaled deeply and hummed. My eyes fluttered shut and I resisted tilting my head to the side, so he'd have better access to my neck, as messed up as that was. *Touch me, kiss me, taste me.* Oh no. Sometimes when my brain got started, it really took a detour.

He moved away, walking over to the window in a few steps. I peeled my eyes open, hoping he hadn't noticed, and picked up the perfume bottle. It was one of those Nest fragrances which I had many of. I brought the travel variety pack, but the scent my aunt had spelled was the only full bottle.

"Sun-kissed hibiscus," I replied, making a mental note to select something different to wear whenever he was around. New rule: do not attract the beast.

"I like it. It reminds me of summer. Since the curse, the weather has been cool like this. I don't know why except that somehow everything about it was designed for our misery."

I didn't want to speak ill of my sister witches, but I still said, "Your mother seems like a real piece of work."

Nighval chuckled and eyed me in a way I couldn't interpret. "You have no idea," he said, and I wondered if he was thinking of the moment we'd shared in her room like I was.

April and Alice shuffled into the room carrying a flowing white gown—my wedding dress. Like the king and his brother, they also had a reprieve from their rat form for a few hours overnight during the full moon.

Normally, I could see their scars through their soft fur, but now old lines from where their flesh had been torn were so much more garish that they were almost hard to look at. Especially since April had a fresh cut on her eyelid that I had a feeling wouldn't heal well. Did they not have stitches? I made myself look at them because if I were going to be their queen, I would not shame or disrespect them.

I made an estimation of the dress as they laid it on the bed. Running a hand over the lace, I realized it was the one thing in this plane that was completely unmarred. But the dress didn't appear new. I imagined they had made this dress for one of Nighval's first brides, executing the artisanship when they could work without ruining the fabric. And then they just kept it, for this very moment. Had they adjusted it for my form or was it still sewn to the measurements of the first witch? I glanced at Nighval. He was staring at the dress, and I wondered if he was having similar thoughts. Perhaps he remembered the first witch this dress was made for and when I considered that, I could almost interpret a little glimmer of melancholy in his eye.

Then his eyes flashed to me, and his face immediately hardened. Any sympathy I might have felt for him evaporated in a blink. "Are you going to stand there while they dress me?"

"I was planning on it. Only an hour to go and you'll be his wife. Technically, there's still time to run. The last thing I want to do is watch my brother's bride flee. Then he might get an understanding of what I went through for the last seventeen years, and I wouldn't want that. Anything to shield my younger brother from any discomfort."

He crossed his arms over his chest and stared at me. He was not going to budge, so I snapped, "Turnaround at least."

He did, returning to his perch at the window ledge, leaning over it with his arms braced on the ledge and his head tilted to the sky. His broad shoulders almost took up the entire breadth of the window, blocking out the moonlight and it took an effort to tear my eyes away from him.

No, brain. We are not making a mistake. In an hour, we'll be a queen and we will have kept our word. I clenched my teeth, swatted the gnats filtering about in my stomach away and hardened my resolve.

My girls didn't seem to notice as they made quick work of dressing me. I discovered the gown had a large V in the back and laces that could cinch the fabric to my figure, which it did, hugging all the way to the knee where it flared out like a modern-day mermaid style dress. There were delicate straps and a long lace train. The curved neckline was modest, but when the girls tugged on the strings at my back, my chest heaved up and out. A line of cleavage appeared, and I grimaced.

Oh God. The last thing I wanted to do was appear like a sexy vixen because, as much as I had agreed to go through with this wedding, all bets were off for the wedding night. A lot was going to have to change in a few short hours for me to decide to sleep with the king. And the good news was I didn't think that he would force me. My aunt had been right. Xavier was a nice man, albeit a little pasty, and he was trying to make every accommodation for me. He didn't even get frustrated whenever I still flinched at him in his rat form.

"Okay, you're ready, Your Majesty," April said, urging me toward the mirror, and the giddiness in her voice didn't escape me as she used my title for the first time. My attendants were excited a witch was finally going through with this wedding.

Nighval heard the pronouncement, turned, but froze when his eyes snagged on the dress. His stare trailed up and down my form and his throat bobbed. Without directly addressing my girls, he said, "Get out." His voice was so rough I started, but the women didn't hesitate before scurrying from the room. When they closed the door, he stepped behind me and stared at me in the mirror. His hand reached for me. A finger slid inside one of the thin straps at my shoulder, and my heart skittered as his rough finger grazed my skin leaving a trail of gooseflesh in its wake.

"What are you doing?" I asked, as the breath caught in my throat.

"The first witch sent here was supposed to wear this dress. You're clever. I'm sure you've guessed that much." He released the strap, and his hands went to his sides, balling into fists.

"I did. And I'm sorry if seeing me in it bothers you." His angular face softened as I said it. I really was sorry. In that moment, my clarity of what it must have been like for him struck me, and I wanted to reach out to him to somehow take his pain away.

Instead, I turned and tilted my head up so I could take him in better. His eyes had a faraway look for a moment, like he was reliving a memory, and then they focused on me.

"The first woman who should've worn this dress was beautiful. Yet, she pales in comparison to you. Another reason for me to hate my brother..." he trailed off as I sucked in a breath at the weird sensation his compliment caused. "*If* you make it down the aisle." His gaze hardened. "Let's go."

He didn't look back as he strode toward the door, expecting me to follow. He held it open, as I passed under the archway. Then he offered me his arm and led me through a maze of dark hallways to the chapel where I would seal my fate.

CHAPTER 13

NIGHVAL

I hated every second of walking the witch to the chapel. I hated seeing her in that dress that had been meant for *my* wife. I hated how fucking perfect she looked. I hated those stupid freckles that dappled her cheeks and nose which also grazed the fine bones of her shoulders and collarbone and were just begging to be kissed. I hated how eager my brother appeared, standing at the altar bouncing on the balls of his feet as we stepped in the arched doors, and he got the first sight of her.

I walked her up the aisle. And when her fingers dropped from the crook of my elbow, I hated that, too. I should recuse myself, but to support my brother and our kingdom, I needed to stay put. I handed her off to him. He held the tips of her fingers, raising them so he could get a good look at her. The chapel only held a small crowd, and the woman garnering everyone's attention seemed so alive, so vibrant in the space, it seemed even smaller with her inside it.

Was I such a selfish bastard that I was considering stealing her away? Taking her from my brother? Yes, I was. After everything I'd been through, the seventeen years of rejection, standing strong against the witches' fear and revulsion, and the weight of the expectation put on me by our people. I bore it all, and she should be my reward. It should be me standing next to her ready to say our vows. I could do it—take her to Lieden Palace, my home on the other side of the kingdom. With my power, it would be a small feat and Xavier wouldn't dare come after us.

The thoughts swirling in my mind made by palms sweat, the sudden anticipation of *what if* sending my heart skipping. I wanted her, that much was clear to me, but what would I do once I had her all to myself?

I was still this monster who she could barely look at without flinching. Even if we somehow managed to break the curse, I saw how she stared at the real me, and I wasn't sure I had the energy to soften my features for the rest of our lives. To hide myself for her or anyone else. No, things were better this way. Xavier won. He was the one who'd negotiated his way to the altar, so there he stood.

Regret curled low in my gut. I should have let him try with one of the witches before this one. There was something about the fire in her eye, her grit and self-possession, the way she carried herself that called to my blood. And her body... I let my eyes trail down her form, and hang on the curve of her ass, accentuated by that fucking dress. As if Xavier sensed my thoughts, he glanced back toward the rows of packed benches, eyes landing on me. He shot a glare full of daggers at me, moving a possessive step toward the witch.

I had two choices. Take her before they completed the vows or leave. Standing here in indifference wasn't a choice. The little, hopeful smile she gave Xavier tipped the scale enough that, with a few motions of my fingers, I was gone. My flight would piss Xavier off, but when was he ever not pissed at me? With the few hours of moonlight left, I needed to find a woman to warm my bed. To quench this relentless stirring the witch called forth.

But my agitation overruled my other flaming emotions. When I was angry like this, the last thing I needed to do was be around a member of the more delicate sex. So instead, I transported myself deep into the forest, to a corner of the woods where the unsavory creatures of my kingdom hid. When I got like this, I spent the night hunting them, eliminating the dredges of society. Murders, thieves, rapists, poachers, demon worshipers, all the miscreants who banded together to poison my world.

Xavier would put them on trial and make them atone in his civilized ways. His justice was another point on which we disagreed. But the fact that I hadn't stolen his bride ought to make any of the actions I took this night forgivable in his eyes. And it was either this or go take care of another thorn in the kingdom's side like Sir Robert Musson, who had it coming eventually. Xavier believed he'd dealt with the man though, so to my mind, this was the preferable option.

And I had to diffuse this energy somehow. When I was done, when I had taken the blood owed to the Goddess, soaking the forest floor, and feeding her with its rich, life-giving properties, I would rest and forget about the witch.

Laughter drew my attention. I narrowed my eyes in the direction of the sound and listened. A crackling fire, and the voices engaged in hedonistic merriment, moon worship, drifted toward me on a breeze. I sniffed the air and caught the metallic scent of human blood. Not moon worship, demon.

This wasn't like the full moon parties held in the fields surrounding Lieden Palace, where ritual and revery were sacred, visceral things. Carnal even. No, I knew the types who found their pleasure, who fed their most depraved desires deep in the shadows of the trees. I'd found them and they were my prey tonight.

Calling to my magic, I stepped into the clearing. As the revelers caught sight of my dark form illuminated by the firelight and the power blazing, glowing blue in my palms, screams rent the air.

CHAPTER 14

AVERY

I walked down the aisle a married woman under the light of a full moon. Oh God, I was a married woman now. A queen, equipped with a crown and everything. More like a tiara, with interlocking rings embedded with channel set round diamonds, and in between the ovals the loops created, yellow pear-shaped diamonds dangled which matched the massive yellow diamond solitaire adorning my ring finger.

Said bedazzled hand wrapped around Xavier's forearm, and he patted it gently. Tonight, he appeared like the king I'd met for a brief moment on my first day in this plane. We had spent some time together, two months' worth, but regardless of the fact that his mother cursed him to look like a half-rat-half-man, he just wasn't my type. Falling in love with this man was an impossible task, and I knew it deep in my bones. Not that at twenty-five, I had exactly nailed down my type. I just knew it wasn't him. Still, we were husband and wife, and no one could say that I, Avery Plath, didn't give it one hell of a go.

The hopeful, beady, human-ish eyes that stared up at me from each guest made all of this worse. So much worse and marrying him was a huge step toward their freedom. A guilty twinge niggled at my awareness. Allowing this wedding to happen would only instill false hope in these people. I stared at my husband as he escorted me down the aisle, then glanced to the guests as I passed them, making a note of a conspicuously missing older brother. Not that I was scanning the crowd for him.

Xavier led me into a long banquet hall, even larger than the dining hall we took our meals in. The ceiling arched two stories over us, and massive tapestries hung between long skinny windows depicting garish battle scenes, fruit trees, creatures I assumed were mythical, humans playing instruments, and old kings and queens standing around looking at each other.

My favorite was of a woman dancing with an arm over her head and the other curved in front of her exposed belly button. Her skirt sat low on her hips and flowed in gorgeous panels of woven gold and red fabric. Her top, which had the same flowing sleeves which cinched at the wrist, hugged her bodice, and fell to the bottom of her ribs. It would have made a sweet club outfit, but in all black, obviously. The red and gold was a little gaudy for my taste. But like everything here, the tapestry was worn, tattered at the bottom, and in need of maintenance.

Xavier noticed I was eyeing it. "You like that one?"

"I like her outfit," I said. "Actually, do you think we could get the tailors to make me something like it?" So far, their clothes were pretty modern—what we would consider vintage, and formal, and I wondered if they got things from our plane. Or had before the curse.

My husband wrinkled his brow as he considered the woman depicted in the panel, then frowned. I gathered he felt the outfit would be queenly and it would be a little breezy for the climate here. "Never mind," I said before he could reply.

I scanned the room. Endless varieties of flowers burst from gleaming silver vases. The stunning arrangements sat on long tables which weren't covered. Seeing the state of the drapes in my room, I understood why. Even the wooden tables had gouges in them and a million more superficial scratches. The flowers were probably the most visually pleasant things I'd seen since I'd been here. Well, those and the jewel encrusted tiara which now sat atop my head.

Leading me to the head of the table where two high-backed chairs were sitting side-by-side, Xavier pulled one out for me, and I sat. Wine was delivered, the guests took their seats, and we feasted.

Later that night, when I judged we had about an hour before the first toll of the bell, Xavier led me by the elbow to my room. His anticipation crawled over my skin and while I enjoyed myself by his side, like I would a childhood best friend or a brother, I couldn't pick up the same vibe.

We stepped into the room, and I moved over to the vanity and began pulling out the pins which held the tiara in place. I set it in the open, velvet-lined box the girls must have set out for me. I felt Xavier's warm breath on my neck before I glanced up to the mirror to see him hovering behind me. "Did you like my vows?" he asked. "I've been working on them for weeks."

Then his hands were on the laces of my dress before I could reply. He tugged, then the bow was unraveled and the fabric holding my chest up relaxed. My hand went to the neckline as my heartbeat ratcheted up. Could he not see the blotching pink skin that was practically hives breaking out across my chest?

Xavier's fingers combed through my hair, which had fallen half down my back, and his other went to the strap the same way Nighval's had done earlier that night. While my body had gravitated toward the fear Nighval's touch elicited, and something tingly that memorized the burn of his fingers on my skin, his brother—my husband's touch elicited an entirely different reaction. *Revulsion*. Interesting, but I filed that away in the never to be explored, ever category.

His fingers moved the strap from my shoulder and his other hand wrapped around the wrist of my hand, still holding up the bodice of my wedding dress. In my ear he whispered, "Show yourself to me, Avery." His wet lips moved on my earlobe, then it was in his mouth, and he was lowering the fabric down my chest.

As the fabric passed over my nipples, my arm, not in his grip, flew up so my forearm was covering them. "I'm sorry, Xavier. I can't," I said and couldn't stop the shiver that wracked my body.

My husband let out a heavy breath and met my eyes in the mirror. "You are a virgin?" he asked, searching for understanding.

"I... uh," I murmured. Did he expect me to be? What was I supposed to say? "No," I said, tentatively. "I've been with a few people. It's just been a while. A *long* while. I'm nervous," I said.

Since time was relative, I wasn't really lying. There was that super hot guy who got my number from the club a few months ago and we hooked up a few times. When he picked me up in a blacked-out Mercedes-Benz

GT-Class Coupe, I fantasized he was secretly a kinky billionaire CEO, and one time my fantasy was that he was an Italian mafia boss. He certainly had the build and coloring for it, but I knew it wouldn't last, because it never did with guys like that and besides, I was coming here to become a queen.

"It's okay, Avery. I appreciate you trying. We can attempt it another day." He ran his hand from my elbow to my shoulder and gave me a soft smile. My stomach clenched and not in a pleasant way. He was a good man, cute, I guessed, but nothing happened *down there* at his touch. Xavier shifted his belt and headed for the door. He tapped the doorframe with the butt of his fist three times like he had more to say, but he turned and left.

I slipped the dress off and threw on a robe, releasing all my tension in a sigh as I slumped into the chair at my vanity. I meant to pick up the refilling make-up remover cloths, but my hand strayed to the crown. Picking it up, I studied it. There would be a day I had to sleep with him. Putting him off would only prolong the inevitable. And I didn't know if being around him more would make things easier or harder.

I went to sleep with the thought bouncing around in my mind. I had to find a way, for the witches, to warm to him. To fall for him, and I had ten months to do it. We were totally fucked.

CHAPTER 15

AVERY

Four months after the wedding.

Xavier came to me again on the next full moon, and the next. Still, I couldn't sleep with him. At least he hadn't tried to make any advances not on the reprieve. That would have been much more uncomfortable.

We'd done all the couple dating stuff except the physical act and the man was determined to make that happen.

"How long are you going to make me wait?" he asked, a new insistent, possible aggressiveness I hadn't recognized before laced his voice.

"I don't know," I said, slipping off my robe and walking over to my bed. This was the same routine every time.

"Avery, the pressure is building," Xavier said, which was new.

"Then jerk off," I snapped.

He stepped forward, wrapping his hand gently around my shoulder. "Not that type of pressure. The people expect me to have wooed you by now. How am I supposed to do that if you won't let me touch you?"

"I don't know," I said, hand shifting to the high neckline of my sleeping gown

"I bring you flowers, I read you poetry, take you for rides to the nearby villages and buy you anything you ask for. What else can I do, my queen?" His hand trailed down the length of my arm. "Your skin is so smooth."

He was right. Compared to their skin, which most of was covered in the knicks and cuts like my helpers. I'd seen his bare torso, and it was the same. Fortunately, his face hadn't suffered the same accidental abuse.

I gently jerked my shoulder out of his hold, even as I took a step back. "Next time?" I asked and could hear the rattle in my voice. There was something about the look in his eye that frightened me. All of this pressure wasn't turning him into a diamond. It was bringing out things in his character that perhaps wouldn't have existed without it. But they say stressful situations bring out people's true character and maybe Xavier wasn't as noble of a man as everyone believed him to be.

He advanced, and I flinched. "You do not want me in this form either, my queen?" Xavier gestured to himself. He was right. He wasn't bad. Many women would be happy with him as a husband. I didn't know what was wrong with me, but I couldn't even make myself go through the motions. I had to go through with it eventually and we both knew it. Maybe if I slept with him, it would trigger some feelings. That happened to some women, didn't it?

I shut my eyes and said, "Okay, maybe we can have a drink first?"

"A drink?" he hissed. "After the kindness I've shown you, you say *okay* to me and want to get inebriated?" He stormed toward the door, slamming his fist into it as he passed, and I jumped. He turned and glared at me. "I'm getting a little tired of being the one doing all the giving."

Guilt, my new companion, nipped at me. Shit. I knew what I needed to do. I was here and married to this man and at some point, we would need to be intimate. If not to produce an heir, then to seek pleasure. I'm sure I wasn't the first woman in an arranged marriage trying to figure things out. Though I was sure none of them were ever given the space and time I was, and many of those women had grown to feel affectionate toward their husbands. Why couldn't I do the same?

I gritted my teeth as I paced the room. The clock on the nightstand ticked away and with each minute, the moon crept across the sky. Xavier wasn't bad. If it were Nighval I could have—oh no. The blossoming thought was as unwelcome as it was true, but I didn't finish it. I hadn't even seen him since before the wedding. But when his finger had traced across my skin, sensations sprung to life, and I was far too aware of his overwhelming presence.

Shaking my head, I made up my mind. I would go to him and force myself to do this. Maybe he'd be amazing in bed and things would change.

As I approached his door, a hushed conversation was taking place. A woman's voice said, "I thought you were done with me, Xavier? Is your pretty wife not satisfying your needs?"

He chuckled in a way I hadn't heard from him before. "Unfortunately, no, she isn't. And I told you, once the curse is broken, we'll send her away, and I'll make you my queen."

My hand flew to my mouth to seal it before a gasp could escape as I placed the voice. *Olive*. What a conniving bitch. No wonder she acted like she didn't want to be friends with me.

"When I saw her and then heard the wedding announcement, I thought perhaps you changed your mind," the woman said.

"Why would I want a woman who has no desire to please me when I have you, darling?" Xavier said.

"You still need to bed her, my king. Do whatever it takes to please her, so she'll fall for you the way I have," she said.

"But she isn't willing. I thought maybe when she agreed to marry me, we were making progress, but she flinches at my touch. I can't force her."

"You can, Xavier. You're king now. If she won't freely give you her love, then you must take it. Do what your brother was too weak to do, for all of our sakes. Show her the man you are like you show me."

They were quiet for a long moment, then fabric rustled and several pieces of material, likely their clothes, thudded to the floor. "We don't have long, my love. Use your mouth," Xavier said, and a few seconds later, his groan was followed by slurping sounds.

I knew I shouldn't be listening, but this was a rubberneck situation. I couldn't tear myself away.

"Oh yeah, baby," he said, and moaned. I jumped as the bell struck once. It rang a second and third time, and a grunt came from inside the room. "Easy, Olive."

"Sorry, my king," she said, and I could tell by the slight change in her voice that her rat teeth had come in. Their footsteps retreated, and I poked my head inside just enough to get a glimpse of them.

I'd never seen any of the rat-people naked, and other than being dusted with the fine rat's hair everywhere, they appeared anatomically the same as humans. Granted, I was a distance from them.

Xavier guided her over to a chair in the corner, pressed her to her knees, and bent her over it. He got to his knees behind her, and she made a pained sound as his hips went flushed with hers and he started pumping, grunting with each stroke. All of it repulsed me. Even the way his thick ankles angled his feet outward behind him as his belly smacked against her furry ass made my stomach churn. Ick.

I'd seen enough. I turned and scurried down the hallway toward the safety of my room.

Oh. My. God. Xavier already had a woman, and he was trying to get me to fall in love with him for the sake of breaking this curse. I thought we'd at least formed a friendship, but this was absurd. That and *his lover*, Olive, had encouraged him to use a stronger hand, coaxing me into submission. I knew her type—total pick me girl. If she lived in my plane, she'd probably be one of those crazies suggesting women give up their voting rights because it made them feel good to pander to powerful men. Eww.

Shock had me panting as I leaned against the back of my locked door. Not that I felt even the slightest glimmer of hurt. That was the thing. I didn't care who Xavier slept with. I just hadn't expected what I saw and heard.

The way he'd glared at me before he stormed away... I knew that look. That was the type of look I usually called a bouncer at the club for. He was slowly gearing himself up to take what he wanted. After that, her words would have convinced him.

I had until the next full moon and then Xavier was going to force himself on me if I didn't let him. I needed to let him. I knew I did. I'd been telling myself that for the last few months since our wedding, and I'd honestly almost psyched myself up to do it, but seeing him railing that rat-woman with his mild paunch slapping over her furry backside was a sight I would never be able to erase from my mind.

Run. I could run away like the women before me, curse be damned. The fact that it would be damning an entire society of people to live for eternity in half-rat form made guilt churn deep in my gut. And then there was what Nighval and the other warlocks would do to the witches when the curse expired. But if I could somehow find this witch who cursed them, *their mother*, maybe I could convince her to release the curse to save her sisters. Yes, that is what I would do.

My mind whirled. I could go now, I wanted to go now, but perhaps waiting until the next full moon would be wise as the castle workers and guards would be distracted during the few hours of the reprieve. That was another thing I learned I could count on in this plane. Those couple of hours a month, everyone seemed to abandon their duties, and no one paid it any mind. Besides, I didn't think Xavier would try anything while in his rat-form. I only had to hope the supposed nice guy inside him held out long enough for me to prepare.

CHAPTER 16

AVERY

One month later

I scanned my room as the moon began its ascent. My backpack lay in the corner of the room near the window, one of the few in the castle with no cracked or broken panes. I had it packed and waiting, stuffed with clothing, my kick-ass makeup kit, and non-perishable food pilfered from the kitchens earlier that morning.

It had been a busy month and since Xavier had taken up relations with his lover again, some of the pressure on me dropped. With that, he even agreed to shift a few of the castle duties Leviticus handled to me which was really too bad since I was leaving. Had he done that and shown faith in my abilities during the prior seven months, when I'd had to fight tooth and nail to make the small changes I had, things might be different.

Actually, who was I kidding. I probably should have seen him for what he was, what my gut was telling me and split like the other witches months ago. That misjudgment I definitely blamed on the Disney movies doing me a solid disservice.

Tonight, I would slip off the first-floor balcony, into the gardens and catch a ride to the first town bartering with my jewelry and the other items which had been inside the drawers of my vanity. All of it was there when I arrived, probably belonging to the other witches before me.

I changed into the most practical attire I'd brought with me, low-worn leather boots, leggings, a long-sleeved crop top which only showed an inch of my midriff and had a built-in sports bra, all black. I snatched out a traveling cloak out of the wardrobe which had armholes for the large draping sleeves and stuffed the valuable items into the inner pocket.

In my month to prepare, I memorized a map of Ras alhague and re-read every single document I'd taken from Samara's room twice. I'd even found Link again and made him pick the lock on the room so I could read the love letters. Anything to get a peek into her psyche. I'd find her and, as a witch myself, kind of, I'd convince her to undo the curse.

My determination outweighed my nerves as I scanned the room which had been my home to see if I'd missed anything when my eyes fixed on the nightstand and the drawer which sat open an inch. Tilting my head to the side, I considered it. In my first month here, when I'd thought that I was in more danger than I was, the danger I was in now, I'd stashed a carving knife in the drawer. Just in case.

Shaking my head, I left it there. I remembered hearing a self-defense instructor say it was better not to attempt to wield a weapon if you didn't know how to use it. I'd be more likely to hurt myself with the thing than defend myself.

I knew I'd never fall for this man, especially not after what I'd seen. And he didn't even want me as queen. He wanted Olive. My efforts had never been so futile. It was time to go.

CHAPTER 17

NIGHVAL

As I crept through the shadows after her, it was hard not to let a smile play at the corners of my lips. It was almost cute the way she tiptoed down the dark alley. Honestly, I was surprised how far she'd made it into the night before I'd sensed her breaching the wards I'd placed on Ravsted. I didn't think she could ride, but perhaps she paid off someone for transportation in a carriage or even one of the dozen motorcars which could be found in the city surrounding the castle for hire.

Something about the way she fled excited my prey drive, a sensation which differed from when I'd hunted the lowlifes on her wedding night or when any of the witches had run before her. Was it the animal in me, enlivened by the curse, or just the way I was? Or was it her? I glanced up at the moon. I had time. I could make a game of it before I delivered her back to my brother.

Cloaking myself with my power, I took a step closer. Then another. When I was so close I could hear her breathing, I splayed a hand across the bricks she leaned against and then edged it toward hers, which was also splayed wide, gripping onto the wall as if it could save her. If I moved a centimeter, our fingers would touch and there was something thrilling about the prospect. Like a fool, I couldn't resist. Gently, I brushed the tip of her finger with my own. She jumped.

"Who's there?" she asked, voice a gurgled cry as she white knuckled the strap of her backpack and gripped her cloak closed at her neck. Her head darted back and forth down the alleyway, only to find it empty. Then she gave a knowing look to the moon. "Shit," she whispered.

The witch scurried down the alleyway, and I kept pace with her. When she reached the end, her head whipped both ways, and she rushed out into the street. Few travelers were roaming the roads, and no one paid the lone woman any mind as they were all off on their own mission to take advantage of the reprieve.

Where was she going? I got my answer whenever her attention shifted to the inn at the end of the street, standing a little off from the others. Had she stolen coin or was she planning to barter with the innkeeper at this hour?

She scurried down the street, keeping close to the right side, looked both ways again and crossed. The handle of the wooden slat door didn't give as she rattled it. She reached for the metal knocker and knocked three times. The witch flicked her gaze anxiously up and down the street when the door finally creaked open and an aging woman with a wrinkled face and a grisly scar similar to my own ran across her nose. She said something to the innkeeper, then shifted her backpack around to the front and began digging inside. Pulling out what looked to be a silver bangle, she offered it to the woman, and gave her a pleading look before saying more things I couldn't hear.

I had a few hours before I turned, and this just wouldn't do. The innkeeper looked as if she were considering the trade, so I stepped out of the shadows, caught her attention, and gave a quick shake of my head that said, *Do not let her in.* The woman's face screwed up into a look of distress and she worried her hands. When the witch understood her trade was being rejected, her shoulders lowered. The innkeeper shut the door with a click, and she lowered her eyes to the handle, which she must hear being locked from the other side.

Then she squared her shoulders and looked past the end of the row of buildings to the open field and the forest beyond. As she made her way through the field, her hands skimmed over the tops of the swaying wheat stalks and she hummed a tune I didn't recognize. Probably something from her plane. It was a nice melody, and she had a soothing voice. I wondered if she even realized she was humming, or this was something she did when she was nervous. She definitely didn't realize she was being followed. Yet.

The squelching of my boot sinking into a puddle of mud shattered the silent evening. Not even crickets chirped at this hour, and there was no way she hadn't heard it. She froze and so did I. As if the wind sensed I had caught her, it kicked up, blowing at her back, toward the tree line, urging her forward.

She spun, and her cloak blew out around her, whipping back toward the trees in a gust. Her arms flew behind her as she tried to get a hold of the billowing garment and as she did, I studied her. The fabric hugged over every contour and dip, almost indecently. I'd never seen a woman wear such a thing. It left little to the imagination, only heightening my desire to chase her into a sharp-edged impulse. Seven months had passed, and our every interaction was still clear as when it had happened in my mind. I wanted her no less than I had the night of her wedding.

"Leave me alone," she cried, and ran for the tree line. As I followed her, the image of that inch of warm skin along her waist that her outfit exposed warmed my mind. I wanted to run my fingers along it and lift the edge to see what was underneath. To see if she'd let me. She wasn't like the other witches, so I had no idea what to expect from her. It wasn't just the way she looked or her clothes. Or the way she painted her face, which was done with painstaking care. Her shocking pink lips, the black lines that swept up on her eyes alluding to the secrets hidden there. The quick mind and passionate soul I sensed lying in wait, needing a man like me to stoke it to life. Goddess, I was eager for the task.

"I know you're out there, Nighval," she said, brazenly stopping to scan the trees behind her, so sure in her rightness.

Hearing her call my name while her voice was laced with fear and a little of that edge she always had snapped whatever restraint I was clinging to. I dropped my magical cloak and let her see just how close I was. Her hand shot to her mouth, and she turned and sprinted through the forest. Her legs were long, but not nearly long enough to speed her away. I let her stay just enough ahead that I could give chase. Her boot caught on a twig, and she went down with a thud, the air bursting from her lungs as she hit the ground.

Get up, I mentally decreed. She did and as she shot a look back at me over her shoulder, I realized what she hid within her eyes. Anticipation.

"Run," I said in a half growl, half whisper. When her body surged forward, things inside me that had long lay dormant came to life in a powerful burst. It was those things now controlling every forest eating step I took as I chased after her. Quickly, I overtook her, seizing her by the waist. I spun her, so she was facing me, hooked my thumbs in the straps of her pack and with a flick, I dropped it to the forest floor. I stepped forward, and she took a step back, scrambling over her pack. I took another step and another until her back hit a tree and she inhaled sharply.

Her chest rose and fell rapidly as her hands went to my chest and instead of shoving me away, they ran up a few inches until her fingertips grazed my collar bones.

Her eyes flicked from mine to my lips, even as her own parted. "Oh my God," she breathed.

What I wouldn't give to know exactly what was in her head at that moment. Except I had a feeling I knew because it was the same thing in my own. Before I could stop myself, I grasped her lower jaw. I tilted her head up, angling mine down over hers. Her hands went to my wrists, but she did not pull them away, so I pressed my lips to hers. My heart was beating so loud, if there were sounds of the forest, I couldn't hear them. The only sensation I had was of her soft lips yielding beneath mine. Her mouth parted.

And then she kissed me back. The witch was kissing me back. My *brother's* wife was kissing me back. But I didn't care. I deepened the kiss.

She moaned as our tongues brushed against each other, and I lost control. Her greedy hands went back my chest and then up and around my neck as I pulled her body into mine, crushing her between me and the tree. I snaked my hand inside her cloak to her waist, to her hip, needing to feel her. A rush of warmth flooded through me, and my blood altered its course, surging between my hips. When I pressed myself into her, my cock was rock hard. She whimpered when she felt it, responding by tilting her hips to meet it. I almost staggered back when she raised her knee to the outside of my thigh. I knew what she wanted, and I gave it to her. I grabbed the crook of her knee and used it to pull us closer together as I ground into her, all the while I took from her mouth what I wanted.

Goddess, she tasted like cinnamon and honey. And a thousand dreams. She was moaning into my mouth as if she felt the same forbidden draw sparking between us. Because we shouldn't be doing this. But I had always been a man who made my own rules, and I was going to take whatever this witch was willing to give me under the light of the full moon.

The word moon, the implication of it, snapped me out of the moment for a heartbeat. I ripped my mouth away from hers and shot my gaze to the damnable cosmic body that had long since crested overhead. I was nearly out of time, and I was going to need a long time to do the things that I wanted to do to this woman. It would be another month until I got the chance if I could find some way to get her away from my brother.

"Why'd you stop?" she asked, breathless. But she tracked the direction of my eyes, which were pointed to the heavens. Like a cold bucket of water had doused her flame, she blanched, dropping her leg. My hands fell, and hers went to her sides before they hugged her cloak around her, overlapping the seam like that could protect her.

"I have to get you back," I heard myself say. I moved my fingers in the familiar pattern and a second later, we were standing in her bedroom. Her body was stiff with tension and as she scanned the room settling on her pack, a little of it eased, but was immediately regained when her eyes landed on Xavier.

"I found your bride," I said, giving my brother a look that I knew didn't hide the disdain I felt at whatever he did that had driven the woman away. He had seven months with her and though she had married him, their relationship seemed to be stalled. I didn't feel guilty for taking the opportunity, and I wouldn't feel guilty when I came back on the next full moon to see what else the witch would offer me. And not because of the curse. Because when she leaned her hips into mine, she wanted *me*. That was an aphrodisiac like no other.

I gave her one last look before I was moving my hands, and I was back in my study. And back in the clutches of the curse.

CHAPTER 18

AVERY

O h God. Oh God. Oh God. What did I do? I had been ready to do Goddess knows what with my husband's brother, the exiled former king. The man who terrified me like no other. The man who stalked me all night then chased me through a fucking forest, pinned me up against a tree, and seemed all too ready to plunder his spoils instead of returning me to his brother.

It was the reason he followed me instead of just catching me and taking me back immediately. Because I knew it was him in that alleyway. I'd felt his presence like a lunar eclipse, creating a creeping shadow over me as I stole away in the night. A man like him would make a game of hunting me. And I loved it.

He was probably the reason the innkeeper didn't let me in. Now that my head was clearing, I could remember her eyes flicking off somewhere behind me before she adamantly told me she had no room, despite the vacancy sign clearly displayed next to the door. He must have given her a look, a message demanding that I be turned away so he could have his little game. A shiver worked its way down my spine. I didn't know what magic he used to lower my inhibitions because considering sleeping with him was something I would never do.

He really was a monster. And I should be grateful for the man who was standing before me, though he saw fit to take other lovers. Yet I hardly blamed him because if whatever pent up frustration he felt was anything near the way I felt when I had been between Nighval and that tree, something had to be done to take care of things.

Though I certainly would not give it to him.

Like Xavier could read the traitorous thoughts swirling around in my head, he said, "What were you doing? And why is it I find you with my brother, again, with that heated look in your eyes?" The way his gaze narrowed as it roved over me, then settled on my throbbing lips, made my stomach swirl. And not in a good way.

"Nothing," I said, desperately

"How are you going to fall in love with me if you're out gallivanting around with my brother?" he asked.

Oh God, indeed. Xavier was right. I was definitely never going to fall in love with him after I made out with his brother. What an idiot. Even if he used magic, how did I let that happen? Clearly, I hadn't been getting enough oxygen, but damn, he was a good kisser. I could practically feel the dampness collected between my thighs, the ache he'd ignited. Had I hoped he'd catch me? How could someone be so utterly terrifying and make me feel that way? Magic. That was the only explanation I kept coming back to over and over again. It was either that or I officially lost my mind.

Xavier knew, and he was furious. Maybe he didn't know that I just made out with Nighval, but he could sense whatever terrible chemistry was between us.

. "I..." I trailed off as both of our eyes landed on my overstuffed backpack that Nighval made sure to bring back with us.

"Did you run? Is that why your pack is lying out in the open?" he asked, his stare becoming dark.

"I overheard you with Olive. She encouraged you to force yourself on me. I was scared," I admitted.

Xavier tilted his head to the side. "What exactly did you overhear?"

"Only that. I came to find you and your voices were muffled. I didn't want to intrude so I left before I heard more," I lied. I decided not to let him know that I knew he had a lover. Best to pretend I only overheard the truth I needed as an excuse. Right now, he still believed we had a chance to end the curse.

He studied me as if he were deciding what to believe. "Avery, you know I wouldn't do that. I've tried time and time again to be patient and gentle because I thought that would make you warm to me, but I can see kindness is not what makes you come alive. I'll give you one month to prepare yourself for your king. I want your body and your heart. On the next reprieve I expect you to be ready to give yourself to me willingly."

I nodded, unable to find the words. Too many feelings were flooding my system.

"Good," he said and scanned the room. "I don't want to have to lock you in here. Now that you know I don't plan to hurt you, can I trust that you'll not flee again?"

"Yes," I said, quickly enough to guarantee he wouldn't consider locking me in here. I wasn't sure I could handle that.

"Okay, my queen. Trust goes both ways. Let's use our next month to show each other we are worthy of each other's trust. Sound good?"

"Of course," I said, wanting to roll my eyes. Sure, I kissed his brother, but he was railing some chick on the side. *Please, just leave.* "Goodnight," I said, hoping he'd get the picture. I needed to be alone and sort my shit out.

That was the wrong thing to say, and it seemed to piss Xavier off, but I didn't care. He shook his head and stormed out of the room, slamming the door behind him. As soon as I was alone, I rushed over to the mirror to see how ravished I looked. My skin had a pink tinge to it and my lips were a little more swollen than normal, but I knew the way I used my makeup differed from how the women did here, especially considering they were rats most of the time, so I could write it off as that.

Goddess, I could still feel him on me.

As I got ready for bed, two thoughts oscillated in my mind. What was I going to do about Xavier in a month, and what would have happened if Nighval had caught me an hour earlier? The latter making my lady parts scream for attention. I was depraved. Still, after I crawled into bed, I hiked my nightgown up and relieved my aching core with the image of a predator dancing in my mind. I'd figure out how to come to my senses in the morning.

CHAPTER 19

NIGHVAL

One month later

Xavier was going to kill me, but I had to get back to her and see if she wanted things to continue as badly as I did. A few motions with my hands, and I was in the hallway outside her room. No noise came from the inside, so I gently tried the knob. It was unlocked. She left it unlocked for me. Tonight, we had hours and the things I wanted to do to her. The month I spent at Lieden Palace was too long to be away from her. Too long to think, to reconsider my actions. Namely why had I taken her back to Ravsted and once there, why I left her with my angry brother.

The truth was, I panicked. Never had I imagined her to mirror my desire and now the way she moved against me was a memory that lived at the forefront of my mind. Tonight, I'd take her and rectify my past mistakes.

My heart skipped as I pushed the door open, then guttered when my eyes landed on my brother sitting cross-legged at the desk where I'd found her reading the book I'd been after months before.

He lifted his head from his hands and said, "I knew it," shooting an absolutely murderous glare in my direction. The expression on the witch's face was horrified as she looked up from her perch on the foot of the bed. Had he threatened her? Was he going to hurt her? I would whisk her away before my brother could do any such thing. She didn't need to worry about him any longer and soon enough my face would be between her thighs, showing her exactly how well I intended to take care of her. Reliving every fantasy I had over the last twenty-nine days. Maybe she'd notice me taking care of her so well that she'd believe me to be something other than the monster I was.

The thought sent a triumphant thrill through me. I was about to reach a hand out to beckon her when Xavier said, "Avery, I believe my brother is under the mistaken impression that you want him. Tell me, wife, do you want my brother?"

The witch glanced between me and Xavier, getting to her feet. He stood and she made her way to his side. I didn't understand. I knew I wasn't wrong about what I sensed. About what she had clearly felt. But even now she shrunk back, looking ready to step behind Xavier if I moved an inch in her direction. My brows pinched together as they lowered, and I knew my visage had become more intimidating by the way her eyes widened.

"No. I don't want him," she said, and she did not stutter. The rejection in the words and in her tone was clear as a bell. Now it was Xavier's turn to triumph, and I knew he was by the devious twinkle in his eye as he crossed his arms over his chest.

"Run along, brother," Xavier said, openly gloating. He even placed his hand on the small of her back, and she did not flinch. I flinched as a jealous gully burst and flowed unobstructed through me.

I bit down on every word that came forward in my mind. I knew she hadn't moved for him the way she moved for me. I knew she hadn't kissed him like she kissed me. Why was she doing this? The witches had finally sent the right woman, and I had four months left. I needed to spend every moonlit second I had in this form with her. I turned my head away from them so I could think for a second and caught my reflection in the mirror. I hadn't tried to shield her from this side of me that night, but it had been dark. Maybe this was too much. I turned back to them and held my brother's gaze as my hand worked at my side. Slowly, I softened my features, the scars, with my magic and then turned to her. Maybe if she saw me the way she saw me the first time—

"No need to do that, Nighval," Xavier said, cutting my thoughts off. "You won't be leaving with my bride this evening. I think it's best you leave."

The way Xavier stood, squared his shoulders, and stepped in front of the witch was intended to impress her, but it only made my hair stand on end. She didn't seem impressed. Her not fearing him didn't mean she found him palatable. And honestly, I was surprised she hadn't tried to run again. We were so doomed.

But if I took her now after she'd made it clear she didn't wish to have me, she would hate me and worse, it would start a conflict I had no business being in without my magic. Still, I wanted to take her. Every instinct in my body was screaming to take her away from this place. Something wasn't right.

As if Xavier knew each of my thoughts, he ushered her with an arm behind his body like he was guarding his possession. Like she was a toy I planned to take. It was my exact plan, so I couldn't blame him.

I stomped over to him and shoved my finger in his chest. "You're making a mistake. The witch can barely keep from cringing when she looks at you, Xavier." He winced because there was no denying the truth of it. "She's confused about her feelings toward me, but she certainly doesn't want you," I continued. "Let me take her."

"I'm not confused, and my name is Avery," she said. "Stop calling me *the witch*. I'm hardly even a real witch, anyway."

I could've sworn hurt or disappointment eclipsed the fear scrawled across her lovely features, if only for a moment, like she *wanted* me to say her name. To know her name. Of course, I knew her name. I might as well have her name tattooed on my right palm. I knew the arrangement of the letters so well.

But I didn't want to say her name. I didn't want the feelings of having it come out of my mouth would dredge up. I didn't want to see her face wrinkle in disapproval as I said it. But it was what she wanted, so I gave it to her.

"Avery," I said. But she glanced away, with hardly a reaction on her face. I gritted my teeth, ignoring the slice of pain her dismissal shot through me. "I don't understand."

"I think it's pretty clear, Nighval. Now do your magic or walk out of here. I don't care. Just leave." He stood firm and pointed at the door. She wasn't going to budge either, so I gave her a last pleading look. Why was she doing this and what was that expression in her eye? If I didn't know better, I'd almost think it was turmoil.

"Just go," she said, so I went.

Since I used the magic to come here, I might as well go to the library to collect another book. I slammed the door as I left. Xavier was wrong for her, and we both knew it. He was being as stubborn as I've been all those years. I supposed it served me right, but the man was going to lock us into this curse for the rest of our days. Did it make me an insufferable fool to believe I, after all the years of failure, had a chance now?

As I pulled a stack of books from the shelves, I debated my course of action. If I took her, and I was wrong, I didn't know if it would be worse for the kingdom or for myself. I paced down the row of books where I had first cornered Avery, letting myself savor the memory, and I knew what I had to do. I wasn't wrong. I only needed more time.

There was an option on the table, but I never thought it would come to this. I never wanted it to. I thought I could do it on my own, find love and break the curse. I saw with gleaming clarity how wrong I'd been. So, instead of going home, I swallowed my pride and went to *her*.

CHAPTER 20

AVERY

"Why did my brother come for you, Avery? The man who is exiled because he couldn't get a single witch to even marry him. But here you are, married to me," he yelled, thrusting a finger into his chest. "And it is my brother who brings out that fire in your eyes. You reject him, but I can see it. Do you think I didn't see both of your swollen lips, your flushed faces?"

I raised my hands in front of my chest. "It isn't like that, Xavier. We talked about this."

"It is, though. He scares you and you like it. What type of woman did I marry?" Xavier's face was red as he tossed back a finger of honey colored liquid he'd been drinking as we sat here waiting for Nighval to make an appearance. As the seconds tore on, a part of me secretly wished he'd show. When he'd stepped through the door confirming every one of my husband's suspicions, my heart seized. The truth was, a part of me wanted to go with him, drawn by some dark curiosity. But my commitments lied here and who knew what the warlock's intentions were. I found myself stuck in a *which is worse?* scenario. I picked the devil I knew.

Xavier stood, poured another drink, and tossed it back as if he were gearing himself up for what was coming next. But it was fine, I was ready for it. I was ready to fully commit to this marriage and atone for what I'd done. Giving into the forbidden pull I had toward the man who stormed from the room in a fit of fury.

As if Xavier could sense my thoughts were not on him, he stepped forward putting himself in my line of sight. "I should have known last time when I saw you with him, but I gave you the benefit of the doubt. I thought about it, you know." He lifted a hand to run it across my cheek. His other gripped my wrist and brought it to his pelvis, guiding my open palm to his erection. His hand over mind squeezed. "I think you are beautiful, and I was very pleased with you the first time I saw you, Avery."

I whimpered as he squeezed harder and used his other hand to pinch my cheeks between his fingers. He leaned forward and placed his lips over my puckered ones and kissed me. When he pulled away, he stared into my eyes. "I won't make the mistake of choosing to be gentle with you again like I did before. I can be rough, demanding. You like a man who's in control in the bedroom. We have four months left, and I think I now know what you are looking for."

"No," I cried, as he gripped my wrist and pulled me toward the bed. "No, Xavier. That isn't what I like."

"I'm not upset, my queen. I aim to please you. To give you the things that you desire. To be the type of man who makes you feel things," he said, reaching for the hem of my top, jerking it upward.

"Please don't be rough," I said, but he lifted the garment over my head and my hands instinctively covered my breasts. He pushed me back onto the bed, crawled over me and took both my hands in his, raising them over my head.

He straddled me and said, "How dare you cover yourself from your king, from your husband. I've been patient with you, but time's up. Are you ready like we talked about?"

"Yes," I said, and his eyebrows raised. "Just not like that, Xavier. You can have me, but not like that, okay?" I begged, and he lowered his forehead to mine.

"If you would have allowed this sooner, maybe we wouldn't be in this predicament. I don't want to force you, Avery, but I will do it."

"I know," I said, trying to become pliant under him and he moved his mouth over my skin. This man wasn't lying. I didn't think he *wanted* to hurt me, and I hadn't fought until now, hoping he'd see it would never happen between us. Or at least just get it over with quickly. But our time was running out, and he only had a few months to change the fate of his people.

On the one hand, I understood. I really did. I spent the last month trying to convince myself to do this very act.

He felt obligated to change the game. "I didn't want it to be like this between us, Avery," he said, tugging my pants down my hips, and his shirt over his head. "I wanted you to want me, but maybe once you know my touch, how good I can make you feel..." he trailed off as he planted wet kisses along my stomach, and I let him, all the while my skin crawled. "How I can take control, how you like, and satisfy your needs."

His thumbs hooked in my panties, and he slipped them off. My breathing hitched, and he glanced up hopefully, but his eyes darkened as he assessed me correctly. It was fear and something less than repulsion, but similar enough that I could hardly disguise it. Still, he pressed on.

"Don't worry, baby, I know what to do," he said.

My knees gravitated toward each other, but his clammy hands pushed them apart, as he commanded, "Open for me." His lids grew heavy as he stared at my very dry pussy. It was going to take a miracle for me to get anything out of this. He placed awkward kisses from my knee to my inner thigh, and tears sprouted in my eyes. I tried to fight them back. I really did, but when his tongue hit my clit, they fell. I jerked, and an encouraged Xavier stroked me with his tongue, then his fingers, then both.

It felt okay physically, but emotionally, I was a wreck. I hated every second of this act that I begrudgingly let this man—my husband—perform on me. If there was some way I could snap my fingers and make myself feel differently, I would. But I couldn't get out of my head.

I'd never caught lasting feelings before with anyone who I was intimate with. There had been an attraction, at least. Not this icky feeling I got as Xavier groaned into me, all the while lapping away. I stared down at him, and my stomach rolled. Was there something wrong with me?

My legs clamped together on their own, which only spurred him on more. But he didn't misinterpret the sob that wrenched from my throat. His head snapped up to me and he took in my tear-stained face. His face darkened in a way that scared me more than Nighval's ever had. It was like in a split second the man, this king, was transformed. I scuttled back on the bed like a crab, my eyes going wide. He didn't say a word, he didn't need to. We both knew what was about to happen. I never should have believed him.

His hand wrapped around my ankle, tugging me toward him. I kicked with my other foot, but he grabbed it, dragging me underneath him. His hands fumbled for the buttons on his trousers, but I wrapped my legs around him squeezing so he was close and couldn't get them undone. He didn't have a shirt on for me to execute the chokehold I'd learned.

He grabbed my breast roughly until I cried out. "That's it. You cry real tears when I treat you nice. I'd rather have you cry out in anger instead. You say you don't want it rough, but I'm catching onto your little game. You want me to fight for it, don't you? Fight for you like Nighval would fight for you. Get your blood heated and take you."

What was he saying? "No," I cried, and beat my hands against his chest as he reached behind me and unclasped my bra.

"That's the fire I was looking for, my queen." He drove his hips into me so hard I grunted in pain and my legs loosened for half a second. His fingers dug into my ankle. He pulled my leg from around him and flipped me onto my stomach. I tore at the covers, trying to drag myself away from him.

He grabbed my thighs pressing me down on the bed with his body over me. The rough texture of his trousers told me he hadn't gotten his pants down, thankfully. I threw my head back, cracking him in the nose, and he gasped. I tore forward again, shooting a quick glance toward the open window. I didn't have much longer before the church bells gonged and it would be a rat-man raping me. That was not going to happen. I had to get away, but he was so strong. Too strong.

Oh Goddess. I knew what I had to do. He had my ankle again, but I kicked out, catching him in the chest, knocking him back just enough that I could dive forward. I wrenched my drawer open, fished the carving knife out from inside and spun to my back in a flash.

A wet, slippery sound shocked through the room, along with a pained cry, and I looked down to where Xavier had thrown himself on top of me. The color drained from his face, and I know mine did the same as both of our eyes tracked down to my hand.

The black stone hilt of the knife was in my white knuckled grip and the silver steel blade had disappeared into the flesh of Xavier's stomach right under his ribs. Blood, a lot of blood, dripped from the wound onto my stomach, and I knew this was bad.

"I'm sorry," I whispered.

His brows wrinkled, but then his confused expression cleared. He didn't move, still resting himself on a forearm over me. His eyes widened, and he stared into my eyes as horror etched his.

"I'm sorry, too. I thought you wanted— I didn't mean to—" he said, then his body went limp over mine.

Oh my God. There was a dead king on top of me, and I was covered in his blood. The blood would be soaking into the bed, probably pooling on the floor beneath the bed, if I had to guess by the amount of it pouring from him.

I killed someone. Shit.

This was not what was supposed to happen. I was supposed to fall in love, but I killed him. Technically, he impaled himself on my knife, but no one here would see it that way.

I had to get out of here. Nighval would find me during the next full moon, so I had to find a way to get back to my aunt and warn the witches before then. Or find their mother, which might not be such a great plan, considering I just killed her son.

Fuck.

I tried to suck in a deep breath. *Okay, step one, get the dead body off you.* Placing my hands on Xavier's shoulders, I heaved. His body slumped to the side and with another shove, he rolled onto his back. I glanced at his face, his dead eyes staring up at the ceiling. Oh god that was a bad idea. I'd seen people close the dead's eyes in movies, so I did the same. As I leaned over him to do it, his arm twitched, and a keening scream jumped out of my mouth before I could stop it.

Shit.

A knock sounded at the door, and one of my helpers called, "Everything okay, Your Majesty?"

Surveying the room for something to shove in front of the door, I called, "Peachy!" I waited for the footsteps to retreat, then I dragged a large chair in front of the door and wedged it beneath the handle.

I had no time to think. The sooner I got out of here, the better. I raced to the bathroom and rinsed off the blood as quickly as I could. Then I dressed and picked up my backpack and stuffed it with all of my original belongings, pocketed some jewelry from the drawers, then pulled the chair away.

I needed to find a different way than the balcony of my study on the second floor I used last time, since in the last month, they'd stationed more guards along my regular routes as if I wouldn't notice. Unfortunately, my third-floor balcony was too high up. I needed to get to the first floor and head toward the garden door. It wasn't the first time I'd gone there late to walk amongst the roses. Sure, I wasn't wearing a traveling cloak and carrying a supply laden backpack at the time, but I didn't know what else to do. It was the best plan I could come up with on short notice and all of my instincts were screaming for me to flee.

Unless Nighval was still here, and I could find him before someone discovered what I'd done. He and Xavier had a bumpy relationship, but I wasn't sure what he'd do if he knew. There was a chance he'd help me, but what if I was wrong? What if he hated me for killing his brother? No, I didn't need him. I was better off on my own.

Throwing the cloak over my shoulders and pack, I raised the hood over my head and slipped out into the hallway. I nodded from the shadow of the hood as I passed an attendant I didn't recognize, then another as I flew down the steps. Down another hallway on the second floor, around the corner to another stairwell. So far, so good. I should have known, but I was so close to the garden door my fingers itched to touch the cool metal of the knob. Only two more turns, and I'd be there. I spun around a corner and ran headfirst into Leviticus.

A whoosh of air left my lungs. "Excuse me," I said, trying to side-step him, but he grabbed ahold of my shoulders, dragging me in front of him.

"Your Majesty?" he asked, pulling me under a flickering incandescent light that hung on an exposed cord in intervals down the hallway.

I tried to look down and away, leaving my face in the shadows. "Unhand your queen," I demanded, but it was no use.

Leviticus said, "Why is there a streak of blood on your face? Where is King Xavier?"

Tears burst into the corners of my eyes, but I held them back. I tried to keep my lip from quivering and giving me away, but I'd just killed someone and the reality of that was crashing into my awareness the longer I stood still.

"I said, let me go." I jerked out of his grip and made to storm down the hall, but a guard turned the corner and Leviticus called, "Seize her."

As Leviticus and three more guards marched me through the hallways, back up the stairs to my room, dread coiled in my belly.

We got to the room, and a gruff guard shoved the door open. Leviticus turned pale as he took in the corpse on the bed. Time crawled as he pivoted toward me. He darted a claw forward, hooking it in the clasp of my cloak. The leather shredded as he sliced, and the garment slid to the floor, revealing my backpack.

His eyes and those of the guards bore into me. Murderous. "This is more than murder, Avery Plath. This is treason."

He slid the backpack straps off my shoulders and discarded it in the room. "Take her to the dungeons," he said, before addressing me. "All you had to do was accept him. Now it will be your head."

A shuddering sob tore from my lips. "But he attacked me," I cried. "He tried to..." but I couldn't continue.

A flicker of doubt ran across his features, softening them for a hairsbreadth before they re-solidified. "It doesn't matter. He was the king, and you were our last chance. We'll be forever cursed and you're to blame. The people will demand nothing less than your life. There is nothing I can do," he glanced at Xavier's body, "and nothing I would do... Go."

The guards didn't blink as they wrapped rough hands around my biceps and dragged me from the room. Twenty minutes later, I was in a dank prison cell on some subterranean level of the castle. Cool grey stone made up three of the walls and rusty iron bars the fourth. They shoved me in, slammed the door, and didn't even speak before turning to leave.

They were out of sight before I had a chance to assess my new surroundings. Not even a cot or chamber pot was in the cell. Only a moth-eaten pile of rags in the corner, and ironically a rat, whose beady eyes poked out from a large crevice in the stone where the grout had deteriorated.

Xavier's last words had been the start of an apology, but I'd never find out what my husband wanted because he was dead. What had I done? I was their last hope, and I'd killed the man I was supposed to fall in love with. I'd cursed the rat people to remain in their half-rat form forever. They were going to kill me.

Everything hit me suddenly and my legs gave out. My knees hit the stone with a crack and while the tears were there, they didn't fall. I was too deep within panic's grip for tears. I knew if I let go, I'd lose it. If I hadn't rejected Nighval, I might have been able to count on him, but he wasn't coming. Not for me. He'd never forgive me for anything that happened tonight. That left only one out. I needed to be strong and hope against all odds that somehow word of my predicament would reach my coven. They'd been able to send my aunt over and pull her back. Surely, they could do it again and bring me home.

PART 2

CHAPTER 21

NIGHVAL

V isiting my mother was the last thing I wanted to do after being faced with another rejection. I still couldn't fathom what had gone wrong, and I convinced myself that it had been Avery's fear that kept her at my brother's side. Or some mistaken loyalty. I blamed him for that. The second I sensed there was something between myself and the witch, I should have confronted him about it and made him give her to me. As far as I could tell, the marriage wasn't consummated, so I'd make him dissolve it and when we broke the curse, I'd reinstall her as queen by my side.

How different would things have been had I not relented to the pressure and given my brother a chance? I'd only needed to hold out for another year and then if I'd failed again, it would have been on my shoulders as it should be for any king. Instead, in a moment of weakness I'd given away my power. I would not do that again, and I would not fail. And there were only four months left.

That's why I had to do this. I'd finally take the carrot Samara had been dangling in my face ever since the first witch ran. The thought of what I was about to do disgusted me. But that didn't change anything. I would take the magic that would give me an edge from my mother and use it on the woman who'd been finding her way into my thoughts more and more. I really was a monster.

The truth was, I could have taken what my mother was offering at any time. My pride had been an insurmountable roadblock. And now, I could use the magic to help my brother to win the witch's heart.

My stomach turned. No, once I got the offered magic, I'd ride to Ravsted and take her, consequences be damned. Little did she know the moment she kissed me back, she'd become mine. Taking her is what I should have done earlier tonight, but now I was standing outside the town deep in the Wildwood my mother had made a home for herself, handing off my Eclipse, the enchanted stallion my father had given me for my eighteenth birthday. I'd made one stop to retrieve the animal, then used my power to deliver both of us to the edge of the wards so I'd have the animal for my journey back to Ravsted.

The small village surrounded her estate and was inhabited by those she deemed worthy, making up her own little fiefdom. In reality, many of them were outcasts or people who preferred to live a more remote lifestyle. Occasionally, members of her following would venture out into the rest of Ras alhague. They were more of a nuisance than anything, though, considering they thought her rule above mine.

I had always let it slide. It was easier to give her that and keep her from meddling with the rest of the kingdom. Still, I never hesitated to exact swift punishment when required. During the past year, they'd become more of a problem due to Xavier's lax hand and avoidant leadership style. It seemed he thought if he ignored the problems long enough, they'd go away. They never did. Samara hadn't been happy with how I chose to deal with her following, but she also hadn't put her neck out for the perpetrators, either.

My magic was only capable of landing me outside her wards, and the time it took me to trudge through the Wildwood to the town felt never-ending. Who knew what she wanted in exchange for the magic and then there'd be another week of hard riding to make it back to the castle and Avery.

As I arrived, I left the horse with a stableboy, paid him handsomely and made my way into town.

My mother's home sat at the top of a small hill in the center of the village. A four-foot wrought-iron fence surrounded it, and neatly trimmed hedges were planted on the outside, creating a nice perimeter. The house had four square white columns on the front porch holding up the two-story overhang. A large chandelier hung down from the center holding a dozen candles which were always lit.

The rest of the brick and wood trim was painted white, and large shuttered windows in even rows were on either side of the front door, which was painted a deep green. By all external appearances, the witch's home was just as pleasant on the inside as it was on the outside, and for the first handful of rooms, that was true, but I knew what lurked beneath the gray slate roof.

As if she was expecting me, my mother, Samara Wrede, opened the door, white silk robes swishing as a mischievous grin lit her finely honed features. Her dark chestnut hair hung freely down her back in a soft sheet, and she held out a jewel encrusted hand in my direction to usher me inside. "My son, you've come to visit your mother. How wonderful."

I followed her inside, biting back a slew of angry and demanding words dying to escape my lips. "Hello, mother," I said.

"It's a bit early for company, but my wards alerted me to your presence in my woods. So I put a pot of coffee on and made some tea cakes since I had some time. These are lemon shortbread, and those are madeleines. You so loved those as a boy, and it was no trouble at all. Wasn't one of your witch's named Madeleine?"

Play nice. She wants to goad you, but you need something from her. I reached forward and put two teacakes on my plate. It had to be about four in the morning, and I had no interest in food or conversation. I wanted the magic and to get the hell out of here.

"Madeline," I said, stuffing a bite into my mouth so I wouldn't be required to respond. Finding Madeline's body was what broke me. She was the last witch from a kingdom she called Russia. In the end, she kept saying she'd traded one hell for another. But I didn't think she had a choice. Most of the other witches had known at least something about why they were coming here.

Madeline arrived completely uninformed, frightened, and alone. It struck me as odd that the coven, who I'd understood were supposed to protect their own, had done that to her. I'd even been suspicious of her and confronted her about it once early on, but she wouldn't talk to me. She hardly talked to anyone or left her room. In my mind, it meant she must have committed some heinous crime to get her sent here. Why else would she cry all the time?

After she'd taken her life, Jetta suggested the woman must have suffered from some illness of the mind that she had long before she came here, but I blamed myself. The day after we buried her, I gave it all to Xavier.

The memory stung as it came and went. As if my mother knew where my thoughts trailed off to, she reached out a hand and placed it gently on my knee as she sat a steaming coffee down at the small table at my feet. "You know you can talk to me, son."

If I didn't know better, I'd have taken it for a loving gesture. But she'd been the one taunting me about it moments earlier, and I wasn't fooled. Best to get why I was here out in the open so I wouldn't snap at something she said and ruin my chance to gain her aid.

"Good," I said. "Because that's why I'm here."

She sat back in her chair and brought her own cup up to her lips to blow on as she watched me over its rim. Did she know why I was here? The curve of her lips suggested she did, but she didn't speak as she patiently waited for me to go on.

"I'd like to take the magic you offered before," I said, and the corners of her lips tipped downward.

"I'm sorry. You what?" she asked.

"Before, you said the terms of the curse were irrevocable, but there was something you could do to make it easier to break. I'm here for it."

"I know what you refer to. But is that any way to ask your very accommodating mother for it?"

She was mad. My pride stepped forward, but I pushed it out of the way before it could intervene. It already had my legs itching to make their way toward the door. I forced my body into a state of ease.

"You're right, mother. I'm here for your help," I said, giving her what she wanted. "I have been unable to beat the curse on my own and Xavier has no chance. I will take whatever help you can offer me." The words, which I knew I had to say if I wanted her cooperation, made bile rise in my throat, which the acidic coffee did nothing to mask. I'd always been one to admit when I was wrong, but this admission was on a whole different level. Just being here felt like I was betraying myself.

"I've been known to give excellent dating advice. Your father and I..." she waved her hand through the air as if she were batting away a fly.

"Before that unfortunate situation which tore our family apart, we were quite the love match. Tell me, this new one," she hesitated.

"Avery," I supplied.

"Ah yes, Avery. Does she not fancy my second son?" I shook my head. "What about you? Does she see your appeal, my darling?"

I leaned over and ran my hands through my hair. My mother stumped me. I did not wish to discuss my or my pathetic brother's love life with her, but this conversation had to end with me getting what I needed out of the vexing witch across from me.

"She has no interest in Xavier and she's admitted she won't ever fall for him. She's different with me, so yes, I think I could win her, but there isn't enough time."

"And the minor fact that she's your queen now and married to your brother. You know, that wasn't your greatest decision, my son."

The coffee cup in my hand shattered, spilling black coffee everywhere.

"I can't imagine the pressure you must be feeling. But don't worry, we'll figure it out," she said, kneeling down to pick up the scattered pieces. She set them on the tray she carried the refreshments in on.

She reached into her pocket to retrieve a few small pouches. Selecting one, she replaced the others, then uncinched the ties and poured a pile of a black powder into her hand. Chanting a few short lines, she spread it over the dark stain on her pristine white carpet, and I felt the magic before the stain lifted and disappeared. Witch's magic was so different from ours it almost mesmerized me.

As she rose and retrieved another cup to fill for me, I asked, "How will the magic work?"

"In order to break the curse, she must fall in love with you, but it doesn't stipulate what you or anything else for that matter, must appear to be. I'm thinking I could infuse the magic into a powder or a capsule perhaps." Her eyes became distant for a moment as she envisioned whatever recipe she'd concoct to solve the problem. As she did the mental work, the lines of tension on her face eased. She enjoyed this, solving problems and exercising her mind to make the calculations using her power required.

"Ah, yes. I know exactly what I'm going to do. Of course, there are a few things I'll need."

"Which are?" I asked, my eagerness apparent in my voice. I sat back, urging myself to calm. Nothing with my mother was ever this easy.

"First, we'll need something of your Avery's, then passionflower oil. I think I have everything else in my shop."

"I brought something of hers. Where do we find the oil?" I asked.

"From the flower, of course!" she said.

I shook my head, my agitation rising. "And where do we find the flowers?"

My mother jumped up and scurried out of the room waving for me to come along. I followed her into her study where she fished out a rolled document from a bin and flattened it out on a wooden table in the corner of the room. When she placed weights on each corner of the map, she pressed her fingers into a strip of land in the most southern part of the kingdom. "They grow there."

My heart sank. It would take weeks of travel without my power to make it there and more to get back to Avery. Time, a luxury I didn't have.

My mother tapped her fingers on the map drawing me out of my dwindling thoughts. "My power will take us, we'll find the flower, I'll make the pill, then you'll be on your way to win your love. I can't wait to meet her."

Goddess, she looked at this as a game, not the fate of thousands of people. Did she have no care that right now she stared at her own son as a mutant being? Or that mothers never got to see their babies' pink toes and laughing bright human eyes instead of the beady black ones all children now had? No, she didn't care. Samara Wrede's entire world revolved around manipulating her way back into the family she'd lost. And like everything with her, there was a hidden cost which I needed to discover before I overcommitted myself.

"Okay, mother. We'll go get this flower, then you'll infuse the magic into a pill. What's your price?" I asked.

She stepped back, like I'd struck her, bumping into the wall behind her. "That's rude," she said. "Why would you say such a thing? You think I wouldn't do this for you out of love, my child?"

The wide-eyed expression on her face might almost be believable if I hadn't been there the night she mercilessly killed my father. One second, her hand lifted toward the sky. The next, it shot down, drawing a bolt of white-hot lightening which speared my father's skull nearly in two. She stood over him and dipping her fingers into the blood seeping from the steaming wound before I could stop her. Xavier, and I were both in shock as we watched her draw symbols into the ground with his blood. I was nineteen and couldn't bring myself to kill my mother. I might have if I'd known what was coming.

"I don't think you do anything out of love, Samara. I think you don't know what the word means," I said, dangerously close to letting this chance, her willingness to give me the magic I desperately needed, slip through my grasp. I gritted my teeth as I awaited her response. Her face twisted through a series of emotions landing on something decidedly sinister. The thing was, I could have tried with my magic, but if the curse sensed manipulation or someone was trying to trick it, it would trigger its permanence. I had to have faith that my mother, being the curse's designer, knew what she could do to work within the parameters of the curse without solidifying our fate.

"I want what I've always wanted, Nighval. I want you and Xavier to act like normal sons. Come visit your mother. Spend time with me and let me be the mother your father never let me be."

"Are you even capable of that?" I asked, genuinely curious if she believed herself to be.

"He poisoned you against me—"

"Considering you murdered him and enacted a curse that doomed an entire kingdom, it seems warranted," I said.

"Son, if I wanted, I could transport us to Ravsted right now. We'd take your witch, and you could force her to be your bride." Her voice rattled as her frenzied energy heightened. "But that's not what I want for you."

I swallowed. The thought of stealing Avery away had been on my mind innumerable times over the last few months, but I hadn't done it. That wasn't how I wanted it to be, but here I was moments away from making a deal with my mother so I could do exactly that. "What did you want for me?" I found myself asking.

"Love, darling. I wished for you to find the love I never did. And if you believe it will be with this Avery, then I'm here to help you. After all, you've never come to your mother over a woman, so she must be the one." I was about to say, fine, let's go, when she said, "Oh, and I want you and Xavier to visit me once a week. Dinner, just the three of us. And when your love bears your children, I want them to come, too. When the curse is broken, you'll have your power back, so it will be no problem for you to manage."

She took in a deep breath and sighed as if she was settled with the terms she'd outlined. I supposed they could be worse. She could demand I move her back into the castle and she accidentally left out meeting Avery, so I needed to agree with it before she came up with something else.

"Got it. Weekly dinners in exchange for the pill. Let's go."

"But it's still night," she said, brows wrinkling in concern.

"Go change. It will be light soon enough. I'm eager to get my task underway."

The corner of my mother's eyes wrinkled in a knowing way. "I think you're eager to get back to your witch and start wooing her." She fluttered her fingers at me as she slipped out of the room, presumably to go ready herself for our journey. "I'll be watching."

Two torturously long weeks later, Samara Wrede placed a glowing blue pill in my open palm as we stood in her foyer. She started working on the spell which would reset the game as soon as we'd gotten back this morning. I knew after transporting us, hunting for enough of the rare flowers, spending several nights outdoors which she wasn't accustomed to and then the power it took to create this object, she must be exhausted. Her skin even seemed thinner if that were possible. My breathing quickened as I stared at the pill. So much magic in such a small space.

"How will it work?" I asked.

"Everything to do with you will be blocked from her memory aside from the day you retrieved her from the witch from my plane," she explained. "Or any other memories that can't be explained without your presence."

"Why not?" I asked.

"It can block or overshadow memories. The magic can't replace them, and she needs to understand how she arrived here, so she'll likely remember you from that. In-between, it depends on how essential the memories are to her experience. The less confusion the better, so you'll have to come up with a clever ruse to take her from Ravsted and get her to Lieden Palace."

"And what will she see?" I asked, a little nervous for the answer because I knew what I wanted my mother's answer to be. Me. No, that didn't matter. All that mattered was getting the pill so I could break the curse. It was foolish to hope for anything more.

"I don't know exactly. The magic isn't that specific. Darling, can you not trust that—" My mother's words were cut short as a courier darted through the door.

"What is it, Luk?" she asked the letter carrying teen, who was also the stable boy I'd left Eclipse with. Luk bowed awkwardly as his gaze tracked up my muddy boots to my annoyed face, his eyes near bulging out of his head as he realized who he stood before.

My mother snapped and he jumped, handing her a folded paper, saying, "Message, matron." My apprehension rose as she quickly scanned the contents, her face draining of color.

The young man bounced on his toes anxiously as if he already knew what the note said.

"Is it true?" she said, assessing him. He nodded, pulling off his cap to wring it in his hands.

"She killed him," she said, slumping against the wall. Luk rushed forward and wrapped an arm around her before guiding her to the sitting room. As they moved out of the foyer, the paper floated to the ground, forgotten. I snatched it up.

It was a note from what appeared to be one of her informants. *The King Xavier Helicanus is dead by the hand of his new queen, Avery Plath. A public execution is scheduled for this coming reprieve.*

My heart started thundering so loud I could hear it in my ears. I stomped into the sitting room to find Luk fanning a pale Samara. "Get up," I demanded. "You have to take me to her."

"I can't," she said.

I leaned over, wrapped my hand around a frail arm and attempted to pull her out of the chair she'd sunk into. "Yes, you can. Just do this one last thing for me, mother."

When she didn't stand on her own after my tugging, and slumped back into the cushion, she said, "I really can't, son. I'm depleted. And she killed your brother. Why do you want her still?"

It was a good question. Family was supposed to be everything. But when I thought of what I'd read, all I cared about was getting to Avery. Now I had the perfect ruse. She'd be sitting in the dungeons, subjected to Goddess knew what. I studied my mother. She did seem more limp than normal. Shit.

There wasn't time to think. I had two weeks to make it back to Ravsted before whoever had taken charge now, likely Leviticus, executed our last chance. I grabbed Luk by the elbow and dragged him toward the door. "To the stables. Ready my mount." When he stared at me blinking, I shouted, "Go, now!"

He skipped forward to do my bidding and when I turned to my mother, intrigue glinted in her tired eyes. Her son had left this world and as the shock wore off, no tears were shed. I guessed we had one thing in common. I patted the pocket which held the pill.

"Thank you," I said, hesitating. She'd just lost her son. Surely, she wasn't that devoid of emotion. "I trust you'll be fine?" I asked her.

"I'll be fine. You'd better hurry." What was unsaid speaking volumes. If Avery died, my mother could do no more, even if she wanted to. Our fates would be sealed.

I nodded, before turning to begin my race for the castle.

CHAPTER 22

AVERY

M y coven witches were going to come. They had to. They were my only hope. That had been my chant for the last month. The thing keeping me from having a complete breakdown. My mantra, my prayer. I just couldn't see my story ending like this.

If my aunt, Cara, and the others didn't come for me by the time the moon reached its apex in the starless night sky, these rat-people were going to Marie Antoinette style lop off my head. A shiver worked its way down my spine. How did I end up here?

Keys rattled outside my cell. I had twenty-nine days for the fear to build. I knew my fate the moment I'd been captured. The sound of metal grinding in the lock set my heart skittering, in quick shallow beats. *Don't panic. They will come.* The hollow words were the only thing keeping my knees from buckling.

The heavy metal grate door groaned as it swung open, and a rather large rat-man stood on the other side, glaring with his beady rat-eyes. Even though I knew the curse wasn't their fault, I hated these monsters with a depth of feeling that was rooted in my soul.

A makeshift stage was set up at the base of the stairs of Ravsted where I'd first arrived. Worn, stained wooden planks lay across scaffolding at least five feet off the stone courtyard. In the center sat a large ominous wood block with a curve carved out of the top about the size of a watermelon.

There were several grooves in the wood which made bile rise in my throat as I took the stair that brought me eye level with it.

About two-hundred onlookers were standing around it, watching with interest as they lined the six of us prisoners up at the back, against a railing which looked ready to give at any moment. Of the six, I was last in the line and when my guard prodded me up the last stair, and I came into view, whispers erupted across the crowd. I ignored them. My aunt would come. Now that I was out of prison and under the moonlight, they would come for me. Still, my hands shook, which was more than I could say about a few of the other sentenced.

The bell gonged once, and my eyes tracked to the prisoners to see their features soften into their human faces except for Anabelle, the only other person in the female section of the prison, who had a dirty brown canvas bag over her head for some reason I wasn't privy to. I wanted to reach out to her, to say something, but what would I say?

She'd already been through so much. I couldn't imagine losing a child the way she had and then being accused of their murder. Over the last month, she'd recounted the story of the accidental drowning at least ten times and the details never wavered, making me believe what she claimed was true. But her innocence didn't seem to matter in this world. Her husband blamed the death on her and here she was, staged to be executed for her alleged crime.

This morning, she seemed settled, resigned to her fate. But now she shook violently and made a crazed humming sound that got louder with each passing moment. Her wrists were bound in front of her. Her clothing was worn and soiled with prison grime like the rest of us.

Another man stood beside her and kept bumping into her as if he was trying to edge past her off the stage, but was hindered by his loosely bound feet. A long, grisly scar ran from his ear, down his neck and across his chest. Without his fur, I could see the skin was red and angry, oozing in a few places.

The man in front of me hobbled forward with a noticeable limp, but otherwise looked unscathed. Even his hair appeared to be freshly combed and he held his chin high.

Several of the prisoners gasped as a broad man clad in brown executioner-style robes strode onto the stage with a curved steel axe.

Leviticus, who seemed to have taken over the kingdom after he'd sentenced me, followed him, making me wonder why Nighval hadn't turned up in all this time. I thought they'd have reinstated him as king, but there was no sign of him.

Leviticus wore a tan jacket and chestnut brown pants. He flicked his dark eyes to me every few steps as he approached. He pulled the pewter caps that were like thimbles off the tips of his fingers, which had been clawed moments earlier, and stuffed them into his pocket. His clothes showed minor wear, making me wonder why more of these creatures didn't use the caps. Someone from below handed him a stool, which he had to bend down to accept.

Guards now stood on either side of me and were between each of the other prisoners. Dripping liquid drew my attention. The first man in our line had a dark stain on the front of his trousers, and urine was splashing onto the planks. With each plop, he released a sob.

Leviticus cleared his throat, garnering the crowd's attention. "Good people, you've come here to watch these prisoners die for their crimes, in accordance with the law. Their sins are grave, their guilt is certain, and their souls are unrepentant, but they will die as men. The executioner will cleanse his axe with their blood by the light of the moon. You may now pray for their souls." Murmurs bubbled up from the crowd, and many eyes closed as Leviticus ended his short speech. He motioned for the first prisoner to be brought forward and to kneel.

As the guard forced the quaking man's head into the depression in the block, reality struck me, and I swayed. A rough hand seized my elbow, righting me.

"Your turn'll be soon, king-killer," his gruff voice sounded in my ear. "Savin' you for last." Then he gave me a rotten grin.

I didn't reply. There was no point. I'd convinced myself it was an accident, self-defense at the minimum, but Xavier was dead, and they'd found me fleeing the scene. I closed my eyes as the executioner raised his axe. A sickening wet noise like in the movies echoed all around and wood thudded as the axe sheered the man's head off clean, sinking into the block. The calm man beside me doubled over, heaving, but his guard latched onto his shoulders, yanking him backward so he ended up vomiting down his front. The foul smell made me nearly lose it.

I glanced back to where the first prisoner had fallen after I heard the scuffle of boots, then the scraping of a body being dragged across the platform. Thump, thump, thump, thump, thump, and they had him down the stairs. His head still lay on its side in front of the block in a puddle of blood and the executioner nudged it with the toe of his boot until it rolled off the edge and cracked into the stones below, causing the onlookers to jolt back.

They shoved the next prisoner into place. "On your knees," the guard managing him demanded.

I looked toward the moon and prayed. I wasn't religious, per se, so it wasn't a deity I prayed to. It was the divine spirit of the moon, the witch mother, the wise women, my aunt, and even mother nature herself. At the rate they were going, my sisters had less than ten minutes, so I prayed hard to anyone who would listen.

I squeezed my eyes shut as the next executions were carried out. The crowd let out a collective scream. Another thud of the axe came in quick succession. I peeked and nearly hurled. Annabelle must have jerked, and he'd missed. Panic clawed up my throat. I gurgled a cry before I got ahold of myself. I'd spoken with her a few hours ago and now she was dead, killed in one of the grisliest ways I could imagine. If anyone told me they still dealt with prisoners this way on this plane, it might have given me pause.

Then the presence beside me was gone. I jumped when the axe thudded into the block.

It was my turn.

I opened my eyes as the guard forced me to my knees in the warm puddle of blood. Leviticus rose from his stool and came to stand beside me. The other prisoners hadn't been given a chance to speak, or even had words said for them. They had conducted the entire procedure without fanfare.

He knelt down so we were eye level. "You deserve so much worse than this, witch." He grabbed a fistful of my hair and forced my eyes toward the crowd. "Your actions sentenced each one of those people to live in their cursed form forever. Not only is your heart full of fear, it is shallow, and darker than a moonless night." The condemnation in his voice hit me like an anvil. I trembled.

As I stared down at the crowd, the blood beneath me cooling, tears streamed down my cheeks. Everything had gone so wrong. The witches had been mistaken when they thought to put their faith in me as a final effort to stop the warlocks from enacting their vengeance. I had been such a poor choice. I loved pretty things, and makeup, designer clothes, and the theater. Fairytale endings and corny romances. I'd have made an excellent queen if my king hadn't been a rat-man and let me have any say. Instead, I'd been no more than a caged bird naively unwilling to see the bars around her until it was too late.

Now here I was, knees drenched in blood, cursing our matron who I was convinced knew what I'd face and sent me, anyway. She said, *don't lose your fire*, and I hadn't. And look where that got me. She should have sent someone else. Someone less superficial, with a bigger heart.

"Are you ready to die, like our king, witch?" Leviticus said, releasing me. My eyes shifted back to him, and a wave of guilt sent me forward, bracing my hands against the block, which was sturdier than it looked. I jerked my hands away like it was a hot poker, but my guard shoved my shoulders forward and my chest hit the block.

A scream lodged in my throat. My lungs pulled in their last sips of air and my mind spun. They weren't coming. The executioner stepped forward. No, no, no, no, NO, NO, NO, NOOO, NOOOOOO!

"NOOO!" a voice rang through the air as the axe whooshed, rising overhead. That voice wasn't mine. Hoofbeats pounded across the stones and Nighval's booming voice cried, "NOOO! Stop," He called again. "Halt!"

I peeled my eyes open to see the dark-haired, scar covered man striding toward me atop a huge midnight colored horse that looked like a Clydesdale. Or maybe bigger. The beautiful animal's glossy coat was gleaming in the moonlight and Nighval wore a fitted suit almost as dark and with crisscrossing straps with tarnished silver buckles. It made the pale skin of his neck stand out in contrast, drawing my eye to the veins in his throat which bulged as the muscles in his jaw strained. I didn't catch his eyes before he swung down off the massive animal and stormed up the stairs.

I got a good look at the fury in their dark depths as he stomped across the platform in my direction. The executioner stood frozen in place, axe raised in the air as Nighval passed. Leviticus stepped forward, but Nighval brushed him away easily. I scampered back, falling on my ass, then scooted backward before I bumped into the boots of the guard behind me.

Nighval didn't hesitate. He knelt down and got in my face so I could feel the vitriol thrumming off of him like a palpable force. So much power—was that his magic? I opened my mouth, but I couldn't speak. My mind was reeling. Did he want to exact revenge for his brother? Was what he had planned for me worse? A violent shudder tore through me.

"You could have had a good man, but now you have me," he said. I really didn't like the glint in his eye, but at least I wasn't dead. I wasn't dead, and the realization rattled through me. He reached forward and cupped my cheek roughly, the callouses on his hands scraping across my delicate skin. Holding up a blue-green glowing pill, similar to a NyQuil capsule.

He pushed the pill between my lips. My hands flew to my face, but he held my cheeks firm, as his fingers pressed further into my mouth until they were practically down my throat. I gagged. He clamped my mouth shut and said, "Swallow."

I did. I swallowed the mystery pill because I had no choice, and he released me. My skin burned from where he'd touched me, and his eyes raked over my face as they waited for the pill to take whatever effect he was expecting.

His face hardened, and he turned to the crowd. "I will fix this. You have my word, in three months' time, you will be free." He said no more before he turned back to me. "Get her on her feet."

Gruff hands were crammed underneath my armpits, and they hoisted me up. The guard let me go with a shove. Before I stumbled, Nighval stepped forward, catching my waist. My hands went to his hard chest and to save my nose from crashing into it, I tilted my head back, only to find myself staring into the darkest hickory I'd ever seen. But instead of anger, they were filled with something else which was cruel, calculating.

We studied each other for a long moment, then he leaned forward, and I flinched, but his lips passed my cheek and stopped so his warm breath was on my neck beneath my ear and my trembling began anew.

"Let the courtship begin," he whispered. With a quick movement, I was in his arms, and he was stomping toward the stairs, down to his horse. He grabbed my hips and lifted me onto the saddle, then swung up so he was sitting astride while I was sidesaddle in his lap. An arm snaked around me, and his other grabbed the reins. I felt him nudge the animal, then we were moving quickly away from the castle.

"Where are we going?" I cried as the horse jolted around a corner and Nighval's arm tightened. He didn't speak and kept steering the animal through the city. When we finally reached the outskirts, he slowed and gave me an assessing look. By now the blood on my prison dress had dried and fatigue from my near-death experience and the month in prison was setting in. I blinked up at him.

"Where are you taking me?" I tried again.

"You should try to sleep," he said, his voice taking on a softer tone. He handed me the reins indicating for me to hold them for a moment and since he'd saved me from certain death, I obliged, despite the fact that he'd said some ominous things to me. A second later, with one arm, he swung a large black cloak around his shoulders, then adjusted it so it was around me, too. What in the hell?

"Nighval, I killed your brother. You just saved me from the axe-man. What is happening?" I asked, handing him back the reins and snuggled the cloak closed so only our hands were poking out. We entered the edge of an open plain and a gust of chilly air breezed by, lifting the strands of my hair, and I tucked back into my captor. "Are you my captor now?" I asked him.

He took a deep breath and released it with a sigh. "Can't you just fall asleep?" he asked, voice a bit threadbare. "Unless that's a game you'd like to play?" He perked up at that, squeezing my side playfully.

I groaned. "I'll sleep once you tell me what is going on."

"Deal," he grumbled. "If you must know, those idiots were about to seal our fate forever by executing you. I made a concession I find very unsavory, to get that pill, which will adjust how you see things. Once it takes effect, things will be different for both of us, and..." He lowered his eyes to my face and an expression I could have sworn was amusement danced there. "And once it does, I plan to show you I can indeed coax a witch's heart into warming to me." I sucked in a breath. "To fall in love with me. Even a king-killer such as yourself," he said, and the amusement shifted into a smug grin.

"If I couldn't fall in love with your brother, I certainly will never fall in love with you," I said, sounding equally as horrified as I felt. His chest rumbled, and I glanced up to see him chuckling. "I won't," I said, staring straight ahead. "We'd be better off trying to find your mother and convince her to let bygones be bygones."

Nighval frowned. "You don't know my mother and you, and I made a deal that you would fall asleep if I told you the truth."

"But you didn't tell me where we are going."

"My home, of course. Now go to sleep so the damn pill will take effect and we can get on with it."

"Wait, what happens when I wake up?"

"You won't remember any of this conversation, of course. Only that I so very bravely saved your life. I'm already off to a good start, aren't I?"

"Oh my God, you really are a monster," I said, tossing the cloak away from my shoulders and twisting. What for, I didn't know. The ground was way down there, and I'd probably break an ankle if I fell off the beast. I had to get away. If Samara had been willing to give him that pill, maybe she'd help me figure out another way to break the curse. But if what Nighval told me was true, I was minutes, maybe seconds from being brainwashed by her magic. The thought of losing control like that terrified me.

"Perhaps, but I think you secretly like my particular breed. Now sleep," he said.

"No," I said, as Nighval tucked the cloak back around us.

"You will," he said. "And you better do it soon, before I turn back into a real monster." The smile he gave me was positively wicked, and I shivered.

This was good because I was not dead. Bad because I had a pill dissolving in my belly that would brainwash me into forgetting what type of creature was whisking me away. But Nighval didn't plan to kill me, and I was gathering all the vitriol earlier that had possibly not been directed at me as his tone had lost some of its edge since we'd gotten out of sight of the crowd.

I glanced around. Ahead of us, far in the distance, was a dense green forest. The road we followed led there. I craned my neck behind me. The city we'd come from was no longer visible. There wasn't a structure or dwelling in sight.

"Why can't you just magic us away?" I asked him, yawning. Shit.

His arm tightened around my waist, and his hand gave my hip a squeeze. "I could, but this is nice." he asked. "I think a few weeks of forced proximity is going to be a boon for our relationship, don't you think?"

"There is nothing you or that pill can do to make me feel anything besides loathing towards you." I had to cling to that thought. Because if he was right, and he somehow found a way to make me fall for him, what would happen then? I wasn't foolish enough, *anymore*, to think there was a happily ever after waiting for me somewhere down the line. He saved my head from the executioner. Now I stood to lose my heart.

"We'll see," he said. "Now be quiet and go to sleep before I tell you all of the things I'm going to make you feel."

"That will never happen, so keep dreaming," I said, squirming restlessly in his arms. He responded by squeezing me closer. So close my body, which wasn't delicate, felt dwarfed in the shadow of his ridiculously huge form.

"Last time we were this near, I recall you had a very different reaction to my touch," he said.

"You were controlling me with magic."

"Is that what you think?" he asked, leaning back a hair to raise an eyebrow in my direction. His low chuckle reverberated through our chests, but I ignored it.

His mouth brushed my earlobe. "Am I not correct in thinking you liked it very much? Or was I mistaking your fear for desire?" he asked. I swallowed, all too aware of the way the vein in my neck fluttered under his scrutiny. *Focus on loathing.* He continued, "I enjoyed it very much, and I came back to give you more. After you had time to consider it, it seems you remembered the nature of the monster chasing you. But don't worry, witch," he said the name he knew annoyed me. I understood it was just to goad me. "Soon enough, the same feelings will stir within you, and you will be mine."

I couldn't suppress the goosebumps that erupted down my neck. He let his mouth linger and his hot breath tease my skin. Did he even want me to be his?

I groaned in agitation, but he ignored me and started tracing idle circles on my hip. Had the horse slowed? It had. Nighval eased it into a melodic trot and the movement was too similar to being rocked, because the warlock knew exactly what he was doing. I leaned my head back against the crook of his shoulder and tilted my head up so I could see him. He was staring off into the distance, probably patiently waiting for me to fall asleep. Maybe Nighval was right, and this plan he'd hatched would be what it took to save both of our people. But how could it work if he used magic to make me fall for him against my will? Surely that was some critical component of the curse, and this would all be for naught.

I studied him, the hard line of his face and the serene, settled press of his wide mouth as he stared at the tree line ahead. How the hollows of his cheeks dipped in, and the bone beneath his eye curved outward at an angle almost too sharp. If it were only a smidge softer, like how he'd changed himself when he'd picked me up, he'd be desperately handsome. If his eyes weren't quite as deep set and his brow weren't so strong, he'd appear much less intimidating. Now I wasn't sure what was worse, the real him or the rat-him.

My eyelids drew down, and I snapped them back up. He couldn't ride forever and if I had to ride with a rat-man, so be it. As if he sensed my losing battle, he brushed a strand of hair off of my face and said with more tenderness than I imagined him capable, "I wish we'd had more time, Avery."

A warm sensation punched into my stomach, almost painfully, before it flooded through me in gentle, cozy waves. I tilted my head back further, and at the edge of my vision, I caught the knowing glint in his burnt caramel eyes.

CHAPTER 23

NIGHVAL

T hank the Goddess the witch was asleep. I needed to think. I had to figure out what she wanted in a man, and become that if only for a few short months, so she'd fall for me. The problem was, she wasn't like the girls they'd sent before. I supposed that was a plus since they'd all run away or... well, never mind that. Still, she had screamed and fainted, so that wasn't new. But she had writhed in passion against me, which was different.

She was picky, outspoken, and didn't know when to let it rest. Xavier had eventually told me she forced him to share the details of the curse and in exchange, she married him, so I understood my brother's motive now.

With our kiss, I'd made it further than I'd gotten in almost eighteen years. I wasn't sure if her knowledge of our curse helped or hurt my case at this point, but hopefully the pill would do its job. It was only a matter of time. Perhaps I should have gotten the pill before to try on a witch sooner, but I'd been too stubborn and now my stupid brother was dead. Plus, there had never been chemistry with any of them like there was with this one. Now that was something to build on and the fragile hope caused my chest to swell.

It was a mistake to exile me and leave the fate of our people in Xavier's hands, regardless that I'd failed each time prior. As soon as I had stepped away for the sake of my people, Leviticus stepped in and bent my brother's ear. And the idiot had been about to execute their last hope. I'd be damned if I'd remain a nightmare for the rest of my long life, much less allow those witches to keep me from my power on all but twelve nights a year. I'd make them pay, but I'd much rather have this woman in my arms fall for me and get my power back without having to wreck the other plane. It would throw off the balance and that would only garner trouble.

Now I had a task on my hands, and I needed to mentally prepare. I glanced down at her. She looked so peaceful when she wasn't arguing or snarling, though if I was being honest, I didn't really mind that either.

Her pink lips parted, and she let out a slight whimper. Perfectly arched eyebrows pinched together and the pupils beneath her eyelids darted back and forth erratically. It took little to imagine the nightmares that haunted her dreams.

"Shh..." I urged, rubbing her waist soothingly. With the care she took maintaining her appearance, she'd probably hate the fact that I was studying her so intently in her current state. But I knew what lay beneath the film of grime she acquired in prison.

I had to have her, and while I wished I could have done it without the magic, there just wasn't time. Too much weighed on this and the urge to make it happen soon was like a drive imprinted in my DNA.

I'd known that much the night I caught her making her first escape attempt. The wind caught that black cloak and, as it soared in the air, I couldn't peel my eyes away from her. I didn't want to think about that inch of belly, her flaring curves, and the way her amber-gold eyes lit with fright and something else more delicious. Then those pretty full lips clamped down into a scowl, and I hated my brother a little more than I did before.

Of all the women over the years, how was this the one that had gone to Xavier? But now the witch was in my arms, and I had my hands on those gorgeous hips and her adorable nose pointed up to me. Long black lashes a few shades darker than her waves of cool brown hair splayed out across her unmarred cheeks, which were dappled with kisses from the sun. I'd hated them at the wedding, but now they were mine, and I wanted to run my fingertips across them, then my lips. One day I would. Too bad whenever she opened those soft lips, which had yielded so willingly, they only spewed venom in my direction.

I tore my gaze from the witch warming my lap and shot a glance up toward the waning moon and stifled a grumble. Gently, I fished around in my pack, fetching the caps for my claws. Soon, I'd need them.

Still, I planned to ride until she woke. Then we would find an inn and rest. I meant what I'd told her. The more reasons I could find to be physically close to her, the more she'd warm to me. Having to share a mount was obvious. In a week or so, depending on how things were going, I'd make sure there was only one room available at whatever inn we stayed in. Whatever it took.

There were no stars in the sky as I made my way through the winding forest path by the light of the moon. Several hours passed since Avery fell asleep and the way her eyes flared right before sleep claimed her suggested the pill had taken effect. I couldn't help the eager jumble in my stomach that I almost recognized as butterflies as her eyelids fluttered. The logging town at the edge of the forest where I'd caught her before was about half an hour away. She could sleep a little longer.

A branch snapped under Eclipse's hoof, and she started. Goddess, the woman felt so good, too good in my arms, pressed against my chest. "Sleep," I said, my hand rubbing idle circles on her waist, dropping a few inches lower to rub soothing strokes onto the curve of her hip.

Something about having her now soothed my soul. I don't know if it was a new sense of control over our destiny or her mere presence. I found myself watching her again as she slept instead of the road where my attention should be focused.

She'd killed Xavier. What type of creature did I hold and what had happened that had driven her actions? When my mother had questioned me for still wanting her after hearing what she'd done, I hadn't understood, but now I had weeks to think on it. I realized I didn't believe her to be guilty. At least, not in the sense that she was some type of murderer. Even now, my instinct was to blame him. He must have done something unforgivable, and she hadn't needed me or anyone else to save her from it. She saved herself which was almost as much of a turn-on as anything else about her. And now that Xavier was dead, there would be no need to annul the marriage. For the next three months, she'd be mine. Maybe longer if I played my hand right.

My hand shifted over her stomach where the pill's magic had taken root. What would it make her see? The pill was a mystery, and my mother hadn't been forthcoming before we'd gotten the news of Xavier. I had no idea if she would see some version of me, perhaps like the image I presented her when I picked her up in the forest, or if she saw her own version of prince charming. Maybe even a lover from the past, from her world, who she missed. There was no way to know. And it didn't matter. It wasn't not like I wanted her to want me. Did I?

In the woods that first night, as her eyes had roved over my notably softened form, I thought I'd sensed approval in her eye. She likely suspected I was her intended and as she'd assessed me and came to a positive determination, I'd be lying if I didn't admit it felt good.

But when she saw the real me in the library, she was terrified. Horrified, even. Almost as much as when she'd seen me as the curse had taken over my form and she understood her new reality. She'd been cold to me ever since, with the exception of the moonlight chase and our picnic.

I smiled as I relived the memory, and a soft groan drew my attention. I turned my attention to the stirring woman in my lap. Wide amber-gold eyes stared up at me, and I said, "Hello, Avery."

CHAPTER 24

AVERY

"Nighval?" I whispered, and my voice became steadier. "What happened?"

The towering man who'd delivered me to my now dead husband stroked my hip in slow, soothing circles. "What do you remember?"

My brow wrinkled, and I stared off into the distance for a moment. "I was..." A full body shudder vibrated through me as I relived the memory, and he squeezed me tight. I turned my head back up to him. "I was about to be executed. I was on my knees, in a puddle of blood, but you... You saved me. I killed your brother, and you saved me. Why?"

His hard features softened a hair, like he was pleased with something. "It wasn't your fault what they were asking you to do. The witches should have told you what you were up against. And my brother—"

"He attacked me," I said. Nighval became stiff as a board behind me and his arm, which was on my hip, snaked around my waist and locked in like a vice grip. "Jesus," I coughed, batting at his hold.

"Tell me what he did to you." His voice held a deadly edge.

"He didn't. Well, he tried to, but—"

"Avery, I need you to tell me what he did to you that made you drive a knife into his stomach. Did he hurt you?" Nighval brought the giant horse we were riding to a halt, his large hand gripped my cheek, raising my eyes to his.

I shook my chin out of his grip. "I'm fine. We had agreed on the next full moon I would give myself to him, and I tried. I really did, but the way he touched me—I just couldn't do it. He was kissing me down there, trying to make me feel good, but I couldn't stop the tears. That made him angry, and he said something about knowing how I wanted it, rough or something, though I don't remember why, and he changed. Then I grabbed the knife from my nightstand, and it was in his stomach, and I was covered in his blood. I promise you, I didn't mean for it to happen." I could feel myself trembling as a flood of emotion hit me at once, and tears streamed down my face.

A gentle hand cupped my cheek, his rough thumb brushing away the tears. "Shh..." he soothed. "You did nothing wrong. What happened was his fault, and if he weren't dead by your hand, he'd be dead by mine. Do you understand me?"

I sniffed and met his gaze. "Really?"

"Of course," he said. "You have my word. As long as you are in this plane, I will never let anyone hurt you. You are with me now."

He nudged the horse, and we were moving again. With the way he said it and the tight hold he had on my waist, I believed him. "Wait, where are we going?" I asked him. "What about the curse?"

That drew his attention. He searched my face for a moment before he answered, seeming to consider his words. "We're going somewhere outside of the curse's reach. You don't need to worry about it any longer. I'll make sure everything is handled."

"Will I be able to go back to my plane?" I asked.

Nighval's lips pressed into a line, and he exhaled a breath through his nose. "No, I'm afraid not. It requires a large draw of power to be able to break the planes and unfortunately, with the few hours we get a month of access to ours, I'd hardly be able to summon enough myself. I doubt I could get other warlocks to do the same."

Something he said made a memory flicker, and my eyes drew to the night sky and the moon dipping below the horizon. "You haven't turned into one of those creatures."

His eyebrows raised, and another grin transformed his face. "No, I haven't. Myself and where I'm taking you are shielded from that aspect of the curse."

"How?" I asked, incredulous.

His grin turned into a smile as we made it to the edge of a small town. "Magic," he said.

The street and the little inn where we stopped felt familiar. Even the way the innkeeper eyed me felt familiar, but I hadn't left the castle grounds since I'd been here, so it must be a weird déjà vu. Besides, the harder I tried to think about it, the sharper the pinch between my eyebrows became. I took a deep breath. *Let it go.* Whatever I thought I remembered wasn't worth a migraine.

Once he made the arrangements with the innkeeper, he ushered me up the stairs, a protective hand finding its way to the small of my back. He unlocked a room, then led me inside. There was a mid-sized bed, a fireplace, and a table with two chairs. There were probably about two or three hours of night left and even though I'd slept as we'd ridden, I was exhausted.

Nighval pointed to a door on the long wall. "There is a bathing chamber through there. The door next to it is to my room. I've called for some heated water to be brought up for you. You may get cleaned up, and sleep some." He pointed to something leaned against the corner near the bed.

"Oh my God!" I screeched. "My backpack." I don't know what inspired me, perhaps my vanity or my obsession with makeup and my other creature comforts, but I crossed the room in a few great strides and threw my arms around the excessively tall man's waist and pulled him in for a hug.

His chest rumbled, and I felt the vibrations with my cheek which was plastered to his broad chest. He grabbed my arms pulling me off of him, holding me still to give me a quizzical expression. "I saved you from certain death, moments before an axe severed your head, and this backpack is what you're ecstatically grateful for?"

I nodded vigorously. "Yes."

"I'm dying to know what is in it now," he said, releasing me so I could rush over to it.

I set it on the bed and pulled a few things from it, namely my violet make-up bag with my skincare routine in it. I ran a hand across my cheek. I'd spent a month in a dank prison cell and needed some serious exfoliation and hydration. Did I smell? Oh Goddess. Maybe he hadn't noticed. Who was I kidding? He probably thought I was disgusting, but it's not like I cared, right?

"I don't know if I've been this happy since I learned I was going to be a queen. I guess I'm not a queen anymore, am I?" I shrugged. "How did you know?"

"Well, I remembered how defensive you were when I used magic to move it to the carriage the day I picked you up, so I figured it was pretty important to you. It was still in your room, forgotten about. I sensed it and had it moved here."

"It is. Thank you," I said. That was really sweet of him to notice it. I figured I'd never get my things back, and I tried to become resigned to that fact as we plodded along while I peppered him with questions. I should have been consumed with gratitude for being alive, but those were the only things I had from my plane and they mattered to me.

"Good. I'm glad I could do something to make you happy." His face was severe, but his smile was warm which sent warm tingles through me the same way riding bundled in his arms had.

"How many more days until we get to where we're going?" I asked, wondering if he'd be getting me my own horse or we'd be riding that towering beast together for the remainder of the journey.

"It's almost two weeks to my home," he said.

Okay, so we were going to his home, in exile. I supposed that was safe enough. When I asked nothing further, he said, "I'll be right here if you need anything. Leave the door cracked so I can hear you and if you get scared, don't hesitate to call out."

I nodded. As he slipped through the door joining our rooms, a knock at my door sounded and two attendants, who looked unhappy to be awoken, shuffled into the room, carrying large buckets of steaming water. It wasn't enough to fill the tub, but I was grateful I'd be able to sponge the blood away, discard this disgusting prison dress, and get clean.

I set out a few towels provided by the inn, stripped down and got to work. There was more blood on me, beneath my clothes than I expected. With each pass of the warm sponge, the water would tint a darker shade of pink until it was almost red. As I rinsed it, then dipped into the clean water, my grip became weak, and my hand trembled a little more violently.

It wasn't long before tears were streaming down my face and my full body had taken up the tremors. Everything from the last eight months hit me like a landslide, taking me down with all the dirt and debris, crushing everything in its wake. I'd been forced to marry a monster, a supposed nice guy, who'd attacked me when he hadn't gotten what he wanted. Who I'd killed, because let's be honest, if he hadn't impaled himself on that blade, I would have pressed it into him.

And right now, I was cleaning away the blood of Annabelle and four other human beings, whose crimes I did not know, whose heads I heard hit the wood planks, whose blood I was made to kneel in. A sob tore from my throat, then another, and another, until ugly tears were cascading down my cheeks and a black hole had opened inside me. How did I end up here? I was perfectly content to bartend and dabble with my half of a theater degree.

I had no power, and I still had that yearning for something more. And look at where it got me. I kicked over the bucket and the bloody water splashed out over the floor, tinting the white towel pink. The liquid reminded me of Xavier's blood spreading, and my sobs redoubled their strength.

Somewhere in the corner of my awareness, I felt a heavy, foreboding presence, but I wasn't coherent enough to notice. Suddenly I was weak. My trembling legs gave out, and I fell. Before my knees hit the ground, big arms were around me and my naked body was hauled against a really hard chest.

"No, Nighval," I said, trying to spit the words out through my gasps.

"Don't worry, I've got you," he said, ignoring my plea. He placed me on the bed, fully nude still, then gathered the comforter around me, wrapping me up like a burrito. He scooped me up, like I weighed nothing, carried me past the pool of dirty water eyeing it, and into his room. I glanced back toward my room. Noticing he said, "Don't worry, your things will be safe until you wake. You need to sleep."

Instead of placing me on the bed in his room, he shifted the pillows around and sat so his back was leaning against them and the headboard, with me in his arms like he was cradling a baby. My tears slowed to a stream instead of a deluge, and I regarded him. "I can't sleep."

He pressed my head into his chest, so the top of my head was nestled into the crook of his neck. The angle made it to where I was staring down the length of his long body. He wore a pair of soft charcoal linen pants, and his feet were bare and crossed at the ankle. Very nice feet, I noted. That brought my attention to the chest that I only just realized was bare, that I'd been crying on. Oh Goddess, I was wrapped in the arms of the brother of the man I'd murdered, bawling into his bare, very firm chest.

And it felt good, the way he was holding me. Stroking my hair like I was something precious, that needed to be comforted at all costs. I really needed to get up and get back to my room. This was inappropriate on so many levels.

"I'm fine," I said, wiggling to free myself, but it was of no use.

"You're not fine, so either go to sleep or keep crying. I don't care. I'm not letting you go. Understand?" The way his one arm was locked around me, like it had been on the horse after I told him what happened, suggested he meant what he said, so I relented, easing into him. I'd come to my senses in the morning.

So instead of trying, I drew in a breath savoring the smell of thunderstorms and firewood that—Goddess—that was his skin. The familiar scent had a comforting quality to it and when I tried to remember where I'd smelled it before my headache threatened to bloom again. After everything I'd experienced, I probably shouldn't be thinking so hard. Instead, I should just let the yummy maleness drifting up into my nostrils wrap around me like a cocoon.

I nestled in closer ready to savor—what was I thinking? I was definitely going to come to my senses in the morning because the last month had obviously messed with my brain, and I was experiencing some serious PTSD right now. It would take time for me to work out all the feelings I had and more sessions while I bawled my eyes out to get past this. Still, I might as well enjoy the warmth this man was offering me. He wasn't prying or making me tell him what I lost it over. He only glanced at the overturned bucket, seemed to understand, and carried me to safety.

I could live with that. Correction. Tonight, I would live with that. Tomorrow, I'd have to explain to him he couldn't just carry a naked woman off wrapped only in a blanket, regardless of how hysterical she was being. But, again, tonight... I snuggled in closer and felt his chin settle into my hair. Tonight, I would sink into the comforting illusion that I wasn't alone.

CHAPTER 25

NIGHVAL

When I awoke, the witch, no—*Avery*—was still asleep in my arms. In the few hours of night remaining, either one or both of us had scooted down, so I was mostly reclined across the pillows, and she was half on top of me, and I had both arms around her blanket-clad body. I'm not sure anything ever felt more intoxicating than this woman nestled into my body, like I was her protector. Last night, I felt her inner struggle as she settled into me, finally giving in to the comfort I was offering her.

As the first sob woke me, I'd resolved to let her go through it. To give her space to work out her feelings, but when the contents of that bucket splashed across the room, followed by that guttural sound which twisted my guts, I had to go to her. Was this what it was like when you claimed a woman? Had I already done that with her and not known it? The way her heart ached, it was like my own was aching right alongside it. Surely not, but in that moment, I would have done anything to take away her pain. Which was horrible because when she found out what I was up to, it would cause her another river of sorrow.

I'd stop that from happening. When I'd taken her, forced her to take that pill, my thoughts had been aimed in an entirely different direction. I had been hurt and angry at her rejection. The memory of how she'd stepped behind Xavier stung, but now as I studied her beautiful sleeping face, something shifted. Resisting the urge to kiss those freckles, I slid out from under her as gently as I could, splashed some water on my face and threw on a change of clothes. After cleaning up what was left of the water, I stuffed the soiled towels in the overturned bucket and placed it outside the door.

This morning I'd give her space to sort things out and let her sleep as long as she needed. I went downstairs to order them to have some fresh water waiting for her and some bread and cheese. She'd come down when she was ready, and I'd be here, ready to go. If I was lucky, maybe I could get her to confide the swirling thoughts in her mind to me. Get her to trust me, because after the way I felt waking up with her, I knew I had to experience that for a hundred mornings, more if I got my magic back.

I'd do whatever it took to do that. When she roared and wailed at me after she found out, I'd take it. Then I'd find a way back into her arms.

CHAPTER 26

AVERY

I awoke alone in bed. The man who smelled so earthy and smoldering was gone. A wave of icy panic shot through me. Oh Goddess, I'd fallen asleep in Nighval Helicanus's, the exiled king, arms. What was I thinking? Now that his brother was dead, did that make him king again? I wasn't sure how all that worked, but since he was fleeing with me across the country, I assumed that meant he wasn't.

I searched the room and didn't see him. I heard no sounds from the adjoining room, and the sun was shimmering through the open window. The sheer white curtains rustled in a gentle breeze, which set the flames dancing in the fireplace. A fresh bucket of water sat near it, and a larger metal bucket hung over some coals. Steam rose in wafts from it, beckoning me. Next to the clean water was another larger pile of towels. Being a former king had its perks. The extras couldn't be an account of my former standing.

I glanced at myself in the mirror and winced. My face was pink, my eyes were red and puffy. So much so that I didn't think I'd be able to apply enough makeup to hide it. Still, I was sure Nighval, though waiting patiently, was eager to get on the road. He had saved my life and let me sob into his chest after all, so I should be respectful and hurry along.

I scarfed down the food that was set out for me and went to work, beautifying myself as best as possible. I sorted through my clothes. None of the chic shift dresses I had would be appropriate for riding on a horse, so I selected one of the workout sets I'd brought to this plane with me. This one was an ombre medium grey fading to a darker grey. Long-sleeves hooked around my thumbs and would look super cool with the charcoal cloak that was laid out across the bed. It was huge, probably his, but with as nice as he was being, I figured he'd let me use it if I wanted. Or he'd wrap us both in it again. A shiver worked its way up my spine at the thought.

Tugging on my boots, I wished they were sneakers, but they'd be perfect for our cross-country adventure and they kind of made me look bad ass. I stuffed my things in my backpack, hoisted it up to my shoulders, grabbed Nighval's cloak, and headed out the door.

Nighval wasn't in the small common room on the first floor. There were a few groups of rat-people huddled around round four-tops, and they eyed me warily as I passed them. Catching the server's attention, I asked, "Have you seen…" I wasn't sure what to call him or if she'd know the man I was traveling with by name. She hadn't been here last night when we'd arrived. Her furry ear twitched and she gave me a curious expression. "Umm… the man I'm traveling with. He's very tall. Incredibly tall. That's how you'd know it was him." I raised my brows at her hopefully.

"His Majesty was out the door hours ago. I'd check the stables," she said, over her shoulder as she retreated into the kitchen. Well, shit. He hadn't left a message or anything. A knot of dread seated itself in my stomach as I reached the door and exited the inn. Surely, he hadn't left me. I had zero resources and no idea what I'd do if he had, except I was near certain that I'd end up back on the executioner's block before long.

No, he wouldn't do that. He wouldn't go to all the trouble to save me, only to abandon me the first chance he got. And there was the defensive way his arm had gripped me that made me think he didn't want to let go. The word defensive wasn't right. Possessive. As I landed on the word, the shiver from earlier turned into full on goosebumps. Good grief, I was practically crushing on my savior. I knew there was a syndrome for people who fell for their captors. Stockholm syndrome or something. Was there something similar for people who were attracted to their rescuers?

When I first saw him in the clearing, I thought he was handsome, but I also felt more than a little intimidated by his imposing presence. His arrogance. Last night, it was dark, or I was bawling, still in shock, and I hadn't really had time to take him in. Despite myself, my curiosity peaked as I went off in search of him.

The fact that he was somehow able to shield himself from this curse and the only person I'd seen in non-rat form in the daylight this entire time. *Magic* as he said. Nerves jumped in my stomach—but I hadn't seen him in daylight. It was still night when we'd arrived at the inn. Just not a full moon. What if it had only been for last night and today he was back to being a rat-man? I hadn't realized how comforting being around another person in human form without the worry of them shifting had been. *Please let him still be human.*

The street was bustling at this hour. Glancing at the sun, I realized I must have slept until almost lunch, and these rat-people were beginning their mid-day breaks. I took the first alleyway next to the inn in search of the stables. Another building sat across the street behind the inn. The scent of sweat, earth, and manure that was distinctly horse drifted up my nostrils. I found the stables. Nighval leaned against the wooden building, standing on one foot. The other leg bent at the knee with the sole of his boot planted on the wall and he crossed his arms over his broad chest.

A flood of relief soaked through me as I caught sight of him. My savior was human still. That brought up another concern. I really didn't like how dependent I was on him. How I was at the mercy of his generosity. If what he said was true, I would never be able to leave this plane. What did that mean for my future? I glanced back at the inn. I guessed I could find some bar in some sleepy town and sling drinks, but that was a far cry from the queen position I'd signed up for. And I'd always be in danger.

Scanning Nighval's body, his face, which was significantly more intimidating than I remembered, I decided it was best to be grateful and perhaps this man would help me figure things out. Nighval was a warlock. Maybe he could get a message to my coven. They could draw me home and things could go back to how they were before I came here.

Water splashed as my boot stomped into the puddle of water which pooled in the middle of the street and my eyes landed on pale skin, not fur, peeking out of that same fitted suit. Thank the Goddess, the towering man appeared as human as I did. My steps almost guttered as a powerful flood of relief hit me. Small victories. Nighval's closed eyes snapped open, locked on me, then widened even as his jaw lowered. His jaw dropped. Who was I kidding? Even with my puffy eyes, I knew I looked hot and this large, very intimidating man seemed to agree.

His eyes ran up and down my body and a little thrill shot through me. Yep, I definitely had a syndrome because the way he was staring at me made me feel good. So good that I couldn't repress the grin that broke out across my face, making my cheeks burn.

"What?" I squinted at his slack jaw, glad I hadn't put the cloak on. "Everyone knows I'm not from here, so what does it matter what I wear? Besides, from what I recall, you didn't approve of my demure white shift dress, and this will be much better on a horse, don't you think?" I asked, blinking my coated lashes at him in mock innocence. His Adam's apple bobbed, but his jaw hardened.

Ignoring me, he said, "I see you're recovered. Are you ready to ride?"

I nodded, following him into the stable. The giant horse was in the first pen and Nighval brought him out into the center of the space, made some arrangements, which included taking my backpack from me and securing it to the animal.

"What's his name?" I asked, holding my hand up above my head near the horse's nose so he could smell me.

"Eclipse," he said, and watched me as Eclipse nudged my hand, lowering his head so I could run my fingers along the gleaming black fur of his muzzle. When he didn't ready another horse, I had my answer to my earlier question.

"We will travel a long distance, like you said. Can Eclipse manage both of our weight, plus my pack?" I asked. The animal nudged the side of my head in what I interpreted as an affectionate gesture and snorted, lifting tendrils of my hair.

I didn't have to see him studying me to know his eyes were still on me. The way they burned across my skin made heat crawl up my neck. "Eclipse isn't a normal horse, Avery."

"Right," I said, turning to him. His hand was raised to me, and I took it, letting him help me into the saddle. So, the horse was like his rider, something beyond normal, something magical and powerful. As Nighval swung up behind me and pulled me to him, settling us in the saddle which I noticed had two depressed areas to make riding together more comfortable.

"You couldn't have gotten me my own horse, then?" I asked. He'd gotten this special saddle after all.

A knowing half-smile crept across his face, and I craned my neck back so I could witness his answer.

"No, a standard mount wouldn't be able to keep up with Eclipse. And I don't have another enchanted animal just lying around," he said, and Eclipse gave another snort I didn't take to be intended as kindly as the one before.

Nighval's thighs, which were on either side of mine, flexed and Eclipse ducked under the arch of the stable doors and trotted out into the street.

"You've offended him," Nighval said, the humor in his rich voice apparent.

"What—how?" I asked, incredulous.

"Eclipse has been gracious enough to let you ride, and that is a high honor. No one besides me has ever ridden him. That you would even suggest wanting to ride another animal is an insult," Nighval said.

"Seriously?" I asked, my intonation displaying my disbelief. Nighval didn't need to answer. Eclipse snorted again and tossed his head back, his shiny mane ruffling as he picked up the pace. Nighval was right. The horse wasn't pleased with me.

"Holy shit," I blurted. "I'm so sorry, Eclipse. I truly didn't know," I said, trying to lean forward to stroke his hair back into place.

Nighval pulled me back against him as he chuckled. "He forgives you. Do you have much experience riding?" he asked.

"No. I've always wanted to learn, but in my plane, everyone has a vehicle, so it is more of a hobby," I said.

"Ah, yes. Before the curse, we had enchanted carriages like the one I picked you up with. Some people have automobiles, but unfortunately, they aren't common, and our infrastructure is somewhat lacking for mass use. And we never believed the curse would go on as long as it has..." Nighval trailed off as if the memory were painful for him.

If I had fallen for his brother, the curse would have been lifted, so I was partially responsible. "Wait, you were exiled because you failed with each of the witches that was sent before me, weren't you?"

"Yes," he said, and it sounded like the word was spit through gritted teeth.

"So, if I were to fall for you, the curse would be broken?" Any would be attraction I felt toward him melted away to be replaced with another red emotion. "Oh my God, it's why you saved me. One last shot at saving your people. You just couldn't resist." Nighval didn't reply. "Are all men in this plane so horrible?"

His arm tightened around me. "Would you have preferred I left you to die, then?" The silence stretched on between us.

"I didn't think so," he said. "And don't worry, Avery. I could hardly imagine someone as flawless as you could fall for such a repulsive man such as myself. Like you said, I failed, given seventeen chances. Obviously, the problem is me." My heart pinched, but he continued, not giving me time to reply. "Hold on tight and try to find Eclipse's rhythm. You'll be less sore later if you do." His voice was rough, guarded.

I offended my rescuer and for whatever reason, it didn't sit well with me. His thighs flexed again, and we were galloping through the open field surrounding the town.

That night when we got to the next inn, he didn't say a word to me as he led me inside and to my room. I slumped to the bed as he passed through the open door between our rooms, dropping my backpack in mine before he did. A door clicked from inside his room, and when I scurried to peek inside, it was empty.

CHAPTER 27

NIGHVAL

W hy did everything having to do with witches have to be such a pain in my ass? The pill couldn't have just made her forget all the parts of her memory that would be a hindrance to me. She was too clever, and I felt her stiffen when she pieced the puzzle together. I should be grateful she hadn't made the connection between breaking the curse and saving her people. Or maybe the pill's magic was somehow shielding her from thinking about the fact that I was the warlock who'd promised vengeance against her coven. That certainly wouldn't paint me in a favorable light. After what she already realized, she would be guarded, and I had less than three months to get her from there to mine.

I wanted to pull at my hair or find a group of bandits to take out my frustration on. But I couldn't because it would be another twenty-seven and a half days before I got my power back for a few scant hours. I hated witches.

Liar, the voice in my head whispered. Okay, I hated all witches but her.

Not speaking to her and storming out of the room wasn't a great idea. Actually, it was a terrible idea. I had to remind myself that while I remembered all the moments we'd shared forming whatever fledgling bond was between us, if my mother was to be believed, Avery remembered none. Only me from the first night she'd arrived in this plane and her rescue. I would be omitted from every other memory of hers in between.

Something about that knowledge made regret coil low in my belly. I was starting from scratch with her. I'd have to establish something between us all over again, and I needed to start by getting some dinner and bringing it to her with an apology. Then lie to her about my intentions, all the while doing the very thing I was lying to her about.

Why did the idea of it make my skin crawl?

I stood in the hallway for a long moment before taking the stairs two at a time. Half an hour later, the innkeeper was following me up to her room with an overflowing tray of food which she sat on a round table barely big enough for two people. In my hand, I carried a bottle of wine and two glasses. In my thundering chest, I carried resolve.

When we stepped into the room, Avery was sitting on the bed, staring out the window with her back to the door.

"Put the food there, then leave us," I said, and the innkeeper obeyed.

The door clicked shut behind the woman and Avery said, "You don't have to be such a dick to them, you know?"

"Excuse me?" I asked, crossing the room to her in a few strides.

The witch turned a tear-stained face to me. That black stuff she wore on her eyes, traced a watery trail down her sun-spotted cheeks and my heart lurched. Had I made her cry?

"The service people," she said, gesturing a hand toward the door. "That's what I did in the other plane. I was a bartender and trust me, if you're rude or dismissive to us, we mark you and... Never mind. It doesn't matter, does it? You were a king, and I'm in a different world, aren't I?"

A fresh stream of tears erupted.

"You don't like my manners?" I asked.

Her eyes widened as she took me in. "You were so gentle with me last night, but you are so harsh with them, abrupt. You should treat them like people, not objects designed to serve you, but like I said, it doesn't matter."

"I'll be better," I said, as that was all I could think to say. "Is that what has upset you?"

"Are you kidding?"

I studied her as understanding came to me. "You're still upset about what you believe my intentions to be."

"Duh," she said.

"Duh?" I asked at the unfamiliar word.

"Yeah, duh. Like, no shit Sherlock. It doesn't take a wizard to figure out my situation isn't exactly ideal. So, go ahead, then. Woo me. When I crumble to your charms and fall for you, what happens then? Will we be king and queen again?" Her pink lips were an angry line, as she raised insistent eyebrows at me.

"You're glorious," I said, and her jaw dropped. I sat next to her on the bed. It groaned under my weight.

"Don't," she said, lifting a hand to push me away as I leaned into her space. I grabbed her hand and placed it over my heart, pressing it flat with my palm. I lifted my other hand to cup her tear-stained cheek and her breathing hitched.

"Even if there were no curse to break, I would still find you intoxicating. You do something to my blood—"

"Don't say that," she said.

"Why not?" I asked.

"Because you've been around me for all of two days and it makes you sound crazy," she said.

I tilted my head to the ceiling and laughed. Of course, that was what she remembered. Two days. She didn't remember our kiss or our picnic in the garden, or before the wedding. Forcing myself to remember that was already presenting a challenge.

I lowered my head and brought my eyes to her gold ones. I lowered my lips so they hovered but an inch from hers, and I could taste the sweet honey of her breath. "I'm not crazy. Any man with a brain would want you. Especially with the way you share your emotions so openly, your fire and cleverness, and that fucking outfit." Being so blunt, so bold with her was risky, but the way her breathing kicked up a notch made me think she liked it, so I kept going. "It only took a few hours to be affected by you, Avery. To be in your thrall."

Her mouth parted. I wanted to lean in and take because I knew she would give despite herself. I really wanted to, but I ignored the sparks crackling across my body and released her beautiful face, standing. Walking over to the tray of food, I opened the bottle of wine and poured two glasses. When I had my breathing under control, I said, "Come eat. We have longer days ahead of us and you need your strength."

CHAPTER 28

AVERY

G oddess above, how did that man take me from crying over the mess of a situation I was in to practically panting and this turned on? The idea of him, his power, his larger-than-life presence made me feel so small, so feminine, and the pretty words he said sent waves of euphoria coursing through me. I was almost drunk on them. For a second, I thought he was going to kiss me, and I swear I would have let him.

I glanced over to where he stood, waiting for me, a glass of red wine in his hand, the other tucked into his pocket. His eyes were searching as they grazed across my face. Maybe I was the crazy one, because I didn't think his words were lies. Well, what he said about his intention was, but his gravitation to me was as real as mine was to him. Maybe he did want to make me his. Would it be so terrible allowing myself to get close to this man? He was dominant—a scary, forceful presence. I had no idea what it would be like to be with a man like that. He was one-hundred and eighty degrees in the opposite direction of Xavier. I hadn't liked that. Maybe I could like this. My core pulsed as if it were trying to remind me I did indeed like this. I liked the fearful thrill of having his full, ominous attention on me.

Shit, it was one thing to role play with the mafia man, but whatever Nighval was, was real. Did this attraction I felt mean I'd have to check my feminist card in at the door? No, I didn't think so. Nighval said he liked my fire. He was drawn to it.

And the truth was, I'd come here to marry a king, to save my people and now here I was, with another chance, though it wasn't exactly what I'd expected. I doubted they'd give me that crown back. I took a deep breath. I could do this. Something about him, his quiet, commanding nature, the way his body moved all stalking predator made me think he'd be excellent in bed. Another surge of warmth flooded through me and, like my thoughts were transparent to him, his eyes darkened.

"You shouldn't look at me like that, Avery," he said in a low grumble.

I stood, crossing the room, taking the glass he extended to me and sat. My mouth was so dry I took a sip, swishing the liquid. Notes of blackberry and oak danced across my tongue. It didn't burn, which meant it wasn't strong. That was good because while I worked in a bar, I wasn't much of a drinker. The last thing I needed was to get tipsy around this man.

Getting naked with him would be easy. The charge between us told me that is exactly what he wanted to do. Coaxing this attraction into something more would take time, and when his lips hadn't crushed into mine, I felt like it meant he was on the same page. We were doing this. I would fall for Nighval Helicanus and save everyone. His people and my people. Easy.

"We should eat before this gets cold," he reminded me. He held my chair out for me, and I sat at the little table the food tray was placed on. He sat opposite me, reaching forward to pile some food onto a plate. He glanced up and found me watching him again as I gripped the stem of my wine glass trying to work up the nerve to take the plunge and let him know it was game on.

"What are you waiting for?" he asked, noticing I hadn't moved.

The corners of my mouth twitched. "For you to woo me."

His breath caught... and I grinned.

CHAPTER 29

NIGHVAL

A ll the riding was getting a little monotonous. Maybe I should
have reconsidered and used my magic to whisk her back to my
Lieden Palace that night I rescued her. We'd been talking on and off since
traveling and she seemed to be making an effort to get to know me, which
was completely unexpected. All of her questions never failed to take me
aback.

As if my thoughts had summoned one, she leaned her head back
against my chest, then I could sense her gaze on my face. "I'm trying to
imagine you as a teenager. What were you like then?"

Another odd question. "Let's see." What was I like then? It seemed so
long ago. "I suppose I was like any other immature and hormone driven
young man."

"No way. I'm not buying it. Tell me something good." She playfully
smacked my thigh.

I huffed a laugh. "I suppose I was a bit more driven than most boys my
age at the time. My father would have told you I lived with my nose in
my spellbooks."

"And when you weren't being studious?" she prodded.

"One solstice celebration my warlock friends Link and Eshan came
to Ravsted to stay for the week. I think we were fifteen that year. They
convinced me that we could glamour ourselves to look older, which we
did, then we snuck out and made it to nearly every tavern in the city
without getting caught. That, as you can imagine, because our tradition
until we came of age. My father never knew." A wave of melancholy I
hadn't felt in a long while washed over me, and I sighed at the memory.

Avery shifted in the saddle, drawing my attention. Instinctively, my hands went to her hips, and I squeezed. The gesture was proprietary, I knew, but she wasn't stopping me. Actually, she let out a little moan as I kneaded the flesh there. "You sore?" I asked, wondering if she was allowing this to distract me.

"Yes, but that feels good," she said, and I'd be damned if a surge of pride didn't well up in my chest. At her command, I handed her the reins and went to work on her hips and her thighs. I kneaded in all the ways I imagined eased her tired muscles, taking care not to let the metal caps on my claws slip.

She leaned back against me a little more, and I couldn't resist asking, "You like that?"

Like she knew exactly what she was doing, she said, "Yes, don't stop."

The words had their intended effect when a surge of warmth made its way to my cock. I had to will the thing not to swell, because there was a good chance she would feel it. I didn't think we were there yet, as much as her playful words indicated otherwise.

I was still human enough to understand that after what she had been through, she needed time. She might think a little fun was what she needed, but I knew in the long run it would benefit both of us if I didn't act too quickly. I needed to let her have time to work out the things that had happened to her over the last eight months. At some point, I needed to try to get her to open up to me. Now we were just trading around light conversation. Since those first couple of nights, she hadn't fallen into a fit of tears and she seemed to be managing her new situation better than I would have expected.

She was certainly managing it better than any of the witches before her. "Don't worry, I won't stop," I said, and I felt a shiver wrack through her. Damn, this was going to be a challenge.

I needed to do something to get my mind off the sensations touching her caused. "Why don't you tell me about this theater degree you never finished?"

She flinched at my words, and I quickly followed up. "I didn't mean that in a critical way. You said that you only had courses remaining. Does that mean you were in plays, in front of a live audience?"

"I was," she said. "Why do I have a feeling you find that hard to believe?"

A laugh burst from my chest. I hadn't done such a thing in I don't know how long. Not since the last time she made me laugh. "Actually, I can believe it. I see how much you enjoy your makeup and dressing up. I can perfectly picture you up on stage being incredibly dramatic."

Avery elbowed me in the side, and I grabbed her arm to prevent her from doing it again, keeping my other hand glued to her hip. "What? I'm only telling you the truth."

"For your information, I was in a play called *My Fair Lady*. It's a very famous play and the female lead is a comedic role," she said, flipping her hair haughtily over her shoulder. "I performed so well our local theater critic said I was a uniquely hilarious Eliza Doolittle, and I blended into the role seamlessly."

"Ah, so why did you not become an actor full time and stop this bartending you speak of?" I asked her.

She giggled, like there was some piece of information I was lacking. "Well, acting wasn't enough to pay the bills, unless one made it big. You see, a lot of us, the bartenders working in the town where I lived, were waiting for our big break. But I was getting older, and the witches approached me. If I am being honest with you, the idea of taking on the role of a queen had a lot of appeal. And the way that I saw it, a queen would be on a stage in a way. She would have to work with the people, speak to audiences, act the part alongside the king. I figured I could do it and things weren't really happening with my other career path."

"I see," I said, and something about her narrative bothered me, though I couldn't put my finger on exactly which part. Maybe it was that this world this magnificent woman had come to me from didn't value her as much as I was coming to. "You made a divine queen."

"Except that I didn't. I was only married for a few months before I became the king killer." Her tone became somber. I didn't like that either.

"Avery, you did what you had to do to protect yourself. I know that will not assuage the guilt you feel, but I wish you would stop beating yourself up about it," I said, and heard her sniffle. I angled my head so I could see her face and notice a singular tear cut down her cheek. I removed my hand from her hip and reached up to brush it away with my thumb. Instead of continuing working on her tired muscles, I wrapped my arms around her waist, squeezing. "If it makes you feel any better, I'm convinced you could do no wrong."

A little half-hearted giggle escaped, and she said, "That's because you don't know me well enough yet. I'm sure if given enough time, I could definitely figure out something naughty to do."

She was deflecting. I recognized it because I myself was adept at doing the same thing. But I wasn't going to let her. Even as tempting as it was to flirt back. "You need to talk about what happened. You can tell me, and I won't judge you. I promise."

"I told you what happened. There's nothing more to tell. And the truth is, I would do what I did again. I don't feel guilty, which is the weird part. Actually, I think I feel guilty about not feeling guilty. All I felt as the life drained from his eyes was relief. Does that make me a terrible person? I know so many people were counting on me to break the curse," she said, and her shoulders shook, as if she were fighting back tears.

Don't worry, you will still break the curse. That's what I wanted to tell her, the knowledge that had been looming between us since she had the realization that we still could. But this wasn't about that, it was about her and her misplaced guilt, so I said, "No, it doesn't make you a terrible person. Well, if it does, then I'm wretched."

"What makes you say that?" she asked.

"The night of your wedding to Xavier, I killed twenty-two people." She gasped, and I could feel her body stiffen in my arms. I chuckled. "Like you, I believed they all deserved it. I found a den of vipers, and I took out my frustration on them."

"And what frustrated you so intensely that you became murderous?" she asked.

Shit. That little slip revealed too much. Or perhaps it hadn't, and this was an opportunity. "I was jealous of my brother. When I saw you, I wanted you for myself. Does that make me a monster?"

I wondered if my admission would turn her away. She would be my wife, that much I'd determined, and it was best she knew the man she was marrying. In the last week, I'd given up the idea of becoming someone else to please her.

Still, Avery was stiff and quiet for long moments "When did you see me, because I don't remember seeing you there?"

My heart jumped into my throat. This was the first admission I'd given her about the depth of my interest, and I was learning I cared deeply what her response would be. "I left before you saw me," I lied. *Do you think I'm a monster? Answer the question.* I had to know.

"Oh." She paused, then her words were thoughtful when she said, "No, I don't think that makes you a monster."

I breathed a slow, relieved exhale. And like she understood the momentary torment I felt, she put a hand on mine, which was still wrapped around her waist and squeezed. "Or if that makes you a monster, then I guess we both can be monsters together," she said.

Her words, as lighthearted as she intended them, made my stomach swirl with excitement. I wasn't used to a woman making me feel this way. Making me feel so lost in every conversation. So eager to hear the next thing that came out of her mouth. What was happening to me? Had my brother felt this way, and that's why he'd pressured her, attacked her? Could he not tell as he touched her, she was repulsed by him? Reading a woman's body language wasn't that difficult. Instead of yielding to her lack of desire, he'd hurt her.

The thought made violence splash across my vision. I meant what I said. If she hadn't done it, I would have. What he did, what he attempted, was reprehensible. And I wouldn't have hesitated. That was the type of monster I was. No trial, no last words. No regard for our history, our sibling relationship, or whatever situation he found himself in. He would have been dead. Simple and final.

Avery let out what sounded like a squeak, and I realized I cinched my arm around her too tight in my haze of thoughts. "Sorry," I said.

"That's okay. I get the impression you don't realize how strong you are," she said in a voice that was dripping with honey.

Goddess, how did she know exactly how to make me feel like this? Like a man, primal and protective. Possessive. One and a half weeks in, I reminded myself. Simmer down.

"It makes me feel good that you can talk to me. I enjoy hearing your thoughts," I told her.

Her fingers threaded through mine. "It is all very strange, and sudden, but I feel the same way," she said, and I almost toppled off Eclipse.

Like the animal sensed my shift, he whinnied, and I noticed the town we were headed for coming into view. We only had a few days left on our journey and it was time to up the stakes. "Not much longer." Knowing full well I was a devious asshole, I said, "I hope we're early enough the inn will have ample accommodations."

Like I planned it, the inn had one room with a medium-sized bed. As we stepped into it, her eyes widened. I thanked the Goddess for the patience she'd gifted me. Making the decision not to whisk us away to the palace was going to pay off tonight. And not for the part of my body that was on high alert every time she looked at me. No... for the future I would build with her. That first night, she'd been helpless in my arms due to her desperate state. Now she would learn their comfort. Learn to lean into me and show me her vulnerability as a choice.

I almost had to frown to prevent my lips from twitching upward as she shrugged, picked up her pack and began her nightly routine, where she removed all of that magical makeup to reveal the clean and innocent face beneath. I loved her in her paint, but I lived for these moments in the same aching way. I had to clear the lump from my throat.

"I'll go find us some food. Make yourself comfortable." Then I retreated from the room.

CHAPTER 30

AVERY

Somehow, I knew with all my flirty comments I'd asked for this, and the Goddess had answered me. Of course, there would only be one bed at this inn. It's not like we hadn't slept in the same bed before. So, of course, I was going to offer him a side of the bed. My best guess was he was not going to stay on his side of it. Something about the thought made flowers bloom in my stomach like one of those time-lapse videos, where you can see the full evolution of the plant, petals unfurling for the sun.

It was too convenient, almost like he planned it. I glanced over at him before he walked out of the room and the corner of his lip definitely twitched. Yep, he planned it. He knew there was going to only be one bed, just like there was only one horse. I was beginning to suspect this ominous yet gentle man who saved me had a strategy, and he was taking all the steps to execute it.

On one hand, there was something about the way he approached pursuing me that made me feel hunted, like a prized animal. He was taking his time, watching, stalking, going through the steps with a clear result in mind. Tonight, it seemed like he had lined up a shot and was going to take it. But it had only been a little over a week and a half and while, yes, I was curious, a little on edge and regularly excited in his presence, tonight he was going to miss. He could woo me a little longer before he scored.

The question remained, was any of this real or was I a means to an end? The attraction was mutual, but love elevated the stakes. What if he didn't want me when this was all over, and why did I care? As long as it broke the curse, at least something positive would have come from me being here. Never mind the damage to my heart. I pondered the thought as I removed my makeup and fished around in my backpack for something decent to wear to bed. The last thing I needed to do was wear what I normally wore to sleep, which was nothing. I slipped out of my workout outfit, peeled off my sports bra and slid into the boy shorts and tank top I selected. I was searching the room for a robe or at least a throw blanket when footsteps sounded in the hall.

Right on time, like he did every night, Nighval arrived, followed by a server carrying a full tray of food. I didn't know why we never ate in the common room with the other guests. Usually, we arrived late and left early, which was why I figured he preferred to eat in our room. Or perhaps it was just more time that he had alone with me, and this was a part of his plan.

"Thank you for your assistance," he said to the server as he handed her a few extra coins. He'd been doing that since I scolded him. I had to give him credit. He listened. But I didn't know what motivated him. That I had told him I worked in a similar position or the fact that he understood what I had been saying. Or even that his actions displeased me, and I got the impression that he wanted all of them to please me. But that's how Xavier had been. Willing to do anything to get me to fall for him. Not only had I not been attracted to him, but something about that eagerness was also a turnoff.

Nighval was different, though. Everything about him was calculating and designed. Like he was hyper aware of every move he made, everything he said. Like how he quickly corrected himself when he thought he offended me when we were talking earlier. Who did that? Who was that self-aware? I supposed a man who had been king for as long as he had before he was exiled would have developed that skill.

The word king, when I thought about it in the context of him, did him justice. And the mere idea coupled with the way he was stalking around the room gave me tingles in places I really shouldn't have tingles considering we were about to be sharing a bed. He hadn't cast his eyes in my direction yet since he'd gotten back, and I hadn't found a robe. I crossed the room, figuring I would just use his cloak and scoot my chair closer to the fire, when a warm sensation traced across the curve of my neck, down my spine and settled onto my ass before I felt it dissipate.

I had enough experience to feel the sensation of someone's eyes scanning me to know that was real. I set down the cloak and cross the room. I wasn't that cold, I was just trying to be modest. Not to tempt the beast standing above me. But in a bizarre turn of events, I felt completely safe with him in a way I never felt before. And while he looked—while I was inviting him to look—I corrected myself, I didn't think he would touch unless I invited him to.

So, I leaned forward in my chair and picked up one of the meaty sub-style sandwiches off the tray, taking a bite. We had been chatting back and forth all day and we both must have been talked out because we finished our meal in silence. No wine tonight, which I ought to feel grateful for. Probably another calculating move on his part. He didn't seem like the type of man who would use alcohol to get what he wanted. He came across too proud for that.

My belly was full, and a satisfied warmth radiated from it, making my eyelids lull as I crawled into bed. There was something satisfying about a big meal after having ridden all day, and I was exhausted. Normally, I slept in the middle of the bed whenever I was alone, but I crawled onto the right side nearest the window, leaving the side nearest the door open. I snuggled down on my side and from the other side of the room, boots thudded to the floor. Fabric rustled, and I expected his weight to shift the bed, but it never came.

There was a small whoosh of a candle being blown out and then the creak of weight settling in a chair. Abruptly, I sat up. Nighval's big body leaned back in one of the wingbacks and he had thrown the cloak over himself. I could tell his feet were crossed at the ankle, as they often were. His eyes were closed, but I knew he could feel me staring at him like how I could feel when his eyes were on me.

"What are you doing?" I asked.

"Sleeping," he said, voice lifting as if it were a question instead of a statement.

"Come on, Nighval. I'm onto you. I heard your little comment earlier, and I know exactly what you're doing. If you think I'm going to ask you to come over here and sleep in the bed with me, you're delusional," I said, flopping back onto the bed, a little disappointed niggle rooting around in my stomach. I totally was going to let him sleep in bed with me before he started with this ridiculous charade.

"I want to respect your boundaries, Avery. I'll happily join you because Goddess knows after riding in that saddle all day I could use a soft bed, but after what you went through... It's important to me you know you are safe with me," he said, and his eyes closed. I could just make out his features in the firelight and he had that expression, like he would not budge.

I gave a loud, exasperated groan. His words melted me, exactly like he planned. "Good grief, just get in and stop being so difficult. I feel safe with you, as wild as it sounds."

He sat up and the cloak slid off his shoulders, revealing his pale skin and the firm muscles of his chest. I'd never seen a man on my plane as well built as him, and I'd seen some pretty fine men in Miami.

I couldn't stop my eyes from ogling him as he stood and set the garment aside. That first night, he'd kept his pants on, but now he wore what appeared to be this plane's version of boxer briefs. They were black, tight, and accentuated the corded muscle of his thighs, among other things I pried my eyes away from. He was like an Armani model, but bigger, darker, and better, especially with that five o'clock shadow I imagined would feel divine scraping across the soft skin of my neck and—bad idea. Still, he was potentially mine if I decided to claim him. And now he was annoyed with me.

"Why would that sound wild?" he asked. The edge to his voice hadn't been there a moment earlier. Something about it intrigued me, like I could affect him so easily. "What is it about me that would make you feel unsafe?"

I swallowed as he walked over to me. I blinked up at him. He stood at the edge of the bed and stared down at me with his arms crossed over his chest. "Well, you are kind of massive. You're wide as a door, packed with muscle, and your eyes and your expression are very intimidating. Especially whenever you're not smiling. It's like you have two different faces. Smiling or scowling, and you wear the scowl ninety percent of the time."

"I do not," he said. Then he gave me a big toothy smile, flipped the covers up, and crawled into bed, propping himself up on an elbow facing me.

"Yes, you do. You are like some type of dark brooding predator man. It's no wonder you scared off many women in the past," I said, and that scowl reappeared. "See, that's exactly what I'm talking about."

"You insult me and then you expect me not to scowl at you? That seems a little unfair," he said, his expression not budging.

I leaned forward and ran my fingertips across the thin line of his mouth. A little of the tension there eased. "You've shown me your softer side, though, and I appreciate that. This hasn't been easy for me, but the way you've been since you saved me..." I couldn't finish my sentence because a wave of emotion crested, threatening to send tears over the edges of my eyelids.

Nighval's face softened as he studied me and his hand snaked out a few inches beneath the covers before he halted its movement like he wanted to touch me, to comfort me, but wouldn't let himself. I didn't understand this because that first night I had no choice in the matter, but it was like now he wouldn't touch me without my consent first.

"We should go to sleep," he said. "Two more long days until we get there. Then you will have your own room, a large bathing chamber, and we will get you some new clothes. I'm looking forward to showing you around where I live. I think you will like it."

He leaned back on the bed resting a hand behind his head, which only accentuated the rock-hard muscle of his bicep. Before his eyes closed, they flicked to me one last time. The way he positioned himself was like an invitation. I'd spent all day either leaned up against him or inches away, but it wasn't as intimate as this was. I could easily nestle up against his raised arm, and I knew it would curl around my waist and pull me into him.

It would feel so good. Maybe it was the fact that he was such a foreboding presence that made me feel so safe. And yes, it had only been almost a month and a half since I accidentally killed my husband, but there was never any relationship there, so it was not like I was moving on from something too quickly. This gravitational pull I felt right now to his warmth was something I did not want to deny myself, even though I knew with the whole one bed thing he'd somehow orchestrated he was thoroughly playing me. As foolish as it made me fill, I supposed I should let him woo me though. I was committed to seeing this through. I'd have to deal with any fallout later.

I hadn't moved, and I hadn't laid down. I was still watching him as the story played out in my head. His eyes snapped open, landing on me and, like he knew exactly what I was thinking, he held his hand out across his chest and gestured for me to come to him.

Wordlessly, I scooted near him and, like I pictured it, his big arm lowered from his head and found my waist, pulling me against his warm body. I was on my side, and he took my outside hand and moved it to where it was over his heart, and he closed his calloused hand over mine. When he had us settled, he made no other moves. Had he gone to all this effort to make sure that we would be sharing a bed just to cuddle? Oh Lord, I was in trouble.

CHAPTER 31

NIGHVAL

T wo days later, and two more nights' worth of excruciating cuddle sessions, as Avery called them, we arrived at my family home

The thing was, I didn't mind them. I loved them. It was just that being so near her all day and then all night was making me crazy with need.

My plan was working. She was comfortable with me and growing fonder by the day. After our mother had cursed us, I never allowed myself to consider that I may find something more. Well, I had for a brief glimmer in time, but after everything failed so dismally with that first witch, I never allowed myself to hope again, even though I tried with the others.

But with Avery, she would just look at me, and the instant pull was there. What I told her was true. I was in her thrall. And it frightened me how much I liked it.

As we rode through the massive iron gates, Avery gasped and gave me one of those very glances. This was the time of day she looked the prettiest. The golden hour, where the sun, still lingering in the sky, highlighted the warmth of her skin. I helped her off Eclipse and allowed myself to take her in. Stable hands came and unpacked my animal companion. I made a point to get ahold of her backpack, so she'd know I accounted for it. Watching her take in the enormous structure, the awe in her eye, made me wonder what was going through her head. Did she imagine herself living here permanently, one day?

We would, of course, live here, but once I had my magic back, we could easily go back and forth between the Lieden Palace and Ravsted in the center of Ras alhague.

I almost felt a little guilty when she said, "It's beautiful."

I knew the estate needed maintenance and when I had my magic all the time, it had taken extraordinarily little effort. Now, everything was a challenge. But according to the witch, Avery would see it in its best form and that, I could be proud of.

Despite the disrepair, vining plants clung to the white marble exterior and wound its way up the expansive three-story building. Much of the banana-colored paint was chipping, but from a distance, the color contrasted beautifully with the white panels that sat on either side of the windows. A blue-grey slate tile roof arched toward the sky with its many peaks and a massive stone staircase rose to the door, wide at ground level and narrowing as one approached the two massive carved doors which stood open.

When I had magic, it was easy to keep the water in the oval fountain at the base of the stairs, but now it sat empty, and I wondered what Avery saw.

"Why is the fountain empty?" she asked, and I decided the first order of business was to get it operational again. "I mean, it's beautiful, but I'd really like to see it when water was squirting out of those fishes' mouths."

"It's undergoing some maintenance," I lied. It would take a few days, but I'd have it running for her. Anything for her. I was learning those words were my newly adopted stance, which wasn't ideal considering I hadn't even kissed her again. That didn't mean I hadn't dreamed of it. Kissing and all the other things I wanted to do to her. "I'll make sure they finish with swiftness."

She gave me a reserved smile, and I sensed a shift in her mood which I didn't think was the state of the palace regardless of how she saw it. I grabbed her elbow and turned her to face me. "What's the matter?"

She shrugged.

"Talk to me," I urged.

"I don't know. I guess I feel this underlying sense of worry. Like everyone on your plane and mine are counting on us. What happens if..." She gestured between us like she didn't want to say the words aloud.

"You know I won't hurt you, Avery." I frowned down at her.

"That's not what I meant," she hissed. Her brow wrinkled in frustration as she looked away, which I found adorable. She was embarrassed.

I had to suppress a chuckle as I ran my hand over the hair at her temple, tucking a lock behind her ear. "You mean what if you can't fall in love with me?"

She gave me an innocent nod.

My chuckle escaped and she frowned. "Why don't you leave that up to me, sweetheart." Taking her hand in mind I drew her toward me and brought her palm to my chest. "I promise you, before our final full moon, I'll have you so utterly dumbstruck with love you won't be able to remember how you ever lived without me." I winked for good measure to which she rolled her eyes. "Come on. Let's go inside."

I lowered her hand and tugged her toward the entrance to my home hoping I assuaged enough of her worry she wouldn't dwell on it.

We entered the receiving hall, and attendants were immediately there to greet us. I handed off Avery's backpack. "Take this to the queen's quarters and ready Her Majesty a bath," I said, noting the attendants didn't blink before scurrying off.

Avery, the queen in question, stared up at me with a mixture of disbelief and curiosity. "But I'm not their queen any longer."

Because I enjoyed seeing that expression on her face so much, I reached out, gently cupping her jaw. Her mouth parted as I tilted her head upward, and unable to resist any longer I leaned down and brought our lips together. Hers moved underneath mine and a light shudder came through our connection. So fucking sweet, ready to yield to me like the first time, but instead of deepening the kiss, I pulled away enough so I could lean and whisper into her ear, "Wishful thinking."

When I stood tall, Avery brought trembling fingers to her lips. Several guards and attendants were unabashedly staring at us. She needed to know that while I'd give her everything she ever asked for, I wasn't my brother. I also wanted the palace staff to know and rumors to spread about the thing I was building with this woman. That they had my assurance I would succeed, she would be mine and the curse would be broken. And how better than to show them?

"Umm, okay," she said, as I smiled down at her.

"Go clean up, and rest. This is Jane," I said, gesturing to the round older attendant who'd become like an occasionally nosy grandmother to me over the years who'd sidled up next to us waiting for her instructions. "She'll show you to your rooms and provide you anything you may require. The staff will have dinner ready in a few hours. I have a few things I need to deal with, so I'll see you then." I didn't wait for her to respond before I sauntered away, savoring the feeling the touch of her lips gave me. The electricity that had stunned her, too.

With the way things were progressing, the next full moon would be the perfect time to have a party. After the fountain, setting that in motion would be my next order of business.

CHAPTER 32

AVERY

There were three significant things I'd learned since arriving at the palace a week ago. One, Nighval was the only one immune to the witch's curse. Every attendant, cook, gardener and passing visitor was still in rat form day and night which made my heart ache each time I saw them. Especially Gran Jane, as she insisted I call her, who had nearly as many scars as wrinkles.

Every time I encountered one of them, my sense of urgency doubled. That kiss given to me in the front entry in front of half the staff seemed to have bolstered their hope, so every interaction was leaden with pressure. *Fall in love, Avery*, they seemed to say. Calculating man indeed, but for whatever reason, I didn't seem to mind as my own anticipation leapt forward with each subsequent brush of our lips.

Thing two, of those rat-people, it seemed as far as they were concerned, Nighval was still king. I hadn't learned whether this was a reinstatement, or they never acknowledged his exile, making me wonder what the rest of Ras alhague's position was on the subject. Either way, this meant Nighval spent much of his time attending to his duties, which included meeting with various rat-people who came and went. Including Sir Richard Musson, who I recalled from Xavier's dealings. Evidently, the man still needed dealing with and the two times he'd come to petition Nighval, he'd left the meeting in a dour mood.

Thing three, Nighval was definitely not Xavier, who preferred to keep me cloistered and pampered. He proved this by heaping a significant number of responsibilities on me the day after we arrived. It amounted to the typical lady of the house type duties, which I'd been prepared to take on, and planning a full moon celebration. He planned to do it himself, but as I eagerly asked for the task when he'd mentioned it, he gave it to me without so much as flinching. Only suggesting I consult the palace steward, a willowy rat-man named Jonas, for assistance and direction as required in regard to their customs surrounding these parties.

Finally, I felt like I had some agency, which was almost as healing as the innumerable tears I'd shed. Not having control over anything made me feel like some sort of sliced in half human being. I knew it had eaten away at my resolve, but now having it back, I could breathe again.

Still, while things were going well and my workload occupied most of my time, loneliness crept in reminding me of the curse's dwindling timeline. I wished we had more time. That it would have been Nighval instead of Xavier who I'd been betrothed to. Getting to know him gave me the most normalcy I'd had since I'd been here.

Since he didn't come to my bed once this week, I actually hadn't gotten to spend as much time with him as I'd grown accustomed to over the last two weeks while we were traveling, and the loss of his constant presence nagged at me.

So when I wasn't working, I found myself traipsing through the empty corridors, searching the vacant rooms for him under the guise of exploring.

The palace overall was amazing. It was surrounded by gardens, had various little sitting rooms, and a sizable library. While the library at Ravsted was stocked with historical tomes, spell books, charts, and ledgers, Lieden Palace's library primarily held books intended for entertainment. Some were from my plane, and others, I was thrilled to discover, were entirely new tales, and I was tearing my way through them with abandon.

It made sense. Castles were places where royals went to rule, while palaces were places where royalty went for leisure and this home was exactly that. Finally, I'd landed somewhere in this plane I might actually enjoy.

I was thumbing through a section of fairytales when I heard Nighval's voice. "Would you find it trite if I told you I've missed you?" he asked, his voice low and midnight kissed.

The flower of anticipation that had been blooming in my stomach before was now an unruly garden, full of heavily thorn-covered rose bushes and night-blooming lilies. "No," I said, breathy and too eager. How was he doing this to me?

His hands were in his pockets as he casually strode down the row of books. When he reached me, he took the book from me and set it back on the shelf. His hands came down on either side of my head, giving me a split-second of déjà vu.

Anticipation curled deep in my belly, and Nighval didn't make me wait. His lips met mine with an urgent heat. All the unacted-upon lust that had been building surged and my kitty came to life, the needy thing that it was. Especially when I was around this intimidating man.

Nighval had been doing this, finding me during the day when I wasn't expecting it and kissing me senseless. That's all he ever did, though. Once, after I'd had a little too much wine at dinner, I'd tried to pull him toward my room, and when he hadn't given in, I tried to unbutton his pants in the hallway. The longer he held out, the more I wanted to get my hands and mouth on the thick length I'd seen outlined in that underwear.

Resisting seemed to be a part of his game, however, which annoyed me. Why not give into what we were both clearly feeling? But maybe men here were demurrer than I was expecting, and I was the horny one. I pulled his hips into me, and I felt my answer. No, it wasn't just me, so definitely a game.

Pushing him away, I said, "You really shouldn't start something you can't finish." I slipped under his arm, my lips deliciously swollen. I wished I had a vibrator because the device would be put to good use. As it was, I would need to sneak away to my room, lock the door, and use my fingers to make myself come because he wasn't going to do it, and I was going crazy.

What was he waiting for? Then it occurred to me, *the full moon party*. So much in Ras alhague happened around the monthly lunar event I bet that's what he was planning to make it memorable.

Expectant jitters fluttered in my stomach as his hand wrapped around my arm. "You don't know what you're asking for," he said. As he loomed over me with darkening features, my heart started beating wildly.

"I do," I said. He did this occasionally, and I was coming to understand I liked the fact that he frightened me, as messed up as that was. Because it wasn't horror like I'd felt with Xavier. It was something else entirely. Something primal. Feeling that heated attention on me from this powerful man was almost too much. My adrenaline surged, and my fight or flight activated. I was an artist, a creative, not a fighter.

Nighval's rough hand wrapped around my neck, and he leaned down so his breath was hot beneath my ear. My back arched toward him in a jerk, but he held me firm. "Be a good girl and go to your room, Avery. Take care of yourself and while you're doing it, you can imagine it's me."

He pulled away, and I swore my face was the color of a stop sign. Jesus, how did he know? He released me, along with a dark, heady chuckle as he sauntered away. Before he exited the library, he called back to me, "I'm looking forward to the party. I can't wait to see what you'll wear."

The door clicked shut, and I slumped into the nearest chair, trying to catch my breath. I didn't know if I'd make it back to my room. I was so wound up.

I glanced at the closed door. I was alone. Oh God, was I going to do this in the library? I threw a second glance at the door, just to be sure. I'd hear someone as soon as they entered, and this chair was facing the outside wall. Screw it.

I leaned forward, reaching for the hem of my skirt. I rucked it up in the center so my inner thighs caught the draft in the room, and I shivered. Sliding my panties aside, I ran a finger through the wet heat, then swirled my clit, all while finding it unbelievable how turned on that man got me.

Just the thought of him. I made another pass, and I moaned. I was so sensitive this would not take long. I plunged a finger inside and my head rocked back against the chair. Using my other hand, I played with my clit and, working my hands in tandem, had my hips rocking up off the chair. A glorious minute later, the tingling turned into gushing pleasure and my inner walls were clamping down on my deeply embedded finger.

"Nigh," I said on a breath as the last wave shocked through me.

I sat there for a moment, panting. Perhaps that wasn't such a great idea, because as the fireworks went off in my mind, I wasn't entirely sure I'd have been able to hear the door. I glanced around the room and didn't see anyone. Shoving my skirt back down, I jumped up, grabbed my discarded book, and fled the scene.

CHAPTER 33

NIGHVAL

I started to leave, but recalled a volume that might be useful in the land ownership case I was working on. That's exactly what I need to distract myself from the rampant desire coursing through me. I changed directions, releasing the door I'd pulled halfway pulled open. I collected the book and was making my way down the row when I caught sight of Avery plopping down into a wingback chair facing opposite the entry. As she tugged at the hem of her skirt, and I realized what she was doing. The fabric made it to her waist and she was pushing her panties aside. My mouth went dry, and I swallowed.

Did Avery know I was still in the room and had a perfect view in the reflection in the window of her achingly perfect pussy? It probably made me a despicable man, but I didn't want to embarrass her, and I didn't want her to stop. I wanted to see how the woman who was my waking fantasy made herself feel good.

My cock strained at my pants as she swirled her clit and then dipped inside. Fuck. Quietly, I raised my hands to brace them on the bookshelf that had shielded me from her quick scan of the room. I would watch, but that is all that I would let myself do. What I was doing was wrong enough, though a part of me suspected if she knew I watched, she'd be even more turned on. She did try to unbutton my pants after all.

I bit my knuckle to prevent myself from groaning as she began working herself in earnest. The way her head tilted back, and her delicate neck arched toward the sky made the urgency I felt soar. I had to figure out how to get out of here so I could get my hands wrapped around myself and relieve this ache.

She was panting now. I could tell she was close by the tremors in her legs. Her eyes clenched shut so tight her face almost looked like she was in pain and her mouth fell open on a moan. I watched her sensual body seize up as the first wave rolled through her. Her orgasm seemed to go on and on and right as I thought it was over, she spasmed again, whispering a word I will never forget as long as I live.

"Nigh," she said.

I couldn't breathe. Couldn't think. Had I heard that right?

My body shuttered with barely controlled restraint. I was one wrong decision away from walking over there, getting down on my knees, and fucking that swollen pussy until she said that word again. And again.

But I couldn't. It felt wrong to take her in this form, regardless of what she saw. Kissing her while I was this creature was bad enough. I needed to wait till the reprieve, despite how willing she was to let me before then.

As she moved her panties back in place and adjusted the dress, I edged a little deeper in the library, wondering what I would do if she found me here. Thank the Goddess, she spared me from that. Her silhouette rushed by with the book I'd taken out of her hand and the door clicked shut. I released a sigh and eyed the door, my focus landing on the little key that was in every door in this palace. I strode over to it, turned it, and tried the handle. Locked.

I knew she'd been doing it, touching herself after I kissed her senseless. I learned she retreated to her rooms after our encounters. The thought of pleasuring myself in the same chair where she had just done the same shot a thrill through me. It only took a second, and I had my pants undone and my cock in my hand. I would worry about the mess after. Now was about release.

With every stroke I imagined that my dick was her fingers plunging deep inside her, showing her what she did to me. How undone I was by her. And like her, it didn't take long until cum shot out of my glistening head into my awaiting palm.

As the last pulse rose to crescendo, I breathed, "Avery."

CHAPTER 34

AVERY

Another thing Nighval had given me since I arrived at the palace was unfettered access to the palace tailor, Fredrik. Though I got the impression the little man was a new transplant from the nearby village I visited a few times. As were a few of the other castle staff.

I'd taken Fredrik over with requests, and together we'd managed to create a modestly sized wardrobe which was some combination of the vintage clothing from their world and the modern style I preferred. At first, I felt guilty monopolizing him, but Nighval noticed how much joy playing with the beautiful fabrics gave me and assured me that Fredrik was more than happy to accommodate.

After research about full moon parties, I decided they reminded me of a bohemian themed wedding I'd attended at one of the hotels on the beach. Draping fabrics, pillows for seating on the floor and bonfires every so often. Committed to the theme, I decided on a gauzy, nearly sheer fabric for my party dress which I felt matched the vibe. I selected several colors of pale pink, peach, and orange. Panels of the bodice wrapped around my chest in a simple wrap style, and thin straps held it up. It cinched at the waist and flowed in an A-line down to where it kissed my bare feet. The skirt was alternating swaths of the different shades, each was free flowing so that as I moved, one could see glimpses of the skin beneath.

If tonight was about the moon, I'd be the sun. It was like Nighval and me. He was the cool, pale presence hunting me, like the moon chased the blazing orb across the sky.

I walked down the stairs and followed the sounds of the music. I'd spent all morning out there making sure everything was perfect., Only when Jonas insisted I let him take over so I could go change and enjoy the party, I relented.

My last two weeks of productivity satisfied something inside me and now I was floating.

Tonight, I'd allow myself to meld into the free-spirited nature of the celebration.

In the distance, firelight glowed, silhouettes moved and danced. The cool grass gave me a chill as I walked, but the closer I got, the more the warmth enveloped me. Around the fires were low platforms with rugs and pillows, set up in even intervals. People were lounging on them, drinking, talking and even a few were giving their partners affection openly, making me wonder what more I would see as the night went on. I looked away, instead checking on the squat tables in between them which were laden with fruit, cheese, and pitchers of the mulled wine everyone was drinking.

I wasn't hungry, and I didn't want to imbibe too much because I suspected where tonight was heading for me, though I could probably use a drink.

The thought of Nighval prowling over to me in his boxer-briefs that night in the inn made my stomach do flips as I wove my way through the crowd to the largest fire in the center. There was a small group of musicians scattered throughout the crowd playing different instruments and though they weren't together, they played in sync, each beat banging in time.

The rhythmic thumping of drums called to something in my blood. I didn't know if it was intrinsically me, or the witch DNA I carried, or something else entirely. It wasn't like the pumping music at the nightclub with the pulsing lights and sweaty bodies. As I took in the multiple bonfires, their orange flames climbing higher and higher, the people dancing around them, some singing the wordless song along with the music, I could see the similarities. I supposed the club was my plane's version of this night, but somehow this was more primal, natural. It called to my inner witch, to my connection with the earth and the celestial bodies surrounding her.

The beat, like my time at the palace, became a part of my healing process. Closing my eyes, I let the heat of the fire radiate onto my cheeks and moved with the music. I felt so warm, so whole, and forgiven as I shared this moment with the Goddess.

Maybe there were things in this plane that were better like the dancing, the Goddess worship, and him. Sympathy welled inside me as I opened my eyes and looked around at the rat-people and the similarly serene expressions on the revelers. In a moment, the moon would rise to its apex beginning the reprieve and they'd have a few hours as humans again.

And when these building feelings inside of me reached their apex, they'd never have to be subjected to that horror again.

I hadn't seen the man who'd break the curse with me yet this evening, and as I scanned the crowd, I found myself searching for the unmistakable man. Then large hands enveloped my hips, and his voice was in my ear.

"I like this," he said. He ran his hands down to where his fingers grazed inside the panels of the dress and scraped against my skin. He kissed my neck as he pulled me back into his chest and we began swaying to the music.

Eventually, he pulled me around to the other side of the fire where a large platform sat, and jewel toned pillows lay in piles. He ushered me up, and I took a seat. I drank him in as he went to a food table beside us and filled a large platter, returning it to our seat, then went after two goblets. Like me, his feet were bare. His loose charcoal linen pants sat low on his hips and a cream linen shirt hung unbuttoned on his shoulders, exposing rows of tight muscle beneath.

When he handed me the glass and sat, reclining back, my eyes were still glued to his rippling stomach. I scooted near him and, unable to resist, I ran my fingertips across his pale skin. He eyed me as I touched him, and I said, "I like these."

"I'm glad, but you better quit before I decide to cut this night short," he said, leaning over me to pluck a bunch of grapes off the platter. He pushed one between my lips, then one between his.

He spent an hour or so alternating between feeding me and giving me panty scorching kisses. I surprised myself by letting him be this affectionate publicly. That definitely would send a message, and I was becoming more and more certain it was one I wanted the people of Ras alhague to see. I was falling for this warlock and fast.

Giddiness zipped through me as I scanned the crowd wondering what they thought of us. I caught party goers watching us. Sometimes they'd approach and Nighval would introduce me. We'd chat for a few short moments before they retreated into the night. Occasionally, I'd notice a slight sneer on someone's face as if they held some resentment toward me over Xavier, or perhaps that I hadn't succeeded yet. Most of the party goers were kind however, and I wondered once the curse was broken, what my reception would be when we returned to Ravsted, because by all accounts, I'd return to my position as queen. Assuming Nighval planned to marry me. We hadn't spoken about it, but he called me Her Majesty on more than one occasion, so I didn't feel foolish to hope.

The longer we sat there, the more my anticipation coiled in my core to the point my hand quivered as I lifted my goblet to my mouth. Nighval's gaze flicked from my hand to the full moon, crested to its highest peak in the sky, and I knew it was time.

"I'm getting tired of sitting," I said, and rose, smoothing out my skirt. "I'm going to walk for a bit." Without asking him to join me, I stepped down from the platform onto the crushed grass. I threw a heated glance over my shoulder at the warlock sprawled out against a pile of pillows with one leg cocked and an elbow leaning on it. Everything about him looked dominant, and so damn sexy. The unbuttoned shirt, the ripple of muscle, the way his dark eyes tracked my every move from deep beneath his brow, unflinching.

I made my way to the outskirts of the fire and stepped out of the clearing. Right would lead me to the woods, left to the palace. The question was, where did I want this to happen? In a bed or on the forest floor.

Left. Better to be in the palace in case I decided I needed to retreat. Who was I kidding? That was the furthest thing that was about to happen. Because he'd been toying with me, as I'd danced and he'd watched me, I'd felt his hot gaze. This elaborate full moon party was meant to end with this. Me beneath him in his bed, and that was exactly what was going to happen, exactly like he planned. He was done teasing.

I climbed to the top of a low hill and glanced back at the pile of pillows where he'd been reclining, which I could barely make out from my vantage point. My pulse started skittering wildly. He was gone.

CHAPTER 35

NIGHVAL

Quiet blanketed the palace as Avery took the stairs up to the front door. My magic shielded me from her view, but I knew she felt my presence as she kept shooting quick glances over her shoulder. Foliage rustled as I brushed up against one of the bushes that lined either side of the stairway. Hearing the sound, she snapped her head in its direction and turned around, darting through the door.

My heart thundered as I crossed the threshold and caught her taking the last few stairs up to the second floor. As I took the first step, wood groaned beneath my foot, and she froze. Ever so slowly, she peered down the staircase and her eyes widened when they didn't discover my presence. I grinned.

"Run," I whispered.

But instead of obeying, she surveyed the space, her eyes darting around the room. Otherwise, she stood frozen, like a startled deer, so I advanced. With each step, the old staircase creaked under my weight until I was almost at the top and almost to her.

"Run, Avery," I said.

Her breath caught, and finally she turned and ran. Her bare feet were quiet across the wood paneled floor as she fled down the hallway. Our rooms were on the third floor in the east wing, and she rounded the corner of the staircase that would take her there.

As she slipped away from the party, I wondered what she would do. How I would get her alone so we could finally act upon this thing that had been building between us over the last month. Like the brave woman I knew her to be, Avery took the lead. In that moment, I was only beginning to understand I'd likely spend the rest of my life following this woman. Chasing her where she led me.

I took the stairs two at a time until we were both on the same landing. Hearing me behind her, she darted forward, trying to skip a step, but I shot my hand forward and grabbed hold of her ankle. I tugged, and she missed the step, but I caught her by the waist before she could crash into the staircase.

"If you don't want to be caught, next time I'd suggest you run faster," I said in a low, heat-filled tone in her ear.

I spun her in my arms and lowered her, so she leaned back on the staircase. I was hovering over her with one leg between hers and my body, about an inch of space between us. I released my hold on my magic, so it was only us. Scanning her beautifully freckled skin, my eyes tracked from her forehead to her lips to the soft skin at the base of her neck, then to her collarbone. I reached up and slid the thin strap of her gown off. Her chest heaved upward, and I brought my lips down to meet it, running them over the highlights and shadows.

Avery tilted her head back, giving me access to kiss her upper neck, the space beneath her ear. Her breath caught as I lightly bit, then licked teasingly. Like before, when I had her pinned to the tree, I felt her leg raise up to my side and her hands wrap around my midsection pulling me into her, closing that gap. I gave her what she wanted.

I nudged her legs wide, so I was settled between them. She bent her knee, mirroring the position of the other one so her thighs were hugging my hips. Gently, I pressed my straining erection into the heat between her legs. Only a few layers of fabric separated us from what we craved.

I rocked against her, and she gasped. The image of her touching herself, sighing my name, came to mind, and I said, "Are you wet for me, Avery?"

"Yes," she sighed.

A wry smile danced across my face, and I couldn't help myself. "As wet as you were when you touched yourself in the library, or more?" She froze beneath me, and I pressed my hips down harder into her as I leaned up to look at her expression. I could just make out the pink on her cheeks, illuminated by the glow of the yellow incandescent bulbs strung at the top of the staircase.

"Oh my God," she bit out. I leaned down and gave her a soft kiss. Still, her arms didn't leave me, and I didn't quit moving in unhurried, undulating motions against her. When I released her lips, she asked, "You watched me?"

Her heated gaze told me she wasn't upset. Intrigued, maybe even turned on.

"I did. I couldn't stop. Watching you pleasure yourself with your fingers was mesmerizing. I can't stop thinking about it, wishing your fingers had been mine. That it was my tongue and my cock." I watched her, wanting to make sure I picked up on any subtle negative reactions or reluctance to my words.

To my surprise, she said, "After you watched me, what did you do?" A playful smile lifted the corner of her swollen pink lips.

"I locked the door, positioning myself as you had been on the chair and then took myself in my hand, all the while imagining it was you," I said. Her mouth fell open as her pink tongue slipped out and ran across her upper lip. Her eyes were heavy lidded as I slid off her. I gathered her skirt in my hand and pulled it up so I could have better access. "I want to touch you, Avery."

"Please," she said, and my hand slipped higher up her thigh.

"Goddess," I moaned at what I discovered. "What are these?"

I thumbed the delicate strips of satin she wore aside, and she watched me. "I would tear these off you, but I'm pretty sure they don't sell them here, and I quite like them."

She gave me a sultry giggle and said, "Tell me what happened next."

I circled her clit until her hips started moving, and then I pressed a finger inside. She was so ready for me. "I imagined my cock was your fingers plunging deep inside you as I stroked myself. When I could tell I was getting close, I squeezed, imagining it was you clenching down around me as you came."

"Then what?" she asked, voice breathy.

Her body trembled slightly, and her heel caught the edge of the step and she pressed herself up into my touch. Hand wrapped around my bicep, she pulled me closer insistently, but I continued touching her how she liked and watching every tremor of pleasure that washed across her face.

"It didn't take long, Avery. When I squeezed, imagining it was you, I couldn't take it anymore. I came into my fist as I called your name."

Avery cried out, and her body tensed beneath me as the first wave washed through her. I could feel her inner walls flexing and clamping down around my fingers. I pressed my forehead to hers as she rode it out.

"Say it," I practically growled at her as she came on my fingers.

Obediently, she cried, "Nigh." A flood of warmth surged through my chest and as she came down, I roved my eyes all over her in disbelief at the wonder this woman was.

Her hand cupped my cheek, and she said again, softly, "Nigh."

I pulled my fingers from inside, and still leaning over her, I sucked the taste of her off them. "You taste so good, Avery. Sweet and earthy, like how flowers smell."

When I sucked every last bit off, I gripped her hip, leaning down to give her a kiss that expressed every bit of chest constricting emotion I was feeling. What a strange thing to feel such euphoria and such an ache at the same time. I pushed myself up to where I was standing over her and she was still half sprawled across the stairs, looking satiated. She started to move, but I leaned down and scooped her into my arms.

"You don't have to carry me," she said.

"I want to," I answered.

I brought her to my room and carefully laid her across my bed. I stepped back for a moment and took her in. She propped herself up on her elbows. The skirt of the dress was wrinkled, a rosy pink blush warmed her cheeks. The little strap was still off her shoulder and the bodice of the gown barely concealed a peaked nipple. I had never seen anything more perfect as I studied my prize. Seventeen long years of disappointment and then there was her. At that moment, I knew I would do it all again. Every single second of it for this moment.

I crawled across the bed toward her. "Let's get you out of this dress. I want to look at you before I take you."

She nodded, pulling a lower lip into her mouth. I leaned over her and tugged the ribbon at her waist and pulled the material that was wrapped around her middle. She adjusted so I could get the ribbon which was doubled around her free and laid it to the side. She slipped her arm out, and I went to work on the other side. A second later she was bare before me.

"My turn," she said. "Strip."

I made quick work of my linen shirt and trousers. Moments later, I knelt on the bed at her feet, my erection jutting out at its target. She leaned back on the bed, watching me.

"Spread your legs," I commanded.

As she separated her knees, a shudder wracked through me, and I had to double my restraint not to jump on her and fuck her like a wild animal. The hair around her pussy was trimmed tight in a little manicured patch so I could see her swollen clit and the slick opening. One day I would lick and kiss and spear it with my tongue, but now I needed to be inside her.

"Tell me what you want," I said, crawling over her, praying it was the same thing I did.

"I..." She hesitated.

Had she never spoken about her desires aloud? "You're safe, Avery. You can tell me what you need," I said, hovering just above her.

She swallowed, seeming to build up the nerve. "Nigh, you've been teasing me so long I just want you inside me. I need to feel you, your weight on top of me, and your," she hesitated again, "your cock filling me. Moving inside me."

"You are everything good, pure perfection, and I am a man with countless stains on my soul who doesn't come close to deserving you, but I'm still going to take you because that's the kind of man I am. Do you understand?" I asked.

"Please stop talking and give me what I want," she said, and brought her lips to mine, pulling me down over her.

I was so wound up, I thought I was going to combust. Simply kissing her sent sparks zapping through my body. I couldn't imagine what entering her tight heat would be like. Everything about the woman writhing beneath me, searching for me with her hips, seemed designed to drive me wild.

Something about speaking to her as I had, hearing her reply in kind, not only affected her, it affected me. I'd never been so forthright with a woman, so expressive. Granted, I never felt the way I felt around her before. It was like being with her unleashed something in me and while dirty talk in its basest sense wasn't anything new to me, it was the way she absorbed what I said, like sunlight and water, and like the flower she was. Watching her bloom under me was becoming addictive.

Fear shot through me, frosting my veins. I couldn't lose her. Panic gripped me. The thought of failing and becoming a monster to her once again drove away the pleasure being this near her brought.

"Nigh, what's wrong?" she asked, using the nickname she'd given me. Hearing it come from those soft lips quelled some of the anxiety the thought of losing her caused.

"Promise you'll never leave me. Promise me, Avery," I said, nestled between her legs, practically begging. When she agreed to be mine, I would finally take her. We had two months left, and I'd waited long enough. So long we were both vibrating for it.

"What?" she asked, and I gave her room to lean up on an elbow. "What are you saying?"

It was a good question. What was I saying? Then I knew. "Marry me?" I asked. "Avery, will you be my wife? Will you marry me? I don't think I can live without you."

"Wow," she said, and kept staring up at me with that dazed expression she wore so often when she looked at me. She said nothing else, and my heart seized.

"Avery, you're killing me. Every second that you don't say yes is like an ice pick stabbing into my chest."

"But what if you're bad in bed, and then I have to live the rest of my life with—" I cut her ridiculous thought off with a kiss. She moaned into my mouth, gripping my shoulder to pull me closer, but I broke our lips apart.

"Do you really think that's possible?" I asked her, giving her a heated expression. Her eyes lulled as if she was imagining what it would be like, then a grin snaked across her mouth. "Marry me, Avery Plath. On the next full moon, commit yourself to me. Become my wife." I held my breath as I awaited her reply, and the seconds ticked on like hours.

"Yes," she said in a whisper.

"Thank the Goddess," I said. "I'm going to fuck you now, Avery."

"Please." She moaned as I ground down into her, showing her how satisfying I found that word. Her hands roamed across my chest, down my sides and across my lower back, and I could have sworn they caught on the many scars that crisscrossed my body. It was only dreaming though, my mind wanting something so badly I was making things up. No, I wouldn't think of that, of who she saw when she looked at me. I'd only be grateful for this moment and everything transpiring between us, because I may not know what visual she saw, I knew who she was surrendering her heart to.

I lifted my hips to enter her, but her hand shot to my cock. She stroked me, swirling her thumb across the slit where pre-cum beaded.

"Nigh, you're huge. I mean, overall, but your dick... Is it even going to fit?" she asked, and more cum leaked out at her words. Goddess, this woman was going to be my doom.

"Yes, sweetheart. I promise you, it will fit."

She groaned as I pulled her hand off me, and I slid my tip through her folds. "You're so wet for me."

"Nigh. No teasing. Please," she begged. I claimed her mouth, thrusting my tongue into it, giving her a preview of what was to come. Her fingers clawed at my hips, pulling them toward her, but I held back, loving every second of her writhing beneath me, needing me.

"You are so perfect, Avery." Grabbing her hands, I raised them over her head, clasping them in one of my hands, and I used the other to grab ahold of her hip and guide myself to her entrance, nudging in an inch. "Does your pussy ache for me?"

She nodded, thrusting her hips upward, but my hand pressed her into the bed. "Do you need me to fuck it until you feel better?"

"Jesus, Nigh, yes," she said, whimpering. "Please make it stop aching."

"Watch me as I take you, sweetheart." I pressed my hips forward, and her eyes almost looked pained as they flashed to mine. I knew it wasn't because my size hurt her. It was because of how slow and deliberate I was entering her.

"You want more?" I asked her.

"You're the one killing me now," she whined, and I gave her another inch.

"That's right," I clipped. She trembled, jerking from where I restrained her, but I held firm.

I slid in deeper, practically shuddering, my control on the edge of snapping. "Your pussy is so fucking wet. Are you always this dripping for me?"

"Always," she moaned, and I rewarded her by slamming home.

"Fuck," I yelled, and captured her cry with my mouth. I wasn't going to give her a choice about how I gave it to her. I was finally inside the woman I'd make my wife, and there had never been a purer ecstasy. Legally, I'd claim her in a month, make her my queen, but tonight I planned to make sure she knew how very claimed she was on every other level a man could claim a woman. I planned to leave the reverberation of it long after we were done.

CHAPTER 36

AVERY

Nighval didn't give me time to come up for air, or even call out. His kisses were all-consuming and the way he drove his hips deep into me, barely pulling out before he shoved in again, grinding against my deepest walls, was a claiming. I knew exactly what he was doing. He was imprinting himself on me in a way I'd never be able to forget. It was so primal, so animal, the way he was driving into me, and I'd never felt more alive and rocked through with pleasure. It radiated from my pussy and my chest, both of which were throbbing in harmony.

Oh Goddess, if I hadn't caught the feels before, I definitely had now. Maybe more than with the way my heart was wildly beating in my chest. He pulled away and grunted with the effort of it. I opened my eyes so I could watch him, all the while my pleasure ratcheted higher and higher.

Never had I imagined any of this. While the man above me lost in his own lust driven haze was so flawed, he was also perfect. And he wanted me to be his wife.

"Nighval," I said, and he caught my gaze. "I think, oh my God," I said as the words began to form in my mind. "I think I—"

"No," he said, and a frightened look crossed his face before he leaned down and took my mouth again. Whatever I'd been about to say disappeared as a wave of pleasure crashed over me and my body went rigid. My heels dug into the bed, thrusting my hips up so I could take more of this sublime onslaught he was giving me. Goddess, the waves kept coming, driving into the deepest part of my core, and I was blinded by the hard rolling sensation.

It felt so good it almost hurt, and as the waves slowed, little aftershocks still jolted through me. He pressed in deep, in a final thrust, and I jerked as it spiked through me, sending off another explosion. He released my mouth and groaned, "Fuck," as his body stiffened above me. His hand had snaked around my ass and was pulling me tight against him as he spilled himself inside me in throbbing, pulsing surges.

When he finished, he collapsed over me, still semi-hard inside me. "Are you okay?" he asked, breathing into my ear. His hand threaded through my curls, and he placed a series of sweet kisses across my face.

"Yes," I said. "More than perfect. You constantly surprise me, Nigh."

"Good," he said, sliding out of me. He was still draped half across me, and he tucked my arm across my stomach and threaded our fingers together. This big, scary man could be so sweet. It was a paradox I could hardly understand.

"I know I should clean you up, but the thought of you sleeping next to me with my cum leaking out of you is too attractive to resist."

Hell, that was dirty. But I'd been drinking herbal pregnancy prevention tea in preparation for when this finally happened, so I figured I could give this to him. "Okay," I said, and his fingers squeezed mine.

Something about the way he'd been while we were intimate, his earnestness, struck me. He was desperate to make sure I was his. It made my heart ache knowing the pain the thought must cause him. That he found himself so unlovable he thought I'd bolt at a moment's notice. That I wouldn't accept him and how wonderful I was learning he could be. I was only now coming to understand how negatively he viewed himself. It was tragic.

If things kept progressing like they were, we would break the curse. It was crazy, and unexpected, and wonderful. Not only would I be a queen, but I'd also get a fairytale love. Perhaps I should back pedal on my Disney hate after all. Sure, the heroine went through some shit to get the prince, but she got him eventually.

How had all of those other women not seen the prize before them, so clearly ready to be loved? I would not make that same mistake. Reaching over, I tilted his face toward mine.

"Nigh, you're not going to lose me, okay?"

He swallowed as he scanned my face. "Promise?" he asked, his voice was guttural and such vulnerability shown in his eyes I could hardly do anything else but agree.

I nodded, as my heart pinched for this perfect man. "Yes, Nighval, I promise."

CHAPTER 37

NIGHVAL

I peeled myself out of bed before my fiancée awoke. The word made me hungry with need. It was too bad Xavier ruined the word bride for me, likely for Avery, too. At least I had fiancée. I'd think of the title until it changed to wife. But the reprieve ended sometime in the night and we both slept through the bells indicating its end. Now when I looked in the mirror, a monster stared back at me. I needed to clean up and get out of this room before I gave into my desires and crawled back into bed.

It was one thing to use my mother's magic to make her see something else and sleep with her in human form during the reprieve. I wouldn't allow myself to have her in this form which meant this next month was going to be difficult. Now that I knew how seamlessly we fit together, restraining from taking her, especially knowing how eager she was for it and the smoldering flame between us, would be utterly painful. Especially since I must keep things progressing between us.

It briefly crossed my mind that I should have allowed her to say the curse breaking words that, for an instant, tried to escape her lips. Then she could hate me, and we could get on with it. Because I wasn't letting her go, no matter what. She was the queen I was promised, and I'd be damned if I didn't keep her. She'd come around eventually and if I'd let it happen, let the curse break with those three words, I'd be one step closer to reclaiming my position between her thighs and in her heart once again.

But after all these years I'd become selfish. I wanted to live for a month under her warmth as her feelings for me built. I cursed my people to another moon cycle for the love of a woman and my weakness. My not wishing to see hate color her eyes against me. I'd done it to prolong that disdain I had coming for another four weeks. And now I was retreating from the room we'd share from now on so she wouldn't wake up and try to pull me into bed. I didn't know how I would resist and the more I ruminated on it, the more fucked I sensed I was.

At least I had enough work to occupy me until I could have her again without restraint. When I awoke and snuck into the bathing chamber to ready myself for the day, I discovered a correspondence from Link sent with his power overnight in our usual spot by the sink. He'd finally made it back to Ravsted to keep an eye on things while I was here and according to the letter, he had Leviticus back on his leash. That was one less thing for me to worry about. The Council of Warlocks, under his guidance, would deal with a few pressing matters there while I was courting Avery, but he'd included a stack of items he felt needed my direct attention. I was grateful for the distraction.

I picked up my discarded cloak and gave my fiancée one last glance before I strode from the room. As I did this, another word floated into my mind. *Chase.* An uncommon name, but a name. The way she'd cried it out last night as I watched her sleep made my stomach swirl with dread. Her face pinched like she enjoyed whatever was happening in the dream. It was the one coherent word I'd picked out of all her murmurings. Could this Chase be a former lover, or who she saw when she looked at me?

I brushed the thoughts away. I had to cling to the knowledge that despite the façade she saw, she was getting to know me. When it all came crashing down, at least we'd have a true foundation to build upon, because choosing to let her fall for myself was the one right decision I'd made in the last eighteen years.

After spending about an hour in my office, I needed to make a trip into Bellfield, the township a few hours' ride away. It would take the better part of the day, but I'd left Avery a note explaining the need for my absence as I always did.

Jonas stepped into the doorframe right as I was collecting a few documents. When I was in residence at Ravsted, people brought their petitions to me, but at the palace I found it easier to venture out into my kingdom. That way I could keep the messy business of ruling out of my leisure home for the most part.

"Your Majesty," Jonas greeted.

"Good morning, Jonas. Perfect timing. Please have Eclipse saddled and brought around front," I requested.

Instead of obeying, Jonas shifted uncomfortably on the balls of his feet. "Actually, Your Majesty, Sir Robert Musson is here to see you." I groaned, but Jonas continued. "This time he has two of his sons with him."

"Where are they?" I asked.

"Waiting at the bottom of the stairs. The guard wouldn't allow them to approach any closer," he said, then fidgeted with the caps of his claws nervously as he awaited my response. Jonas was right to be nervous, too. I despised the entire Musson clan, Sir Robert being the most unagreeable of them all and every time they came around left me in a foul mood.

Xavier releasing him with a hefty fine and a royal decree had been a mistake. Had it been up to me, I'd have executed him while he was stuffed in some dank hole in the prison. But now he was out, and I hadn't found a good excuse to get him back in that hole. Hopefully, he'd give me one today and then I'd do away with him.

"It's fine, Jonas. I'll see them on my way out," I said, throwing my cloak over my shoulders. On second thought, I slid behind my desk and opened the case holding a few ornately designed daggers and knives which had been gifts to the crown over the years. I selected a few and clipped them into the buckles of my suit so they'd be visible and threw the cloak off one shoulder to emphasize the point before heading out the door.

Sure enough, Sir Robert, and his two eldest sons whose names I forgot, were standing at the bottom of the stairs in front of an expensive carriage led by a pair of blonde mares. Sir Robert paced back and forth glaring up at the door every few seconds, face reddening by the minute. The oldest son leaned against the carriage and cleaned his teeth with a claw as he fiddled with its cap with the opposite hand, seeming all together uninterested. The other son made nervous glances between the two as if he were the only one cognizant of their dire situation.

Upon his last visit, I'd not so politely suggested he not come to me unless the situation warranted it. I couldn't fathom what they were here for now that would be worth the risk of my wrath. Sir Robert's gaze caught mine as I stepped outside. Mixed with the crisp scent of the approaching cool season winds, a pungent spicy aroma which I knew to be the man's fragrance that he liberally doused himself with wafted through the air reaching me all the way at the landing I now stood upon.

The two guards on either side of the door stepped forward as I approached him, and I held up a hand to halt them. I made my way a third of the way down the stairs and watched as Sir Robert unabashedly took the first few steps. "Why are you here, Musson?" I asked before he could ascend another step. "I thought I told you if you came here unwarranted to disturb me, you were a dead man, so whatever you have to say better be good." I folded my arms over my chest as I stared down at the man whose face nearly resembled a bruised tomato.

His hands went out to his sides, and he guffawed as if that weren't possible. "You and your witch were gone by the time my wife, and I arrived at the party last night. See we had some trouble with our invitation—"

"You weren't invited," I said.

"Actually, that's the problem. Your family and mine have held a tight alliance over the years, and your lack of respect for that, for me and my position is beginning to grate upon my patience," he said, piquing my interest. Hopefully, he'd dig himself a hole so deep he couldn't get out of it, and I'd be done with him.

"And what do you plan to do about it?" I asked, raising my brows at him.

Sir Robert took a wary step down as I took one forward. Only four steps were between us, and he didn't seem to feel that was enough. "Don't think it goes unnoticed how you shun us. My wife and sons suffer as you sully our reputation. Your fool of a brother kept me in prison for a whole month all over a simple misunderstanding."

"You weren't paying your workers again, Musson. Xavier told me you'd been seen whipping a man for... what was it? Oh, yes, not making his daily yield. So, it seems to me, if your family suffers, they should be looking to you. Letting you live has been a kindness from the crown. One I'm not overly inclined to carry on."

Musson took another step down, which I mirrored. "I..." he shuddered. "I only wished to ask that Your Majesty and your witch grace us with your presence at a dinner in your honor in our home. Seeing you there, so soon before you break the curse would be a boon for our reputation."

"You've come to my home to invite me and my fiancée to dinner to restore your reputation?" I asked. Now I was so close to the man his scent nearly made me gag. Was he perspiring? The cool morning air was almost chilly. Sir Robert's nerves were getting to him.

"Your fiancée?" he said, which drew the older son's attention. "We heard you and the witch were behaving very friendly, but it's only been a month since she was almost executed. Lori said after what the poor thing has been through, there's no way she could feel something so quickly."

"Are you doubting me, Sir Robert? Because that's where it sounds like your train of thought is headed," I said, my curiosity quickly dwindling. I could hardly execute a man for a dinner invite. I needed to get him off my property so I could get on with my day.

"Unless you're not making the progress your actions seem to proclaim," he said. The smug look on his face told me he thought he'd won.

What he'd done was step dangerously close to the line. The only reason I was holding back was because I knew what he said to be false. Otherwise, it was almost enough to force my hand.

"No, we won't join you for a celebration in our honor and if you don't leave, I'll keep your head as a souvenir. This is your last warning." I stepped toward him, letting him move back so as to not get run over.

He made it to the gravel drive, and I pushed past him as I headed to where Jonas had Eclipse. The man had a death wish as he charged after me calling to my back, "Rumor has it you used your magic to make it look like she was enjoying herself. Some even say you forced yourself on her in hopes of making her fall—"

Sir Robert cried out as the dagger I sent flying embedded itself in his upper thigh. I'd never been accused of hurting a woman like that. I was this man's king and that was good enough as treason for me. I charged toward him, drawing another double-sided knife needing no further excuse to rid our plane of this man. Musson staggered back, pulling on the dagger, making more blood ooze from the wound while out of the corner of my eye I saw his eldest son, Bobby from what I recalled, open the carriage and was fishing around inside for something.

Metal shrieked as the young man pulled a sword from its sheath as the other son stood frozen, mouth ajar. Bobby cried, "Get a weapon, Tommy!"

Tommy didn't budge as he watched me grab a fistful of his father's thinning hair and drag his face to mine. Through gritted teeth I said, "That was your last mistake."

At the edge of my awareness, a feminine scream carried across the breeze as I sliced a gaping whole across Sir Robert's throat. The man clawed at the gushing red line before dropping lifeless to the gravel. Tommy, seeming to find his voice, yelled, "Stop it, Bobby. That's treason."

Bobby, however, advanced, lifting the long steel blade in my direction as if he were capable of using it against me. "You should listen to your little brother," I cautioned him.

"You care for her," Bobby said, voice dripping with accusation as he pointed the sword in my direction. "Father was right. You're an abomination. We were much better with Xavier as king and that bitch king killer murdered him. You just killed our father for saying what everyone else is thinking." He thrust the blade at my head which was clouded with a haze of murderous crimson.

I darted back to give myself time to think. I didn't want to kill this kid in front of Avery. That had been her scream I heard. I shot a glance at the window on the third story. Sure enough, her silhouette filled the center pane, one delicate hand was pressed to her neck, the other pressed against the glass. Shit.

The boy was of legal age, and I couldn't allow him to live. He knew the choice he made raising a weapon against his sovereign. My hesitance cost me, and the boy showed more skill with the weapon than I'd anticipated. A swift, albeit jerky move and the blade sliced across my shoulder making a shallow cut. It stung for a moment before I allowed my rage to take over.

This was who that witch in the window was signing up for. I had to resign myself to it. Power thrummed through me, just below the surface itching to get out, but hampered by the curse magic. It didn't stop the heightened state my magic gave me or my physical strength.

"You're dead," I said, spinning forward, knocking the flat edge of the sword with the brace on my forearm so it went wide. Bobby dropped the weapon and his hand darted for a dagger at his belt, but I beat him to it, wrestling it from his grip. "You don't get to threaten a king and live." I shoved him hard, and his back hit the carriage. The varnished wood whined at the impact. I almost backed away thinking of her, but the vitriol in his eye I couldn't ignore.

I fished out the two other knives stashed on his person then dragged him by the collar to the opposite side of the carriage, hoping it would shield Avery from what I was about to do. Bobby, thrashed in my grip and my fingers slipped. He darted forward, but I was on him, tackling him to the ground.

"Abomin—" His words were cut off as my knee drove into his back. Then his hair was in my hand, and I had his head pulled back to expose his neck. Reaching underneath, I made a hard cut and felt the warmth gush onto my fist. The traitor went through a series of convulsions before going limp.

I knelt there for a moment, letting my breathing even out. This was how I ruled, and I didn't regret it. But as I took in the blood pooling beneath us, just outside the shadow of the carriage my heart sank. I dared a glimpse over my shoulder, and I could swear our eyes met.

Yes, this is the real monster you're going to marry. I watched as she backed away from the window into the darkness of the room before I stood and approached the last Musson son.

"Tommy, you made the right choice today, and I won't forget your loyalty," I said. And it was true. This wasn't the first time I'd killed someone's loved one.

Tears streamed down the boy's face, and I remembered the day I'd lost my father. Tommy had to be about my age when it happened, though the circumstances were vastly different. He held his hand out to me. In it was the first dagger I'd thrown which had been lodged in his father's leg. He held the hilt toward me in a shaky hand, stained with blood. "Thank you, Your Majesty."

Taking the weapon, I slid it back into its sheath. "I don't like that you had to see that, but you're the man of your family now. And I could not allow them to live."

Tommy nodded, though the tears didn't cease. "I know," he said, then made his way to the carriage, climbed atop to the seat where he would drive the horses. He gave one last glance at me, before snapping the reins.

One day, I'd take the time to check in on the boy, but now I had a larger problem to deal with. Wiping my hand on my pants, I made my way up the stairs to see if I had any hope remaining or if what she'd seen had sealed my fate.

CHAPTER 38

AVERY

I knew who Nighval was, theoretically. I knew he had killed people. He'd told me as much. Seeing it, however, was a different story. And he knew I saw it and he was coming for me.

Last night, he'd been desperate to make sure I would never leave him. I agreed to marry him, which gave me giddy flutters as I'd recalled our evening when I woke. But now... Now, I needed a few minutes alone to think. To reconcile what I saw with the loving and passionate man I'd been with the night before. That was why I was scurrying down the hallway back to my rooms.

I made it to my door before the sound of heavy boot strikes thundered up the staircase, headed in my direction. Slipping inside, I snapped the door shut and spun the key in the lock until it clicked, and I could breathe. Footsteps stomped through the hallway, approaching nearer and nearer. I crossed the sitting room before slipping into my bedroom. I started to shut the door when a loud banging sounded from across the chamber. When I didn't answer, the door handle rattled.

"Avery, let me in. I need to talk to you," Nighval said. The desperate pleading edge in his voice made the hair on the back of my neck stand up. Would he break down the door? Did I want him to? Part of me did. Fortunately, the rational part of my brain was winning out.

"Go away. I need some time to think," I called across the room to him.

The door handle rattled again more viciously before it stilled. "Avery," he growled. "Please let me explain."

"I know who that was, Nighval. I know Xavier released him. And I remember that you—" Goddess. I brought my hands up to cover my eyes as a sharp pain burst behind them. I felt like something was at the edge of my memory, but it just wouldn't come through. Something to do with that man Sir Robert Musson and my fiancé.

"He committed treason—" he started to explain, but I cut him off.

"And his son?"

"Yes, and his son. I couldn't let them live. Please open the door."

"I said no," I reminded him rather loudly.

We sat there at a stalemate for long moments before a crash which sounded like a fist splitting wood shot through the room and Nighval yelled, "Fuck."

I expected another outburst, but none ever came. Eventually, footsteps retreated down the hall, and I was alone.

The sight of blood called the memories from my near execution to the front of my mind bringing up a swell of dizzying emotions. Images that just wouldn't quit. The decapitated head rolling across the planks, Annabelle with the bag over her head, and now the sight of my future husband kneeling on what had to be a rat-man around my age's back, wrenching his head back by the tuft of fur and slitting his throat as his clawed hands wildly tore through the air for a target. I couldn't see a great many details from the third-floor window I watched from, but my brain filled in the details I couldn't make out.

How could he do this? Life was so much harder for them in that form and Nighval had been spared from that. Yet he showed them no mercy and took their lives. Even seeing the rat-curse slip off the men as death claimed them was a new horror I'd relive in my mind.

At least they would be buried as men, because the thought of seeing the rat-people in human caskets was too horrible and surreal. It had heat rising up my neck. I fanned my face as perspiration beaded on my forehead. I had to get a window open or I was going to pass out.

Get it together. My world swayed, and I reached a handout to grab onto the footboard of the bed for support. I just needed to lay down. Between the headache that sprung up out of nowhere and my overactive imagination, I had to turn my brain off for a while.

Flipping back the covers, I crawled in and pulled them up over my head, creating a dark cocoon. I lay there in shock for a long while until I recognized the scent enveloping me was of the man who had triggered these fraying emotions. I threw the covers back and looked down at the shirt I pulled from Nighval's closet to put on after I found my party outfit in a wrinkled heap on the floor. I had thought it so romantic, wearing his clothes after what happened last night, but now as the scent permeated into my awareness, I questioned my decision.

Still, I couldn't bear to take it off. I liked that scent, and I liked the man it emanated from. There it was. I had laid here for hours and while I felt more than a little emotionally disturbed by what I'd seen, I still wanted him. And, he wanted me, too.

I crawled out of bed and walked over to the mirror to take a good look at myself. My soft waves were a rumpled mess, and my day-old makeup was a little smudged. Tilting my head to the side, I took in the pink flesh of my neck from where Nighval's stubble scratched me as he had ravished me last night. I even still felt his presence between my legs. Just the thought of the act and how savagely he had taken me made heat pool there.

Something about my tousled look was ridiculously sexy and as I assessed myself, I willed myself to acknowledge a hard truth. There were things about the man that I was falling for that scared the shit out of me. Things that he did that I completely disagreed with and that when I was queen I would work to change.

Namely the God-like justice he seemed to believe he had the right to take. None of that was going to stop me from falling for him though. I just wasn't sure what that said about me. Because the more that I allowed my memories from last night to eclipse the ones from this morning, the more my need for him became a living thing.

I saw his note this morning when I got out of bed that he had to make a visit to the nearby town today. I rushed to the window to see if Eclipse had been taken from his stable that I could just see from that vantage point. The stallion was coming across the yard when I noticed Nighval descending the steps to confront the men below.

Was he still here or had he continued on about his day? Suddenly the urge to speak with him, to see him and touch him and let him know that he hadn't broken what was between us was a driving urge in my gut. I knew what he was thinking. *Please don't ever leave me.* I knew where those words came from and turning him away would only reinforce them.

I needed to think, and I deserved that space, but our fledgling relationship was in such a fragile place, with so much expectation from the outside world put on it that I questioned my decision to not open the door to him.

As if he sensed thoughts of him were burning through my mind, a rap at the door sounded along with his deep timber. "Avery, Jane says you haven't left your room all day. May I please come in?"

The beating of my heart ratcheted up as I crossed the room to the door, even as anticipation coiled low in my belly. "Avery?" he called, his deep voice rattling in concern as he tugged on the handle.

I grasped the little metal key, giving it a few swift turns and stepped back as the handle spun down and the door burst open. His presence was foreboding as he pushed into the room, and he was breathing in long heavy breaths like he was fighting himself for control. I slipped around him and shut the door before coming to stand before him and putting a palm to his chest.

"Are you going to let me explain now?" he asked, sliding his hand over mine to grip my fingers.

"What did they do?" I asked as he squeezed.

His voice was gruff when he said, "Treason."

"Nighval," I scolded because I knew that wasn't the entire story.

"They said some things that were impermissible."

"About?" I pressed.

"You. And me," was all he said, but his brow wrinkled in a pained way.

"I see." I stood there for a long moment trying to process this new information. I had a feeling Nighval wasn't going to share more, regardless of how much I pressed because he wanted to shield me for whatever hurtful words had been spoken. But I had enough of an imagination to figure out what they would have said. To many on this plane I was the traitor, branded a king-killer. Another witch who failed to break the curse and end their suffering. Some people probably hated me and still wanted to see me dead.

His Adam's apple bobbed as he swallowed. "I didn't know you were standing there, but this is the way in this plane. You must come to accept it."

I frowned. That wouldn't do, but I understood changing things would take time, and I give it my all to work toward that new future. "The truth is that nothing you say will convince me to accept what you did—"

"Avery," he said. The way my name came out from deep within his chest caused me a new physical ache.

"If you would let me finish, what I was going to say was, but I understand who you are and you have shown me that you are capable of change. You have shown me that you value my opinion, and will take it into consideration as we go about rebuilding and ruling this kingdom."

"I will," he said. Then as if he was only now putting together the implication of my words, he drew in a harsh breath. "Does this mean you still plan to be my wife?"

The words were too bottled up in my chest for me to force them out, so I nodded.

The relieved expression on his face was so sharp it had me standing up onto my tippy toes and threading my fingers through his hair so I could pull his head down to brush my lips against his.

He gave me an achingly sweet kiss before stiffening. "Avery, we shouldn't—"

I hummed against his mouth as I claimed it again. "We should."

He pulled back, gazing down at me with scrutiny in his eyes. "I imagine you're sore..."

Another kiss. "Mmm... In a good way. Don't you want to claim your make-up sex?"

His lids became heavy as the expression on his face became almost pained.

I traced my fingers across his grimace. "I promise you won't hurt me."

His hands wrapped around mine as I ran them up his hard chest. He'd changed into a linen ensemble which I determined was his around the house clothing and the feel of his strong body beneath the soft fabric was delicious. I had the sudden urge to taste the salt of his skin. I ran my tongue along the edge of his exposed collarbone and up the side of his neck. He heaved a breath trying to grab my hands between us, which I glanced at.

"Nigh, what's wrong?" I asked, not understanding. He appeared to have cleaned any blood off of them and he wasn't injured as far as I could tell. I didn't see what the problem was. The fact that he was actively resisting made me nervous, and I didn't like that one bit. I needed him, to feel him and to let him show me that everything was all right. A chill shot through me. Was he upset with me for shutting him out? Surely not. "You're not upset with me, are you?"

"Nothing is wrong. You were the one upset with me only hours ago. I don't want to take advantage of you." He pulled my hand up and kissed it.

"Well, I want to take advantage of you. Right now," I said, letting insistence flood my voice. I wrapped his hands around my waist, and he teetered forward. I wanted him to know he wouldn't hurt me. I liked how he'd made me feel, the ache and oh how I craved more. Goddess, I was aching and this hard-to-get thing he was doing was killing me.

"Nigh, I need you *right now*," I demanded since he didn't seem to get it the first time.

That seemed to snap his control. He groaned as his hands ran down the outside of my legs. He caught the edge of his borrowed shirt, pulling it up as his palms rubbed back up my thighs. When his hands reached my ass, his big fingers wrapped around me and he squeezed so tight it almost hurt as he pulled me against him. I gasped in his mouth.

"Yes, that's what I need."

The way he kissed me, I knew he had given in to whatever he had been fighting. His misplaced guilt at being with me after what he did this morning and then the weight of the disapproval he knew I felt. But sharing this right now was the healing I demanded. Lifting me, I wrapped my legs around his waist as he carried me to the bedroom.

"You look so fucking hot in my shirt," he said, laying me down on the bed. He pulled his own shirt over his head, his muscles flexing and rippling. I was drooling. Then he kicked off his boots and peeled down his pants before crawling over me. I started to lean up so he could pull his shirt off me, but his rough hand shoved me back down to the bed. "I want to have you while you're wearing it." He pulled it up so it was resting just under my breasts and the soft curve of my stomach could be seen. Then he moved a leg between mine, nudging it out, so I was spread wide for him.

His dark eyes licked across my skin before his fingers followed them. Chills traced behind his touch and he gave me a wicked grin as he watched them erupt before lowering himself onto me. Then he once again claimed my mouth as he thrust himself against me.

I was practically panting when I pulled my mouth away from his and demanded, "Inside, right now." I didn't think I could take anymore foreplay.

"You're still mine?" he asked, sucking at my earlobe as he brought my hand over my head.

"Yes," I breathed.

"Swear it?" He raised my other hand to join it and he pinned both of them there with one of his.

"Jesus, yes, Nighval. Please," I begged.

"Don't you dare shut me out like that again. Not knowing what you were thinking made me fucking crazy. I don't know if I can handle it again. Do you understand me?" he asked as he used his free hand to pull my knee up and then grab his length, positioning it at my entrance. His head brushed through my wet folds, and I whimpered. Geez, it had only been for a few hours, making we wonder what he'd be like if we ever had a real blow up.

He nudged me before pulling right back out and the sounds that came out of my throat were more animal than human. "Do you understand me?" he demanded, his grip on my wrists tightening.

"Yes, Nigh, yes, I understand," I eked out between ragged breaths.

When I finished, and he was apparently satisfied, he rewarded me by slamming home.

CHAPTER 39

NIGHVAL

As the weeks passed, I could sense the curse breaking words on the tip of her tongue. I thought what she witnessed would have at least slowed down progression by a month or two, but it seemed to have the opposite effect as she had somehow accepted my darkness. Surrendered to it, and I found that intoxicating.

I was a lucky bastard. There were a few hours where I convinced myself I had royally screwed everything up. Since then, I'd broken my vow not to have her in this form. Repeatedly. But how could I say no to her? She had not only forgiven me, but she had been wet and wanting. And I'd been so hard, and she begged so prettily. After that first time I'd slipped, every time after that got easier to give in to my desire.

And each time I collapsed on top of her with her arms wrapping around me pulling me close, I sensed she was spiraling as intensely as I was.

The question was, how much longer did I have until it happened? Until she realized how she felt, and everything changed. Three words spoken from the heart were all it would take. I narrowly held her off the realization at the full moon party.

At first, I'd been angry with myself for keeping the words at bay, but since I'd given into my weakness and we had make-up sex, as she called it, I was enjoying showing her how very thoroughly I planned to love her. With each encounter, my regret seemed to fade since I greedily enjoyed everything she gave me during this stolen time.

Still, I needed to hold it off until our wedding night, which was at the end of this week. It made me a manipulative asshole, but I wanted to make sure she was bound to me before those words crossed her lips and my world came crashing down as the realization of what I'd done mowed her down. Tying her to me would give me time to re-win her heart and rebuild the trust I destroyed.

That thought made my stomach clench, but I should enjoy this, enjoy her and what we had before Samara robbed another thing from me. "Kiss me," I said.

Avery stood on to the tips of her toes, wrapped her fingers around my neck and pulled me down for a mouthwatering kiss. Everything between us was so new that each time our mouths met, my thoughts immediately jumped between my legs. It took an absurd amount of restraint to stop from taking her every chance I got.

I knew she wanted it, too, that we needed to keep building these moments between us. That was why we were going on an adventure today.

Eclipse strode up to us, and I held out a hand for her. She took it, and I helped her onto him.

"Where are we going?" she asked.

"It's a surprise. Did you bring what I asked you to?" I asked, swinging my leg up behind her until I was flush with her back. I looped my arms around her and grabbed the reins.

"I did, but where on earth are we going where we would need towels? Wouldn't a picnic blanket have made more sense?"

I cleared my throat. "You were supposed to bring both."

"Oops," she said. I look down to see a guilty grin on her face.

"It's fine. We will make do. As long as we have each other," I said and kissed her cheek as I nudged Eclipse forward.

The grotto was about an hour away and as the blue water came into view, Avery gasped, covering her mouth with her hands. "Oh my god," she said. "This place is beautiful."

Large shafts of sunlight danced between the holes in the canopy, causing the rippling blue water to sparkle.

"Okay, now I see what the towels are for, but you didn't tell me to bring a bathing suit," she said.

I slid off Eclipse and held my hands up to her to help her down. "It's just us. Do you need one?"

"I see what you're up to," she said, her voice full of humor as she poked my side. "You're just trying to get me naked."

"When am I ever not trying to get you naked?" I asked, pulling out a bottle from one of the saddle packs.

"Good point," she said. "Well, in that case, what would you like to eat first?"

I almost choked on the water I had just taken a sip of. "Avery," I scolded. "Don't tempt me."

"Is it deep?" she said, peering over the rock ledge and ignoring my comment.

"Yes. It's nearly bottomless all the way up to the edge. There's a rope ladder over there that is still in good condition. And there's a wooden one across, leading to that overhang."

Her hands went to the hem of her fitted midriff exposing shirt, peeling it off. And, of course, as was often the case, she wasn't wearing a bra and her perked brown nipples hardened as they hit the air. She didn't hesitate before dropping her loose pants and then slipping out of the lacy panties she called a thong.

In a few strides, she was at the edge. She threw a playful glance over her shoulder before turning toward the water and diving in. I walked over to the edge and looked down at her to see her treading water. Her beautiful golden skin visible through the clear water created the most inviting contrasts.

"It's warm," she called.

"I thought you'd like it," I told her, and went to get the towels to set them at the top of the rope ladder.

"How did you know?" she asked when I came back into view.

I followed her lead and stripped. There was something about standing naked at the top of this rock ledge and staring down at her that made me feel invincible. Like a god.

"You told me about where you were from. About how much you liked the ocean, and while the ocean used to be accessible to us from here when I had my power all the time, this is the best I could do for now." I jumped in and then swam out to the center. She followed me.

"That was sweet," she said.

"Would you still think I was sweet if I told you the other reason I figured you'd like it is because you keep looking at the fountain longingly? Like you want to get in it. So really I'm just trying to save you from embarrassing yourself," I said. Her mouth fell open, and I let my teeth show as I grinned at her.

The edge of her hand smacked the surface of the water, and a wave hit my face. "Rude," she cried.

Shooting my hand out, I grabbed ahold of her wrist and tugged her toward me. Then, without warning, I put my hand on the top of her head and shoved her under the water. She came up sputtering and laughing. Before she could retaliate, I pulled her toward me, wrapping her legs around my waist, and I kicked backward until I was at the wall so I could hang on to the wooden ladder with one hand.

I guided her onto it, and she crawled up giving me the most enticing view. Then I got an idea. When she was almost at the top, I came up behind her and grabbed her by the hips. I pushed her shoulders down to where her chest pressed against the cool, smooth stones.

"How?" she asked. "Oh." She got her answer as I lowered myself to where I was eye level with the softest part of her.

I hooked my arm around the side of the ladder to brace myself and used my other hand to spread open her thighs. Gooseflesh dotted her skin, and I blew hot air onto her folds. She squirmed.

"I'm going to eat you now," I said, hovering an inch away from what I so desperately wanted.

"Okay," she said, and as soon as the words left her lips, my tongue darted forward, licking across her slit. I dipped lower and circled her clit with my tongue, teasing and sucking it until she was making little gasps. I went back and forth until her thigh shivered beneath my palm.

I moved my hand further up so I could separate her cheeks, and I glided my tongue over the other tight hole. She tried to bolt up, but I planted my face and shoved her down with my free hand and as I worked licking between her ass and her pussy, she began whimpering in earnest. I thrust my tongue deep inside her and she cried out as her legs went tense in front of me.

"Oh, Nigh," she bit out, between pants. When her breathing evened out, she said, "I've never had anyone kiss me *there*."

I knew precisely which *there* she was referring to by her little surprised jump. "Did you like it?" I asked her, helping her onto the ledge. She rolled over and propped herself up on her elbows. I drank her in, from the impression of the rock which made a pattern on her flushed skin to the drizzle from her wet hair which traced down across her breasts, some sliding off and some pooling in her navel.

"Yes," she said, though her grin was a little sheepish, but she leaned forward, licking her lips, probably steeling herself for what she believed I expected her to do for me. Sure enough, she said, "Come here so I can return the favor."

"You don't have to," I said, crawling onto the platform and then over her. In a single thrust, I was inside her heat. Just the taste of her had almost caused me to explode, a few slaps of our wet flesh, and I was seeing stars.

When I gathered my bearings, I rolled off of her, the chilly stone cooling off my overheated skin. Propping myself up on an elbow, I watched her savor the sensation of sunlight beating down on her. Her serene face shed any of the worried tension it occasionally carried. She was so beautiful like this, experiencing the simple joys of life, and I suddenly wanted to know everything about her. *What were you like as a kid? What happened to your parents? How many lovers have you had? Were any of their names Chase?*

Damn my spiraling thoughts.

I'd done a decent job of preventing the nagging question from eroding the time I spent with her. That didn't mean it still wasn't in the back of my mind and the question it brought up. Soon enough, I'd know who she saw, or didn't see, and then some past lover would be the least of my concerns.

I kept my mouth shut for fear of what would come out of it and adopted a prone position beside her, closing my eyes. I don't know how long we laid there, but eventually she rustled beside me and then was out of sight. There was a splash, and I looked up to see Avery swimming across the grotto.

I let her swim for a while before I joined her. We spent the rest of the afternoon enjoying the picnic she brought and even offered Eclipse an apple and some carrots she had thoughtfully packed.

As she dropped the towel, I noticed a thin red line across the back of her thigh and my heart went cold. I glanced down at my hand and sure enough, one of the caps must have come off in the water. Dread sluiced through me, and I rushed over to her and knelt down to inspect it. The blood was dried, and it was barely a scratch, thank the goddess.

"What?" she asked, craning her head around to see what had captured my attention. "Nigh, that's just a scratch. I probably got it on the stones. Don't worry about it, okay? It will heal and be gone in a week."

Her gentle hand cupped my cheek, and she tilted my head up toward her. She leaned down and gave me a kiss. "I'm not breakable, okay? You need to quit treating me like I am."

If she knew where the scratch had come from, she would be horrified. I should never have allowed myself to sleep with her except on the full moon, but I was so weak. She was someone I couldn't resist and at the first opportunity, I caved with hardly a fight. I truly was the monster she thought I was.

As I stood, I vowed to myself and the goddess that I would not give in again until our wedding night. That meant six more days. And nights. I could do that. I would make up some excuse about wanting our wedding night to be special and stay away.

If I had only allowed her to say it that night, this would all be over with, but I couldn't stand the thought of her hating me, though I knew it was inevitable. I still felt awful, but the decision gave me some comfort. And as we rode back to Ravsted, I thanked the goddess that the cut hadn't been worse.

CHAPTER 40

AVERY

Nighval had been gone the last few days, and I was aching to see him. I stared at myself in the mirror, alone in my room. This wedding would be different. It was to a man that I had more than warm feelings for, who I knew in the depth of my person felt the same as I did. Had it been me and him in the beginning, what would have happened?

But I couldn't let myself think of that. By the end of the night, we'd save the people on two different planes and be basking in this thing that had grown between us against all odds. I couldn't wait to see him. And for him to see me.

I'd designed my dress this time and though Nighval hadn't seen me in the other, this dress would be one of my creations. The white fabric was embroidered with sequins and pearls, full sleeves, a high neckline, and hit just below my breasts so it exposed a sliver of my tiny midsection I knew he liked. The bottom also hugged my curves down to where it flared out at the knee slightly in a subtle mermaid cut.

It hardly revealed any skin, but with the way it showed my physique, I knew he'd love it. A part of me wanted to take over and design his tux, but this was important to him, and I imagined after everything he'd experienced with the other witches, he would want some say.

Like the full moon party, he wanted the moment we said I do to be when the moon was at its peak. I loved his reverence for the goddess and the significant role nature played in his life.

I started for the door, but at the last minute rushed over to my makeup kit and wiped off the bright pink I was wearing on my lips, changing it to a lighter shade. I took another glance in the mirror. Perfect.

I walked out into the garden. A little pathway had been created with white rose petals that wound through the flowers to a small marble gazebo. Inside it stood Nighval and a priest I'd never met. The wedding would be just the three of us, and I love it.

Like I imagined, Nighval's tux was a longer 1940s style with a squared off bottom and a classic black bow tie. His eyes lit up as he saw me, and the world was silent for a moment. My heart thundered in my ears and then the sounds of crickets singing came into my awareness.

This had been the craziest year of my life, but with each step forward, the more confident I became in my decision. He was the right man for me. He held out his hand, and I took it. He turned to the priest.

I tried to follow along as best I could, but the vows differed from my world, and even the ones I'd spoken to Xavier. When the small ceremony was over, Nighval dismissed the priest.

I craned my head up to him. "So that was it? What do we do now?" I asked.

His grin was positively wicked. "I thought we could have some fun."

He knelt down wordlessly and took off my shoes, then he stood and spun me back toward the path. The white rose petals had disappeared and an iridescent glow that seemed to shine like moonlight beckoned me toward the forest.

Not fully understanding what he expected, I turned around, but he was gone. Only my white satin heels remained in the gazebo with me. My breathing hitched as I stepped down the three steps to ground level and followed the path. With each couple of steps forward, the glowing light seemed to retreat deeper into the forest, drawing me away from the palace. I looked up to where they led, recalling the decision I had made on the last full moon.

My heart hammered as I realized the game my husband had set up for our wedding night. This was another hunt and, like our chase up the stairs into the palace, I knew what he wanted. Tonight, I would let him hunt me. I would let him take me on the forest floor. Tonight, we would break the curse.

I swallowed the lump in my throat and took a step forward. I had not chosen the right outfit for this type of adventure. As if he realized it, the fitted fabric eased, and I looked down to see my dress was gone, replaced with a simple white nightie that came to mid-thigh and nothing else.

My nipples hardened as the breeze lifted the corners of the nightie and the anticipation curled low in my belly. I got to the edge of the garden, and I turned back to the gazebo. Nighval was back, standing in what looked like black leather pants, boots, and a fitted black jacket with countless buckles and straps similar to what he wore when he traveled, but more battle ready. He had his arms crossed over his chest and when my eyes found his face I saw him mouth the word, *Run*.

Thank goodness I was in decent shape. I took off sprinting. If he wanted a chase, I would give it to him. But as I looked to the ground, at the surprisingly soft moss which made up the trail, I realized he was leading me in a certain direction. By the looks of the rest of the forest, my feet would be torn to shreds if I veered off the path.

I sprinted around a corner. In the distance at another bend, I caught the sight of a black-clad man leaning up against a tree and my heart jolted into my throat. I started to pause, but realized it was him. He was leaning against one shoulder and his feet were crossed at the ankle. He had a smug look on his face as I approached, and I flipped him off as I sprinted past. I wondered how long he would make me run when I heard footsteps behind me.

I glanced over my shoulder, and he was only casually stalking forward, which irritated me to no end. I hadn't even kicked it into high gear yet. I took in a long breath, and increased my pace. When I looked back, he again was out of sight which made my nerves jump and my awareness of my surroundings heightened. The trail ahead seemed to curve in a circle. I slowed as I followed it and when I made it around the thick tree, I saw where it led.

The moss rejoined the original trail crossing right in front of him. Cocky bastard. And his point wasn't lost on me. Somehow, everything led back to him and always would. Especially after this curse was broken, and he got his power back.

The thought of being married to such a powerful man sent chills down my spine. I wasn't going to let him taunt me, though, and I knew he wouldn't let me get hurt. As I slipped back around the tree, I caught one of his eyebrows raised. I took a tentative step off of the moss and before my foot touched the ground, new moss appeared beneath it.

Smiling, I darted forward into the uncharted forest.

CHAPTER 41

NIGHVAL

"Got you," I said, as I overtook my wife. *Wife.* I never savored a word like I did that one. She spun in my arms and her thumbs ran across the edge of my jaw as I lifted, then wrapped her legs around my waist. Her slip was in tatters, and her feet were bare and covered in dirt, but I knew not a scratch marred them. I used my power to make sure that her flight across the forest floor would cause her no harm.

I had her pinned to a tree, like I'd done what seemed like a lifetime ago, and she was writhing beneath me. Our hearts pounded in unison from the chase, and she lowered her eyes to mine. The sparkle in them told me she was close, possibly standing on the edge of that precipice, ready to topple over and fall in. The glimmer of it I saw the first night we were intimate had turned into something stronger, but I didn't want her to drift into love. I wanted her to plummet into the depths of it in such a way that would scar her heart. Bind her to me so thoroughly we might make it through what I knew would happen once she did. Because knowing her, she was going to be furious.

She leaned forward to give me one of the kisses she gave me so often now that made me want to tear the remaining scraps of her slip away and bury myself inside her to quench the thirst they afflicted me with.

She would let me, but I needed to slow down and focus on her needs. I needed to push her over the edge. It would happen tonight, and the thought made a volcano of anxiety erupt in my chest. I didn't want to gain her love then immediately lose it. My chest felt like it was on the verge of collapse. When she pulled away, her eyes searched my face.

I shouldn't go there, I shouldn't ask, but the way she was looking at me, the way she looked at me during the ceremony, I had to know. Was it him, this Chase person, me? Someone else entirely. A man who was a total fiction?

I took a deep breath and asked, "What do you see when you look at me?"

She released a delicate chuckle. "What do you mean?"

"I mean, what do you see?" I pressed, knowing the moonlight illuminated my features like they did hers.

Her smile was warm as she said, "Well, I see your lips that I like to kiss, full when you're smiling, but thin and hard when you scowl."

I grinned at her. "What else?"

"I see your hard jaw and proud nose." She ran her finger across the bridge of my nose as her other hand played with the hair at the nape of my neck. "And this scar," she said. My heart stuttered, then exploded in a thundering chorus I battled for control over.

Still, my eyelids slid closed as she dragged her finger across the scar from my nose, down across my cheek. Her lips lightly followed it, then grazed my eyelids in soft, barely there kisses. "I can't see your brooding dark eyes now, but I see the hard line of your brow and this scar," she kissed it, "that runs from your hairline to here."

I released her waist, letting her slide to the ground. Grabbing her hand as she started to trace her finger down my scar, I fell to my knees. I forced my eyes open and stared up at the woman who'd unknowingly captured my soul with a touch. Mercy, I wanted to cry. What wicked magic—the witch saw *me*. Avery was looking at and falling in love with *my face*. I'd been told the pill would change how she saw things and it had. Just not in the way I expected. She shouldn't have remembered the scars, but somehow she did. The best I could have hoped for was her falling for the softened version of me, but this was better and worse all at the same time.

Chase. Had I been such a fool worrying over nothing? My mind had immediately twisted it into something dread inducing when maybe it hadn't been a name after all. Maybe she'd murmured something from a magically blocked memory, the one of our pursuit the night she'd tried to run from Xavier, and it was threatening to seep through in her dreams. It was too good to be true.

Dread and elation coiled in my chest, weaving tight braids around my stuttering heart. I should be grateful to have this exquisite woman look upon me so adoringly, but I knew when she fell and the curse was lifted, dissolving with it the magic's power, she'd see me and feel about me as she had before. Damn witches and their curses. A woman always knew how to hit you where it hurt. I really hated them. At least the consolation would be that my people would be free, but I'd be a tattered scrap of a man left in her aftermath.

I shouldn't be so dire. My heart would be shattered, but I'd find a way to win her back. I'd vow my life on it, and she'd promised.

She gave me the sweetest look, and I sank a little deeper under her spell. "Husband, you look so desperate. Why, when I'm your wife now?"

There would be no hesitation. Though my heart was a thundering war drum, I wouldn't flinch. "Because, Avery, I've fallen desperately in love with you, and I'm terrified you won't feel the same. I've never wanted anything more in my pathetic life."

"Nighval, I..." she said, raising a hand to her throat.

I tugged on her other hand, so she met me on her knees. "Shhh," I said. "You don't need to say anything. Just let me make love to you."

I kissed her then, fingering the edges of her slip, lifting it over her head so she was bare before me on the forest floor. My magic created a soft bed of bright green moss that I carefully laid her down on. I made quick work of my clothes as she watched me as I lowered myself over her. When I planned this hunt, I imagined I'd chase her through the forest and take her as roughly as I did that first night, but the love welling in my chest demanded I savor her. Savor every second gifted to me.

She was ready for me as I entered her familiar warmth with a gentle stroke, and she gasped. Then I kissed her, in slow languid motions, kissing and licking her lips, her jaw, her neck. Her fingers threaded through my hair, and I slid into her again and again. Her tremors started, and I moved in the way I'd learned she'd liked stroking over and over until she seized up beneath me. I pressed our foreheads together and breathed in every exhale as I guided her through her orgasm. When she settled, opening her eyes, I started moving again.

"More?" she asked, her voice still breathy with need.

"Yes, my love, more." I rocked, nudging against that deep spot that sent her over the edge, making sure my pelvis ground into her deliciously swollen clit. "Like that?" I asked.

"Yes, please," she said. Soon her body jerked, and she bowed off the ground. I held her still, moving as she rode out her pleasure once again.

She was shaky when she came down and she looked up at me with glazed eyes. I nudged my cock, still rock hard, deep inside her and her eyes widened. "More?" she asked again, but this time a hint of a giggle laced her voice.

"Yes, wife, more. I'm going to make you come until you believe you can't live without me like I can't live without you."

A lust-addled grin lit her face. "Why?" she asked.

I chuckled and thrust into her, wiping the smile from her face. Leaning down, I said, "Because I love you, Avery. And I would do anything to keep you."

Her face was full of wonder as she stared up at me and in that moment, my chest had never felt so full, like I could soar. "You make me feel like I could—"

She cut me off with the most earth-shattering words I'd ever heard. "I love you, too, Nighval."

I felt the truth of her words as the air around us began vibrating. Building. Then a tidal wave of magic burst through the clearing. The momentum of the curse blowing apart threatened to lift us off the ground, so I clung to my wife, letting my full weight press her naked body into the moss bed. I tried to take in what was happening. My heart jumped to my throat as blue streams of light, much like my own magic, lit up the area beneath the canopy radiating out from where our chests touched.

We'd done it. I could hardly believe it. A hot tear traced down my cheek, as relief flooded through me. I buried myself in her hair, keeping perfectly still as the last waves of it rolled out.

It had to be past the time when the third bell would have rung, and while the moss was still coating the forest floor, my power had been gone. It rushed back to me in a flood that had me thrusting my hips forward into this glorious creature underneath me. For fear of what she would see, I said, "Close your eyes, my love, and let me finish inside you."

She obeyed, and I started pumping into her with renewed vigor. With the elation I felt from her love, from my freedom, from all the good things that would come of this. I'd never felt happier in my life, and it was all because of her.

I leaned over her and kissed her neck, murmuring the words I needed her to hear. Needed her to never forget. "I love you, I love you, I love you." Her body shuddered underneath me and broke and this time I erupted with her, surging my release deep inside my wife's clenching walls. Deep inside the woman who loves me.

When the pleasure subsided, I leaned up on my forearm. It might have been foolish, but I was curious if she'd felt the release of the curse, too. I grinned as her eyes fluttered open, landing on me.

Then she screamed.

PART 3

CHAPTER 42

AVERY

"Get away from me," I screamed, backing away from the monster that was above me. A flood of memories crashed into my mind, and my brain was an instant tangle. Crab crawling far enough away, I scrambled to my feet. I bent over to snatch my discarded nightie and held it to my breast to cover myself from him.

"That fucking pill." I staggered back and my hand flew to my chest. "My fucking heart, you monster." And he was a monster. A scarred, devious, deceitful, wicked man, more than any rat-man I'd ever encountered. There he was on his knees in human form, curse fully broken, having captured my shattering heart with his trickery.

Nighval held his hands up to me in supplication. "It isn't like that. We love each other. You're my wife, Avery." For each step he took toward me, I retreated another step back.

"I remember everything," I screamed, and my back bumped up against a tree. I turned around and screamed at it, remembering the day I had fled from Xavier and Nighval had hunted me. Then chased me through the forest and pinned me up against a tree. I had fallen in love with him without having remembered who he really was. Because of that pill he forced down my throat.

"Yes, and we're free. You did it, Avery. There is such a vastness in your heart, you saved us. Our love has spared everyone."

I sneered at him. "You told me you would do it. You told me I would forget everything, and you would make me fall in love with you. I'm such an idiot. Goddess, I'm such a fool." Nighval took a few steps toward me. "Get the fuck away from me."

"Avery, I promise everything that has happened in the last two months has been completely real."

"Don't you lie to me. You drugged me. Where I'm from, men go to jail for that." A sob escaped my throat, and I threatened to double over. "You broke my heart." I couldn't help the tears streaming down my face. My chest felt like someone had torn it wide open and the culprit was standing mere feet from me, mouth agape.

"Avery, I will do whatever it takes to make this right. I wasn't lying when I said I love you, and I will do whatever it takes to keep you." Nighval ran his hand through his dark hair.

"Are you seriously kidding me right now? You think I could possibly want to be with you after this? If you do, you are fooling yourself. What did you think was going to happen whenever I came back to reality and realized what you'd done? That the sex was so good, and I was such a simp for you I would just accept everything? Not fucking happening, buddy." I turned and stormed off, back toward my husband's palace. My *husband*. It was my second marriage in a year, and this one wasn't off to a better start than the first. I had to get out of here. To start, I had to get back to the palace and regroup.

"It's not what I wanted. Because of the way my mother structured the curse, you were never going to fall for me in a couple of hours one night a month where I could be a man for you. But remember the way you felt when I kissed you in the forest? I knew there was something between us, but we just didn't have time. And you were so afraid of me, Avery. I went to her, and I told her I couldn't do it without her help. I'd run out of time and choices. So, I groveled, and she gave me the enchanted pill.

"But her magic allowed you to see me as I was and still fall for me. I didn't know that until tonight. I'd been too afraid to ask you what you saw. She told me it would only alter what you perceived, so it would be possible. But when you saw me, you fell for *me*, Avery," he said, breaking off. Tears fell from his face as he sat there naked, on his knees in the chartreuse moss. I almost felt sympathy for him, almost saw his beauty as the moonlight played across his pale skin, except I was the victim here. He continued, "And she gave it to me, knowing you would hate me afterwards. Please don't let her win."

"Who?" I asked. "Oh my God. You got the pill from your mother." I watched as his face blanched. I was almost impressed. I knew what he had to give up to take the pill from her. To ask for her help. All the while, he must have known that I would hate him, and he did it anyway.

He did it to save his people and while I respected that, it didn't change the roiling rage I felt toward him—the devastation threatening to break me apart. I didn't think I could ever see him the same again. He shoved a Matrix style blue pill down my throat in front of a crowd of people who'd been chanting for my death moments earlier, then carted me off on that horse, admitting everything to me knowing I would forget.

"Tell me what to do," he begged.

"Okay, Nighval. You want to know what to do? Fine. I'll tell you. Use all that power that you have been storing up for nineteen years and send me home." I crossed my arms over my chest, hugging the ruined nightie, standing my ground.

His eyes flared, and he got to his feet, picking up his discarded clothes. He slipped on his leather pants and boots, then threw the rest over his shoulder, so I could still see the scar covered muscle of his chest. I guess he was done being on his knees for me. That didn't take long.

The change in his expression cemented that thought. How his face darkened, and the sure way he stepped toward me. I was smart enough to know not to run, though that's exactly what I wanted to do. He liked that too much. So, I backed up until I bumped into another tree. Fuck.

He was on me in a second, his hand threading through my hair, tilting my head up so our gazes could connect. "You promised me you'd never leave me. You wouldn't shut me out. You promised me, Avery. I understand you are upset, and I will do anything in my power to make you happy. Anything to build back the trust we've lost." I started to repeat my demand, but he said, "Anything but that."

His scarred face lowered so it was inches from mine, and shivers wound their way through my body. "You are mine, and I am yours. And I will wait until you choose to forgive me, my Wounded Heart. But until then, we have a kingdom to set to rights. And I can't imagine the woman I married would cower away from such a challenge." His hand tightened on my jaw and my mouth opened. "Unless I was wrong about you?"

Goddess, he knew exactly how to get under my skin. How did I let this happen? And my stupid body sure liked the dominant male thing he had going on. I was half trembling because I was scared shitless of him and what he was capable of, and half trembling because he was so goddamn hot, scars and everything. If I ever got back to my plane, they were definitely going to make me hand in my feminist card.

"So, you're back to being king now?" I asked him, refusing to cower or submit.

"That's right. And now, you're my wife, which makes you queen." He towered over me, watching me as the information sank in.

"And your home is the palace for the kingdom. I'm guessing there's no chance we can annul the marriage?" I knew the answer, but I asked anyway because it would needle him.

A deep angry laugh burst from his chest, and he stepped away, releasing my cheek like he saw what I was doing. "No chance, sweetheart."

Okay, so I was back to being queen again, and by the position of the moon, my husband would never turn into a rat-man again. "The witches are saved, right?" I asked, just be sure.

He nodded. "Yes, I'll send a message in the morning."

Then he held out a hand for me, which I stared at, unable to move. "A fucking message? You mean you could have sent a message this entire time?" I was going to be sick.

"Come," he said. When I didn't budge, he added, "If you're a good girl, I'll include a message from you, too." Hope welled in my chest until he followed it up with, "As long as you don't beg them to take you back." A smug grin darkened his face. Of course, he'd monitor what I sent.

"You are such an asshole." He withdrew his hand and stood there blocking the path. As he watched me wage the war in my mind, I swore the brambles and briars lining the path around me seemed to be growing. Sure enough, his hands subtly moved at his waist in an unmistakable warlock pattern.

"You wouldn't," I said, as the vegetation seemed to be crowding me in further, edging me forward, toward him.

"Ouch!" I cried and stumbled forward. I glanced behind me to see where a single branch with a sharp pointed thorn stuck out right to where I was standing. The pinpoint on my ass still smarted.

"Come, my queen," he said, choosing a different tactic. "That's what you wanted isn't it? Now you're queen, to a king who's heart you hold. Who you love and makes you feel as no other man would, Avery. A man who wishes to give you—"

"Will you just shut up," I said. I had to think for a minute. If I really considered things, my predicament wasn't terrible. I felt betrayed and heartbroken, but I knew in my bones Nighval wouldn't force himself on me and after what these poor people had been through, they deserved for their world to be set to rights, as Nighval put it. And maybe I'd eventually convince him to send me back. Better to play along for now.

"Okay," I said, placing my hand in his. "But do not misinterpret my willingness to work beside you as my forgiveness. That you will never earn."

A devious grin lit his face, and he jerked me forward, sweeping me into his arms, and I gulped down a sharp breath of air. "I won you once. I can do it again," he said as his hands moved beneath where his arms held me. In a blink, we were standing on the top of the stairs at his—our—palace.

Uniformed guards stood as men, not rat-men, on either side of the main entrance and, as we appeared before them. They gave a prideful look to their king. He still wore that smug smile and he nodded at them as a man full of self-congratulation, because he'd won. He'd beaten his mother even though he had to ask for her help. She'd given it to him for whatever unfathomable reason and now he was carrying his naked bride with only a ruined garment pressed to her chest back to his home. Fortunately, the men hardly spared me a glance, probably because of the possessive nature of their ruler, so my modesty was spared.

"What are you doing?" I hissed, feeling much like the spoils of war. I had no intention of letting him plunder me, however.

"I read about marital traditions in your plane. Isn't it proper for a man to carry his bride across the threshold of her new home?" he asked, and he did just that. A few strides and my husband had carted me into the palace and made his way up the stairs toward the room I had been using.

Thank goodness he didn't appear to be headed toward his room, because that was another thing that was not happening.

"Yeah, that was a thing from like fifty years ago. These days, women aren't such damsels. Sorry to burst your bubble."

"How reassuring, because I'm not sure a damsel could handle me, sweetheart. You, on the other hand, seem able to take me just fine." He kicked my door and strode into the room with all the authority of the man that he was. Walking over to my enormous bed, he tossed me onto it. Literally tossed me so that I bounced a foot in the air when I hit.

"What the hell?" I yelled after him as he abruptly turned and stalked out of the room. He didn't answer me, only leaving the echo of his chuckle in his wake as he retreated down the hallway.

I sat up from where I had been discarded on the bed. The moon was nowhere in sight, and I could see a faint glow edging up on the horizon. I don't know if it was my exhaustion, my exertion from the chase, my wedding, or the fluffy bed I was now lying in, but everything hit me at once, and I felt like the bed might swallow me up whole.

I threw the nightie to the side and crawled into the covers, uncaring that someone may come in here in a few short hours and find me in this state. I needed sleep, and I needed to think. That was when the tears came. I didn't realize I was such a crier, but I never had a broken heart before. I never went through what I've been through this past year before. Until now, I had lived a relatively pain-free life. I lost my mother, but I had been a baby when that had happened, so my aunt had been my caretaker, and I didn't know any different. I lost no other relatives. I never lost a friend, like other kids did either. The truth was, even though the witches prepared me to come here as best they could, I was so sheltered. I just never realized that until now.

To give my husband credit, he had helped me work through some of the trauma that I experienced since I had gotten here. Held me as I relived those horrible nights I went through to get here. And I thought I had found somewhere safe, only to have it ripped away from me.

I had never been upset about not having power, but now I wished I had inherited it. Because I would use every shred to rain hellfire down on his mother. Except she must be one powerful witch if Nighval couldn't spare the world from her existence. But from what I understood, he had only been nineteen himself when she cursed them. Maybe now he could unalive her. Surely, he was powerful enough. That was definitely something he could do to get back in my good graces.

I don't know how long I lay there with tears streaming down my face, when I heard soft footsteps approach. The covers rustled and his weight lowered onto the bed. My heart seized up. "Get out," I said.

"No," he replied, and I felt his body shift and his warmth was near my back.

I sobbed. Just the proximity of him was robbing me of breath. "Please, just leave."

"No," he repeated. "What type of man would I be if I left my wife alone, crying on her wedding night? I'm not leaving you." He emphasized this by snuggling an arm around my waist and pulling me flush against him. A chill drifted in through the broken seals in the windows, which direly needed maintenance, and the fire had long since died. I hated how good his warmth felt, how much like home it had already become, almost as much as I hated him.

Knowing there was no point in resisting when this man made up his mind, I released an exasperated sigh and closed my eyes. I wouldn't realize until later that morning whenever I awoke alone that his mere presence had stopped the tears.

CHAPTER 43

AVERY

Jane swished into the room sometime the next morning. The rising sun peeked in through the curtains and while I had stopped crying, an overwhelming sense of dread settled in. How had I let this happen? How had I been so stupid?

I replayed the events of the last couple of months, and I realized I should have noticed little things that might have led to questions which might have led to the truth. But I was so relieved to be with him, to be safe, to feel heard and comforted, so stupidly desperate, that I'd been willingly blind.

How had the curse made me see everything so differently? How was Nighval spared, but the other rat-people who lived here weren't? I can't believe I'd fallen for it.

And him, a man, a warlock, who was clearly a predator, who loved chasing me, and taking what he wanted, who acknowledged he didn't deserve me, had been the architect of it all. The image of him flashed through my mind. Tall, the overpowering sense of dominance that he exuded, and those scars. Now that I had my memories back, I remembered the first time I'd seen him with them in the library, I had been terrified. His nearly black eyes and all of that power that just radiated off of him. How had I fallen in love with that? *Because he's super hot, and sweet, and gentle, and so utterly male—shut up*, I scolded my wandering thoughts. And why did, in his absence, my chest twist and pinch in such a painful way?

But it hadn't been the first time I succumbed to his dark charms. I'd let him almost ravish me against a tree whenever I knew full well who he was, so maybe I was a bit to blame, too. But that still couldn't make up for the sense of betrayal that seemed to seep into every cell in my body.

Be logical. I needed to think about things in a practical context. The curse was broken along with my heart, and I needed to get the fuck out of here. I knew I promised him I would rule alongside him, but these people weren't my problem. As far as I was concerned, they were guilty of collusion. Not only that, when I got back to my plane, I was going to get on Wikipedia, find out where ole' Walt's grave was, and go there and spit on it. What a complete and total sham.

I was building up the case so firmly in my mind against everyone I believed to be guilty, I winced when Gran Jane said, "Your bath is ready."

I dragged myself out of bed. As I padded by the mirror, I glanced at my reflection. The tip of my nose was an angry red, my eyes were bloodshot, and there were bags underneath them. I never had bags underneath my eyes. The chilly air peaked my stupid nipples, and they were probably wondering where the skilled man who squeezed them so nicely was. I still felt his presence lingering between my thighs. I assessed my backside for marks and thankfully there were none, then ran my fingers through my hair, finding a leaf in all the tangles.

I held it between my fingers for a long moment as Jane stood staring at her feet, waiting patiently. Her eyes flicked up to meet mine. "What are you looking at?" I snapped, and then immediately felt guilty for it. "Sorry."

I crushed the leaf in my hand and tossed it into the wastebasket. The steaming water stung for a moment as I lowered my most sensitive area into it. I leaned back, dipping my hair. Dutifully, Gran Jane poured some shampoo in her hands and began working it through my waves. She paused momentarily, and I glanced up at the mirror sitting on the vanity so I could see her. She looked lost in her thoughts for a moment, as if she had something she wanted to say, but was unsure.

"Just say it, *Jane.* I'm exhausted, and I don't have the energy to play pretend with you. If you have something to say to me, just say it," I said, leaving of the Gran intentionally.

Her lips pressed into a disapproving line, and she continued lathering my hair. "I see that our queen is upset with our king and—"

I spun around her to look at her face. Water and suds sloshed to the tiled floor. "Are you kidding me right now? If you are about to stand up for him, just save it. But why would I expect anything different from any of you since you're all his accomplices?"

Before I knew it was happening, the old woman had my cheeks and her hands, and she had brought me face to face with her. "I will never have a day where I am not grateful to you for finding a place in your heart for that man. Tomorrow, whenever you leave, I will get to see my grandson play with his toys in broad daylight as a little boy because of your big heart. So yes, if you want to hate me and any of the rest of us for following our king's lead and trusting him to do what is best for his people, then I can't stop you. But you are queen now, and instead you are acting like an entitled brat."

"But—" I tried to interject.

"No buts. That man may not be perfect, and you may feel betrayed right now, but he loves you. I have never seen him so transformed. Look at him next time you see him. After eighteen years of women, perfectly flawless women, looking at him with such horror, do you not think he would believe it's true? That he was utterly unlovable. And right now, the woman he has found such a rare gift with, who loves him back, is doing the exact same thing."

"You knew him before the curse?" I asked, speaking my suspicion to life.

Gran Jane nodded, gesturing for me to dip my head back so she could rinse the soap from my hair. A contemplative expression crossed her face and she nodded as she rubbed conditioner through my locks and then pinned it into a bun at the top of my head so it could soak in.

"I did. I worked at this palace my whole life. I was here when that which killed their father, and here to deal with the aftermath of that. The curse affected everyone, but sometimes I think it affected His Majesty the most."

A knot built in my throat, and I tried to swallow it down, but it stuck. "I guess that's a lot of pressure," I said.

"Damn right it is. I can imagine what you're going through isn't easy either, the shock that you must be feeling, but you will come around.

You two need each other," she said, eyeing me with that old wise woman expression I was coming to expect from her.

"Hold on, you said we would leave tomorrow?" I asked, only then sifting that out of everything she had said.

"Yes, now that the curse has been removed, there is much work to do. His Majesty wishes to return to the capital as soon as possible to begin setting our world to rights." Gran Jane squeezed a sponge over my shoulders for the final time and reached for a towel, gesturing for me to stand. I stepped out into it and let her wrap me in a fluffy cocoon.

"Okay," I said, taking over toweling myself off. I wrapped my hair up with a towel and then threw on a robe so I could apply a minimal amount of makeup.

"Will you be taking breakfast with your husband this morning, Your Majesty?" She asked, reverting to a more formal tone. I guess she was done lecturing me. Technically, as queen, I probably shouldn't have tolerated being spoken to that way, but I actually found her frankness refreshing, even if I disagreed. I wasn't being a brat. I was hurt.

"I will," I said. I refused to back down from a challenge, and I would not hide. I would keep my chin high, dine with my husband today, figure out where that bitch of a mother of his lived and then when the time was right during the journey, I would sneak away and find her to let her know exactly what I thought of her blue pill. Then I would force her to send me home.

Dressed, and with a plan of action, I felt determined as I strode from the room.

CHAPTER 44

NIGHVAL

It tore at my soul that I had hurt her, but that scream had gutted me. Of every scar, every injury I had ever experienced, nothing split me in two the way the judgment, the horror in her eyes had. When she'd asked me to send her home, to her plane, the words ripped through my heart like debris from a cyclone.

Still, I thought if she could just see how earnest I was, how honestly and truly I loved her, I could make her see, but that was of no use. She didn't care to hear it. Exactly as my mother had planned. As the memories flooded back and she saw what I had done, her heart had iced over. I knew it would take time for it to thaw, and I was determined to wait it out, but that didn't mean I didn't resent it. Did she think I wanted it to happen as it had? The pill was a last resort. And hadn't I suffered too? Not that my suffering had ever mattered.

If we didn't need to leave within the next day, I would spend the night hunting down the foul things in this world just for the release it would give me.

Avery stomped into the room and before I could stand to hold out a chair for her, she dragged it a few feet back, plopped into it, and scooted forward, glaring at me all the while. I tried to keep a grin from my face, but I could hardly do it. I knew she was angry, and hurt, but she hadn't sent me away last night, which was a triumph, and as my arms had wrapped around her, her tears had waned.

"Good morning, my Wounded Heart. How did you sleep?" I asked.

Her glare darkened into a scowl. "I got a lovely scolding from Gran Jane. Aside from that, I'm fine. Not that you need to be concerned with my state of being."

I couldn't help but chuckle. Jane had worked at the palace for as long as I could remember. The old woman was the closest thing to family I had now. Well, besides my new wife.

I reached over under the corner of the table, hooked my fingers under the lip of her chair and pulled it, so she was closer. As I wrapped my fingers around her wrist, she tried to tug it away, but I held firm. Whenever she finally relented, I used my thumb to rub soothing circles over her pulse point.

"Did any of Jane's wisdom happen to sink in?" I asked her, knowing my taunts would get under her skin. Her eyes narrowed in my direction, and her fingertips edged toward the knife sitting by her plate. We both knew the exact intention of the gesture.

Bringing her wrist to my lips, I kissed it. "We both know you aren't going to do anything with that, sweetheart, so let's not pretend." I kissed her wrist again, this time letting my tongue trace over her throbbing vein. "You are so beautiful when you're angry. And I admire your tenacity." I brought her pointer finger to my lips and placed it between them. She tried to pull away, but I held tight and sucked on the tip of her finger. "We could skip breakfast if you like, and I could fuck you on this table instead." I raised an eyebrow at her.

She gave a forceful yank to her wrist and said, "I'm dry as a bone."

I chuffed. "You're a liar is what you are."

Staff brought in heaping plates of breakfast foods I knew Avery liked and placed them before us. "I figured after last night you would be hungry," I said, nodding to the ridiculous amount of food on her plate.

"Would you please stop talking?" she asked, stuffing a bite of pancake into her mouth.

"Are there other things you would prefer me to do with my mouth?" I asked her.

"What is wrong with you?" she asked, her face screwing up into the cutest agitated expression.

I looked at her with seriousness then. Her eyes softened as she took in my change in tone. "I have never tried to make you think I'm a better man than I am. And I don't wish to disregard or minimize your feelings, but I would do what I did again."

"You're a fiend," she said.

"I am a lot of things. A monster, as you say. But as I walked through my palace this morning, as the sun rose, and saw the faces of my people as human, with sunlight on their skin, I knew I would do it again in a second. I would wound us both again in a second, without hesitation. You and I will recover. That's also the kind of man I am. I will not sit here and allow you to act like you don't like it. That you didn't fall in love with everything that I am. Maybe you saw things differently because of that spelled pill, but you knew who I was at my core, and you gave yourself to me willingly." My blood was thrumming, and I knew if I didn't get out of here, I'd do or say something I'd regret. I was moments away from grabbing her, pulling up her skirt and proving to her exactly how right I was. And I knew she wasn't ready for that.

Wood scraped across the stone floor as I pushed my chair back from the table. "You have the rest of the day to pack. Tomorrow, we leave at dawn." I gave her a last glance as I stormed from the room.

As I got to the door, wrenching it open, she said, "You didn't finish your breakfast."

"I've lost my appetite," I said, slamming the door with a crack behind me.

CHAPTER 45

NIGHVAL

"You mean to tell me you're not going to just magically transport us there? I thought you were powerful," she said, carrying her pack down the staircase that led to the gravel drive the next morning. Attendants followed behind with an overstuffed trunk, and I chuckled, knowing despite her aching chest, she was present of mind enough to pack her many creations.

She dropped the pack at my feet. Even as she looked up at me, somehow, she still looked down her nose. Warm rays from the breaking sun danced across it, making me want to relive what it was like to kiss that beautiful face. I really needed to play my cards right and get back into her good graces soon, so I could do it again.

"We have a few stops to make along the way. I figured the proximity worked for me once before. Perhaps it will work again." I shot her a wink because I couldn't resist.

"You are conniving and despicable," she hissed.

I wanted to press her angry lips to mine. Instead, I held out a hand to help her into the carriage. "I'm being honest as I was before, and you're the one who fell in love with me. What does that say about you?"

She groaned, but I could tell there was an edge of humor in her voice as she put her hand into mine. For this trip, we would take a larger carriage that had an insert to go between the benches so it could transform them into a makeshift bed. I didn't want to use my power because I had some things I needed to do along the way, and I wasn't lying whenever I said I wanted the excuse to be near her. I craved her touch.

"I've been asking myself the same thing. Obviously, I was a fool. But I'm not anymore so no need to worry about that. And since I still have my memories intact, your ruse will not work on me," she said, raising a defiant chin.

I huffed a laugh. "We'll see."

I crawled into the carriage behind her as Eclipse strode up beside it.

"I thought now that you had your magic back all the time, the carriage wouldn't need a horse to pull it?" she asked.

"Eclipse will accompany us, but we will ride in here and the carriage will travel by my power. It doesn't require much."

"So why can't you ride out there on him?" she asked, glaring at me from across the bench.

I moved my hands in the familiar pattern, and the carriage jolted forward. I pulled the curtains back, pinning them so we could enjoy the beautiful countryside as we rode. "We've been over this, Avery. I wish to be in my wife's company as much as possible."

"Well, your wife doesn't wish it." She crossed her arms over her chest and looked out the window.

"You'll come around."

"That's what Gran Jane said, and I assure you I won't."

I sighed. "After I realized the curse was more or less permanent, I spent about six months wallowing. Then one day, I woke up determined, as if something had shifted in the night. The Council of Warlocks met, and that's when we decided to use a binding blood oath to sway the witches who'd yet to respond to our request for aid. The council members collected drops of blood from every warlock we knew of, and I traveled to your plane to meet with the Council of Matrons. I made the oath to the Goddess sealing it with our combined blood. It bound every Warlock to make good on the promise of revenge if the witches didn't produce a witch bride within six months.

The first one's name was Lisa. I told you on the day you married Xavier that she was lovely. I was nineteen and naively hopeful. Back then, I didn't have all of the scars. I met her on the full moon like I did with you, and her eyes brightened as she took me in, realizing I was to be her king. But then when the curse took over, and she saw me transformed, she..." I didn't mean to trail off, but the memory dredged up old painful things I had spent nearly two decades trying to forget.

"She saw you and screamed like I did, didn't she?" Avery asked, filling in the gap. I cleared my throat simultaneously loving and hating that she knew me so well. There was almost a glint of pity in her expression as she watched me. "What happened to her? And the other women?" When I only frowned, she continued, "We have to find them and help them."

I shook my head. "They don't want our help, Avery. And it's in the past. They would have made their way in this world by now, but if any of them come to us asking we'll offer them our aid. I promise." She didn't look satisfied, and I sighed. "My point was, I got over it. And you will, too."

Her eyes watered, and she brought her sleeve up to catch an errant tear. My pain was visceral to her, and I didn't understand why she kept herself from me. How could she flip from her curse-breaking love to this damnable distance? The betrayal lingered like a cloud between us.

How could she not understand, especially after what I told her? After what Jane told me she shared. Could her heart be this hard? Had I broken it that completely? I studied her profile as we rode, sorting through the months we'd been together.

I had branded her heart as she had mine. We were truly one now, but now she hovered at the edges of my reach.

The silence and my wild, running thoughts overwhelmed me. I worked a pattern with my hands, then was riding in the fresh air atop Eclipse.

I gave her space the rest of the day, only interacting with her to take our meals and to slide in the center bench in order to make the bed. I rode outside until the wind picked up, becoming brisk. It took nearly as much power to halt the carriage and restart it, so I cast the spell and a second later, her scent drifted into my awareness.

Her head snapped up in my direction as I reclined inside the carriage at her back. She was shivering and glaring at me. My fingers itched to bring her into my body. "Cold?" I asked.

"I'm fine," she bit out.

"Liar," I said, and gave into my desire, pulling her into my arms as a blanket appeared at my command. Her trembling stopped and, while her body was stiff enough to tell me she would allow no more, she didn't push me away. So, I pulled her closer, and we slept.

CHAPTER 46

NIGHVAL

A week of traveling had done nothing to soften Avery's heart. She was still nearly as angry as she had been the morning after our wedding, and I desperately hoped I hadn't miscalculated. Still, I had things to do and a certain witch to pay a visit to.

"Where are we?" Avery asked, stepping down from the carriage the next morning. I had halted our journey, pulling off of the well-worn dirt road just at the edge of a clearing to our north. A dense woodland sprung up from the open field, dark and ominous, mirroring what lived inside.

Avery eyed the forest and the eight-person guard who joined us the night before. I owed my mother a visit, and I would not take my new bride. Getting her to stay put would be a challenge, but eight highly trained people on horseback ought to be able to keep her in line.

"The Wildwood," I said, raking my hand through my hair. At the word, her attention snagged. Perhaps bringing her this way had been a mistake. I could have brought her to Ravsted and seen to my duties another way, but at least I had been able to hold her every night without resistance. And for now, that was enough. "Don't worry. You're safe. The carriage is warded, and your guard will protect you while I'm gone."

"Wait, you're going to send me into that forest and then leave me?" she asked and made a more detailed sweep of her surroundings before handing me one of the two wraps she made. Now that I had my power back, I could cast the simple spells needed to keep food at a safe temperature on the road, among other things. This was one of the few things that had made my new wife happy, as she, I learned, had very unusual eating habits she claimed were perfectly normal in the witch's plane.

"We will ride together for a distance, and then yes, I have some things in the area I need to attend to. I will be back before nightfall."

"If I am supposed to be your queen, shouldn't I be attending to these things with you?" she asked, stuffing another bite into her mouth.

"We've been over this, Avery. There will be plenty for you to do whenever we reach the castle. Besides, as I recall, the last time you saw me exact my justice, you weren't keen."

"Won't you even tell me what you're doing?" she asked.

I sighed. I spent every day last week cleaning up the messes Xavier created while he'd been in control of Ras alhague. Some of the members of my kingdom required a firm hand. The last thing I needed was for my new wife to see that side of me again. She'd forgiven me about Musson, but she'd been under the influence of the pill's magic then. Now wasn't the time to add any additional strain to our relationship, and I certainly would not let her meet the witch that had cursed her own children.

When I didn't respond, she said, "If you want to rebuild our trust, tell me." A smug expression took root on her pretty face, and she knew she had me. But I wasn't about to give this up without getting something back.

"Let's get on the road. We can discuss this in the carriage." I nodded to the surrounding guard and then held the door open for her, helping her inside.

"I'm getting really tired of sitting," she said. "Another week of this?"

"Tomorrow, we can ride Eclipse. Just bear with this for one more day, okay?"

She nodded as she settled herself on the bench. "So, you were going to tell me what you've been up to, specifically where you are going out there." She peeked out the window. By now, the thick canopy of the forest was blocking out most of the light and the air was still and cool.

Avery shivered as a brisk gust blew in through the window. Her waves lifted on the breeze, and she pulled her cloak tighter around her.

"I will tell you," I said, and she perked up, "but I want something in return."

Her shoulders slumped. "What?"

"Let me kiss you," I said.

"No," she said, not skipping a beat.

"Well, if you're not planning to act like my wife, I don't really see any reason to treat you like an equal partner. I'm a greedy man, Avery. I want it all. A queen, a partner, a lover. Everything I've earned."

My voice had taken on an aggressive glint, and her eyes widened. I continued, "If you want to be included in my world, then I need you to include me in yours. I slipped off the bench, getting to my knees before her. Under her cloak she wore one of the loose shift dresses she favored, claiming they were comfortable for lounging, and this was probably the only time I ever felt grateful for the things.

It was time to move things forward. I ran my hands up her calves, hooking them under her knees, separated them, and yanked her forward so her body was close to mine. She released a small gasp. My hand slid its way up her thigh and my other fished out from under her dress to curl around the base of her neck.

"Kiss me," I demanded, gravelly need apparent in my voice.

Her eyes flashed from mine to my lips and a pained expression crossed her face like it hurt her that she wanted me. And she did want me. I could feel it as her legs trembled on either side of my hips. I leaned forward. She didn't move as my lips brushed hers for the first time since our wedding night. She sat frozen. I broke the kiss, pressing my forehead to hers as I stared into her amber flecked eyes.

"Enough, wife," I growled, and her lips parted. The second she leaned forward, I was on her, crushing my mouth to hers, barely letting her come up for air. With a hand still up her dress, I moved it to her ass and pulled her against my growing need. She moaned into my mouth, then her hands threaded through my hair, traced across my shoulders, down my chest and across the muscles on my sides. Needy fingers made quick work of the buttons of my shirt and then her hands were on my scar covered skin.

I unclasped the cloak from around her neck as I rocked into her. It slid off her shoulders, and I snaked my arm around her waist, lifting her so I could tug the dress from underneath her and up her torso. She lifted her hands as I pulled it off and threw it to the side. "Goddess, Avery. Do you ever wear a bra?"

I consumed her neck and collarbone in a trail down to her peaked nipple. Taking it into my mouth. I sucked and nipped and her grip on my hair tightened. As I moved to the other one, my free hand went to undo my pants. In a second, I had them down my hips and my erection free and ready for her. I had to be inside her.

Pulling away, I took myself and my hand and looked down at her. Her warm skin was a blotchy pink in places from my onslaught and her chest rose and fell in quick breaths. She leaned back slightly, propping herself on her hands, and I pulled her, so her ass was on the edge of the seat. Sliding my finger inside the band of her panties, I moved them aside so I could see her glistening cunt.

Running my finger through it, I said, "Still so fucking wet for me, sweetheart." Avery moaned as I brushed against her swollen clit. "You like that. You want more?"

"Yes," she said, and I knew a part of her hated saying the words. Hated giving in to what was between us, but I didn't care. I was going to take anything she gave me, because she was mine and she needed to know it in the deepest part of her.

With her panties pulled to the side, I lined myself up and then cupped her head, angling it so she could watch me as I penetrated her. "This," I said, smacking her aching center with the tip of my dick, "is mine. *You* are mine, Avery."

"Please," she said, whimpering with need, and I gave her what she wanted, sliding inside until our bodies were flush. But this time I didn't give her time to adjust to the size of me. Pulling back until I was almost fully out, I slammed back in. Again and again as we watched. With every thrust, her breasts bounced, and I couldn't get enough of the sight. I couldn't get enough of how she jolted, making little pleasured sounds every time I fucked into her.

Right when I thought I was going to die from the sensation of it all, she spread her legs wider for me and wrapped them around me, trying to pull me closer with her heels, like she couldn't get me deep enough. I was already fucking her like I wanted to crawl inside her.

Reaching my hand between us, I found her clit and circled, increasing the intensity with every pass until her sharp cry split the cool morning air. That was all it took, and I was spilling myself inside her as violent pleasure shocked its way through me.

When it subsided, I didn't move. I wanted to stay inside her forever with her limbs wrapped around me and my face pressed into the crook of her neck.

"I love you," I said, and placed gentle kisses on that smooth skin then kissed up her jaw and placed a soft kiss on her lips, but froze when they didn't kiss back.

I sat back, concerned that maybe I had hurt her. I brushed a sweaty strand away from her face, scanning it. An icy current surged through my veins as I took her in. "You didn't tell me to stop. You said ye—"

"That's not it," she said, and a flood of relief hit me. "Get off. We shouldn't have done that. It doesn't change anything."

The pain of her rejection lanced away any elation or afterglow I might have felt. As we put ourselves back together, I couldn't help but feel a little piece of my heart harden over.

"Then why did you let me?" I asked. My voice was a weak, wounded thing. Brittle.

"Because I'm a glutton for punishment, obviously. And that was more than a kiss, so you owe me answers." She was angry. At herself or me, I wasn't sure, but it was more than before. I shouldn't have done that. I should have waited. I could practically see the wall going back up, shutting me out.

I slumped back on the bench, resigned to give her what she'd bargained for. "Xavier was only king for a short time, but during that time he and his advisers did some things which aren't important, but they created some dissent. There are a few pockets here and there where lords were showing through their actions that they may not consider themselves under the crown's jurisdiction any longer. Not as bad as Musson, but a few are nearly, so I'm dealing with them."

Avery wrinkled her nose, but I continued. "The curse brought with it a certain heightening of our animal nature. My people evolved. Became more territorial, aggressive, part beast. I may have failed seventeen times, but when I ruled, it was with strength. I did what it took to protect them from each other and themselves."

"Then why did you let Xavier take the eighteenth and final chance?"

I shook my head. "That much failure can shake any man's confidence. I thought maybe the people were right, wanting my brother to have a chance. Maybe we should have done things differently. But that doesn't change the fact that we are here now, the curse is broken, and I am king. I will not tolerate any question of loyalty with my subjects. So, I've been visiting a few of these lords and affirming their loyalty or bringing them to heel."

Avery's throat bobbed. "Does that mean you used force?"

"In some cases." I was silent for long moments, giving her a moment to process the information.

"Did you kill anyone?" she asked.

"Not this time," I said, crossing my arms over my chest. "But I will again. I have killed many. It's not like you have no blood on your hands." I shouldn't have said it, but I did. And I didn't regret it. If she wanted to put me as the bad guy, that was fine. Her love had renewed my confidence, brightened my dark soul, and I knew I would win her back. It was only a matter of time. I just hoped I still had a heart to give her when it happened.

She didn't even flinch at my accusation, however, as if she'd made peace with what had transpired between her and Xavier. She only said, "Tell me where you're going today. Another lord to threaten?"

"I'm going to meet with my mother. I told her I would come when the curse was broken. It was a part of the deal. I expect she wants to see me suffer. I think the only reason she gave me the pill was because she could see I had feelings for you."

"Oh," she said, and her brow furrowed in concern. "I'll go with you."

"No," I said, and worked the spell to slow the carriage with my hands.

"But—"

"I've already told you more than I wish to. You're not going. The last thing we need is for you to fall under her scrutiny and become a part of her machinations. You're safer here, so please, just stay in the carriage until I get back, okay?" I gave her a pleading look as I stepped down from the carriage.

When she begrudgingly nodded, I looked at the forest's canopy, hoping to get a gauge of the time. From what I saw, the sun was nearly overhead. I motioned for a female guard to approach. "Her Majesty needs a moment of privacy in the woods. I will give her a half hour. Stretch your legs and take care of your needs. Then the carriage will move, see that she is on it."

"Yes, Your Majesty," the guard said. "I will see that she is back in the carriage by then. You have my oath."

I nodded and then turned to see Avery struggling to retrieve her pack as Eclipse approached. The hard set of her jaw told me she wasn't happy that I would be leaving her behind.

"Here," I said, lifting the pack from the back of the carriage, assuming she needed some fresh undergarments. "I'll be back by nightfall, and I'll tell you what transpired. Sufficient?"

A deadpan stare was all I received in response. It was foolish of me, but I leaned forward, needing to kiss her one last time before facing my mother. My lips were met with a cool cheek, and a wife who turned away.

As I mounted Eclipse, she eyed me and said so only I could hear, "That won't happen again."

I barked out a laugh. "I'll enjoy proving you wrong once again, my queen." Then I nudged Eclipse, and we rode away toward my mother's wards.

CHAPTER 47

AVERY

What an arrogant bastard. What had I been thinking? There was something about that man that made me stupid crazy with lust. My thoughts continued to swirl as I trudged through the dense forest in search of somewhere to change that would give me a little privacy from the guard who shadowed me.

After walking about five minutes in the direction Nighval had ridden off, I scanned the area, noting the guard was within view. "Would you mind giving me some privacy?"

I thrust an angry finger in the direction of the carriage and the woman gave me a knowing smile and turned to give me space. "I won't be far. If you need anything, just shout," she called over her shoulder.

"Thanks," I yelled back. As if I'd need anything from these people. His people. I plopped my backdown in a little clear area between two massive pines and knelt in the bed of soft needles, opening the zipper to fish out a change of clothes.

How dare he not let me go with him to see his mother? The curse affected me, too, so I deserved to go. I had a whole litany of things to say to that witch and my husband had no intention of ever giving me that closure.

A breeze picked up, blowing in the direction Nighval had gone and it almost felt like a beckoning. Did Samara sense I was here, in the Wildwood? I knew she made her home somewhere in this dense forest, but I didn't know where. From what I recalled from when I'd tried to run from Xavier, there was a town shown on the map about ten miles off the road which ran through the center of the Wildwood which must be where she lived. Now, because of Nighval, I knew the direction.

I slipped out of my dress and soiled panties, pulled on a fresh pair and opted for leggings and a sweater. I was about to slip on my flats when a bulge in the pack reminded me that I had packed my boots in it. An idea struck. I glanced in the direction of the carriage. The guard was still out of sight.

Just because Nighval didn't take me, didn't mean I couldn't go. And maybe she'd send me home. My heart pinched at the thought of leaving my husband, but it wasn't real. None of it had been. Sure, he enjoyed my body, but who did what he'd done? When he'd given me that pill, the anger, and bitterness on his face was undeniable. I wasn't sure who it had been directed at, me or the people about to execute me, but now I no longer cared.

My heart thundered as I laced up my boots. I threw my cloak over my shoulders and hoisted up my pack. I needed to slip away quickly. The guards would be after me soon.

My boots nimbly hit the forest floor as I took off in a dead sprint. I could probably run full out for about ten minutes, maybe more, before I'd have to slow to a jog. Back in Miami, I'd done some fun runs and my record time was sub eight minutes for a mile, and I could do a five-kilometer race at that pace. But now I was in heavy leather boots and carrying a large pack. Still, in about twenty minutes, I'd be nearly three miles from the carriage. How far could the witch's home be?

Hearing my name called from a distance drew my attention away from the seconds I focused on counting as I ran. They'd given me longer than I expected before they started searching for me. I felt a little guilty, as I heard the female call out, "The king will kill us if we've lost you. Please, Your Majesty..."

Her voice trailed off as I ate up more ground and a guilty twinge nipped at me. I knew Nighval would be furious when he returned to learn I wasn't there or when I showed up at his mother's home without his permission. But perhaps it would be better if he wasn't there. Then I could bargain with her.

I suspected my husband was strong enough to send me between planes with ease, but was keeping that from me. It had to have something to do with him having both a warlock and witch's blood.

I'd been thinking about the Metonic moon cycle. I was almost certain it had played a part in his birth or his conception—Samara wouldn't have failed to use that. She seemed like an incredibly calculating woman much like her son, though her end goal remained a mystery to me.

But if Nighval was right and his suffering was her goal, then what better way to create it than sending me back to my plane? I was ready to cut my losses and be done with this. Hell, maybe I'd move to another country and start anew when I got back. Move to Italy and find an actual mafia man. Wait, that was actually a terrible idea. I already had a guy that was something to that effect, and I was running from him.

I hated the way that thought made my chest ache. I promised to rule beside him and after the way he'd been in the carriage as I'd stupidly let him in for a brief glimmer of time, his claim had been so intense. Would he tear a hole in the planes to get me back?

No, he wouldn't. Because if he did, that would have to mean—no. I wouldn't think about that. I wouldn't surrender no matter how big of a sob story he told, or how good the sex was. Or how comforted I'd felt in his arms, telling him my darkest secrets.

The week-old ache welled up in my chest and a tear spilled over the edge of my eyelid before I could brush it away. I had to be five miles now. I stopped and leaned against a tree to catch my breath. I no longer heard voices still searching, and the carriage had to be long gone by now.

What was I doing? More tears fell. He loved me. The thought bored a hole right through me. He'd messed up and went about it in the wrong way, but we fell in love and saved an entire plane of people from living as monstrous rat people for the rest of their lives. How could I be so stubborn?

My grief brought me to my knees. I saw that look on his face as I'd screamed like all the others had. And again today, when I'd pushed him away. Ever since his mother put that curse upon them, every incident seemed designed to chip a little more away from his heart. Yet it was still big enough to love me. Now here I was running again, either toward her or away from him, I wasn't sure.

Shit. Even if I ran the five miles back, he'd know what I'd done.

Panic gripped hot claws around my throat.

Leaves rustled nearby. Too close. My head snapped up in the sound's direction. *Help me, Goddess.* A six-foot wraith-like creature slithered across the ground not ten feet from me and gaining in my direction. Nighval warned me to stay in the carriage. Did he know about these things?

Slowly, I rose to my feet, lifting a hand, palm facing it to let it know I wasn't a threat. "It's okay, I'm leaving." I'd heard of witches using spectral beings as barrier protections. Maybe these things were tied to the wards Nighval referred to that surrounded the edge of his mother's land.

Two inky black, barely corporeal shapes appeared behind it. Each figure was humanoid in a blurry way and identical. Three more rose from the ground, and I realized they were appearing, encircling me.

If these were Samara's creatures, maybe they would take me to her, and I could explain to Nighval if he was still there. Or maybe they were spelled to kill on sight. When the first one, as if sensing my questions, bared its pointed black wraith teeth that definitely looked like they could sink into flesh, I had my answer. They advanced, and I ran.

I was unsure of which direction I was going. All I knew was I headed away from the deadly things that slithered across the forest floor behind me. The deeper I went into the forest, the more brambles and briars I encountered, but the pine floor was soft and easy to run on. I darted around a tree, and my cloak caught on a thorn, tearing. I tugged, ripping the fabric free, and continued.

Had I not already worn myself out trying to escape the guards, I might have been able to make it. Exhaustion and my heavy backpack were weighing me down. A clawed hand swiped and caught one of the dangling straps, but I jerked sideways, and it lost its grip.

Another swipe and it caught hold again. In a swift move, I unclasped the buckle at my chest and thumbed the backpack, all my precious possessions gifted to me by my aunt, off my shoulders. The backpack hit the ground with a thud and lighter now, I hooked a left in the direction I believed the road to be.

My lungs felt like I'd drank battery acid, and the raw sensation deep in my stomach told me I couldn't continue much longer at this speed. As it was, my legs were jelly, becoming sluggish. The toe of my boot caught on a tree root, and I didn't have the strength to skip forward and land on my feet. My ankle twisted, and I went down hard. The air left my lungs in a whoosh, and I rolled, popping up on my feet.

Adrenaline must have shielded me from the initial pain, because when I stepped on my twisted ankle, fire shot up my leg and it barely would bear any weight. Glancing over my shoulder, the wraiths neared, surrounding me. I hobbled to the nearest pine tree. Its trunk was about a foot around and limbs about as big as the head of a baseball bat jutted out in every direction. I could climb them like a ladder. I wasn't sure if the things could follow me off the ground. It was worth a shot.

I scrambled up the tree, pulling myself up with my arms and steadying myself with my good foot. The wraiths hissed at the base as they watched me climb, but didn't follow. Their arms were like Gumby's though, long and stretchy, and one swung, catching on my boot. The sound of its claw scraping down the leather made a scream tear from my throat, but I managed to kick it off and scamper up a few more branches out of their reach.

Since I'd fled, the light coming in through the few holes in the dense canopy dimmed. Outside, it may still be daylight, but inside it appeared as if it was past dusk. So much so that the glowing blue that suddenly appeared drew every eye in the vicinity.

A wraith shrieked as a neon dagger flew end over end and pierced its throat. My eyes darted in the direction it came from. In a whirl of black was Nighval, hands out, palms face up, glowing with blue fire, or more like power, essence. He was fury unbound, his black hair moving with every turn as his blue light became a sword, slicing through wraith after wraith.

My husband was terrifying, deadly, and incredible. Beautiful, and he was going to be livid with me, but I'd never felt more in love. The limb I was leaning on groaned and snapped. I plummeted toward the ground, smacking branches as I fell. When I thudded on the soft ground, Nighval shot me a glare as if my fall was a distraction. Then his palms unfurled, and two glowing balls shot out, slamming into the chest of the final two wraiths.

He stormed over to where I lay beneath the tree next to the broken branch and crossed his arms. "Wow," I said. I was married to an action hero, albeit a darkish one.

There was no love or affection in his black eyes as they glared down at me. "Get up," he bit out between his teeth.

"I can't. My ankle," I said, gesturing to where I could already feel swelling inside my boot. I needed to get it off soon or it would be more painful. I unlaced my boot and tried to tug it off, but the angle hurt too much.

"What are you doing?" he asked, still not budging from his towering stance.

"I have to get it off before it swells too much. Here, help me," I said, and he immediately scoffed.

"Don't be an ass, Nighval. Grab the heel of my boot." He approached, and I held my foot out to him and he palmed the shoe. "Gentle," I said, and he swiftly yanked, ignoring my warning and white flashed across my vision, but the boot was off.

"Is it broken?" he asked, only looking mildly concerned, as he knelt down at my feet. An oily substance was splattered across the black attire he was wearing, which I only now realized was made from thick leather.

"No, I think sprained." Angry purple bruises were erupting, and swollen tissue engulfed the little bone, which usually jutted out on both sides.

"I take it no more running then?" he asked, and a smug grimace played across his features. He was hurt, and he was going to act this way, like he did to the other women who pushed them away, to me now. My hand went to my stomach. I was going to be sick.

Leaning over, I heaved, but nothing came from my empty stomach. Nighval only watched, disinterested.

When I righted myself as the sensation passed, he asked, "Are you finished?" He stood, assessing the stains on his clothing, and leaned down, holding out a hand to me. I took it and in a swift movement, he yanked me up and over his shoulder like a sack of grain.

"What are you doing?" I asked, and instead of an answer, I received a stinging smack on my ass.

"Shut up," he said, and must have been working his hands because a moment later, we were standing in the intense late afternoon sun on the steps of Ravsted.

Scarred human faces were everywhere, many who gasped as their sovereign and his queen materialized before their eyes. He didn't address them as he made for the steps.

"This isn't how I envisioned this going," he grumbled as he strode up the stairs, taking them two at a time.

My chest thudded against his back with each step, but I managed to ask, "What exactly did you envision?"

Our subjects sat on the stairs, and on the landing, dipping their bare feet in the two fountains which sat on either side of the main entry to the castle. They were operational now, and I wondered if he had done that for me or if someone on the Council of Warlocks had already been to work on the castle, restoring it while we traveled.

No one made eye contact with me as we passed, but their gaze fixated on him, mouths ajar, and I could only imagine the smug smile he wore. The predator and his prey, hunted, captured, delivered. Even as undignified as I felt, I could still appreciate what a man he was, the pride, strength, and sheer sense of will with which he carried himself.

He didn't speak until we crossed the threshold and the guards nodded as we entered, one stepping in front of him to clear the way.

Once we made it to a familiar corridor and we were alone, he said, "I thought maybe you would be in a beautiful dress befitting of your station, with a crown on your head. I'd wear mine and we would walk hand in hand up the stairs, announcing to the world that you, my love, were the new queen and my wife."

"But instead, I'm in a tattered cloak with a damaged ankle and you're in gore covered battle leathers carrying me over your shoulder like a fresh kill." I could almost laugh at the irony.

Nighval chuckled, sensing it. "This will make a far better story in the long run, and honestly, I think it is just as effective, if not more. Do you think anyone will question my authority after rumors of our grand entry spread?"

"No," I said, resigned to my husband's primal need to be the alpha. To put me in my place after I had wounded him by running. Apparently, some of the animal stayed in them after the curse was lifted, so I'd give him today, but if he thought he could do this regularly, he had another think coming.

He stormed into the room I had occupied when I'd first arrived and dropped me onto the bed. "Your things will be here in a few days when the carriage arrives. Until then, you'll have to make do."

"My backpack," I said, only now remembering I had to abandon it and would probably never see it again.

Nighval groaned. "Don't tell me you lost it in the Wildwood?"

"It doesn't matter," I said, as the ache in my ankle and chest coalesced into an overwhelming sensation of pain and tears burst forth from my eyes. "I'm sorry," I said, wiping my cheeks with the corner of my cloak.

Nighval gave me a hard look, sat on the bed, and took my ankle in his lap. His hand made signs around it, occasionally touching the swollen tissue with his fingers until the swelling was reduced by half and the purple bruises had become an ugly yellow. The pain was significantly decreased when he stood and walked to the door without turning back.

"Nigh, I'm sorry," I said, as more tears fell.

He stopped short, but didn't move to face me. "Don't bother with an apology. You ran from me, Avery. From me. And it's worse because you knew what that would do to me." He spun then and the look on his face, the agony, gutted me. "Do you have any idea how humiliating it was to hear from the witch who had cursed me, my own mother, that my wife was being chased by her wards through her land?"

I shook my head because there was nothing I could say.

"Answer me!" he said.

"I know. It was a mistake. I wanted to see her, but you wouldn't let me. I needed to—"

"You needed to what? Beg her to send you back?" I flinched as he said the damning words, and his expression showed me he saw the truth of it. He shook his head, the gesture a defeated thing. "A heart for a heart, Avery. If that's what you wanted, it worked. You win. You fucking shattered mine."

I jumped up from the bed, tearing off my cloak, rushing over to him. He held his arm out, and a glowing blue wall of his power stopped me from coming any closer. "Nigh," I begged.

"Don't call me that. Go to sleep. If I could send you back tonight, I would, but you're stuck here until my power has regenerated. I'll want to be at full strength since I've never crossed the planes with anyone else, which will probably take a week or two. Tomorrow, we'll figure out where you can live until then. I need to rule from here, so probably the palace."

"But—"

"It doesn't matter." He waved me off and walked out the door. It shut with a click, and I took a testing step. He'd released me. When I opened the door and stuck my head out into the hallway, he was gone.

It was all I could do to make it to the bed, and crawl inside its warmth. How did I end up here? When the curse was broken, I felt betrayed, shocked, but had that really been heartbreak? And if it was, what was this? The thing inside my chest which kept relentlessly beating was a charred heap, raw, and tore open with each thud. It had taken trying to run away to make me realize I'd been wrong to keep pushing him away. To understand what he'd done, and that he loved me. Too late because I didn't see how we could recover from this. I didn't see what I could do to melt the thick enamel which now encased his shattered heart.

And like I'd wanted, he planned to send me back. A sob gurgled up, and I tried to swallow it down. I really did, but another followed it too closely they both spilled out, followed by an onslaught. Finally, I realized I landed exactly where I needed to be, with the man I loved, who loved me back, and in the position I'd desired and the wish I'd been asking on and off for the better part of a year would be coming true soon. I couldn't leave him. I had to do something to convince him I saw how wrong I'd been.

The bed felt like it could suck me into its depths, like my hopelessness swallowing me whole. I lay there drifting in and out of sleep, tears ever present, but always waiting for him to come. He'd never left me to suffer alone before, but part of me knew this time it was different. He wasn't coming.

CHAPTER 48

AVERY

I awoke with steadfast determination. I would not let him send me back. I threw the covers off even before any attendants roused me and opened the curtains. Somewhere in all of my wallowing clarity had struck. I was a queen. I had a responsibility to my people, and I had a husband who desperately needed me. Who loved me. We had hurt each other, and I found a way to get over the sting of his betrayal. He would do the same in time. And until then, I would put my acting skills to work and play the role of a badass queen. At least the place was clean now, so I was already one step ahead.

The door creaked on its hinges and April's familiar face popped in. I grinned at her broadly. I didn't know if she knew what transpired between me and the king. Actually, who was I kidding? I was sure everyone knew about our entry spectacle. But I didn't give a flying fuck.

"April," I said, striding over to her and taking her hands in mind. "It is so lovely to see you. I was in need of a familiar face, and we have work to do."

She stepped back, blinking, and followed me into the bathroom.

Alice came in shortly after her and in an hour my girls had me cleaned, dressed, and I had even allowed them to apply a selection of makeup from this plane to my face. I assessed myself in the mirror. Aside from my puffy bloodshot eyes, I looked damn good.

The first order of business would be to redecorate this room, if this is where I was going to stay, and it was for the time being because I would not let Nighval send me back to the palace. Eventually I expected we would share the same room, but I knew forgiving me would take time.

In the meantime, this would be a beautiful space for me to live in and then a guest room one day. Or perhaps a nursery.

I surveyed the room. "April, Alice," I called. They both scurried out of the bathroom at my request. Curiosity danced in April's eyes, while the timid Alice wrung her hands at her waist.

"I want these curtains removed and replaced immediately. The inner curtain should be shear and cream, the outer lilac velvet floor-to-ceiling." I turned to the bed and the large rug that lay beneath it. "Get rid of that rug. I want six to ten samples of floral rugs and shades of cream and other pastels. Same with the bedding, but that should be all cream and in varying textures. Bring a selection of throw pillows."

"But His Majesty said that you would be returning to the palace today," April said, voice cracking.

"His Majesty is mistaken," I said, and gave them another more forceful smile that let them know I was, in fact, the boss.

"And what of the furniture, Your Majesty?" Alice asked.

"Leviticus owes me quite a few favors, assuming His Majesty hasn't gutted him." I looked at the women who appeared taken aback. "He is still here, is he not?"

"Yes, Your Majesty," April replied. "I believe he and the other advisors are meeting in the council room with the king this hour."

"Perfect," I said, and without another word, strode from the room.

While I was absolutely confident and determined to go through with my mission. The room I walked into gave me pause. It didn't matter how I felt, though. I was channeling a badass queen.

There were no empty seats at the table which held twelve men, including my husband. *Typical.* Nighval's eyes tracked me as I entered. Mine passed him, landing on Leviticus. This man had watched me kneel in blood and was prepared to watch my head get lopped off after telling me I deserved worse. When they had caught me trying to escape after I had accidentally murdered Xavier, he hadn't flinched before throwing me in prison, so I would not flinch now. I understood he'd reacted as any advisor to a *murdered* king would, yet my grudge toward him held firm, and I wasn't going to bypass my desire to assert my authority.

Holding my chin high, I walked over to him and addressed him directly. "Get up," I said, and the room went silent.

"Pardon?" he said, as if he didn't hear me. His muddy brown eyes widened as he took me in. I had the girls weave the crown into a braid at the top of my head so there would be no question about my authority. The lower half of my hair hung and loose waves down my back. I wore a demurrer cream dress that had long fitted sleeves, a scoop neck and hugged my figure, flaring slightly at my lower hips. It swished with its own command as I walked.

"I didn't stutter." I gave him a wicked grin. He glanced between me and Nighval. My husband only raised a single brow as if this entertained him and he didn't remove his eyes from me.

Leviticus shuffled to his feet, holding the chair out for me. "Of course, Your Majesty. I'll send for another chair."

I took the seat to the right of my husband offered to me by the cowering man, who would now become my errand boy. "No need. I have some tasks for you."

"Your Majesty?" he asked, shuffling between his feet as his voice cracked.

"I'm sure you remember whenever you offered me your services. I know a lot had happened since then, but I imagine the offer still stands?" I asked, piercing him with my gaze. I would have melted him if I could. This humiliation would be sufficient, however.

Nighval had told me about him, how he'd squirmed his way into Xavier's council. I didn't think he was unscrupulous per say. More ambitious and self-seeking. My wise husband had always held the man at arm's length, but now that he had been assigned to the council, it would be difficult to remove him without just cause, so I figured this little scene and his subsequent busy work I was planning to give him would keep him occupied.

"Of course," he said. "I live to serve." He forced a smile, and I got the sense that he knew exactly what I was doing.

"Good. After lunch, I would like to meet with the best furniture and tapestry makers. Bring in designers or whatever you have in this plane.

The state of Ravsted is unacceptable. I understand the warlocks will be seeing to its maintenance, but any changes to the decor will be done by me."

"But, Your Majesty, I understood that you would be returning to the palace. You—"

I cut him off. "It seems there is some misinformation flying around, so let me clarify that for you. My husband, and I weighed that as an option when we considered how best to restore this kingdom." I reached across the table and wrapped my fingers around Nighval's cold wrist. He didn't recoil which I considered a win. "We have decided there is much work to do here, so I will be staying indefinitely to rule by his side. Now go and do as I ask."

As Leviticus shuffled out of the room, I turned and addressed each of the remaining men. "I'm Avery," I said. "Your new queen."

CHAPTER 49

NIGHVAL

I thought my chest was going to burst open as the most beautiful woman I had ever seen stormed into the council room with all of the authority of the Goddess herself. With her gold crown and that cream colored gown offsetting her glowing golden skin, she looked the part and as she commanded Leviticus out of his seat, I could have sworn my soul left my body.

When her warm fingers clasped my wrist, I didn't understand how a broken heart could still beat the way mine was relentlessly pounding in my chest. When she removed them, it was like she had removed something that was intrinsic to my person, and I felt the loss acutely. I wanted her to put her hand back, the sadist that I was. I didn't care that she'd hurt me. I knew her running was no less than what I deserved for what I'd done to her.

I couldn't even hold on to my anger. She'd hardly spoken to me for over a week as she marinated in hers. All it took was a single touch, and I was back under her spell, willing to forgive her. That was how weak I was. But instead of revealing it, I wanted to see what she would do. Somewhere in the night, she had transformed into the steely creature, and I was desperate for more of it.

I was king. I could swoop her out of her chair, mid-council introductions, take her to my room and let her know exactly how forgiven she was. Or better, send the men away and take her on this table and make sure everyone knew our relationship had made it through. But with my power, we would have long, and healthy lives, and I'd have time to do that later. Now I wanted to watch her. Savor her, making her point, showing me what a divine queen she would be for me. Showing me all the reasons to keep her by my side.

The men finished introducing themselves, and I finally spoke. "Those four you haven't met are warlocks, if you didn't guess. Plus Link, they make up the Council of Warlocks. These five, plus Leviticus—" I gestured to the men on the opposite side of the table from her. "—are the human council. We were just discussing how best to move forward with the restoration of Ras alhague now that our power is returned to us."

"Very good," she said. "My focus will be on the castle and its grounds to start. I'm sure the crown had a level of responsibility for the public areas of Ras alhague, but the more we can spread our coin around in our restoration efforts, the better off my subjects will be. As I am unfamiliar with much of your plane, I'll humbly consider any direction or advice you may offer and am grateful for the opportunity to work beside you during this process."

Several members of the council sat slack-jawed and a few of the mages eyed me with a new level of respect, including Eshan who Avery hadn't met.

Link, who hardly ever met a female he couldn't charm, said, "We're honored to be in your company, Your Majesty. And you have my respect. Anyone who can tame our ruthless king is an ally of mine." He said it, of course, for show in front of the others. They'd formed a tentative friendship in her time here before.

I knew the look he gave her wasn't meant to ruffle my feathers, but I wanted to throttle him as my wife blushed beneath his gaze. She'd never seen him in his human form. I cleared my throat and gave him a pointed look. "Thank you Link. Please, let us continue."

The amount of work to do was mountainous, but after two and a half hours, a plan slowly took form. When we broke for lunch, Avery strode from the room without looking back. I sat at the head of the table until everyone but Link and Eshan remained.

"It's nice to finally meet the woman who has your balls," Eshan said, as he stood stretching out his lean form and the three of us exchanged a look before they burst into laughter at my expense.

"I hope you two are lucky enough to meet a woman like Avery one day. And I'll be the one laughing as she tightens the vice."

CHAPTER 50

AVERY

I shouldn't be listening. It was wrong, but I couldn't resist. After I had left, I changed my mind and doubled back, thinking of how he had been so amiable during the meeting and inclusive of my ideas. And no one had even brought up what happened with Xavier. It was as if it hadn't even happened at all. Maybe now was a good time to bring up some other concerns I had. Namely, the ridiculous amount of testosterone on the panel and the barbaric practice of beheading.

But when I passed through the hallway and crossed every member, but the two who I knew to be his longtime childhood friends, hearing them conversing inside, I couldn't help but listen. Little did they know I did not, in fact, have a hold of his balls, or any other part of him at the moment.

I heard shuffling from the inside of the room, but it didn't sound like footsteps were approaching. They must be adjusting from sitting for so long.

"I thought since the curse ended, she hated you?" Eshan asked, piquing my attention.

Nighval sighed. "Have you ever met a woman who drives you mad and brings you to your knees at the same time?" He paused. "That is what I married."

My heart leapt into my throat.

"If she becomes too much for you, I'd be glad to take on the challenge," Link said.

"If you look at her again, the way you did in the meeting today, I'll rip your heart out, understand?" I couldn't tell if Nighval was kidding. Maybe spying on the warlocks wasn't such a great plan.

"Don't get your feathers ruffled, Nighval. You know Link is only taunting you, right Link?" Eshan said.

"Honestly, she is extraordinary. I didn't know you had it in you to get such a specimen to fall for you. I thought we were doomed," Link said. His voice held that slippery seduction I'd come to understand was his personality. It definitely matched his fully human appearance. With his angular features, cool light skin, shoulder-length pale blond hair, and sparkling grey eyes, he'd be a shoe in for a scarred, after the war Draco Malfoy role, assuming he could act.

"I can't believe you got Samara to give you that pill. After Xavier was killed, I thought I was stuck that way forever. When I felt my magic come back to me, I dropped to my knees and wept," Eshan said, and my heart squeezed.

Eshan, Nighval's other dear friend, seemed to be the polar opposite of Link in appearance with his deep umber skin, and the tight curls he wore cropped close to his skull. He came across more reserved than either Link or Nighval and his thoughtful hazel eyes seemed to hold an entire world behind them like those people who call themselves old souls. I wondered if the comparatively fewer scars he had marring his skin was due to his gentler nature.

I remembered Link from before, now that the pills effect was gone, and I was glad to finally meet Eshan. I hoped they both would be around regularly so I could get to know them.

"Do you think now that we have all this power, we could kill Samara?" Nighval asked.

"I don't know. She's powerful. More so now than she was whenever she cursed an entire plane," Link said. "What did you have to give up to get the spelled pill?"

"Well, outside of a lot of groveling, I had to promise to visit her once a week for the rest of my life. Now, do you understand why I want her dead? The witch wants to watch my heart bleed out of my chest weekly, like hers had."

"Does Avery know?" Eshan asked.

"No." His voice dripped with hurt. He didn't speak for a while and neither did the two other warlocks. "The day before we returned, she ran. She wanted to leave me. To find Samara and have her send her back to her own plane."

"Goddess, Nighval," Eshan said, and though I couldn't see him, I could imagine the man placing a comforting hand on the other's shoulder. The warmth in his voice told me much of his character.

"Would you believe me if I told you I haven't spoken a word to her since I delivered her to her room yesterday late afternoon? I have no idea what's going on inside her head. I didn't know she'd do that today. Honestly, I'm afraid of what she'll say. Does that make me a coward?"

"No," Link said, and huffed. "She gutted you. She had to know what it would do to you, and she did it anyway. That's some cold shit."

"Link," Nighval growled in warning. "She is my wife and your queen. I would watch my tongue if I were you. Besides, it's my fault, not hers. She's only reacting to my betrayal."

I didn't need the reminder as chills prickled across my skin. It was too much. The way he was taking the blame for my misguided actions to protect me. If I heard anymore, the tears would come back, and I needed to head to the kitchens to have my first of many meetings with the cooks. Then hopefully Leviticus would have the meetings lined up for me, and I could get to work. That was what I needed to distract me until my husband forgave me.

Eshan was saying something about Nighval needing to talk to me as I slipped away down the hall. I could only hope my actions this morning had been enough to keep him from taking me back to the palace.

I reached the doorway which led into the kitchen when I heard my title being spoken by a male voice. I paused and flattened myself against the wall as my breath caught. Something about the man's tone gave me pause.

I'd met the head cook on a few occasions during the months I'd been here before. Then Nickola had eagerly taken his new queen's menu suggestions, but based on the grumble in his voice he wasn't as keen now as he said, "But His Majesty has never had a problem with the food I served before."

The edges of my lips quirk downward. Had he only been playing along nice before because everyone had been coddling me in hopes I would break the curse?

He continued, "It's only that my cooks aren't used to the strange food she prefers. When she was here before, I spent half my time experimenting with recipes and training them. We hardly have enough staff to cover that extra labor meeting her needs would require."

That's when a decidedly whiny female *humph* joined the chorus. Olive. Why on earth was she still here? "I agree with Cook. Why do we have to change our ways for her?"

Leviticus let out an extended sigh. "Nickola, all I am asking is that you meet with her and try to make some accommodations. We can see to adding the additional staff you require. Our king has made the witch his bride and things will go much more smoothly for all of us if we complied. It seems she is here to stay and if you remember, His Majesty does not rule with a lax hand the way his brother did."

I knew exactly what Leviticus was referring to. I watched my husband execute two people without blinking for speaking ill of me.

"You mean to tell me that that woman can get away with killing a king and then come in and order your staff around?" Olive asked, an insistent demand in her voice.

"Firstly, they are His Majesty's staff. I am only tasked with managing them. Second, I am unsure His Late Majesty's welcome will be extended to you now that the new queen and reinstated king are in residence."

Olive huffed. "You can't kick me out. Where else will I go?"

"That is not my concern, but I think you should make haste with your plans to do so before His Majesty catches wind of your presence and does so himself. You should bear in mind our king's power has been fully returned to him, and I imagine he will be very protective of his new bride."

My heart was thundering so loud in my head that it was almost hard to hear them over its roaring beat. I could hardly believe Olive was still living here, much less thought she might have some sort of sway with any of the council members. At least, Leviticus seemed to understand where his loyalties lied.

"If I may interject, there is wisdom in your words, Sir, and I will be sure to pass them along to the staff in my care," Nickola said, which made a little of the tension which had been building in my neck ease.

Unfortunately, Olive didn't seem to have received the message because she shrieked, "But she killed my love. Is no one going to do anything?"

"A word of caution Olive. It seems our queen was telling the truth at her claim that she was defending herself. His Majesty was quite adamant about that in the meeting this morning and he will not permit any sentiment to the contrary. Our queen is also a curse breaker and has the heart and the ear of our warlock king. Sir Robert Musson and his son, if the rumor is to be believed, were executed on the spot for their disparaging words about Her Majesty. So, as you make your way out of the castle, I would urge you to seal your lips," Leviticus said. It was finally enough that Olive spoke no more.

Urgent heel strikes snapped into the stone getting louder, so I peeled myself off the wall and made to seem like I was just approaching the doorway. We met under its arch and Olive's tan skin blanched as her gaze met mine. Then as if surprising herself, she dipped into a low curtsey, murmuring, "Your Majesty."

"Olive," I greeted. As she rose there was an unmistakable tremble in the hands she clasped at her waist. Before, when I bumped into her in the hallways she had been much more confident, smug even. This was the woman who encouraged Xavier to force me, which had gotten him killed. I hardly knew what to say, but I was her queen so I had to say something. Or at least dismiss her from my presence.

I think I was as startled as she was, so I said the only thing I could think to say which was the truth. "I'm surprised to see you here still. With Xavier gone, I didn't think you had a reason to stay." The implication was clear. *Leave.*

My claws had accidentally slipped out and a look of horror flashed across her face as it became apparent we both understood exactly what I was talking about. Her delicate hand came to her mouth and her auburn ringlets bounced as she bobbled, unable to speak. I stared at her until she finally found her words and said, "If I may, I was actually just leaving, Your Majesty."

I gave her a polite smile and said, "You may," though *please do* was on the tip of my tongue. With that, she scampered away down the hall, and I entered the kitchen.

Eyeing Nickola, I said, "I trust Leviticus has prepared you to expect some changes." I figured it was best to just rip the Band-Aid off, and I might as well use what I had overheard to my benefit. "I gather that the changes I plan to make will require additional staff so Leviticus and I will see to providing that for you right away. I know you must be excited to learn something new."

Nickola blinked a few times in stunned silence as I plastered a smile on my face and shifted my attention to Leviticus who was giving me a knowing grin. Yep, he knew I heard them speaking. The man was a total politician, as was my initial suspicion. And I was glad that he knew I overheard them because that meant we knew where each other stood and that would make the rest of what I planned to do that much easier.

"Of course, Your Majesty," Nickola said, holding out his arm to welcome me into his domain.

"Great," I said. "Let's get started."

CHAPTER 51

NIGHVAL

A very had been working tirelessly for a week now, meeting with nearly every merchant in the city and nearly all the castle staff. I hated to think of the bills that were coming, but it made her happy and driven. And while it would be a considerable sum, technically, we had the coin. Maintenance had fallen by the wayside during the nineteen years of the curse, and our coffers were full.

I was due for my weekly meeting with my mother, and I wanted to see my wife once more before I left. Something about being in her presence bolstered my mood, even though we hadn't officially reconciled yet. She seemed pleased enough I hadn't sent her back to the palace and we hadn't broached the topic of sending her back to her plane. It was like she planned to ignore it until it went away, and I was still enjoying watching her.

She ran her hands through her hair as I approached and continued pacing in front of several design boards lined against a wall in the sitting room she'd transformed into an office.

"Good afternoon," I said.

"Oh, hi, Nighval," she said, not removing her attention from her work.

Since I yelled at her, she had taken to using my full name again, and every time she said it, it was a reminder we needed to reconcile. That I needed to pull her back into my arms, and forgive her. But she was done apologizing, and she seemed so unaffected that I didn't know what to do. All I knew was that being around her eased the ache in my chest that not having her with me each night caused.

What if she was only doing this to be queen again? It's why she originally came here from what she told me. While I desperately wanted to place my heart back into her care, I was too petrified to do it for fear I was reading the situation wrong.

Lost in her thoughts, she said, "Which of these do you prefer? I can't decide."

I looked over the four samples she was pondering. Each arrangement contained fabric samples, mockups for tapestries, swatches of rugs, and paint colors.

"Which room is this for?" I asked.

"The banquet hall. I'm leaning toward the green because it signifies new growth, but I like the blue as well," she said. "I'm pretty sure we can rule the red out. I'm so sick of that color. It reminds me of blood and outdated royalty. We need something new and fresh, don't you think?"

I thought back to when I had saved her, knowing that was the memory she relived. Why she hated the color. "I think I favor the blue, but, of course, if you decide on the green, I'll be happy with that." I touched her elbow, and she turned, finally regarding me. Her eyes widened as if she only then realized I may have approached her for a reason.

"I'm going to see my mother," I said.

"Oh. Are you sure you don't want me to go with you?" she asked. I appreciated her willingness to come. I suspected it wasn't because she wanted to escape *this time*, but she wanted to be there for me in solidarity. I still hadn't figured out what changed, however, and until I understood what she was up to, I planned to watch it play out. That tear in my heart was too raw. Still, I longed for her to mend it.

"Will the banquet hall be ready by the next full moon?" I asked.

An eager grin lifted the corner of her lips. "It can be if you felt we had a need for it."

It would be a month since our wedding night, and we hadn't had a formal reception. This would be the perfect time for our reconciliation. An idea formed in my mind.

"Yes, I think it's time we invite our court to pay their respects to their new queen. The warlocks can take care of delivering notices and transportation. Will you be able to manage everything else, with Leviticus's help, of course?" I gave her a wry smile. Since the council meeting she barged in on, she occupied every waking hour of the man's time with tasks.

The wiry man scuttled into the room, stopping short as he saw us. I gave him a once over. His hair was unkempt, a pale purple shadowed his eyes, and he fidgeted like Avery had him utterly frazzled. I chuckled internally. Good.

"Well," she sighed, but her eyes were bright, betraying her words. "Of course, I can handle it." Avery eyed the waiting adviser, then me, unable to suppress the grin which kept attempting to sprout. She'd just gotten her stay in our world extended indefinitely, though I hadn't officially said it. Knowing her, she'd consider it a victory. And that elation would overpower the fatigue she must be experiencing with all this work.

While she was a one-woman motorcoach, I suspected with everything she was doing, she needed help, but was too proud to ask for it. That was fine because I knew the perfect person to offer her support. Avery had been here for almost a year now and hadn't had the opportunity to establish many female friendships. And while, to my knowledge, the various curious visitors, castle staff, and tradespeople had heeded my warning and treated her with kindness and acceptance, I don't know that she had warmed to anyone.

Jetta Proudfoot, daughter of one of the oldest warlocks in Ras alhague, Hager Proudfoot, could be a little abrupt upon meeting, but she was a steadfast and loyal friend.

"Perfect. I'll see you this evening for dinner." Before she could reply, my magic was working, and I was gone.

CHAPTER 52

AVERY

The hour bell gonged through the hallways of Ravsted, echoing off the stone walls. My eyes shot to the bronze clock I'd temporarily borrowed to use in the sitting room while the other more interesting one was at the watchmakers for repairs. It was the first room Leviticus brought me to when he first gave me a tour of the castle, and I decided to turn it into my office. I'd cleared out all the furniture and had a plush gold rug brought in along with a simple desk with side drawers large enough to store my stacks of paper.

I kept every object on the shelves and had them each dusted or polished. Otherwise, only two other chairs in the room were sitting beside each other in front of my desk. I found a warlock to fix the windows which had previously leaked, and along the wall beneath them were a dozen color boards for the varying rooms in Ravsted.

I had only addressed the spaces that were used the most frequently. Meeting rooms, reception rooms, the banquet hall, my room, and then, of course, a hall of guest rooms. We'd need more rooms to be brought up to the new standard now for the party. I jotted down a note to get with Leviticus about that.

I wanted to do Nighval's room, but I was too frightened to bring it up and he hadn't said anything. I hoped he didn't take it as a slight, but my husband seemed as impervious to my efforts as he'd been to my apology. At least he hadn't forced me to go back to the palace, so I wasn't planning on complaining. And now he planned to announce me to the kingdom as his queen. That was a good sign, right?

The borrowed clock ticked loudly, reminding me of the time. It was the dinner hour, and I was expected. Occasionally, others joined us. Despite that, this was one of the few times I had unfettered access to my husband when he wasn't off on some important mission, so I wouldn't miss it.

I glanced down at my attire. He hated these shift dresses, but they were easy to move in, and I didn't have to worry about looking perfect. I liked to wear them as I worked, because I found my gym apparel got too many strange looks. Giving myself a once over in the mirror above the small fireplace, I decided this would have to do because I didn't have time to change. I was already late.

Skipping through the hallways, I wondered how much of my advice the cooks had taken this time. It seemed incremental changes with them worked the best to bring them to my way of thinking. If I had to eat another heavy stew, I might retch. Tonight, I expected a lighter chicken broth soup with vegetables and orzo like pasta I taught them how to make and a salad. I wasn't a great cook back home, but I watched enough cooking shows to fake it well enough. That and my aunt had me chop so many vegetables growing up as a child and do my fair share of the grunt work in the kitchen, I wasn't afraid to dive in.

My upbeat mood, which was spurred on by my productivity, immediately stuttered as I rounded the corner to the dining hall and caught the sight of a lithe woman speaking to my husband. Her black hair hung in a glistening sheet down to the two tight globes that were her ass. The way she moved her hands as she spoke, and the demure set of her shoulders told me she was an elegant woman. That, and the glittering blue dress she wore that hugged her physique, but seemed to cover everything. A thick matching belt accentuated her curves, cinching a waist as narrow as mine.

I stepped into the room and my heart dropped as they turned to me. Her face was even more beautiful than I could have expected. Her alabaster skin was nearly flawless if it weren't for a single scar which ran from the corner of her lip down her jaw. Her lips were as red as an apple, and just as shiny. Bright blue doll-like eyes were rimmed in a thin ring of eyeliner, and I had to figure out what she was using for mascara because her lashes looked amazing. She was giving me total Maleficent vibes, and I hated how perfect she looked standing next to my equally severe husband.

My jealousy flared in twisting waves. I was late, and they were chatting and having an enjoyable time while I had been busting my ass. I was queen and my aunt taught me never to apologize for myself. As I tried to glide into the room, I remembered what I was wearing and, in that instant, decided I would burn every single shift dress I owned.

Still, I kept my chin high and said, "Thank you for waiting on me."

And because I knew Nighval wouldn't embarrass me, I walked up to stand beside him and placed a hand on the small of his back and a possessive hand on his forearm, so our bodies were nearly touching.

Nighval tilted his head down toward me and raised an eyebrow before addressing the woman. "Avery, this is my dear friend, Jetta Proudfoot. I asked her to come here because as a warlock's daughter, she is familiar with our world and the expectations of official gatherings. I thought you could learn from her, and you might need the help. She is a valuable resource, and I know you two will get along splendidly."

Oh my god, this woman was my worst nightmare come to life. Here I was trying to win my husband back over and he brought this stunning woman because he thought she needed to teach me things because apparently, I wasn't doing a sufficient job. Every hair on my body bristled. This was going to take a hell of an acting job to make it through this dinner, and then I would get rid of her.

I held out my hand to shake, not thinking, and then at the last minute turned it so my palm was facing the ground. How embarrassing allowing this woman to disarm me, but weren't people supposed to kiss royalty's hands? I mean, I hadn't seen anyone do that here, but I could pass it off as that, right? Amusement danced in Jetta's eyes, but she dutifully took my hand and pressed her red lips to it. When she pulled away, she left a lipstick impression on my hand, and I thought my head might explode.

"Pleased to meet you, Your Majesty," she said.

"Actually, my wife prefers it if those in her close circle call her by her given name, Avery. I know you two will work so closely together titles will become cumbersome." Nighval looked awfully proud of himself, and I didn't know if he brought this woman to gloat or what exactly was going through his mind, but this *Jetta* was not in my inner circle, and I had a suspicion she would never be. I barely even had one. April and Alice seemed to still like me after learning I'd killed Xavier and then there was Link, who was friendly with me before. At least until that little conversation when Nighval had confessed to them what I'd done.

"Your Majesty is fine for now," I said, blinking sweetly, to which Nighval shot me a frown.

I ignored it and gestured to the table. "Please, let's sit. I've been working with the cooks on some new recipes. I've been looking forward to what they've prepared for us all day."

Nighval held my chair out, and I sat immediately, reaching for a sip of water to soothe my parched throat. Across the table, Jetta had the audacity to remain standing until my husband walked around and held her chair out for her as well. I had to gulp down the liquid, so I didn't spew my water across the table.

"Thank you, Nighval," she said, her sultry velvet voice dripping with sweetness. Then she turned to me and said, "Avery, you have quite the catch here. I hope you know how lucky you are." She patted his hand in a way that was almost mothering if she didn't ooze sex.

Unclenching my teeth, I said, "I am quite aware of every glorious facet of the man I have married." His hand was atop the table, and I reached over and threaded my fingers through his. Worry lines creased his face and his gaze darted between us as if he were questioning the decision he had made.

Damn it. Here I was, lost in my jealousy and the man whose heart I was trying to win back had done something he believed was nice, and I was treating this *dear friend* of his rudely. I really needed to shake it off. That didn't mean I was going to let go of his hand, though.

"So, Jetta, I understand we have a lot in common," I said, not that Nighval had ever mentioned this woman. It wouldn't hurt to act like he had though, and then I wouldn't appear blindsided. The way she was looking at him out of the corner of her eye, I suspected he was the one thing we had in common. I parked that thought train at the station. "My Aunt Esmeralda raised me. She's a powerful witch, so I grew up around magic, too, but didn't have any myself. She had the foresight to include me in many of the lessons as a child in case I ever had a daughter of my own who I passed on the gene to."

Nighval's hand squeezed slightly when I said the word daughter, but his expression didn't falter, and I wondered if he realized he'd done it. Did he want children? I wondered if he had ever thought of it.

Jetta's eyes softened almost enough that I couldn't exactly hate her. "How smart. It does seem we have a lot in common. And it will be my pleasure to get to know you this week as I share the customs and expectations of our world as we prepare for the feast."

Scratch that. I was officially not a fan.

A mind-numbing hour later, dinner was over. Dessert had been served. Each item barely met my new standard, but that was progress. As we stood, Link sauntered into the room, as if he were the king himself.

"How was I not invited to this dinner? And with such a beauty?" Link said, taking Jetta's extended hand, placing a kiss upon it. He turned to me and bowed low, his tone decidedly colder as he said, "Your Majesty."

It seemed Link's opinion of me had dropped since the council meeting and since whatever else Nighval had told him. Unfortunately, I agreed with him, and this was my fault. I wanted to bring it up with him and let him know we were on the same page and that I planned to fix it, but he was adept at avoiding me. I needed to have the council members on my side, including each warlock.

"Jetta, Nighval," Link glanced at me and reluctantly added, "Your Majesty, can I interest you in a nightcap?"

Before I said something I regretted, I excused myself and slipped out of the room.

Back in my room, I paced, stewing. Throwing open my wardrobe, I yanked every single shift dress off its hanger and tossed them out into the hallway. Then I tore the one I was wearing over my head and pitched it into the fireplace. The dress smoldered atop the embers, but didn't catch. I'd have to fish it out of there later and throw it away. I was too tired to clean up a bunch of soot, so I sat on the bench at the end of my bed and stared at the open wardrobe.

JENNIFER M. WALDROP

Tears threatened to spill over the rims of my eyelids, and I looked at the ceiling, determined to keep the salty liquid in my eyes and not let it fall. I would not be defeated by them. The way I saw it was I had two choices. I could put on something enticing it go down there and make them all like me or I could crawl under the covers and try again tomorrow.

I walked over to the hanging clothes and pulled out a sleeveless navy jumpsuit the palace tailor and I created. I threw it on, reapplied some soft pink lipstick, and pinched my cheeks. Though not as sultry as Jetta, I still looked good. With my warm coloring, the bright jewel tones washed me out, but a dusty navy, which Nighval would like, made my skin glow.

As I approached the room they'd retired to, voices drifted through the open door. "Don't worry, Jetta, she'll warm up to you. She's passionate." I could hear the smile in Nighval's voice, like he was proud of his unruly wife. Still, annoyance bubbled to the surface, knowing they spoke about me behind my back.

"She probably feels threatened. Look at you, Jetta. You're a vixen," Link said, his voice a tease.

"Why would Avery feel threatened?" Nighval asked, and I had to give him credit. His confusion seemed genuine.

"There is no threat," Jetta said. "That was a long time ago and only a brief tryst, Link. We're both much happier now that we have found what works for us."

I knew it. They had been a thing, but at least it was old news. I stepped into the room. Jetta and Link were at opposite ends of a long, tufted leather couch against a wall with a painting of a hunting scene. A large red rug sat off center beneath it, and next to an overflowing bar cart, Nighval reclined in a black leather wingback chair that had to be custom built because he didn't dwarf it like one might expect. Surface level scratches marred each piece of furniture and looked like someone attempted to buff them out with leather oil and did a decent job.

He must like this room, so I decided I'd leave it as it was. Some things I could come in and change, but sometimes imperfection made a place feel like a home. I sauntered over to the cart and poured myself a finger of a deep brown liquid, as I'd noticed that is what everyone else was drinking.

"What works for you?" I asked, wondering how much she'd disclose.

Jetta didn't blink, saying, "For me, women. For him, you."

It was embarrassing how relieved I felt, but it was short-lived.

She glanced up and down at my figure, eyebrows wrinkling. Nighval was used to my unusual outfits, and I knew this jumpsuit would confuse her. "What are you wearing?" she asked.

I gave her a sweet smile as I perched on the arm of the wingback Nighval sat in. "It's called fashion. Maybe as we get to know each other, I could teach you?"

Link spit out the sip he'd just taken, and Nighval's warm hand encircled my waist as he leaned forward. Jetta's eyes flashed, before she erupted in a fit of laughter. Her annoying mirth was contagious, and a chuckle escaped my lips. Soon I was clutching my stomach, shaking with humor. I wiped beneath my eyes and regarded her.

"Does this mean we're friends now?" she asked.

"Only if you tell me where you get your mascara," I said, and a puzzled expression crossed her face. After her laughing fit, the product hadn't even run. I looked at my own black smudged fingers, then to her clean ones with envy. "Mascara. You know, the stuff you put on your eyelashes. I had some from my plane that my aunt had spelled to be refilling, but I lost it in the Wildwood with the rest of my backpack."

Link leaned forward. "What were you doing in the Wildwood?"

Nighval's arm around my waist squeezed, and I patted his arm. Link already knew and was trying to test me. But he didn't know I knew. "I was doing something really stupid that I deeply regret, and I activated Samara's wards. They chased me, and I had to get rid of it because it was too heavy, so I dropped it. Now no more magic makeup."

"You had magic makeup and lost it?" Jetta asked, and I nodded. "That's a tragedy." She winked at me, and I knew she'd glazed over the difficult part of what I'd said on purpose. Perhaps I could be friends with her after all. Goddess, as the warmth at the thought of a friend flooded through me, I realized how lonely I'd been without. And this woman Jetta, my new friend, was here at the behest of my thoughtful husband.

Still her words didn't stop Link from interrupting my happy moment by giving me an assessing look.

"That backpack was your queen's most valuable possession, so it is really no trivial matter," Nighval chimed in, his fingers rubbing familiar, comforting circles on my waist, and I wanted to sink back into his lap.

But I suspected his soothing caress, probably unconscious, would stop the moment I did, and he'd be back to the avoidant man I'd been living with for the past week.

"Hmm..." Link patted his forefinger on his mouth. "Our queen's most valuable possession is missing. Sounds like a job for a warlock."

His tone was jovial. Was he coming around? "It isn't important," I said, giving him a weak smile.

"It sounds terribly important. My guess is Samara's monsters brought it back to her. Nighval, you didn't think to ask her about it when you were there?" Link asked.

"If I had, she hardly would have returned it. You know my mother. She can and will use anything she can get her hands on to hang over my head. I'm surprised she hasn't mentioned it yet," Nighval said.

"Then perhaps she doesn't have it. I'll make it my mission to deliver your backpack to you unharmed, Your Majesty." With the proclamation, Link stood and bowed low.

He gave me a cocky grin and refilled his glass, making me wonder if the warlocks had a higher tolerance to liquor than humans did, or was it their size? As I learned during the council meeting, that attribute wasn't just reserved for Link and Nighval. All of the warlocks were broad-shouldered towering men, yet that was the only common thread between them besides their power. Still, I'd yet to see any of them act remotely tipsy.

Already, I felt the effect from a few sips, but I wasn't much of a drinker. Watching people slur in a high-end bar for years made me uninterested. "Thank you, Link. But it's just stuff. I don't want you to go to any trouble or put yourself in harm's way. Those wraith wards are no joke."

He chuffed, as if he disagreed, but didn't argue. I stood, stretching. Fatigue weighed down my limbs, and I yawned. "I think I'm going to head to bed. I have a lot of work to do to get ready for this event."

Jetta stood, following my lead. "*We* have a lot of work, *Your Majesty*." This time when she said it, I knew it wasn't a taunt. A tentative friendship blossomed. She linked arms with me, and we strode from the room.

CHAPTER 53

AVERY

J etta's guest room was in a different wing of the castle than mine, so I parted from her in the hallway, and headed to my suite. My heart felt lighter than it had in weeks. When Nighval wrapped his arm around my waist, it was the first contact he'd made on his own since I tried to run from him, and it released a flutter of dancing butterflies in my stomach.

I turned the handle to my door, which was warm, and glanced down to see a fine stream of smoke flowing through the gap between the door and the uneven stone floor. I cracked the door open, and smoke billowed out. The fire in the chimney was ablaze and dense smoke was pouring into the room.

No, wait. The rug had caught fire, too. It must have sparked minutes earlier. I slammed the door shut and sprinted down the hallway, running into Nighval's big chest as he and Link rounded the corner coming from his sitting room.

His strong hands wrapped around my shoulders, and he held me at arm's length. "Avery, what's wrong?"

My mouth failed to operate for an eternal second, and he stared at me with concern etched on his face.

"Fire," I said, and pointed in the direction of my room. "My room."

He and Link shared a glance. Then in a blink they were gone, and I was left rushing back to my room. When I arrived, Nighval was standing at the door and his jaw was set, expression locked in deep concentration. He contained the smoke first, his power with a glowing blue halo encapsulating the discolored air, pressing it down. Across the room and through the dome of smoke, Link stood at the window. His own power, which was more aqua, had blanketed the smoldering rug.

All I could do was watch the warlocks as they worked to smother the fire and push the trapped smoke up and out of the fireplace. When it cleared, a fine layer of soot coated everything. The walls, the once white bedding, even the clothes in the open wardrobe. Thankfully, I'd hardly had time to unpack and most of it was undisturbed in a chest by the window.

Link's boots collected soot as he crossed the room, leaving a trail of shoe-shaped stone in his path. "You did this on purpose?" he said, giving me an incredulous look.

As if it hadn't occurred to Nighval, he gave me a wary glance.

I rolled my eyes. "Why on earth would I set a fire in my room on purpose, Link? And then immediately come find you two. That doesn't even make any sense."

"Maybe, you didn't want to sleep alone in your room anymore and you needed a way to trick this bull-headed warlock into giving you somewhere else to sleep," Link said, giving me his best mischievous smile.

It actually wasn't a terrible idea. Well, it was a terrible idea, but it would probably have worked.

"Thank you, Link. That will be all," Nighval said, interrupting my thoughts, and I turned to see him drilling me with a dark gaze I couldn't interpret. Link gave a quick bow and then tracked down the hallway, leaving a path of dark prints.

Nighval surveyed the room from the hallway and then noticed the heap of discarded dresses outside the door. He picked one up and studied it, and then turned his attention to me. I couldn't help the blush that rose on my cheeks.

"Why are all of your favorite dresses out here?" he asked. Something like anger mixed with hopeful curiosity flitted across his face.

I considered lying, but I had a feeling he'd see right through it. Instead, I stepped into the room and urged him to shut the door because I didn't want to have this conversation in the hallway. But I was so frustrated. He shouldn't have just dropped a beautiful woman on me without giving me a warning first.

"I don't know, Nighval. It's your fault." I waved at the now dead fireplace. "In my plane, I had a fireplace in my condo and if I wanted to use it, all I had to do was press a button and it sprang to life. And it wasn't even for warmth. It was just there because it was pretty. How was I supposed to know that if I threw a dress onto it, the whole room would catch on fire?"

"That doesn't answer my question," he said, crossing his arms. "And it certainly doesn't make it my fault."

"Well, if you hadn't brought Jetta without giving me a heads up, I wouldn't have stormed into my room, taken off my dress and thrown it into the fire. So, here we are and now you see that it's your fault—"

"You threw all of your favorite dresses out into the hallway because you were jealous?" His voice went low and gravelly as he said the words.

"Well, nothing else I'm doing seems to be working, so I figured I need to dress like a *vixen*," I spit the words out and my hand immediately went to my mouth. Crap.

Nighval's expression jumped through a series of emotions before landing on amusement. "So, Link was right, and you did this on purpose trying to get into my bed."

"What?" I blurted. "No, I didn't." Holy cow. Surely, he didn't actually believe that.

"I think you did," he said, stepping toward me, a taunt playing on his features. I swallowed as I tilted my head back at the menacing man hovering over me.

"You know I didn't," I said, but his smug expression made me question myself. He wasn't gaslighting me. That wasn't like him. Then it dawned on me. This was a game. Was he ready to reconcile? He rubbed at the back of his neck, causing a peck and bicep to flex beneath his fitted black shirt. My pulse skittered.

"I think you did. I think you missed me so much, and I didn't give you what you wanted, so you threw a fit and caused a fire. Very naughty, Avery." In a swift motion, he leaned down and hoisted me over his shoulder. This time, I kicked my feet and beat my fists into his back.

"Put me down, you caveman," I called as he carried me down the stone corridor, all the while desire pulsed through my body in a dizzying wave. He responded by giving me a swift smack on my ass, which had a decidedly different feeling than when he'd done it in the Wildwood. A second later, that same hand slid up my inner thigh, and rubbed teasingly close to the part of my body that was actively responding to his utter maleness until my struggle dissolved into me wiggling, trying to get closer to his devious fingers.

"This is what you asked for, so who am I to deny you, my queen?" he said, stomping through the hallways with purpose. The electric lights flickered as we passed as if they were reacting to the power of the man carrying me. He got to the end of the hallway where there must have been a door I couldn't see. He kicked it open, stepped inside and then slammed it behind him. A few more giant strides, then we were through another door into a smaller, darker room.

As he turned, I saw a massive four-poster bed draped with a navy velvet coverlet. Every piece of furniture was black, even the rug. The walls were exposed grey stone and long sapphire satin curtains hung on each side of huge windows which opened onto a balcony beyond. A single flickering lamp sat on the nightstand, faintly illuminating the area nearest the bed. The space was haunting and gorgeous. I could only assume this was his bedroom. Much more somber and reserved than the simple elegance of his suite at the palace. More *him* and something about him bringing me here felt intimate, like peeling another layer back from the mysterious man I'd fallen for.

Still, I asked, "Where are we?"

"My rooms. Isn't this where you wanted to go?" he asked, still keeping me hoisted over his shoulder as he pulled the curtains closed.

"Why am I here?" I asked, voice turning into a whisper.

He turned and then a few more footsteps and we were in front of his bed, which he lowered me none too gently on to. I landed and immediately propped myself up on my elbows. He stood at the side of the bed with a shit-eating grin on his face, his fists planted on his hips reminding me of the man he'd been when taking out the wraiths with all that power. The same power that snuffed out a fire a moment earlier without him breaking a sweat.

Just the thought of it made flutters erupt in my core because all of that power and the man who wielded it belonged to me. I could practically see it shimmering in the surrounding air, like a teakettle about to explode.

His voice was guttural when he said, "Have you figured out why you're here, Avery?"

I swallowed, really hoping I did. Pulling my lower lip into my mouth, I nodded.

"Then tell me," he demanded.

I didn't hesitate. I knew exactly what he wanted, so I assumed my role in this game, and said, "I've been a bad girl."

"Goddess, Avery," he said, running a hand through his thick hair, never taking his eyes from me. "You've been very bad. And do you know what I'm going to have to do now?"

I brought my hand to my neck and ran it down my décolletage, down the seam of the jumpsuit's V-neck, then between my breasts. His eyes tracked the whole way, and I continued my path across the smooth fabric further down until my fingers disappeared between my thighs.

"Punish me," I said, unsure of where the words were coming from. I only understood my intrinsic need to give him something he felt he'd lost. Show him I knew I'd hurt him and that I was willing to do what it took to rebuild it. To surrender to what was between us.

"That's right," he said as his eyes darkened and lulled and his need for this, for me, became apparent. I didn't know if he could resist even if he wanted to and suddenly, I felt powerful, in control. This was probably how he had felt in the carriage when he knew I couldn't say no to him.

Then his hand went to the bulge in his pants, and he rubbed what was beneath. My mouth fell open at the thought of him. Of tasting him.

I sat up and crawled over to him, getting up on my knees so we were chest to chest and my fingers went to the buttons of his shirt. He watched me as I loosened each one and then pushed the fabric off his broad shoulders. My fingers went to trace the scar that ran across his pectoral when he grabbed my wrist. His other hand wrapped around my head, and he brought my eyes to his.

"You don't get to touch me like that until you're forgiven. Until you've earned your penance," he said, and his eyes went to my mouth.

"What's it going to take, Nighval?" I asked, using his full name, and he flinched.

His thumb traced over my bottom lip. I parted for him. I flicked my tongue out, licking his thumb, and he slid it into my mouth. I sucked and swirled around it, hoping that the imagery would drive him wild.

"Want to make it up to me?" he asked, and I nodded eagerly.

"Good," he said. "Then get on your knees." He pointed to the rug at his feet, the veins in his forearm snaking up his skin and over the corded muscle.

Jesus, I was dripping for him already. I could hear my heartbeat in my ears as I got off the bed and lowered myself before him. The ache between my thighs increased tenfold as I unlaced his pants exposing his V muscles. I tugged the waistband down over his thighs. His heavy erection jutted out, bobbing as my finger scraped over his heated skin.

He ran a finger through the strap of the jumpsuit and as he tugged, it slid off my body in a blur. I looked down. I was bare. Next to me on the bed, my clothing and shoes were in a neat pile. He tilted my chin up to him, surveying my shocked expression.

"You know every facet of me?" he asked, self-satisfied and unapologetic. Then he grabbed the base of his cock and ran the tip across my cheek. "I'll only ask you to do this when you're bad, Avery. So be a good girl and suck me."

A part of my heart cracked because he thought doing this to him was something I would only reluctantly do. He was so wrong. I had dreamed about getting his cock in my mouth since the first time I saw it. And now I understood why he had been hesitant at the grotto. Deep down, this beautiful man didn't think he was enough and when I ran from him, I'd reinforced that belief.

His words, however, were still confident and so hot. He'd had years of practice being king, in control, dominant. I never had a man talk to me the way he did, and I didn't know how I was going to get through this without touching myself.

My lashes fluttered as I beamed up at him and ran my lips over his tip without opening them. Then I removed his hand and wrapped mine where his had been and licked up his entire length. When I got to the tip and the pre-cum beaded there, I craned my head back so I could meet his eyes, and I licked across his slit. Hot, salty, masculine flavor burst onto my tongue, making my eyes roll back in my head.

Scar riddled shoulders shuddered and his fists clenched at his sides. "Fuck," he bit out. He was breathing through his nostrils like a bull, like he could barely contain himself as he stared down at me. Like there was a part of him that was still hesitant, holding back, and that wouldn't do.

"You mean this as a punishment?" I asked, blinking up at him with the best doe eyes I could muster, and he gave me a brooding nod in response. A strong hand threaded through the hair at the base of my neck and a subtle grimace ghosted across his face like he was torn between wanting this and feeling guilty for asking for it.

"Poor choice, Nighval. This can't be my punishment—"

"Why not?" his voice laced with hesitance as he asked.

I gave him a wry smile. "Because I love it," I said, and took him into my mouth.

CHAPTER 54

NIGHVAL

O ur game shattered as Avery's mouth wrapped around my cock and then sank down on it. She was so perfect for me. She liked this. Loved it, she'd said. Her confidence, and the way her eyes blazed as she stared up at me, had me throbbing, wanting to do to her mouth what I had done to her cunt that first time. Claim it. Reclaim her and make sure she knew exactly where she belonged.

I reached down and grabbed a handful of her breast squeezing and rubbing at her nipple and she groaned. I felt the vibration all the way up my spine as she kept working me. I leaked for her as I cupped the back of her head and pulled her onto me deeper.

She jerked, gagging, as her beautiful amber eyes became glassy. "Deeper," I said, and pressed in slowly and she opened her throat for me. "So good," I breathed. "Just like that."

A smile tried to form on her lips, still wrapped around me like she enjoyed how she pleased me. I pressed in again and again until a fire built low in my groin. Tapping the tip against the back of her hot throat, I chased that feeling until tingling sensations spasmed down my cock, spreading through my body like the buildup right before a fight, but so much better. The nails on one of her hands dug into the flesh of my thigh and the other disappeared below her waist. Then her hips were moving in time with my thrusts. Goddess, she was touching herself.

Her nails bit into my thigh harder and her mouth all but quit working as her eyes squeezed shut. A whimper from deep in her throat ripped through my control. A surge of hot cum shot into the back of her throat. I pulled out just enough that I knew my release would coat her tongue before pressing back in, riding out the pulsing waves. The way bliss relaxed her features as she tasted me, swallowed what I gave her, sent shocks of pleasure through me.

I rode her mouth until the last wave subsided, and a rare moment of peace covered me like a heavy blanket as the throbbing eased. Pulling myself out, I tapped the tip of my dick, still glistening, on her swollen lips. Her tongue darted out to collect what remained, and she looked up at me with glazed eyes.

"Am I forgiven?" she asked. The sweet submissive act brought me to my knees. I cupped her face and kissed her gently.

I wanted to grovel and beg her to never hurt me like that again and somehow get her to promise me that her heart would always be mine, but I knew I had to trust her and to have faith in what we had built. What we would continue to build. Instead, I said, "Sweetheart, you'll always be forgiven."

She attempted a grin, but her yawn overtook it. Still, I said, "Let me make you feel good."

Shaking her head, she said, "You did, Nigh. Just feeling you lose control like that because of me—you make my world tip upside down and sideways. I never knew it could be like this." A blush crawled across her cheeks as she stared up at me, wide-eyed awe relaxing her features. Gooseflesh broke out across her shoulders, and I pulled her closer, lending her my warmth.

I smiled, hardly able to imagine such a divine creature could feel that way about me. "Tell me what you need, Avery. I'll give you anything." *Anything.* If she asked me to send her home, in that moment, I would have been powerless to deny her and found a way. The thought of her possibly wanting that sent a shiver wracking through me, and I gently pinched her jaw, tilting her head up at me. "What do you wish? Tell me, and I will grant it."

Her eyes flared, and she went stiff as if she seemed to understand the unstated meaning of my words. She searched my eyes for a long moment and said, "Hold me. That's what I want."

Obeying, I got to my feet and lifted her into my bed. I peeled my pants the rest of the way down my legs and crawled in next to her. As she drifted off to sleep with her head on my chest, her fingers tracing my scars, claiming me, a sense of wonderment bloomed in my chest. My wife, the other half of my heart, was here to stay. Against my mother's carefully planned odds, I'd won.

CHAPTER 55

AVERY

Nighval was gone when I woke and a little pang of disappointment hit me, making me regret not taking him up on his offer for more pleasure last night. Someone had opened the curtains and dust danced in the rays of sunlight streaming in through the window.

Throwing the covers off, I got up noticing someone had also brought in my trunk and moved a small desk and my vanity items into the room, which were now soot free or perhaps only replaced. Wow, I slept through it all. Was it the exhaustive week I had or being with him? I suspected it was the latter.

With all my shift dresses abandoned, and everything that was in my wardrobe covered in soot, I was stuck with the smaller selection of what my trunk protected.

Rifling through it, I fished out a few things and went to the bathroom to ready myself for the day. Despite the fact that I was running late for breakfast, I took care with my appearance in case my husband sprang anymore former lovers on me.

The outfit I chose was on the more experimental side of my collaborations with the palace tailor. I slipped on the dark charcoal sweater I cut into a crop top, and a thick jersey-like black fitted skirt which sat high on the waist and had two slits that came to my upper thighs exposing the black leather boots which laced up to the knee. They were new, a modern take on combat style, with a three-inch stacked heel and shiny gold eyelets that ran up the front. The shoemaker had given me more than one strange look as I'd explained to him what I wanted, but these were worth it. With the frayed edge of the top, the heavy eyeliner, and the boots, I looked like a punk rock princess.

Jetta glanced up from trying to stab a grape, which rolled around defensively on her plate, as I walked into the dining room. A grin transformed her frustrated expression into one of pure mischief.

"Is it true?" she asked, leaning forward as I took a seat across the table from her.

"Is what true?" I asked, already dreading where this was going.

She caught the grape and plopped it between her red lips. "That you set a fire to your room so Nighval would have to come save you and take you back to his bed?" Her eyes were wide, curious. Was she impressed?

"Oh my god, no, Jetta. I didn't start the fire. It was an accident."

Jetta huffed in disappointment. "I hardly believe you. Link said you seemed very eager when you found them."

My face flamed. "I was in a panic."

"He said Nighval dismissed him rather abruptly and one of my attendants said she saw him carrying you through the hallway over his shoulder," she said, and now her grin turned into something liquid as she tapped her finger on her pursed lips.

I wanted to crawl under the table.

"So, it is true," she teased. "Our king is a very deserving man, so I hope you were able to give him what he needed."

"Are you always so forward?" I asked, and she only hummed like the question amused her. We chatted about our similar childhood experiences, and the differences between our planes as we finished breakfast.

As we stood, she gave me a once over. "Another new outfit, I see."

I returned the scrutiny, taking in the fitted emerald sweater dress she wore which had a deep V-neck and black leather laces that held her chest from spilling out. Barely.

When we arrived in the Great Hall, the designers were already waiting with their samples, along with furniture makers and other artisans. I ushered Jetta over to where Leviticus tapped his foot impatiently next to the color boards I had gone over with Nighval.

"Good morning, Your Majesty," he said. "You've made a decision?"

I had made the decision, but I still looked at Jetta for her input. She studied the options for a few moments, then said, "I think I prefer the green."

"I do, too, but Nighval prefers the blue," I said. "There's just something about it that isn't coming together for me."

She picked up the blue color board and set it on the banquet table in the middle of the room. The table was massive, and all of the varnish had been sanded off down to the raw wood. The craftspeople were waiting on me to make a decision for the new stain. It was the one piece of furniture I decided not to replace, and many of the surface level mars had been removed with the sanding, but the deeper ones I felt would be a symbolic reminder of the past.

Jetta pointed to a man holding a box of fabric swatches and gestured for him to come to the table and set them in front of her. She rifled through the box of material and pulled out a smoky navy and another lighter, silvery blue. She laid the second swatch over a more turquoise one on the color board and then laid the navy next to it.

"I think this one would work, but we need to play with tone more. What if we covered the existing chairs with this darker swatch and used the lighter one for the accent piping?"

I picked up the silver, folded it around a pencil, and set it against the dark navy. "I love it." I walked over to where the stain colors were laid out, and the dinnerware. "The table should be this charcoal wood dye, white plates on these pewter chargers. And we'll want the larger silver candelabras to be polished and set between each bouquet."

The people scurried off to do as I had requested. It would take a small village worth of upholsterers to make the chair covers, but the people needed the work, and I imagined new chairs would have been much more of a challenging request. It was a clever idea on Jetta's part.

"You are very good at this," I said.

She gave me a toothy grin. "I spent years trying to keep my father's estate on the mend. Despite the curse, I refused to let things fall into disrepair, even though everything felt hopeless."

As she said it her fingers brushed the scar on her chin and my eyes skipped over the other silvery remnants marking her otherwise smooth chest. I appreciated Jetta's strength. Few people here had been so fortified and she was a teenager whenever it happened. I could hardly imagine what that would have been like. When I was a teenager, I was busy thinking about boys, what university I would go to and the upcoming Smashbox holiday color palette release.

She hadn't noticed my gaze, or she was used to it because she didn't flinch, only saying, "You're good at this, too. How did you learn?"

"I was a theater major in my plane, but I never finished the degree. Along with all of the acting classes, I was able to take things like set and costume design and stage makeup. I wanted to act, but I turned the other things into a hobby and would help backstage when I could," I said.

"Well, that explains the outfits." She laughed behind her hand as she eyed what I wore.

"You're just jealous," I said, but a barely noticeable flinch crossed her face, which made my heart squeeze. "I think after the event, we will deserve a break. If you want, we could use the time to make you a few pieces. Just think of how prestigious it will be to have clothing designed by your queen. You will definitely be at the height of fashion."

"I think we need to meet with Fredrik tomorrow and you can design our dresses for the reception," she said, as her hands went to a steeple in front of her chest, fingertips tapping in order from small to large.

I glanced at the awaiting craftspeople. We would have a lot of decisions to make today, but we could squeeze it in. "Leviticus, bump the meeting with the chefs until after lunch tomorrow. Have the two best tailors meet us right after breakfast. The florist can wait until Thursday, and we can schedule our fitting for Friday so they can make any last-minute adjustments." I took a deep breath and released it slowly and looked to my new friend. "We've got this."

Appointments and lunch came and went, and it turned out Nighval was right. Jetta proved to be an effective tool, and more than eager to work alongside me without stopping. Part of me expected her to be work-averse, AKA spoiled, but she wasn't remotely. She didn't even shy away from making decisions on things I delegated to her, which gave me a little room to breathe, and I was excited about designing our dresses.

I was determined to come up with something that would drop Nighval's jaw to the floor, and Jetta had briefly mentioned that one landowner's daughter would be here, and she was hoping to catch her eye, so I imagined she had a similar vision for her attire.

As I freshened up for dinner, I still hadn't seen my husband. Only Jetta and Leviticus greeted me when I entered the dining hall later that evening.

Leviticus, who was seeming to warm me even though I was running him ragged, pulled out my chair so I could sit and then took the open seat to the right of me. "Good evening, Your Majesty," he said, handing me several sheets of paper. "We need to go over the list of special requests from the guests. Many of them will be staying in the guestrooms, and we should try to make accommodations for them."

I looked over the list. I was used to accommodating food allergies, but some of these items seemed more like a celebrity dressing room rider. Attendants filled our glasses and brought out salads while I skimmed through the items.

"Who is Lord Gram Billings?" I asked.

Jetta leaned forward. "Why?" she asked, eyes wide with intrigue and amusement. Leviticus only settled back in his chair with a sigh, lifting his wineglass to his lips.

"Because he is requesting that he only be served food that is green." I pushed the paper across the table so Jetta could read it with her own eyes and then turned to Leviticus who was chuckling under his breath. "Does that mean he will only eat lettuce and broccoli? Like, is he a vegetarian?"

Leviticus shook his head. "This isn't the first time he's been to Ravsted. The cooks will know what to do."

"Which entails?" Jetta asked, arching a brow.

"Which entails using food dye to color his food green," Leviticus answered.

I almost spit out the sip of water I had taken. "Wait, like you mean if he has a hard-boiled egg, the chefs will dye it green? Or they will dye a piece of chicken green?"

"Exactly. And just wait. It gets better." Leviticus flipped to the third page and pointed about halfway down. I read over the request, unable to bite back the laugh.

"Lady Janelle Danforth is allergic to doors that open inward and the sound of her husband chewing. I guess we could seat them at opposite ends of the hall, but do we have to honor all these requests?" I asked.

Leviticus sighed and Jetta jumped in. "If we can, we should." Jetta skimmed over the paper. "Within reason. Like this request to have the event three hours earlier is obviously not something we are going to consider, but if the Lady of Lakely Manor will only use lavender scented bath products, we should try to accommodate that."

"Can she not bring her own?" I asked.

Jetta frowned. "As their queen, it would endear you to them to accommodate as many requests as possible, especially if they are insignificant things. You remember what life has been like for us for the past nineteen years?"

She gave me an apologetic smile, and I appreciated her gentle way of delivering to me the words I needed to be reminded of.

"Yes, and after the unfortunate situation you found yourself in after Xavier's death, endearing yourself to our people would please our king very much," Leviticus said.

You mean when you threw me in prison for a month and were about to lop off my head? That's what I wanted to say, but it seemed that all that was in the past. Forgiven. To give the man credit, he was working his ass off. Maybe that was his way of trying to make up for what had happened. So instead, I said, "Speaking of my husband, where is he?"

Leviticus shifted uncomfortably in his chair. "He and the mages had some work to do outside the city. Unfortunately, he had to leave immediately when he received the news early this morning. He did not tell you?"

"Umm, no," I said. Perhaps he tried, but considering that I slept through an army of attendants this morning, maybe I hadn't heard it and he chose to leave me in my sleep coma. "But I understand, of course," I said, throwing it in for good measure.

If I tried to press, I suspected he would not tell me what exactly it was that drew them away, so I would wait to ask Nighval when he returned. Worry swirled in my stomach. My husband was powerful, capable, and from what I'd seen with the wraiths, nearly invincible. That thought should have comforted me, but my mind flicked to the name Samara Wrede. She was more powerful, and I hoped whatever it was he was dealing with had nothing to do with her. Still, I wanted to demand answers. As if Leviticus suspected it, he shoveled a massive bite of pheasant into his mouth. Then another as he side-eyed me warily.

I had a feeling that I occasionally teetered on coming across like a brat. I had lived all this time in another plane not realizing the suffering of an entire people, and the more I experienced here, the more flippant and superficial I realized much of my life was. I thought I knew everything they'd gone through, but I realized that I hadn't really known their pain. Granted, I understood you couldn't compare trauma, and since I arrived here, I'd certainly had my fair share.

I reached over and padded his wrist. "No need to worry, Leviticus. I won't force you to disclose the king's whereabouts to me. He will tell me when he returns." I offered him a smile. His features visibly softened and his grip on his knife relaxed.

We finished eating, and then each took a page of requests. Leviticus passed out pens, and the three of us made quick work, approving or denying our guest's wishes, and sorting them into categories so they could be delegated to the proper attendants.

After we finished, out of habit I found myself wondering in the direction of my old room. Nervous energy danced through me as I changed directions and went in search of the dark suite that belonged to my husband—us now.

The thought of slipping into his bed, surrounding myself with his glorious scent was delicious and as I used a soft cotton cloth to remove my this-plane makeup, I wondered if he would appear at some point in the night.

That was when I noticed what looked like a folded notecard propped against the mirror hanging above the vanity in the bathroom. In a scrawling script the name Samara Wrede was stamped on the outside of the elegant stationary. I suspected this letter arrived via her magic. How interesting. Had she always communicated with him this way? I couldn't stop myself. I had it in my hands and was breaking the wax seal before I could think better of it.

> *My dearest Nighval,*
>
> *Word has come to me that to celebrate your perseverance, you've planned an elaborate reception and nearly half of Ras alhague will be in attendance. I want to offer you my congratulations because I must assume that you've managed to win the witch's heart once again. And in such a short time. When I informed you of her flight in the Wildwood, the hopeless stricken expression on your face was almost more than I could bear, but I knew you could do it.*

My heart guttered as I read the words. The proof of the damage I'd done and in front of her of all people. The sudden overwhelming guilt made me nauseous, but I kept reading.

> *You have not mentioned this during our dinners, and I wish for you to know I welcome you to bring these troubles to your mother in the future. Or better yet, bring her. Please consider this my formal invitation. I'm already going to feel quite foolish meeting my daughter-in-law for the first time at your wedding reception. But I do understand the whirlwind of a new love.*

Goddess, this woman was laying it on thick. If I didn't know the history and that she was the bitch who'd cursed an entire plane, I'd have read this and thought she was a doting mother. Fortunately, I did understand her character and how ruthless she could be.

> *One final thing, son. I'm sure you can imagine my shock as with each passing day, I sort through my correspondence,*

and realize I've received none from you. I imagined as the architect of your love story, I'd have been at the top of your guest list, so I'll make another assumption—and allow you to correct this oversight. I know you and your new bride would never dream of offending your mother.

With all my love, S.W.

I stood there clenching the note in my hand as dread sluiced through my mind. That was a threat. Samara wanted to come to the reception, expected an invite, and I knew what Nighval was going to say. Absolutely not. Apparently, he wisely had omitted it from any conversation during the few visits he'd had with her since we broke the curse.

As I folded the letter, I walked back into the bedroom and placed it on my nightstand, eyeing it warily in hopes that the magic that had deposited it in our bathroom wasn't going to whisk it away in the same manner before I got a chance to show it to Nighval.

I crawled in bed, running through excuse after excuse. They all were some elaborate version of, *No, you can't come because you're completely unhinged,* which wasn't really going to work. Eventually, with all the thinking, it seemed I'd tired myself out because I awoke sometime in the night to find the other half of our bed empty. In the sliver of moonlight creeping in through the break in the curtains, I made out the impression of the note still lying on the nightstand. I sank back into the covers, willing my thoughts to drift away from tomorrow's problems as my husband's scent surrounded me, lulling me into deep, fitful sleep.

CHAPTER 56

AVERY

By Thursday afternoon, I still hadn't seen my husband and his absence was becoming an acute ache in my chest. I only now realized that we hadn't gone this long without seeing each other. Even when I had been upset with him and he with me, we had seen each other every day. Otherwise, every task this week had gone according to plan.

Well, except for the note burning a hole in my pocket as it had done the last several days. There was nothing for it. Even if I had known what to say, I had no idea how to get a message to her. I thought of bringing it up to Jetta, but I didn't suspect she'd have more of a clue than I did, and I wasn't sure how Nighval would feel about me sharing.

Leviticus was an advisor on the council, so I figured he was safe to tell, but with our history, I didn't trust him completely yet. So, I resorted to carrying it on my person, in hopes that Nighval would return home or I'd bump into another warlock and they would get a message to him.

Moments earlier, Jetta escorted a team of florists out of the garden, leaving me with a rare break, which I took. Blushing roses were in full bloom, and their sweet scent wafted through the air as I walked down the rows. The sun was out and hanging in the sky-high overhead. Moisture beaded across my forehead, and I gathered my hair. Twisting it, I secured it with a clip I fished out of my pocket. I had become acclimated in the last year to the cool air, and it seems since the curse had been broken, it was becoming progressively warmer, which I loved. I missed the balmy air of Miami.

I lifted my arm, lamenting the faded gold of my skin. When I'd come here, it was a rich, warm color, but had faded somewhat being out of the sun and my usual tan lines I had year-round were nearly faded. I had half a mind to go back to my room, find something I could fashion into a makeshift bathing suit, slip it on and then go float in one of the fountains. I held my arms out to the sun, closing my eyes as I stared up at it, enjoying the warmth it gave me. I could only imagine the reputation I would get if I did such a thing. But I suppose I could play the role of a mad queen. It would probably amuse my husband.

I stood there like that for a long while until my skin became warm. That meant enough sun. The last thing I needed was to be a glowing terra-cotta for my reception. Or worse, get a funky tan line. I noted the little building where Nighval, and I sat and read one afternoon, what seemed to be a lifetime ago. The sun was at just the right angle that the bench would be in the shade right now, and I made a beeline to it.

I sat and leaned against the cool stone wall and enjoyed the passing bees and butterflies, and the birds chirping throughout the garden. It was so beautiful here, and as I watched Ravsted be transformed, knowing that I was a part of it, sent a warm wave of joy through my chest. I wondered what I would do when I finished my work. I mean, on the one hand, I would be living in one of those old castles that in my plane were no longer residences, but turned into museums, or art galleries. It was a far cry from my condo, and as I sat in the shade, I realized it was the first time that I didn't mind it. Sure, there were some things here that were still circa 1800s, like the outdated modes of transportation, and the lack of modern plumbing in some of the inns that I had been to. At least the castle had been outfitted with that little bit of modernity.

But I wasn't a scientist, or mechanic, or whatever other profession would be needed to bring Ras alhague into the future. I was queen though, and I knew what was possible. And somehow the warlocks were able to transfer things between planes occasionally, so perhaps there were things I could do to make this plane a better place. A sense of rightness flooded over me as I sat with my thoughts until gravel crunching somewhere behind me drew my awareness into the present.

CHAPTER 57

NIGHVAL

A very lifted her arms and face to the sun to bask in its warmth, and I stood there for long moments, taking in her beauty. It had been a rough few weeks keeping myself away from her, then reconciling, and then having to be away so soon after.

When she moved behind the garden hut, I stepped to the corner, so I remained out of sight. "Do you remember the last time we were here?" I asked her.

"You didn't want me to see you," she said, her melodic voice drifting around the corner, and I followed it.

I grimaced at the memory. It was true. The thought of her seeing me in that form had made my skin crawl and my pride gutter. "You're right. Before, when I made you watch me transform, I had been resentful of you and my brother. I wanted you, and I was angry that I couldn't have you, so I was an asshole. But that day, for some reason I was just so eager to share something with you, and I didn't want you to see me as a monster."

"I'm yours now. What are you going to do about it?" she asked.

I chuckled and leaned down to scoop her into my arms. When I sat back down on the bench her legs were straddling me to wear her knees were on either side of my hips, and I leaned back against the cool stone. She rested her head on my chest, and I put my arms around her.

Just feeling her peaceful breathing against me was more than I deserved.

"I've missed you," she said.

I kissed the top of her head and smoothed out her loose curls. "I've missed you, too, Avery."

"It's not over, is it?" she asked, shifting uncomfortably, like she had more to say.

"It is," I said, squeezing her tighter.

"What about Samara? You'll continue to visit her weekly for the rest of her life?"

Sighing, I rubbed soothing strokes up and down her back. "She lost, and she knows it. I will visit her weekly until I can figure out another solution." She wiggled in my lap, and I could tell something had her unsettled.

I tilted her chin up to me so I could see her face. "What's wrong?"

"I just feel like she's this looming threat that's out there. From what you said, she's unpredictable, and I have a feeling she will not let this be." Worry lines creased her forehead, and I wanted to take away the stress the thought of my mother caused her.

"You have a feeling?" I asked her.

Fishing around in her pocket, she held up a folded piece of stationary I recognized immediately as the familiar dread at any mention of my mother stabbed through me.

"Well, a feeling and this showed up on your vanity a few days ago. I read it," she said, as she handed it to me, and I felt my brows narrow. As a flash of fear darted through her eyes, I unclenched my jaw, took the paper and flipped it open, holding it out to the side to read the contents which I did without a word.

"Nigh," she said, a nervous edge to her sweet voice. "Are you upset I read it?"

"No, I'm upset that her meddling has upset you."

"I don't think she's going to let us live out our lives in peace and this is just the first of it. I've been wracking my brain for some way to get out of it. I've got nothing aside from cancelling the entire thing." Her shoulders slumped as she spoke and my hands went to their sides to sooth her.

"We're not cancelling. This celebration is important to me and my kingdom. I'm introducing the woman who loves me enough to break a curse to my people. This is symbolic, and they need to see you in a new light," I said, knowing we both were fully aware of what I was referring to without needing to mention it. "We will stand together to close a messy chapter in our history, and I'm not letting that woman stop me," I said with finality.

"But, shouldn't we respond?" she asked, before worrying her lower lip between her teeth.

I held the paper to the side away from us, and with a thought it burst into blue flames in my palm. Avery, still in my lap, jumped which positioned her hands on my chest and her body angling nearer to mine which I took advantage of by pulling her closer. I grinned and she said, "I take that as a no."

"That's right. She does not get our time or our worry. And if she tries something, we'll be ready. I'll have the Council of Warlocks ward Ravsted. We'll be safe."

She gave me an unsteady smile. I decided the best course of action was to change the subject and put that minor disturbance behind us. "You and Jetta seem to be getting along better," I said, and she huffed as I placed a gentle kiss on her jaw.

"I was ready to smack you for bringing a gorgeous woman at first, but you're right. I do like her." She gave me a bashful grin. I stole the two inches between our mouths and kissed it off her lips.

"I'm sorry I had to leave so suddenly," I said. "I have to go again before dinner, but I needed to see you."

"Will you always be gone so much?" she asked, and my heart pinched.

"No. I have another of Xavier's messes to sort out this afternoon. My brother actually deeded the same plot of land to two different landowners if you can believe it. At some point, they must end." I leaned in and nibbled up her delicate neck causing a little shiver, but she continued her questioning determined.

"After the reception, will you take me with you?" she asked. That question I'd been waiting for. Dreading.

If I took her, she would see the sometimes-heavy hand that was required to rule this magic-filled land. But she knew who she married, and she hadn't backed down from it. I should give her more credit. She was, after all, straddling me unabashedly in the garden where anyone could walk up on us.

I moved back so I could look at her and there was no mistaking the lazy, lust filled expression in her eyes. I needed to hurry up and give her this, so I could add the rose garden to the list of places I'd taken my wife. "There will be times when you are needed here, but yes, I will take you when I can," I said.

At my agreement, she straightened and took my jaw in her hands. "Thank you," she said, and gave me a long, lingering kiss.

When she pulled away, she asked, "How long do I have until you're gone again?" A mischievous smile lit her face, and she ground her pelvis down onto my swollen cock.

My dark chuckle rang through the garden as I slid my hands up her thighs, lifting the layers of her skirt so I could get to her firm ass. "We have more than enough time for me to show you how very much I missed you."

CHAPTER 58

AVERY

Tonight I would greet Ras alhague formally as its queen, for the second time. Jetta and I had been over every list a hundred times and there was nothing left to do but get ourselves ready.

Jetta came out from behind a screen in her room, which we'd turned into a full-blown dressing room, even going as far as stringing lights around the full-length mirror we'd brought in. I waggled my eyebrows at her breasts, which were currently defying gravity in the gown that we had designed for her.

"Wowzers," I said, and she adjusted them, so they'd stay put.

I finished filling in my eyebrows and went to slip on my dress. When I came back, Jetta dragged me in front of the mirror. "Damn," I said. "We look good."

Her gown was a deep red satin, with a balconette style bodice, a belted waist, and hugged her hips, running straight down to her ankles where her nude strappy heels were exposed by a single slit which ran to mid-thigh. Attached to the wide shoulder straps holding up the top, was a matching cape which brushed the floor. I talked her into doing a heavy, smokey eye, and nude-pink lipstick which I had to create by blending several shades from her palette of makeup from this plane. Her dark hair was pinned back on the sides and ran straight down her back. She was giving off futuristic commander vibes, and I loved it.

I, on the other hand, was channeling Guinevere energy. Lush navy velvet crisscrossed my chest and sat off my shoulders, so my glowing décolletage and upper back were exposed. Each strip of the velvet was trimmed with gold stitching and the sleeves were past my fingertips, but a large slit ran up the center to my inner elbow. The bodice hugged my curves and low on my hips, I wore a braided gold rope belt. The skirt flowed gently down to my feet, and to make the dress a little more modern, the front panel was unattached and two large slits came to my upper thigh similar to the skirt I wore earlier in the week. I had to show off my new boots. The shiny gold grommets carried the theme through, matching the gold crown which sat upon my head.

My hair was half up, and the loose strands floated in gentle waves over my shoulders. I kept my makeup simple and natural, relying on the warmth of my skin and the pink and peach color palette I had selected, and only a dusting of gold glitter on my eyes.

"Of course, we do," she said, grinning at her reflection before her eyes caught on mine. "What's wrong?"

"Nothing," I said, and she shot me a frown that said, *liar*. "It's only that half of these people still probably hate me for murdering Xavier."

"But you didn't murder him, and the talk of your heroic defense of yourself has been circulating," she said, winking. I'd heard murmurs of this, and I knew my friend had started the rumor. "Besides," she continued. "I think you'll find people are more curious than anything."

"Yeah, but I'm still nervous. What if I get cornered by someone who really liked him, therefore really dislikes me?" I asked. She turned to me, taking my hands in hers. I felt my face blanch. "Like that lover of his, Olive. I told you about her, right? I caught her complaining about me to Leviticus and the kitchen staff, and essentially had to ask her to leave the castle. She was still living here."

"You didn't tell me that, but I'm aware of her, as are many of the Ladies who will be attending tonight as she tended to proudly overshare about her affair with the newly risen king. From what I heard, she'll be attending on the arm of a lower lord who, in an attempt to gain status for himself, and misinterpreting any importance she might have gained from her former liaison, has taken her as a lover."

I raised a curious eyebrow. "Interesting," I said, though the story was not fully disposing of my worry.

Jetta shook my hands, squeezing. "Trust me, no one would dare say anything. The worst you'll get will be a sideways glance which will be quickly hidden. I'll be near and make sure to show you who to steer clear of. And once I introduce you to my friends, everyone will know not to mess with you."

Her sly smile gave me the impression I was about to be inaugurated into this plane's version of a bitch pack which was perfect as far as I was concerned. Having a group of women who had my back would feel really good. The thought excited me so much that a pang of melancholy hit me as I thought of the witches in my coven I'd enjoyed a close friendship with growing up. Yes, that would definitely be welcome.

"I'm in," I told her.

She spun me back to the mirror. "I mean look at you. You deserve to feel as confident as you look, my queen," she said.

"Thanks, my friend," I said, and she nodded.

"Ready?" she asked.

"Let's do this," I said.

Butterflies danced in my stomach as we made our way to the Great Hall. According to Jetta, everyone who was anyone would be here.

The guests would be arriving through massive wood entry doors at the long end of the hall. Once they were gathered and Leviticus made an official announcement, Nighval and I, along with Jetta, Link, and Eshan, would enter through a discreet door beyond the dais at the opposite side of the room. We rounded the corner, and I caught sight of my husband. Our motion drew his attention from the conversation he was having with the warlocks, and his eyes tracked up and down my figure, landing on my boots. I knew it was unconventional, and I loved designer heels as much as the next girl, but these just made me feel powerful. And I needed to feel that way tonight. When the corner of Nighval's lips tipped up, my stomach swirled for an entirely different reason.

"You like?" I asked.

He nodded and approached me, bending down to place a gentle kiss on my neck. As he did, his hand slipped inside one of the panels and grazed against the warm skin of my thigh, giving me goosebumps.

"I like this a lot," he said, his hot breath tickling my neck. "You look like a queen. *My* queen."

I grabbed ahold of his wrist before he could get carried away, and Link cleared his throat. "I believe you two are expected momentarily, so cut it out," he said, crossing his arms over his chest and frowning.

Nighval sighed and pulled away, giving me a chaste kiss on the lips, and offered me his arm. I had designed his tuxedo. The midnight fabric stretched over his broad shoulders and was cut perfectly to accentuate his narrow waist and long, muscled legs. Underneath, he wore a simple white button-up shirt and a thin satin tie in the same shade. The style was far more modern than anything the other men here wore and made him look that much more impressive. If he had sidled up to the bar dressed like this back in my plane, I probably would have been struck speechless. With his dark hair and chiseled features, even without considering the scars, he was intimidating. A work of art.

"What?" he asked, noticing me ogling him.

"Just enjoying the view," I said, and a satisfied smirk appeared on his face as he patted my hand hooked on his arm.

The way he soaked in my appreciation for him made me realize I needed to spend more time telling him exactly how perfect I found him to be. That would be easy because he was painfully gorgeous. Not even the imperfections marking his skin could take away from it and really, they only made him come across that much more masculine and so freaking sexy.

I leaned toward him. His arm lowered, dropping my hand to hook around my hip and he angled his head down so he could hear me whisper, "That suit makes you look so hot. I can't wait to get it off you later. Or maybe I'll make you fuck me while you're still wearing it."

My bold words brought warmth to my cheeks and that same heat flared violently in his eyes as his hand tightened on my arm. Before Nighval could pin me against a wall and take me up on my offer, and for a second, I really thought he might, Link said, "Keep moving, people."

I flashed my eyes back at him and he had a slightly amused, slightly annoyed expression on his face. Leviticus's booming voice could be heard through the doors, announcing us. I gave Nighval a wink before we stepped into the party.

As we walked on to the dais, and Nighval caught the first sight of the room, he stopped, swiveling his head to take everything in. "I thought you were going with the green," he said.

"I wanted to surprise you. And Jetta helped me make a few changes to the blue color palette that brought it together. What do you think?" I asked.

"Like you, it's perfect," he said, and then leaned down to kiss me. When I finally came up for air, I turned my attention to the gathered crowd, many of which were staring at their sovereigns who had just been making out in front of everyone.

"At least they know now that there's no love lost between you two," Jetta said as she and Link came to stand beside us. "Come on." She waved a hand to usher us down the steps and pointed to the chair at the head of the center table. "Dinner will be served shortly. Then you can accept your guests' well wishes."

"Actually, I have something I'd like to say first," Nighval said, and grinned down at me.

As he clasped my hand, lights flickered and a cool breeze floated through the room, raising my neck hairs. Was this his power? I glanced up at him and he seemed to sense it, too. Something was off.

Shit. I'd been so worried about how the populace of Ras alhague would receive me, I'd nearly forgotten to worry about *her*.

Lightning crashed, and the air in the room shifted as a new energy entered, blowing through any security the Council of Warlock's wards made around the space. You could almost feel them breaking down as the texture of the air crackled and cooled like a quickly forming thunderstorm.

In a blink, Nighval dropped my hand and his were in front of him, glowing blue. Next to him, Link's were glowing in his aqua. I scanned the room searching for the cause of the disturbance, noticing many of the other warlocks present had readied their power, including Eshan, whose hands were cloaked in a vibrant grass green.

Then, out of a mist, a striking chestnut-haired woman appeared standing atop the center table. The crowd gasped. I instinctively moved to my husband's side as his hand moved in front of me.

"Shit," Link said.

"Is that who I think it is?" I asked in a whisper.

"Yes," he replied, and Nighval shot him a glance, stepping forward.

Reading whatever the glance meant, Link stepped beside me protectively. "Don't worry," he said. "Nighval will take care of her."

"What are you doing here, Mother?" Nighval called to the woman, clearing a path as she strode down the table.

Each time she reached a flower filled vase, or one of the beautiful silver candelabras, she kicked out, catching it with her foot and it went flying. Guests dodged as she kicked place settings in their direction.

When she got to the end of the table, she planted her hands on her hips and stared across the open expanse to her son. "I guess my invitation went missing. Did you not receive my letter?"

Double shit.

I had to do something. Surely, we could settle this without bloodshed. The last thing I wanted was for the people of my kingdom to come to my wedding reception and get hurt. I stepped forward. Link tried to grab my arm, but I jerked away before he could get a hold of me.

I threw my shoulders back and set my jaw as I took my place beside Nighval. "It was my oversight," I said, and her icy blue eyes locked on me. Then a wicked smile erupted on her face.

"I've been dying to meet you, my dear," she said, hopping down from the table as if it were a single step. She sauntered over to the bottom of the dais, and made to take the first stair, but Nighval held out a glowing hand in her direction.

"Not another step," he said.

"Nighval," I beckoned, tugging on the sleeve of his jacket, but he kept his eyes locked on her as he angled his body in front of mine.

"How did I raise a son with such poor manners? At least your bride knows when to submit."

"You didn't raise me," he growled. "Now get out." Nighval motioned for the warlocks to advance.

"I think not," she said, not budging as they moved nearer to get a more direct line on her. "Your slight will cost you, and until you come to accept me, I'll make you suffer." Her voice took on a crazed tone and as her hands lifted, I saw Nighval share a glance with Link and Eshan.

Samara tossed a black silk pouch up into the air and sent a spear of power after it. When it struck, a cloudlike fog tore across the ceiling as tiny bolts of lightning danced within it causing the lights to pop and go out. Shrieks came from the stunned crowd as they were overtaken with darkness as only the glow from the warlocks and the remaining candelabras lit the room in eerie shadows.

Nighval's voice boomed as he yelled, "Get down."

Her face twisted with barely restrained anger as she noted the location of each readied warlock. "The insolence," she hissed. As the crowd dropped, several bolts of lightning shot out from Samara's hands, aiming toward the magic wielders who raised colorful shields as the power blasted into them.

"Stop this, Samara," I begged. "It doesn't have to be like this. We can get you a place setting and continue with the celebration." I didn't know exactly how I would pull that off considering she ruined half of the main table, but if she would just stop this, we could manage. This woman just wanted acceptance for who she was, just like Nighval. But he had never turned into a lunatic like this witch.

Her eyes pierced into me through the darkened room, and a full body tremor wrapped through me. "It's too late, child." She didn't break eye contact as a geyser of power shot toward the dais. Would she really kill us? I knew she wanted to scare us and satisfy the gaping hole in her chest where her heart should be, but I didn't think she would actually kill her last remaining son.

Link and Nighval darted forward to throw up a protective shield and when her blast hit it, white-blue flames exploded from the impact. The crowd screamed, many of them were crawling beneath the tables as the warlocks battled the witch.

I stood there stunned, before Jetta's smooth fingers wrapped around my arm. "Come on," she said, tugging. She pulled me back further onto the dais, so we were shielded behind the two large thrones that sat there. I peeked around the corner to see more explosions. It seemed even a few of the guests were lesser mages and were blanketing groups of guests with protective spells.

A surge of energy, much like a miniature nuclear explosion, surged out from the middle of the table, but instead of a mushroom cloud following it, the space where Samara had been, was vacated.

Jetta cried out from beside me and Samara's fingers wrapped around her face, digging into her pale skin. Her face went ghostly white, and her eyes rolled back in her head before she dropped to the floor.

"No," I cried and swung my fist toward the witch, but before it struck her jaw, it froze in midair. Then she grinned and darted a hand forward, grabbing ahold of the hair at the back of my neck.

In a blink, we were standing in the middle of the room on top of the table where she had first arrived, and she had a dagger pointed at my throat.

"Hold your fire," Nighval called, and the warlocks lowered their magic-encased hands. "Let her go."

"Maybe this will teach you to show your mother a little more respect," she said, and began chanting some incoherent magic I didn't recognize.

A prickling sensation zipped through my body before agony chased after it, and a scream burst from my lips. The pain lanced through me like every bone in my body was being broken at once and then I was weightless. Samara's hand still gripped the hair at the back of my neck though now I was dangling from her hand in a much smaller form. An instinctual panic shot through me with a severity I'd never experienced before. *Flee*, it bellowed. *Flee, flee, flee.*

Something was very wrong.

CHAPTER 59

NIGHVAL

W atching that witch's dark power dance over my wife was what
nightmares were made of. Horror etched itself into my bones as
I watched the woman I loved transform into a six-inch-long rat. Mother
or not, I was going to kill Samara Wrede.

Pretty amber flecked eyes were now beady, black, and terrified. I wasn't
sure if she understood what had happened to her or if she was even still
her, but before I could beg or do anything to get my wife back, they were
gone. I wanted to fall to my knees and bellow, but I was king. I could not.

Within a few seconds, Link and Eshan were at my side, and the other
warlocks joined them. I glanced over to Leviticus, whose face had taken
on a sickly hue. "Get them out of here," I commanded. The frazzled man
nodded and went about ushering the guests out of the room.

"She'll take her to the Wildwood," Link said.

I scraped my nails across my scalp. Avery was still alive. I had to remind
myself of that, so I didn't crumble inwardly.

"We should go after her," Link said, with a little more urgency.

"We need to think. I don't think Samara will kill her or cause any
permanent damage." Just thinking about everything Avery had been
through until this point made me sick. The thought of her going
through anymore suffering because of me and my family made my
stomach churn relentlessly. I had felt murderous before, but that was
nothing like I felt now.

Before she sent that first blast, I felt an ocean's worth of power inside
me trying to crack open. I should have smashed the dam holding it back

before she flinched. Now we were at her mercy. I knew what she wanted. She wanted me to come groveling.

"If there's a spell where we can all channel our power together. If we could somehow get to her house without her knowing—"

"We'd have to dismantle the wards, and that is witch magic," Link said, cutting Eshan off.

"We could set fire to the Wildwood and try to flush her out," Hager said.

"Quiet," I boomed, and all eyes trained on me. "That isn't what she wants. She wants me to go there and beg. She wants to play nice, like we're one big happy family. We might have been able to take her by force before, but she has my wife now. I have to go to her alone."

Out of the corner of my eye, I saw Jetta was struggling to get to her feet. I rushed over to her and helped her up. Darkened veins rose to the surface of her pale cheeks, caused by whatever spell had rendered her unconscious.

"What happened?" she asked, disoriented. She leaned onto me for support, and I ushered her over to the group. Immediately her father wrapped her in his arms and began using his power to heal the damage Samara had left.

As he worked, she eyed me. Then her eyes widened. "Where's Avery?" she asked, voice insistent and more than a little panicked.

I shook my head, and she gasped as her hands flew to her mouth. "No," she said beneath her breath.

"My mother will keep her alive, to lure me to her. I need to go. I can transport myself to the outside of her wards, and then I'll have to get to her on foot," I said.

"Nighval, I know you're not going to want to hear this, but you need to let her calm down. Rage has taken over her mind and there will be no sense talking to her now. She's too unpredictable. Go see her tomorrow. Let her sleep and come to her senses. She won't hurt Avery," Jetta said.

When I looked like I would not listen, she stepped forward and wrapped a hand around my forearm, squeezing. "Please trust me."

"How do you know?" I asked.

"Because I'm a woman, and I know there is no sense trying to reason with us when we are furious." The corner of her mouth tipped up in a sad smile, but she was right.

I didn't know what I was going to do with myself having to wait to free my wife. Every minute she had to stay in that form would be a nightmare for her.

I patted Jetta's hand. "Okay," I said, and without another word, I turned and stalked out of the room.

I didn't sleep. I spent the night pacing in front of the bed I shared with her. She had replaced the old, time-worn bedding with new, fresh fabrics in the same coloring and style as they were before. My thoughtful wife. She changed some things, but she left other things as they were, always knowing exactly which things made an impact.

As I wore a path and the rug, I decided I would never leave her at Ravsted without me once I got her back. I didn't care what she saw me do. I was keeping her by my side from now on. Nothing else mattered. I should have immediately grabbed hold of her and transported us somewhere safe. That was my mistake. And now the hours I spent without her were as much a punishment to me as knowing what she must be going through.

As soon as the sun peeked over the horizon, I transported myself to the edge of Samara's ward in the Wildwood. She spelled them to recognize my essence since we'd made our agreement to give me access, but I wasn't sure it still held, so my gaze was ever wary.

On foot it would be about two hours to the heart of the wood. Rustling sounded in the distance to my left. I jogged toward the sound, not wanting to be caught unaware. A small hunting party made up of four burly men trudged over an overgrown trapper's trail. The first two carried a long pole between them and a wild boar carcass hung upside down, bound by its legs. Another had a deer over his shoulders and the final man had a rope with a few rabbits strung through the eye, much like one would see a catch of fish.

I fell in behind the men, unbeknownst to them. It seemed like these woods were ever changing, shifting, and watching, but the hunters knew the way. It was easier to follow them and would likely save time.

When we entered the village, they shuffled down an alley and into a side door of a little stone building that belonged to the village butcher. My boots clapped onto the cobblestones of the narrow street as I charged toward the grand house at the end of the lane.

Kicking the wrought iron gate open, I strode across the yard and up the steps. My hand tugged the brass knob, but it didn't budge, so I beat my fist against the wood, making the knocker clank.

My heart raced as my vision clouded when she didn't immediately answer. We both knew I was coming, and we both knew she was in there with my wife.

I beat against the door with another series of muffled curses and paced over to see if I could get a glimpse inside a window. I was about to punch my fist through the glass when the door creaked open.

My mother had a slew of servants, but it was her smirking face that appeared from behind the door. It always was when I came to visit. I stomped over to her and slammed my hand into the wood, which tore it out of her grip before I brushed past her and entered.

When I turned around to glare down at her, she clicked the door shut and faced me, crossing her arms over her chest.

"Where the fuck is my wife?" I demanded, between gritted teeth.

"One might think you would be a little kinder to your mother," she said.

"If that's what you think, then you really are delusional," I said as she paced past me and down the hall. I followed on her heels. "Is she still trapped in the hold of your magic?" I asked, dread swirling in my stomach.

She shrugged nonchalantly, running a fingertip down the wood paneling of the hallway. She'd chewed her nails to the quick, I noticed, and what looked to be chemical burns were on the back of her hand. "You'll see soon enough. And you haven't even asked me what I wanted."

"I don't care what you want," I said, losing focus on the words I had told the warlocks last night. I knew I needed to play nice, but seeing her smug expression, my self-control slipped. I needed to get a hold of it with urgency for Avery's sake.

As if sensing my thoughts, she asked, "Are you sure?" Her voice dripped with poisoned honey.

I released a sigh as we turned the corner, taking a passageway that led to the workshop at the back of her house. We crossed the perfectly manicured lawn and entered the building through the solid wood door.

The room was dim and musky, and the foul smell of urine and animal waste drifted into my nose as I entered. "Why are we here?" I asked her. In the center of the room there was a large stain covered table and innumerous jars filled with varying items, from volcanic ash to what appeared to be blood.

"I thought you said you wanted to see your wife," she said, pressing her lips together and regarded me as if I had lost my senses.

I was going to burn this place to the ground once I got Avery back. Jetta was right, and my mother was much calmer, but it horrified me to think that the woman I cherished most in the world spent even an hour in this god-awful building.

"Come, darling," she said. "No need to panic. She is unharmed. The last thing I would do is hurt my daughter-in-law." The grin she gave me as she stepped around the corner made me wonder if the copious use of whatever magic she had siphoned from the earth had somehow corrupted her mind. She seemed to be getting worse the more time elapsed.

I followed her, stepping around the corner and as I took in the cages, my stomach dropped. My throat went dry as panic seized it, and I swallowed. "Are those all humans?"

I don't know what shocked me more. Her ambivalent attitude or the fact that dozens of little wire cages were stacked on top of each other and in each of them was a rat.

Samara picked up a tin, flipped the lid open and began handing little pieces of dried fruit to them. As her hand approached, they rushed to the front of the cage and their tiny pink fingers reached out and took the fruit before bringing it to their mouths to nibble away at it.

My blood went from ice to boiling in a split second. I grabbed her by the neck and slammed her face first into the wall. Before she could move,

I had a dagger made from my power digging into her side. My actions surprised her, and though her hands which were planted on either side of her head on the wall were glowing white, she didn't move.

I leaned down to whisper in her ear. "If you do not release her right now, I will drive this dagger into your liver. Then I will take my time as I fillet you before cutting out your eyes and shoving them down your throat. After that, if you're still alive, I'll see how hungry your pets are."

To emphasize the point, I pressed the dagger in deeper and a trickle of blood trailed down her cream robe.

"How dare you?" she hissed. "Let me go this instant."

I tightened the grip on her neck, digging my nails into her delicate skin. If I changed my angle slightly, I could crush her windpipe. We both knew I couldn't kill her, though. What she did to Avery was witch's magic and possibly a dark form of it. I needed her to turn my wife back into a human.

Before I could stop her, her finger flicked once, and the sound of creeping metal filled the room. I glanced over at the cages. Every single door sprang open, and the rodents tentatively approached the edge. They were practically identical and within seconds, as they discovered their newly found freedom, they began hopping out of the cages, hitting the floor, and scurrying past our feet, squeaking, hissing, and crawling over each other as they went.

In my shock, I loosened my hold on her neck. Samara used that to spin around and shove a blast of hot power into my stomach, wincing as my dagger dragged a thin line across her side. Her power clad hand met the black fabric of my shirt where her power burned me with such force I flew into the opposite wall. I slid to the ground, clutching my stomach.

She hovered over me, gripping her side. "Why could we not just be a normal family?" she asked, as she teetered back to the part of her that seemed to earnestly want to be a mother. I only needed to wait another few moments and she'd be back to the conniving witch who'd tricked my father and murdered him before my eyes.

I clutched my stomach, and the magic burns I felt blistering beneath the fabric. My insides felt charred as I glared up at her. "Because you're an unpredictable psychopath."

She twitched and her eyes became glassy for a moment before hardening into the pale blue ice I usually encountered.

"That's unfortunate," she said, surveying the creatures squirming into cracks beneath the baseboard and under the door.

She started to walk away, but halted when I got to my feet and asked, "What about Avery?"

She spun. "I released her. Just as you asked." She waved her arm around the room at the fleeing creatures.

"I'm going to kill you," I said, raising my hands to draw on my power, but whatever she did to me had guttered it. Only flickers rested in my palms. Not nearly enough to make good on my threat.

"Not that you would ever take my advice, but if I were you, I wouldn't be spending precious time threatening me whenever you should be hunting for your wife," she said.

I darted forward to grab hold of her, but my fingers met the air where she had stood. Shit. I lifted my shirt to inspect the wound and winced as I pulled away the fabric and skin. A few places I could see down to the sinew of the muscle. I wasn't sure if any lasting damage had been done to my internal organs. It didn't matter. Samara was right. I needed to find Avery.

The irony and the horror were not lost on me as I knelt to the ground trying to scent which of the creatures had that familiar sunshine and floral smell. Surely, I'd be able to recognize it. Hissing came from the table, and I looked up to see a couple of the creatures tussling over the open tin of fruit. A few others were still working their way around the edges of the room, but one stood in the doorway, blinking its black beady eyes at me.

"Avery?" I asked, feeling more than a little insane. How had the woman reduced me to this? But I'd endure this and limitless humiliations for my wife. Tentatively, I crawled toward the animal, but as the board underneath my knee creaked, it darted away into the lush green grass of the backyard.

I shot to my feet and ran after it. The blades were thick and tall, and I could only see the top of its back as it ran toward the hedges. I had to get it before it made it out into the city. There were endless blood chilling possibilities. Horrifying things that could happen, from being caught in the jaws of a stray dog or under the wheel of a carriage, to poison, or a rat trap. And there were also an endless number of places to hide. If she got out of my sight—no, I couldn't let that happen.

Keeping light on my feet, careful to not accidentally bring my boot down on one of these cursed beings, I chased after her.

She fled between the metal rods of the fence and darted under the bush and into the nearest street, running along the buildings. A woman stepping out of her building, saw the rodent, screamed as she jumped back, slamming the door shut before it could run inside.

A second later I saw her with a broom in hand, peering out of the window of her shop. Avery ran, and I followed. Around corners, down alleyways, until she got to the door of the stables at the edge of town. She skittered beneath the wood panels though when I peered inside, I lost sight of her.

I threw the door open, pushing past a stable hand who immediately barked at me to get out. I vaguely recognized the youth as the one who'd delivered the message of Xavier's passing months earlier, but I didn't have time to think on it. He must have recognized me, or at least was intimidated by what he saw, because his mouth fell open and he plastered himself against a wall.

I ran my hand through my hair. In each of the four stalls there was a horse munching on a basket of hay, and beneath it was a pile of straw. I slid into the first stable and was about to rifle through the pile when the boy shouted, "Out, you varmint!"

I shot out of the stall. "Where did it go?"

My cursed wife was nowhere in sight, and the boy was back to looking like a gaping fish. I grabbed him by the shirt collar and drew him to me. "Which way?" I growled.

He blinked, dumbfounded, but his head seemed to clear as I rattled him. Then, wordlessly, his finger jutted out toward the open door.

I grumbled as I released him, but when I got to the alley, I lost her trail. A niggle of doubt crept in. Was it her, or was I creating a narrative to ease my fear?

No, I wouldn't doubt myself. Over the years, I honed my instincts into a fine blade. That was her. She was the only one who had hesitated before acting like a normal animal, which would make sense because her curse was new.

There was no telling how long the others had been under Samara's spell. I closed my eyes and drew in a deep breath through my nose, trying to take in any information that my enhanced senses, which still lingered from my own curse, could detect. The wind down this alleyway swirled, making it nearly impossible for me to detect which way she went.

I looked back at the direction I had chased her from and moved in the opposite. It was a fifty-fifty chance.

I didn't know how long I jogged through the village, but as I made my third lap, my hope was dwindling. I leaned against a brick wall in an alleyway out of view from the passersby who were already gaping openly and lifted my shirt. What was left of my skin was angry and red and the exposed flesh was oozing and trying to scab over. I should have stopped and healed myself, but I didn't have the time.

I lifted my hands to work the healing magic when a guttural scream rent the air, making my hair stand on end and my instincts go on high alert before I could take care of my wound.

"Avery?" I yelled, hoping she'd call out again. The sound of her terror would haunt my dreams, but at least it was an indication that she had somehow been transformed back into a human. She screamed again. This time the sound was muffled, but it was enough. I pinpointed its direction and followed it.

The scream echoed in my mind, leading me toward her. As I raced nearer, the sounds of rough male voices came from the depths of an alley. I darted around the corner and came upon the three hunters from earlier, all facing a corner, taunting, and jabbing at their prize.

Golden-brown skin peeked out from between them, and I almost staggered, the blinding rage was so potent. The last dregs of my power chased down my arms and two glowing balls of fire magically appeared in them. I was consumed with ending them. I didn't think they had hurt her yet, but that they had even gotten close to my wife demanded their death.

I flicked my wrists and the magic shot toward the outer two. Blue light burst through the alleyway as it slammed into their backs. Their cries as the power hit them, searing off their flesh, was a melody I would savor long after this day. Avery's eyes widened as the fire consumed two of the men before her.

Now that I could get a good look at her, she seemed relatively unscathed, but she had one hand wrapped protectively across her breasts. The other gripped a sharp rock she held at the apex of her thighs, which were clamped tight together. Blood coated the rock and the tips of her fingers, and a purple and red mark swelled on her cheek.

"Nighval," she said, the sound of her panicked voice cut like broken glass.

"It's okay," I said, pulling a dagger from the sheath at my thigh. The burning men fell to the ground at her feet, writhing and screaming as the flames consumed them and she pressed back into the corner. The other man glanced between his fallen companions and spun to face me. A large gash bled across his temple and there was a gaping wound at his neck, but it hadn't been enough to kill him.

I grinned. "Did you do that?" I asked.

She nodded, even as fear filled her eyes, momentarily displacing me. I wasn't sure if I was now scaring her or the fact that I had so easily killed two men without flinching had, but she would have to accept me if she was going to stay at my side as I set the kingdom to rights.

I shot forward, grabbed the man by his drab, greasy hair and brought his eyes to face me as I slit his throat, finishing the job my wife had started. Blood sprayed onto my already soaked tunic, and I dropped him to the ground with the others.

"Look out!" she screamed, as a searing pain stabbed through my chest. I spun, but I was too late. The fourth hunter was standing at the end of the alleyway, loading another crossbolt. I lifted my hands, calling upon the fire magic as another bolt sailed through the air. Still, the magic left my hand and the last thing I saw before my knees cracked into the ground was the trader catching fire.

CHAPTER 60

AVERY

A sob tore from my throat as I rushed to Nighval's side. He landed face down, pushing the shafts of the arrows so they protruded out his back. I went to my knees beside him and rolled him, so he was on his side. The front of his stomach was covered in third- and fourth-degree burns, and his shirt was in tatters. Two metal arrowheads stuck out of his chest. One from beside his sternum on the right, and the other—no. It couldn't be.

Why had I never learned anything useful, like first aid? I glanced around for something to stop the bleeding. The diamond shaped razor blades of the arrowheads looked like they could shred whatever they touched, and my husband's blood gushed out, pooling at my knees.

I tore at what was left of his tunic and rolled it up into a ball to press it to his chest wound. The thing was soaked in a few seconds.

"No, please, no," I cried as I hovered over him, trying to staunch the blood.

I scanned his perfectly imperfect face. His lips were becoming a deadly blue tinge. "Nigh, please, don't leave me." I leaned down and kissed them as I begged. They were already cool.

If there were other men with the four that Nighval had taken out, I wouldn't have noticed them. My only focus was on my husband and my collapsing world as his life quickly slipped away before me. "NO!" I scream-sobbed. I closed my eyes, and I begged the spirit of the earth that gave the witches their magic to intervene. To do something. Anything not to let this man be taken from me.

My breathing was coming in quick, shallow gasps now. This was the part in the story where the heroine was supposed to discover she had magic all along. I opened my eyes to stare at my powerless hands, only to come face to face with the bitch whose fault this was.

Samara squatted across from Nighval's failing body and she had a finger pressed to his pulse. She was probably making sure he was dead. All thought escaped my mind as I launched myself across him at her. We tumbled backwards as my hand went to her throat. My fingers were around her, and I was squeezing with everything I had when a blast of energy sent me flying backwards.

I slammed into a wooden door and the cracking sound bit through the alleyway. I hung in midair where I had hit, and I could feel warm blood trickling from a gash in the back of my head.

I sucked in a deep breath to refill my lungs. "Don't you touch him," I sputtered.

"Easy, my daughter," she said as she pulled a vial from her pocket. Her hands moved, and the arrows disappeared.

"I'm not your daughter," I hissed, all the while mesmerized as I watched her roll him to his back, bite off the cap of the liquid and pour it onto his wounds. His skin sizzled as smoke rose from the wounds and the smell of burnt flesh made its way to my nostrils.

"What are you doing to him?" I demanded, still dangling from where her power held me against the door.

She ignored me, rolling him over to his stomach, pulled out a matching vial and poured it into the wounds in his back. When she was satisfied and they quit hissing, she positioned him face up once again.

Assessing his stomach, she frowned. Then her eyes drifted to me for a second before returning her gaze to her son and she placed her hands atop of each other over his chest. Darkness spread from her palms over him, cloaking him and then eventually her.

"Samara," I cried. "What's happening?" I shook my feet, kicking and wiggling until I finally fell to the ground with a thud. I raced forward before halting at the edge of the inky fog.

Reaching my hand out to run it through the black smoke, my fingers met a substance as solid as stone. She had encapsulated them inside, without me.

Tears streamed down my face as I ran my hands across the fog dome. Tiny vibrations resonated off the surface, and I could feel the sound of her chanting more than I could hear it. I didn't know how long this went on or how long I circled them when the fog shifted to grey, and then white. It swirled into a vortex that lifted into the sky until it had completely dissipated, and I could see the mother and son once again.

Samara sat on her knees, still in the same position she'd been in when she blocked me off from them, but her cool blue eyes were distant.

"Samara?" I asked.

I moved forward, stepping in front of her face, but as her eyes flicked up to mine, she slumped to the side onto her hip. "Samara? What happened?" I asked a little more insistently, but she fell forward, her forehead slapping into Nighval's bare chest. I sucked in a breath as her head rose with the expanding chest. A guttural sound burst from my lips, and I went to my knees beside them.

I ran my finger along his neck and found a steady pulse. I bit out another sob. "You're alive."

I bent down and kissed his forehead and every beautiful scar on his face, then I gently eased Samara off of him. She too was alive, and apparently, she exerted herself so much she passed out. My discarded rock lay near Nighval's dagger on the stones a few feet away. My fingers itched as I crawled over to the blade and wrapped my fingers around its hilt. I was making my way over to the unconscious witch when a voice came from the end of the entrance to the alley.

"Oh, my goodness," a gentle voice squeaked. The woman plastered her hand over her mouth. Her stare went from me to the knife in my hand, to the six bodies strewn about.

I set the knife down and raised my hands, palms outward. "It's okay," I said, and she nodded, taking a step back. "Please, I need your help."

I stood and took a few steps toward her. She didn't move, but her brow wrinkled, and I realized what she was seeing. Since I had transformed back into a human, I hadn't had a chance to find any clothes. I was standing in an alleyway completely naked with a bunch of dead bodies, the most powerful witch, and her warlock king son unconscious at my feet.

"They're alive," I said. "But I need to get them to safety. Fetch a carriage. And some clothes."

She hummed a nervous sound as she turned around and scampered away. I picked up the knife again and considered taking this opportunity. I had a feeling we would never get one again, but Samara had just saved him. Granted, it was her fault we were in this mess, but killing her like this seemed a little cold-blooded. And besides, there was a witness now.

I couldn't bring myself to do it, and I hoped it wasn't a decision I would regret later. As I sat there turning the thoughts over in my mind, and wondering when Nighval would wake up, voices and the sounds of hooves and wheels clattering across the cobblestones came into my awareness.

A single horse came into view, pulling behind it a small carriage as requested. The woman and a boy who looked about seventeen jumped down. The boy started as he realized he passed a dead and charred body. As his attention focused on his king and the witch, his eyelids peeled back.

"What the hell, Sadie?" he asked the woman.

"It's the king," she squeaked.

"I know it's the king. He was in father's stable earlier chasing a rat," the boy said, his strides becoming more confident as he passed the two still breathing bodies and went to the other three at the end of the alley. He nudged the one whose throat was slit so he could see his face.

"Who is it?" Sadie asked.

"The Hoover brothers," he said.

Her nose wrinkled and disgust. Apparently, they were as unsavory in the daytime as they were at night. "Clothes?" I asked, hopefully.

"Oh, yes," Sadie said, and fetched something out of the carriage. She handed me a bundle, and I slipped into the too big dress, grateful to be covered.

When I finished dressing, I saw Sadie and the boy were inspecting Samara and Nighval. I had no idea how we were going to get my large husband into the carriage. Hopefully, the three of us could do it. "How are you going to—" I started to voice my concerns aloud, but the boy's hands began working as strain concentration sprouted across his features.

Sadie opened the carriage door as Nighval's body hovered and drifted into it. Then Samara's moved in a similar fashion. Once the two were inside and arranged in a somewhat dignified resting position, the boy approached me.

"I can take you to the witch's home," he said.

I shook my head. "No, we need to drop her off there and then I have to get the king back to Ravsted." I could tell a protest was bubbling on his lips. "You must. This is an order from your queen."

If his eyes had been wide earlier, now they were bugging out of his head. "Yes, Your Majesty," he said.

He ushered me to the seat where he would drive the carriage. I assumed he didn't have enough magic yet to operate it without the horse, as Nighval had, and the effort of getting the bodies into it seemed to have taxed him to his limit. I squeezed a slack-jawed Sadie's arm as I passed. "Thank you," I said.

The moment my butt hit the raised seat exhaustion flooded through me. I wouldn't allow this young man to see me break down, so I kept the tears behind a fragile dam.

I would be strong because that was who I was now. If we could survive this, we could survive anything. I didn't think after everything, Samara would mess with us again. Perhaps that was naïve, but I had hope. My love had been a few heartbeats away from leaving this plane and now his heart was beating strong, and we were on our way home.

CHAPTER 61

AVERY

Two heart-breaking months passed, and he still hadn't woken. We returned to Ravsted after nearly a week of me and the boy, whose name I learned was Luk, traded off driving and sleeping. I'd been nearly as panicked after a few days watching my comatose husband as I was as I watched him bleed out, but I held out hope the Council of Warlocks would know what to do. They hadn't and seeing him like this wasn't getting any easier to bear. In fact, it was becoming worse.

I had him, his body anyway. It was like some awful repeat of Khal Drogo, and I definitely wasn't about to smother him with a pillow or walk into a fire and make baby dragons. I didn't have any special eggs, magic, or anything else of value. Only this crown and this gaping hole in my chest where the man I sat vigil for day and night remained.

But I was a hopeless romantic and whatever waking sleep paralysis he was under had to end at some point, right? I'd tried kissing him, to no avail. I'd screamed at the ceiling, trying to call the healing power of the Goddess down. The warlocks pooled their power and sent a message across the planes to consult the witches. No solution. My aunt had even sent a note of condolence, but I was still so bitter at her and the witches for not helping Nighval originally, for sending me without telling me about the curse, and now for not having a solution, I'd skimmed it and thrown it into the fire.

My husband lay there, open eyes fixed blankly on the ceiling, heart beating, but not really there. Not the same.

Eshan stepped into the room, clearing his throat, and I tore my gaze away from my husband's still body. "Avery, the council is waiting." He approached, holding a hand out, which I took. He tugged me to my feet and clasped both of my shoulders, giving me a little shake. "You're stronger than this, my queen."

A tear snaked down my bare cheek. "Some days are harder than others." I shook my head as more fell. The gentle man's rough thumbs clasped my cheeks and brushed away the moisture.

"I know it's not the same, but we miss him, too. Link and I grew up with him as a constant fixture in our lives. You couldn't have a better friend than Nighval, outside of whenever he was in prince mode. He could be a real dickhead then."

I huffed a laugh. Eshan and Link had been telling me about their adventurers throughout their youth. They'd been inseparable since they met, and they'd even learned to control their magic together. I thought of Luk and hoped he had a friend like that. When Nighval woke, I'd make sure he took the boy under his wing.

"I can only imagine," I said.

He put his arm around my shoulder and urged me toward the door. "Come on. We'll get through this together, and I promise you, we will figure out a way to get him back."

I nodded, sniffing. I had to have faith and there was still work to do. Jetta stayed after the reception and if it weren't for her, Link and Eshan, I'd have been lost. Even Leviticus didn't seem unaffected watching me suffer and attempted to cheer me up from time to time, bless his heart.

It took all of my willpower to let Eshan guide me down the hall toward the conference room. He ushered me inside and sat me between him and Link, who reached over and gave me an assuring squeeze on the knee.

The council greeted me. Only a few of the older ones were brave enough to make eye contact. Leviticus, who I had invited back to the council in Nighval's absence, leaned forward, reciting off the first item on the agenda. Then the next. More repairs, the state of the different provinces, requests for aid, disputes needing intervention from the crown, tax reports from the magistrates and a million other things I didn't care about. It's not that I wouldn't care about it if my husband weren't in some sort of frozen state like Han Solo in the other room.

My voice was weak, on this side of breaking when, as the meeting neared its end, I said, "And what of the fate of our king?"

The men on the council shifted uncomfortably, many of them averting their gaze. Jetta's father, Hager Proudfoot, locked eyes with me in a show of bravery. Shaking his head, he said, "We haven't found anything yet, Your Majesty."

"But you are still looking?" I asked.

He looked away then. "We're doing everything we can."

I didn't think he was lying, but I wasn't sure they felt the same urgency I did. I rose from the table and my chair scraped loudly across the stones. I leaned over and slammed my fists on the table and impressed a demanding look at each one of them.

"Let's get one thing straight. Until that man is walking among us once again, he is your priority." I pointed an angry finger in the direction of the Chapel where Nighval lay under heavy guard. My voice broke as I yelled, "Do you understand?"

A chorus of "Yes, Your Majesty," rang out.

"You're dismissed," I said, desperately waiting the long seconds it took for the men to shuffle out of the room.

Still a few lingered and Link must have noticed my trembling, my barely contained anguish bubbling to the surface. "Go," he said, waving off the men who were hoping to get a private audience with me. I looked down at the table, closing my eyes, and when the footsteps retreated and the door clicked shut, I let a sob escape.

I was about to collapse back into my chair in a heap of tears when strong arms wrapped around me and pulled me into a hard chest. "Shhh," Link said. "I've got you."

"Today sucks," I said, as I blubbered into his chest. Noticing the darkening fabric, I said, "I'm going to ruin your shirt."

His chest rumbled beneath me as he laughed. "Anything for my queen."

"I'll go get Jetta," Eshan said, in a hushed tone intended for Link.

I sobbed and sobbed and when I finally calmed, Link pulled me away from his chest, tilting my chin up toward him. "I feel like such a weakling. I'm supposed to be queen, bulletproof, but I can't even keep it together through a boring meeting."

He smiled. "Do you know what I thought of you the day you walked into that council meeting and made Leviticus get up and proceeded to take his place and participate as an equal to your husband?" he asked, and I shook my head.

"Outside of the massive pang of jealousy that zapped through me, I thought to myself one day I'm going to have a wife like that. I had never given much thought to settling down, but seeing how you changed my dear friend, and what a love like that can do to a man, I decided I wanted something like that for myself. I promise you, I'm not the only person here you have inspired. You don't give yourself enough credit."

A tear, for an entirely different reason, tracked down my cheek and he wiped it away with a finger. "Avery, Samara intended this punishment to be particularly cruel. I don't believe she will let this go on forever. We are just going to have to bear it a little while longer, okay?"

"But Samara put him in this state, and she won't even respond to us." I could feel another wave of tears coming on, but I held them back as the hopelessness I felt settled around me.

Link ran a hand through his icy blonde strands. "I don't think she wants him dead, Avery. She'll come around. We'll get Nighval back. I promise."

I nodded. "Okay," I said.

"Good. Now if I know anything about Jetta, she is about ready to force feed you. So, shall I carry you and then tie you down, or will you be walking yourself?" He gave me a smirk, and I huffed, but walked through the door.

Out in the hallway, we ran into Jetta and Eshan. Link nudged me toward them as if I were some sort of ball to juggle, and said, "I never had a chance to give you your wedding gift. I feel like now is as good a time as any and you need cheering up because I know you're going to love it."

Before I could protest, the tall man was dashing down the hall.

I glanced at Jetta, and she shrugged as if she had no idea what he was talking about. Lunch was already served whenever we got to the dining room. It seemed Jetta had the cooks make us a selection of my favorites and they sat in little piles in the middle of the table for the three of us to pick through at our leisure.

Observing my wary gaze, Jetta jabbed in the direction of the wrap sandwiches and said, "Eat at least one."

"I second that. Link seems like a nice guy now, but you haven't seen him when he's on a mission. Have no doubt that he will tie you down and force feed you," Eshan said, humor at the edge of his voice.

"Fine," I said and put a few items on my plate. The first five bites tasted like sawdust, but eventually my taste buds awoke. I had eaten about all I thought I could when Link sauntered back into the room full of his usual swagger. He shoved the place setting which had been waiting for him beside me to the side and plopped down a huge, wrapped present.

"Open it," he demanded, then leaned against the table, crossing his arms. A self-satisfied grin lit his face, as if he knew I would love what was inside. As if he knew this little moment of sunshine was so desperately needed to clear the clouds away, if only for a moment.

"Oh my God." I was actually going to cry again. This was getting a little out of hand. "You guys have been too good to me," I said, standing to get a better angle to unwrap the gift.

Jetta leaned back in her chair with a curious expression on her face.

Eshan said, "You're our queen, and more than that, you're our friend."

Jetta made a puking sound. "I know, right? Big sap," I teased.

I made quick work of the gift wrap, and Link handed me a switchblade, and I cut open the seam of the box. I eyed him as I reached inside, feeling around. My hand was met with cool leather that felt worn and familiar. There was a loop of the stiff material with mesh on the interior at the top and on the sides... my hand ran down further, and I gasped.

"Oh my God," I said with even more emphasis than before. "How did you find it?"

"What is it?" Jetta said, getting to her feet, coming to stand near me.

I pulled my hand from the package and threw my arms around his waist, squeezing so hard I hoped it would convey my gratitude. When I released him, I turned around to see a too curious Jetta had tipped the box over and was pulling my backpack from inside.

She turned it over, inspecting it. "I heard about this thing. Doesn't look like much."

"It's not the pack itself, but what's inside." As glee brightened my features, a wave of guilt surged over me. How could I be feeling any sort of joy whenever the man I loved was frozen in some sort of magical stasis?

As if sensing my deteriorating thoughts, Jetta ran her hand up and down my arm. "He would want you to enjoy this. You're allowed to have happy moments, too."

I nodded and looked at the warlock. "Thank you, Link. This is the best gift ever, and I hope it wasn't too much trouble."

"Nothing is too much trouble for my queen," he said, and the earnest, yet self-assured grin he gave me might have been dangerous if I were any other woman. Link was gorgeous, as were Eshan and all the other warlocks in their own unique ways. Including Jetta's father, who was a total silver fox. Nighval was the most handsome of all, though, and the most powerful. It's not something he ever would admit, but I could tell, and so could everyone else. And Jetta was right. He would want me to enjoy this moment and make something beautiful despite the soul-crushing circumstances.

"Jetta, if you promise to let me do whatever I want to your face, I'll take a break from standing vigil this afternoon and go back to him after dinner," I said.

"Only if you agree to eat dinner," she said, smirking.

"I will eat dinner." I held up one hand and crossed the other over my heart.

"Done," she said, and hoisted the backpack off of the table, looping her arm through mine. "You'll need to do your best work because I'm meeting a certain someone for dinner, which means you guys will have to make sure Avery keeps her promise."

Link and Eshan agreed and watched as she tugged me out of the room.

An hour later, we were sitting in her room and the contents of the makeup bag were strewn across the vanity in her bathroom. "I need something for my cheeks," Jetta said.

She selected a few of the small Nars compacts, flipping each over to read the names of the shades. "Let's see. Will it be Sin, Desire, or—" She burst into laughter.

"What?" I asked, making my mascara face as I coated my lashes with my favorite waterproof black.

"This one is called Orgasm," she said when she finally contained her giggle fit. "So strange. I wish I could visit your plane."

I gave her face a once over. "Definitely Orgasm," I said. "I think Desire would be too intense for you. Too pink. You need something softer that will make your pale skin glow. And after you use that," I handed her another compact with a shimmery finishing powder, "dust some of this lightly over the highlights. You can also use it on your collarbone and the top of the girls."

She did as I said and caught my gaze in the mirror as she was assessing herself. Noticing my somber expression, she turned and wrapped her fingers around my wrists. A tear trickled down my cheek, carving a path through the powder, and I gave her a weak smile. She pulled me into her arms and said, "We'll get him back, Avery. I don't know how I know, but I do. My intuition about these things is never wrong."

CHAPTER 62

NIGHVAL

Like everything my mother did, this scheme of hers was vicious. Her vindictive power washed over me, and my body seized as a bone-deep chill bit through every cell. When Avery rolled Samara off me, the terror lacing her expression before she realized I was alive caused my heart to split in two.

And now, she didn't understand that I could hear her, that I could see her when she came close. That I could feel every tear that fell onto my face. Feel every time her warm lips brushed against my cool ones. She didn't know that as she sat beside the small bed which they'd brought into the space to lay me upon and she buried her head into my chest as she gripped my arm, that I felt it all. I was grateful they hadn't put me in my own bed since that at least gave her a place of refuge, because I knew so very acutely this was killing her.

I heard every conversation, from the guards to her own incoherent mutterings. I heard her scream and wail to the heavens, to the Goddess, and to the warlocks. I would have laughed if I could. I'm fairly sure half of them were afraid of her, and I knew all of them were doing everything they could to discover how to break this curse.

I heard it when Eshan told her she was stronger than this and from the corner of my vision, saw his arm around her, supporting my queen, as he helped her from the room so she could rule our kingdom.

I was grateful for my friends and how they were supporting her. I had lost track of time, though I knew only a few months had elapsed, but I longed for her suffering to end. I wasn't sure I could bear another of her sleepless nights, the pacing and moaning, her tearful sobs. Some nights she kept them at bay, and I could see her sitting beside me with a blank expression on her face, like she had physically spent all the emotion she kept bottled inside and had nothing left to give. Her breathing would change on those nights as her head rested on my chest, and I would know she was asleep. Sometimes, either Link or Eshan would sneak into the room, work a spell, and carry her away. Presumably back to our bedroom.

The days that followed were the worst ones, because she would be angry that she was taken away from me, but rested, so the anguish would spring back to life again with renewed energy. And the cycle would repeat. Last night had been one of the bad ones, and I hoped my friends would be able to get her through the meeting today.

"Do you think he's ever going to wake up?" one of the guards posted at the door to the chapel asked.

"I dunno," the other replied, and I tuned them out.

Every one of their idiotic conversations, I heard, too.

I heard everything. I heard it all and could do nothing. It wasn't like it had been with the rat curse and my heightened senses, some of which still lingered. This new torment was maddening, being trapped in one's mind. I heard every footstep, every breeze, birds chirping distantly through the window. I even thought I heard the castle groan as the temperature dropped overnight.

I heard the familiar crackle of magic as the witch whisked into the chapel on a power-filled breeze. I couldn't see enough of the room in my periphery with my frozen gaze to catch sight of her.

Two thuds sounded which I suspected were the guard's bodies dropping to the floor, before footsteps clicked across the stone. Fabric rustled as the intruder swished toward me.

"Hello, son," Samara said, stepping into view. Her rich chestnut hair was piled atop her head and her big blue eyes softened as she stepped over me. While one could tell she was older by the way she carried herself and the definition of her features, hardly a line etched her smooth creamy skin, the only trait I seemed to get from her.

That and we shared the same defined jaw and pointed chin. I knew it made me look severe, but on her it gave her a delicate edge.

Otherwise, I had my father's hair and eye coloring, and Xavier had gotten hers. A slim hand brushed from my temple down to my cheek, where her thumb gently caressed.

What do you want? I thought, hoping somehow, she could hear me. *How could you do* this? I screamed internally. *I won. I beat you and you still couldn't let it be.*

I wanted to rail and rage and cast her down. As soon as the curse had been broken, I should have rallied the warlocks and gone after her. That was a mistake I wouldn't make again. If I ever get out of this.

"You should be dead," she said, in a matter-of-fact tone. I watched her as she petted my hair and traced every scar with the pads of her fingertips. "You've become quite the man despite everything I've thrown at you. Maybe you are just more deserving than me." She gave a dramatic sigh as a single tear threatened to tip over the edge of her eyelid.

Why are you here? I asked again, though I knew she couldn't hear me.

She leaned against the bed, over my body, resting her hand on the other side of my chest and brought her face down enough so we were eye to eye. "I'm here to say goodbye," she said.

So, she could hear me. *But, why? I don't understand.*

"All I ever wanted was to be a mother—"

You could have stayed in your plane and done that, I thought, interrupting her.

She huffed and gave me a knowing smile. "I wanted sons. I wanted powerful, beautiful sons. Have you ever wondered why the witch and the warlock planes are separated? Why we don't breed?"

I had wondered this, but I cleared my thoughts to allow her to continue.

"All you have to do is consider the power you hold, son. You are my legacy. You are everything that I was trying to create. You allow yourself to be held back by what is known about the warlock's power, but you also carry the power from my blood. If you wanted, you could move between planes and even take your new wife."

That is why you didn't let me die? You could have let me die and had another son.

Sadness eclipsed the vision of the future in her eyes. And I felt perhaps I understood where it was coming from. And then I knew. I knew what she was planning. "No, Nighval. You were the goal. You were the child I wanted to have. You may not have known it, but I've spent years watching you and no other son could replace what you are."

Her words twisted the long forgotten knife lodged in my chest. In that moment, it seemed we shared a lifetime of regret, caused by the prejudice of my well-meaning father, and my vicious, vindictive mother.

"I spared you, you know."

From what? I mentally hissed.

"Heartbreak. I believe your wife sees every part of you, the goodness, and the flaws. Everything that you are, and she loves you for it. I've seen it these last two months as her heart has broken for you. I loved your father. I know he painted me to be a monster, and maybe I am, but you'll never experience the loss that I did. That is what I spared you from."

In a strange way, I understood what she meant. She honestly believed that her curse which turned me and the rest of my people into monsters had somehow protected me and my heart. The woman was mad. Cursing an entire people to protect her child was an insane thing to do, not to mention she'd apparently found a way to spy on us all this time. And she was lying to herself if she denied the role vengeance played in her actions. Still, her words gave me a brief insight into what it would have been like to be raised by a loving mother. The type of mother Avery would be to our children.

I had been meeting with Samara. Eventually, if she would have behaved appropriately, I might have even brought Avery to meet her. This was her fault. She was the one who couldn't control her temper. My anger boiled to the surface.

None of this would have happened if you hadn't stolen my wife away and turned her into a rat.

Her sadness transformed to fury in a blink, and she grabbed my cheeks, pinching them between her fingertips. "None of this would have happened if you invited me to your reception."

Power corrupts, I thought before I could think better of it.

"What?" she asked, knitting her eyebrows.

You asked me if I knew why the planes were kept separated, so, I answered you. Power corrupts. And somehow, you got too much of it.

As I thought the words, her expression seemed to tilt, not just the angle of her head, but like I had shattered something inside her. Or set a truth free. We stared at each other for long moments before she said, "Yes. Perhaps that is true. I hope you will wield yours better than I have mine." She stepped away and brushed her hands down the front of her dress, smoothing out the fabric.

"Goodbye, son," she said, and a crackle bit through the air and she evaporated into a mist.

CHAPTER 63

AVERY

While the afternoon had been fun, and my freshly makeup face looked amazing considering how red and puffy it was, my situation felt endlessly hopeless. I spent my days beside him and my nights dreaming of smiting that bitch mother of his. How could she do this to her only remaining son for finding a love she never dreamed possible for herself? He was wild, frightening and had done some unspeakable things, but was so much better than her. And he was mine.

A fresh round of tears welled, and I doubled over with the weight of it. I couldn't get the cycle of repetitive thoughts out of my head. The dwelling was going to kill me. I should be stronger and have faith like Link. But I didn't. My chest ached like nothing I'd ever felt before, and when that sensation wasn't threatening to tear me in two, a murderous rage hijacked my thoughts.

Footsteps sounded. The clicks of a pair of high heels approached me. Jetta. I'd played along this afternoon, and even ate dinner. What did these people want from me? She wanted to help, but I wasn't in the mood.

Without looking up, I said, "Go away."

"If you insist," said the witch, whose voice I'd recognize anywhere. My head snapped up to take her in. Samara Wrede was here in my fucking castle. Again. *How* dare *she*?

"You better explain to me what you're doing here before I have every warlock in this plane hunt you down and end you." I was growling, gnashing my teeth as I shot to my feet.

Samara murmured a few words, and her power halted me. "You do not wish for my help?"

381

I was too lost in a rage filled stupor to consider what she was saying. "I think you've already helped enough," I hissed. "If I could, I would draw a lightning bolt from the sky and roast you like you did their father," I said, pointing to where Nighval laid prone carefully tucked beneath a blanket on the small bed he occupied. "Actually," I continued, "I would seize you, and tie you to a spit and roast you like the animal you are and warm my hands by the fire as you screamed."

Something about speaking the imagery made me feel the slightest bit better.

"So, based on your garish comments, am I to understand that you do not want the gift I'm here to offer you?"

"What do you have that I could possibly want?" I asked.

Before I could spit anymore vitriol, she said, simply, "Life."

I glanced from Nighval to Samara. "What do you mean?"

She shrugged nonchalantly, as if we were about to bargain over a sack of grain. "I spoke with him earlier," she said, and for a second, I thought she had fully lost it.

"You did what?" I stuttered.

"When I came here earlier, we spoke. He has been conscious this entire time, aware, listening." She smiled as she stepped toward him, and I moved to step between them, but her magic still had ahold of me. I sent a shocked glance in his direction. His eyes were closed. Ever since she had put him in stasis, they had been open and distant. Fear gripped my throat, and it squeezed so hard I could barely swallow.

"What did you do to him?" I demanded.

"I didn't want him to hear this conversation—"

"He deserves to hear every bit of this conversation. And you mean to tell me his mind has been fully active, but he has been unable to move or communicate?" I asked, sure the dumbfounded expression was apparent on my face.

She nodded, and guilt banged through me like a gong. That meant he had heard every bit of my pain. Knowing him, unable to do anything, unable to comfort me, it must be slowly killing him.

"You are a massive bitch," I said, gnashing my teeth at her.

"I don't expect you to understand my choices, but I would have expected you to be intelligent enough to realize that if I had not done what I had done, his heart would not be beating right now. Furthermore, I wasn't strong enough then to finish bringing him back from the brink. I am now," she said, pushing the sleeves of her black gown up her arms.

"You're insane. None of this would have happened if it weren't for you. He never would have been in that alleyway if it weren't for you," I said.

"And he wouldn't have met you if it weren't for me." Her smile was self-satisfied as she breezed over to him, rendering me unable to move. She touched his chest, smoothing the fabric. "One day, when you have children, you will understand."

Samara Wrede was totally off her rocker if she thought in any way anything she had done made her a good mother. I was readying myself to send another verbal lash her way when electricity crackled through the air, drawing toward her.

"What are you doing?" I asked. Panic clawed down my chest as I struggled against the magical hold she me in.

"As I said, he would have been dead if it weren't for me. And now he will live because of me." Power shimmered in the air, continuing to ripple toward her as she placed her other hand on top of his chest and began chanting. The lights flickered, some of them went out while others popped and flared as their glass bulbs broke.

With the last pop, the room went dark and the light from where her palms touched Nighval flared, and her chanting stopped. Her eyes flashed to mine for a brief second and she said, "Take care of my son."

Samara's body seized violently, like she was having some sort of attack before it went limp. Her hands slid off his chest as her eyes rolled back in her head and she dropped to the floor, her head cracking as it hit the hard stones. The power she was using to hold me back dissolved, and I rushed forward as Nighval lifted off the table, drawing in a massive inhale. He gasped for several seconds as if he were drowning. When he finally caught his breath, his head snapped in my direction.

Then he was on me, running his hands over my hair, across my cheeks, down my shoulders, around my waist and pulling me into him. Then his hands retraced the movements like he couldn't believe I was real. "Avery," He moaned, his voice hoarse and desperate.

"I'm here," I said. "I'm okay."

I stood up on the tips of my toes, trying to kiss him, but he went to his knees, pulling me with him. Cupping my face, he finally gave me the kiss that I had been searching for. At first, it was tentative like I was something breakable, but as I returned his kiss with more urgency it became heated, all-consuming. Savage. His fingers raked up the sides of my skirt and plunged beneath, as if touching my skin was some type of cure he desperately needed.

I pulled away. "Nigh, your mother," I said, pointing to the far side of the bed.

"She's gone," he said, then shot an agitated look toward the two guards getting to their feet at the door. One had a small trickle of blood running down his temple and some bruises already blooming from where his head smacked the floor when Samara incapacitated them. The other appeared unscathed and was only now realizing their king was an animate being once again and on his knees in front of their queen with his hands inside her clothes.

When his eyes tracked back to mine, we shared a grin, and I knew my face had tinted pink.

Nighval stood, pulling me to my feet, and he walked me over to the guards with his arm around my waist, tugging me into his side as if he couldn't bear to remove the contact.

He assessed the bleeding man. "Go take care of your injury. And you," he said, to the other. "Get a message to the council that the king has returned, and I will meet them at first light in the council room. On the other side of the bed, you will find the witch Samara Wrede. Her body should be prepared for funeral rites, so please see to it that she is brought to the morgue. Instruction will follow within the next day. Now I have a queen to attend to."

His commanding presence sent a wave of relief crashing over me. I was no longer alone.

Nighval didn't wait for their response as he directed me out of the room, brushing past them and through the hallway in the direction of our suite.

"She told me she talked to you earlier today," I said, deciding on that line of thought from the dozens that were popping up in my mind.

"She did. She came not long after you had left," he said.

"And?" I asked, nudging his side. "What did she say?"

He grinned as he looked down at me. "First, she took credit for finding you. She told me what she was going to do today and some nonsense about the type of man I was, almost like she was proud she created me. She also told me I am much more powerful than one might expect, but we both know that, don't we?" he teased, giving me a wink, which caused flutters to erupt low in my belly.

As if he sensed my sensations, he said, "Don't worry, sweetheart. We're about to take good care of that."

His words and the feeling of finally coming home after having been without him for two months made my knees weak and, as they nearly buckled, he swooped me up into his arms and carried me the rest of the way.

Light from the full moon danced in through the open window and a breeze blew in, lifting the sheer curtains. Nighval placed me gently on the bed and flipped off the lamp on the nightstand. His pale skin seemed to glow in the moonlight as he tugged his shirt over his head. There wasn't so much as a scar where the arrows had pierced through the flesh of his chest, striking his heart.

He took my feet, slipping off my shoes gently and tossed them to the floor. He crawled across the bed and lifted my shirt over my head, unclasping my bra, pulling it away. He didn't touch, however. He only grabbed the waistband of my skirt and my panties with his fingers and pulled them over my hips and down my legs until I was laying bare before him. I reclined back on the pillows, letting him take in his fill. Letting him see that every inch of me was his.

CHAPTER 64

NIGHVAL

A very reached up with one of her legs and nudged the waistband of my pants with a toe. "This is hardly fair," she said.

I moved off the bed and slowly unbuttoned them, giving her what she asked for like I always would. I wasn't nearly the masterpiece that she was, but if she wanted to see, who was I to deny her?

I rolled my pants down my legs and stepped out, then crawled back across the bed to kneel before her. I hadn't even touched her yet or kissed her since we'd been back in the bedroom, but I was rock hard just from seeing her.

"Did you miss me?" I asked, having witnessed the answer, but I wanted to hear her say it.

"Desperately, but you already know that, don't you?" she said. A glint of melancholy flashed across her perfect face.

"I will never be able to express how sorry I am that you got caught in the crossfire of my family drama. I should have killed her as soon as she arrived. Seeing the way she hurt you, how you suffered every day, I will never forget—"

"Nigh, she was your mother," she said, and her voice held a world of pain for me. "You don't need to—"

"I do, Avery. I need to tell you I will do everything in my power to make this world a better place for you. I'll make up for every tear you cried and replace the ugly memories with something beautiful."

Her face glowed with what could only be love as her eyes glimmered up at me. She sat quietly, waiting for me to finish and when I said no more, she asked, "And how exactly are you going to do that?"

JENNIFER M. WALDROP

I couldn't help but grin because she knew exactly how to play this game. The Goddess had made this woman for me, and I suspected she felt the same way. Even her sentences fit perfectly with mine the way our bodies did. Like we always knew what came next in this easy rhythm we'd found.

I crawled up her body, tracing my fingers up the smooth skin of her legs, up over her hip, her side, the side of her breast and to her neck. I settled my weight on her and gave her the gentlest, heartfelt kiss. Tonight wasn't a claiming, or even about sex, really. This was about finding each other once again, the way we always would. This was about stripping every horrible thing that had happened to us away and starting new. This was healing.

As I kissed her, I rocked my hips gently, pressing my needy erection down into her. She nudged my leg with hers, sliding it under mine and wrapped it around the back of mine so her toes ran up the hair on the back of my calf, like there wasn't a part of me she could stand not to be touching.

I moved my arms under her shoulders so that I could cup her head from behind, and I continued to explore her mouth as I moved against her. It wasn't long before her hands were raking against me, demanding more. I could feel the word on her lips, but I wouldn't let her speak. Her lips belonged to me, not her words.

As I slid against her center, I could feel the warm wet heat gathering there, and I knew she was ready for me. Barely separating our chests, I eased back and pressed into her, catching her moan with my mouth. Her feet pressed into the backs of my legs as she pushed herself on to me, her hands dragging my hips down. I rocked over and over, slow, but relentless. When I finally pulled away so I could see her, I watched the pleasure build on her face.

I had spent two months watching her hurting. I needed to see her feel good. As her eyes fluttered closed and her breathing picked up, I pressed in deeper, knowing it would send her over the edge. Her eyes squeezed shut and the cutest grimace of pleasure crossed her face, and I drove in until she cried out, "Nigh."

I stilled and pressed my forehead to hers to give her a moment to recover. A sheen of sweat coated both of our bodies now and as I moved against her, our skin slid so perfectly against each other's.

Reaching behind her, I got ahold of her knee and pulled it up, pressing it towards the outside of her chest, changing the angle because I needed to be even deeper inside of her. She gasped as I punched into her inner wall. I pressed up onto my hand and kept stroking into her.

"Oh God, Nigh," she moaned. Her face tensed again, and I could feel her inner walls gripping around my shaft. I wanted to last forever, for this never to end, but the sensations were too good. Building too quickly and with each tap against the deepest part of her, delicious prickles erupted from the tip of my cock until I couldn't hold it back any longer.

Pleasure shot straight up my spine as I erupted inside her, in pulsing waves of plane altering bliss.

"I think I transcended space and time," I said, and she laughed. She nestled into me, but I sat up.

"Here, let's get you cleaned up." I went into the bathroom and turned on the water to fill the tub. I found a bottle of stuff that smelled like flowers and sunshine and poured it into the water. Then I picked her up and carried her back, setting her on the counter as we waited for the tub to fill. I grabbed her makeup case, which Link told me he found. I guess he had found time to give it to her while I had been out and my gratitude to my friends swelled once again in my chest.

I rifled through the bag. "Which one of these concoctions will remove your makeup?"

Avery leaned over and pointed to a box of pre-moistened wipes. I pulled one out and it immediately replaced itself, and I shook my head at the witches from her plane. "Close your eyes," I said, and she obeyed. I went to work at first smearing, and then removing all the paint from her face until her beautiful freckles were completely exposed, and I could kiss them, which I did over and over.

"Nigh," she said, giggling. "The tub."

I turned to see the tub was nearly overflowing already, and that was without us in it. But what good was it to be king if I couldn't make a bit of a mess whenever I wanted to? I picked her up off the counter and plopped her into it. Water gushed over the sides, splashing to the ground, and I gathered a selection of products I was more familiar with and set them on the little bench next to it where a washcloth and some fresh towels also sat. Then I climbed in, my large body making even more of a mess of water all over the stone floor.

"Oh my God, I can't believe you did that," she said.

"Believe it, sweetheart," I said, squirting soap onto the cloth and then fished under the water to grab her foot. When I had a hold of it, I tugged her toward me and she slid, her head dipping fully into the water. Whenever she came up, she was sputtering and dashed her hand forward, splashing water in my face.

My hand darted out to grab ahold of hers, and I pulled her toward me, so her chest was against mine and then I went to work, washing her back, then lower until she started squirming against me.

"Stop it," I said. "We just did that. You need to let me take care of you."

She sighed and then rested against me. When I finished, I spun her around and worked on her front, before easing her forward so I could wash her hair. I picked up a jar and a brown mud-like substance was inside. I held it out to her. "What is this?" I asked

She seemed very amused as she said, "That's a face mask." And then her eyebrows shot up. *Oh no.*

She turned around in the tub and dipped her fingers into the jar I extended. She swiped a pass down the right side of my face, and then the left before I could stop her.

I tried to move my face out of her reach, but she grabbed my chin and said, "Stop resisting." When I stilled, she continued, "This is good for your skin. And plenty of men in my plane use products like this."

"My skin is what it is, Avery. And besides, I'm not vain."

She rolled her eyes and continued to spread the mud around on my face. "It's not about being vain. It's about taking care of yourself, and I love your skin exactly how it is. And you deserve to be taken care of, too."

When she was satisfied, she got another scoop and spread it across hers and then, seeming to relish in my discomfort, leaned forward, and kissed me. Then she turned around and laid her head back against my chest, and I wrapped my arms around her.

"How long do we have to leave this stuff on?" I asked. If I were being honest, I could hold her like this until the water became frigid.

"I can't see a clock, but about ten minutes. Then we'll wash it off and put on some serums. Then we can go to bed," she said.

After about five minutes, her breathing became steady, and her head lolled to the side. I waited another five and then gently nudged her. "Avery, wake up."

She looked up at me with a satisfied drowsy expression and let me wipe off the mud from both of our faces with a fresh washcloth. I got out of the tub, and lifted her, dried both of us off and allowed her to direct me about the potions. After the fourth one and her submission to my waning patience, she let me tuck her into bed.

I had never bathed a woman, but something about taking care of Avery that way was perfect. I had a feeling it was something I was going to want to do regularly, and not only for the unfettered access it gave me to her body. My beautiful wife deserved all the care that I could give her. Now that Samara was gone, and she confirmed what I had suspected for a long time, I'd use every extra ounce of power gifted to me by the goddess to give my queen the happy memories she deserved.

CAROLINE THE CRUEL

CHAPTER 1

"Hold still, Cara." Emmy giggled, raising the stolen tailor's shears awkwardly hooked around her adolescent fingers at Caroline's temple making her tremble. "If I give you a jagged crop because you're wiggling, it's your own fault."

Emmy's bright blue eyes met Caroline's silver in the large, gilded mirror they sat in front of. Mischief lit Emmy's features, and a self-indulgent smile crept across her sun-speckled face. The all-too-familiar expression sent a flood of dread charging through Caroline's limbs, which crashed into the walls of her stomach before settling there in a gurgling pool.

"Please, Emmy. I don't want to cut my hair." Fat tears dripped down Caroline's pale face as chunks of her onyx locks floated down to the floor.

"Stop crying." Emmy poked her in the shoulder with the point of her scissors, eliciting a cry. "This is your punishment. You chose. I'll give you a cut, or I'll tell father what you did to Cook."

Hot shame burned on Caroline's damp cheeks and her mind drifted.

Her and Emmy had made a game of forcing their cooks to eat the meals which dissatisfied them, heaping on seconds and thirds until the cooks were rubbing their protruding bellies and dripping with perspiration. The punishment, which had been Caroline's idea, was an effective tactic to improve the quality of their food.

It wasn't her fault the entire kitchen was preoccupied with feeding the envoy from Veetula here for the Peace Ball. Feeding her and Emmy should be a priority. The portly older man they called Cook, who had the unlucky task of feeding them on more days than not, served Caroline a rabbit stew with chewy bits and a flavor that made her insides roll.

Caroline suspected the soup was from the day before—and it hadn't *smelled* spoiled. Before Cook served them, an attendant came and fetched Emmy. *Too convenient.* Emmy's mother, the Queen of Everstal, requested her only daughter's presence, probably to gloat over the blonde-haired princess in front of their foreign guests.

The intuition in Caroline's heart told her that Cook would have never served Princess Emmy day-old soup. She hadn't meant to be vindictive, but when he'd set the bowl down in front of her, pin pricks crawled up her neck to her cheeks and her teeth ached like they might crack, she was clenching them so hard. Cook should have seen Caroline's ire, and replaced the bowl immediately with something more palatable, but he had been too busy to notice.

After one bite, Caroline spit a slimy piece of rabbit on the cold stone tiles and pushed the dish across the table in protest. A passing castle cat called Red jumped down from his perch on a windowsill to inspect the food which had splatted into its domain. The castle cats were blue and orange, speckled and striped, but they were all called Red after Roskide, the red castle which was the crown of Everstal. Red took a sniff of the discarded meat and turned its nose to the ceiling, flicking its tail disappointedly as it sauntered from the room, which set Caroline seething.

"Cook, come over here right now and take your punishment." Caroline stomped her foot twice and crossed her delicate arms across her still flat chest. She motioned with her chin to the steaming bowl and even Cook wrinkled his nose.

With a shaky hand, he picked up the spoon and brought it to his lips, blowing across the contents. Cook shot her a wary glance and slurped the rotten stew.

"All of it," she insisted in the most terrifying monotone a fourteen-year-old girl could muster.

Emmy clicked her scissors open and closed, snapping Caroline out of her memory and back to the present. "Cook had to be taken to the infirmary," Emmy said, prancing around the room, circling Caroline like a shark. "You know what that means, don't you? You need to be punished."

"The infirmary?" Caroline swallowed the knot in her throat. She didn't mean to make him that sick, but he *had* planned to feed her the foul dish.

Cook had been retching whenever she gushed out of the little dining area where he served them their meals. The man hadn't made it two steps past the table before he heaved the contents of his stomach onto the floor. The smell had been too much for her. A guilty little tingle crawled across the back of her shoulders.

Emmy brought the shears in front of Caroline's face with a final clack, closing them a little too close to her nose. "I will give you a choice, Caroline," the older girl said haughtily, pursing her lips into a prim pout. "You can either let me finish your haircut, or I will tell father."

That's how Caroline found herself sitting in front of her half-sister, and all her beautiful onyx locks littering the floor around her feet.

She wiped her clammy palms down her skirts. The motion soothed her rowdy gut, which was still churning from the stew or the debasement, possibly both.

Emmy picked up one of the longer strands and twirled it between her fingers. Then she let a crazed cackle escape. "What is Father going to think? You're no longer his raven-haired love child."

Caroline had favored her mother, the beauty who King Thom Dallimore had taken as a lover on his final campaign against Manula fifteen years ago. He took one look at the raven-haired woman and fell in love. Caroline resulted from their union and when Queen Cerise discovered the king's lover, she sent her own spies to locate the woman, and then she sent an assassin.

King Thom never confirmed it was his own queen who was responsible for the death of his love, but he knew in the way a king knows those things. That unspoken suspicion was why Caroline, his illegitimate daughter, was allowed to live in the keep alongside his other child, Princess Emmaline, his heir. He was the king after all.

His two daughters were opposites in all things: coloring, beauty and in temperament. One girl had the love of her father, the other her mother. One was soft, the other all angles.

Caroline's lovely sister, who was two years older, despised her for having the king's heart. It was a rift she appeared to ignore on most days. And because Emmy was the heir, when it was not *most days*, she was untouchable. She used that advantage against Caroline every chance she got.

Caroline ran her fingers through her shorn hair. It stuck up in little tufts, making her cheekbones poke out even more dramatically and her large silver eyes bug out of her face like an insect. She could only blink at her reflection as numbness eclipsed the searing of the fresh wound given to her by her half-sister.

"I don't know, Emmy. Let's go find out if Father still loves me." Caroline shrugged and pulled her sagging body from the stool. She kicked the hair with the toe of a satin slipper, and put it out of her mind, stomping off in search of the king. Emmaline skipped eagerly behind her.

King Thom was in the training yard when Caroline and her sister found him. Sweat glistened off the brow of the brawny man as he removed a layer of steel plate which he always wore during his sparring sessions.

The patter of footsteps drew the man's attention. Her father lifted his head in the girls' direction as they approached, the start of a grin was replaced by a deep frown. He ran his sturdy hand through the spiky mop that sat atop Caroline's head.

"Oh, sweetheart, what have you done with your beautiful hair?" He sighed, resigned to the antics of children.

Both Caroline and the king had loved her hair. He had told her one night after they had read stories that her hair was exactly like her mother's. A shiny, almost iridescent black, long and stick straight. Heavy, beautiful hair that seemed to absorb all the light and attention it received. It was the one thing that had made her feel pretty, special even. And now it was gone.

Caroline's lip trembled as new tears sprang to her eyes. She tried to tell on Emmaline in the past, but the other girl's mother always came to the rescue. It was no use.

"Oh, don't cry, my darling. It will grow back," the king soothed, petting his daughter.

"But what about the ball tonight?" Caroline brought quaking fingers up to her forehead.

"I suppose we'll have to get you a lovely bonnet," the king teased, testing the resilience of his youngest daughter.

A small grin cracked across Caroline's face before she fell into a giggling fit with her father.

Emmy, who had been quietly observing them, huffed, and stormed out of the training yard.

CAROLINE THE CRUEL

CHAPTER 2

C aroline's pride swelled, making her chest full. Another year had passed with no conflict between Everstal, her father's kingdom, and Veetula, the frozen kingdom to the north. The peace ball represented everything good her father was, the event marking the fifteenth year since King Thom Dallimore had ended the centuries long conflict between the two enemies. No one had believed it possible and now each spring, either Everstal or Veetula would host the other for a full week of gaming, drinking, feasting, and dancing.

It was their turn to host, and while it was typical for the red castle to be covered in roses, for this event Queen Cerise brought in crates of different flowers, fruits and vegetables and commissioned sculptures to be made with the bounty. She was even invited to help, but Caroline decided decorating wasn't her thing. Not that she was going to rebuff the rare kind gesture from the queen.

Caroline almost bumped into a topiary that wasn't usually there. Roskide was in full bloom. She circled the statue plucking a strawberry from a live vine and sunk her teeth into the ripe end. Bright sweetness burst into her mouth mirroring the rush of giddy flutters that lifted her spirits, almost making her forget about her hideous hair.

Caroline tried to catalogue who would be in attendance and which royals would be missing. She would make her father proud and represent Everstal well, even though she was the bastard princess.

Agna, their queen, had four children. Twin girls, Lissa and Leeza, and Natalia, who were married off to princes from far away kingdoms Caroline couldn't pronounce. A fifteen-year-old son, the heir, Jaden, who was rumored to be just as dashing as the other men in the Ivanslohe line, never attended for 'security reasons', which she supposed made sense. And the fertile queen expected another child within months. Carrying a child to full term at her age was a delicate thing, so she was excused.

That left King Hollis in attendance, along with his younger brother, Prince Breicher, and several royal cousins and other important men and women and their families whose names weren't important. Caroline had only gotten brief glances at them, but the rumors had been true. With their blazing sapphire eyes, an Ivanslohe trait which could be seen from across the room, their rugged features, and tall, broad stature, they seemed like warrior princes from a storybook. Butterflies danced in her stomach. One day, she might meet Jaden Ivanslohe, the handsome prince, who was only a year older than her. And since her father had united their Kingdoms, who knew? Maybe one day one of those blue-eyed royals would sweep her off her feet.

Caroline tapped her toes anxiously, unable to stand still as she and Emmy waited on their parents. It was the first time they were allowed to attend the festivities, which culminated in the glamorous dance in Roskide's Great Hall set to open in less than an hour.

Emmy was on the dancefloor, preening before an invisible gentleman, who'd apparently asked her to dance as she was now twirling in his invisible arms. The queen had gone all out for Emmy's attire, having Everstal's finest dressmaker customize a multi-layered, red, chiffon gown befitting a sixteen-year-old princess. Twisted flourishes and sashes adorned the monstrosity. It was supposed to bear a resemblance to one of the thousands of crimson roses that were scattered about Roskide and the surrounding villages, but Caroline thought Emmy looked more like a melting cake.

With each step, Emmy's tightly coiled blonde locks bounced. When she finally ended the dance, she swayed over to Caroline and tugged her wrist. "Come on, Cara. Your hair is fine. The guests will be here soon!" she whined. "Don't you want to dance with me?"

"You were doing fine without me," Caroline said, reaching up to her shorn hair, which her attendant had battled with a curling wand for over an hour earlier. Her stick-straight hair had finally submitted, and the tuffs bowed into each other in submission. At least she was still able to wear the silver rose pins her father had gifted her.

"Stop touching it. You're going to make it worse." Emmy swatted Caroline's hand away from her damaged mop.

"I think Alma singed the ends," Caroline groaned.

"I told you, you should have left it spiky. It was rather interesting that way at least."

"It looked like I'd been struck by lightning."

"Mother says I should apologize. She said a woman's hair is an important part of their identity." Emmy fingered a shiny blonde curl. "So, I guess I'm sorry. Forgive me?"

Emmy's eyes bulged and watered, and her lip gave a little practiced quiver. Caroline had seen her rehearse her apologies and the mock sweetness she delivered them with in the mirror loads of times. She still couldn't hold a grudge for long, though. Caroline always ended up forgiving Emmy. They were sisters, after all.

"It's fine, Emmy. It will grow back," she said, frowning.

"It will." A self-satisfied smirk crossed Emmy's face.

The way her sister could get away with anything grated on Caroline, but she did her best to plaster a fake smile across her face. It was just hair. She should brush it off as casually as Emmy did and not let it get to her.

Emmy perked up. "Good. Oh, see what they've made for us!" She dragged Caroline on the dais where two smaller thrones were sitting adjacent to the king and queens, the latter who'd entered from a discrete door behind the podium.

"Hello, girls," Queen Cerise greeted. "Are you excited about tonight, seeing all the guests in their finery?"

Caroline narrowed her eyes, not ignorant to the fact that the queen had said *girls,* but addressed her inquiry only to her daughter.

"Oh, Mother, do you think they'll love my dress?" Emmy made several twirls, and the cake dress took flight, turning around her in the air.

"No one will be lovelier," Queen Cerise praised her daughter, eyes shining with the pride only a mother could possess.

"What about Caroline?" Emmy prodded, pressing her lips into a prim smile, and gestured for Caroline to spin. Caroline didn't want to spin. She didn't want any more attention than necessary.

"Go on," the queen demanded, mimicking her daughter's circling hand gesture.

Caroline smoothed the simple grey silk that hung limply on her boyish figure and turned in a quick circle. Emmy had developed womanly curves by the time she was fourteen. Caroline had no shape to speak of and was still sprouting toward the sky. Every comparison made between her and Emmy was like a dagger twisting a little deeper into her wounded ego.

"She looks nice, doesn't she?" Emmy pushed. "Besides the hair, of course."

"Caroline looks..." The queen hesitated, wrinkling her brow, searching the room for an escape. "Oh, there you are, dear," she deflected as the king joined his family on the stage.

"What do you think of your thrones, my darlings?" he asked, motioning to the two custom made wooden chairs on either side of his and the queen's.

Emmy sashayed over to hers, surveying it. The king's artisans had carved elaborate blooming crimson roses and thorn-covered hunter vines which appeared to be sprouting from each plank of wood. Gold leaf topped the tip of every petal and thorn. Emmy plopped down, wiggling her butt to settle in the seat, and looked out to the empty room as if she were looking over an awaiting crowd of her subjects. "It's perfect!" She clapped her hands together excitedly.

"Caroline?" King Thom asked, eyebrows raised.

Caroline savored the texture of the smooth wood as she ran her delicate fingers across it. Her throne wasn't as ornate as her sister's. It was taller and narrower, like her, and it would take her years to grow into. Delicate vines crawled up the two three-sided posts, which supported a back panel that was shaped like a diamond.

Other angular shaped geometric patterns were carved into the surface reminiscent of thorns, and a single rose, painted an iridescent black, was carved into the face of the backrest. Silver trimmed the edge of the petals and the linear grooves which ran down the arms and legs of the chair.

It was less elaborate than Emmy's, and she might have thought less effort and cost had gone into making it, but her father had taken great care to instruct the craftsman of its every detail. A tear came to her eye and her heart didn't feel like it could fill any further. Never had she received such a gift.

"You don't like it?" He bent down eye level with his daughter, his heavy brow furrowed in concern, misinterpreting her reaction.

She shook her head. "No, Father, it's perf—"

"Your Majesty, something's not right." A voice echoed across the empty room as Torac, the head commander of Roskide entered with six heavily armed guards at his heels.

Caroline had known the stout commander since she was a child. She couldn't remember when she'd seen Torac so rattled.

"What is it, Torac?" King Thom's ruddy skin turned sallow, causing a chill to run up Caroline's spine.

"The guests seem to be... *missing*. At first, attendants couldn't find them in their rooms, or the gardens. They should have been getting ready for the festivities, but their belongings are gone, too. We spotted a caravan leaving the city." Torac flexed his hand over his short sword as he paced before his liege.

"And no one noticed?!" Queen Cerise demanded. She gathered her skirts in a white knuckled grip and turned toward her husband.

Swearing under his breath, King Thom rushed over to one of the lower, narrow windows in the Great Hall of Roskide. The castle was built into and atop a sagging mountain peak overlooking a wide bay and the harbor city to the south. To the north, rolling vineyards and farmland stretched to the river which separated the kingdoms.

The Dallimore family took advantage of the strategic hilltop location, carving caves and tunnels through the mountain under Roskide in a fashion that the deeper one ventured into its belly, the more lost they might become should they not know the way. The design had kept many Everstal royals safe over the years, and the king and queen had schooled the girls on its intricate, winding layout since they were children. In Roskide, hide and seek took on a whole other level of difficulty.

Caroline peeked over the ledge around her father's shoulder to see the dust being kicked up at the gates by a fleet of horses and carriages, leaving the city at a pace which suggested they were fleeing. How they'd been able to get outside of the sphere of the king's power without detection, she couldn't conceive. It had been the use of the Gift, the ability of the ruling

Dallimore to seize the will of another, which had stopped the war. By King Thom's actions alone, they had fifteen years of peace and prosperity between the kingdoms. To Caroline, her father was only second to the Gods. All powerful, undefeatable. To see him in a panic like this—

King Thom spun, grabbing Caroline by the arm, his grip wrenching a whimper from her lips. "Run, hide!" he commanded as he released her, shoving her toward Emmy.

Stomach flip flopping, Caroline followed her older sister across the room, and behind the dais toward a favorite escape tunnel they frequented during their games. A booming groan stopped them short. Caroline glanced back to see a ruby-toned dagger protruding from deep in her father's shoulder.

Rosenwood. Any other blade could wound a Dallimore, but with a weapon crafted from rosenwood, a wound would be fatal. Even if it didn't hit anything vital.

A chilly hand wrapped around Caroline's wrist, tugging. "Come on, Cara," Emmy pleaded as she ducked through the opening.

"But what about Father?" Caroline whispered as she followed Emmy into the tunnel.

"Don't worry about Father. He'll use his power to compel them to turn themselves in. This will be over soon." Emmy's voice shook, betraying her confidence, and silent tears flowed down Caroline's waxen face as she crawled after her sister through the narrowing passageway.

All Caroline could see was the red of that dagger as they ran, taking little used pitch-black corridors beneath Roskide in which even they became lost from time-to-time. Had Emmy not seen it?

"Ouch!" Emmy cried, as a thud sounded in the cramped space. Her sister ran headfirst into the underside of one of the many stairways that dipped over tunnel sections here and there. "It's the stair over the west passage. We missed the opening. Turn around. It must be close."

Caroline ran her fingers across the cool stones, searching for the insignificant crack which split the wall right above the alcove, a spot

Emmy defaulted to when she was being lazy at their little game. Hiding spots were bound to be repeated, but due to how difficult this one was to find, it was a favorite of Emmy's.

"It's here," Caroline whispered.

The girls squatted down and tucked in deep. Caroline leaned against Emmy, trying to stave off the chill of the subterranean passageway and her chattering teeth.

They sat for what felt like hours, unflinching, barely letting a breath escape. The silence would have been deafening if it weren't for Caroline's roaring heart. How could one be so cold, but sweat at the same time?

"We should probably split up," Emmy said, finally breathing.

"Shhhh..." Caroline hissed.

"Wouldn't Father have come to find us by now? Or at least sent Torac?" Emmy's voice was feebler than Caroline had ever heard it, causing the sick feeling twisting her insides to wring even tighter. "What if something happened to him? And I'm the only living Dallimore. You should go—to distract them."

"He'll come. We just need to stay here."

Footfalls sounded from the direction of the overhead stair. An ominous sense caused Caroline's trembling to begin anew. If the source of the sound were friendly, they wouldn't be taking such care to be silent. It wasn't her father.

Soon, breathing accompanied the steps, and as they approached the crack that the crevice laid beneath, they stilled. Caroline's heart jumped into her throat, and she swore the hammering was audible. She reached back to grab Emmy's hand, hoping for her sister's reassurance, but Emmy had tucked herself impossibly far back in the little cave, leaving Caroline between her in the opening.

"I can smell your fear, little princess. I can hear your breathing."

Caroline swallowed. Trying to still her pumping lungs, realizing the man only thought he'd found one of them. Emmy must be holding her breath. She should have done that, too. How stupid could she be?

"Come out, come out." The sound of steel dragging across the stones set Caroline's nerves alight. So much so that she didn't feel the toe of a boot land on the small of her back until it was too late.

No, Emmy wouldn't.

A scream tore from her lips as she burst from the cave with a thrust from behind.

How could Emmy do this? Give her own sister over without a fight. The betrayal stung harder than the smack of her cheek against the chilly stone as she hit the wall opposite the hiding spot. Hands swiped in the dark, grasping for her, as she scrambled with all her might to escape their clutch.

Getting to her feet, Caroline leaped in the opposite direction and started running. She was quick and nimble, she reminded herself as she sprinted. And she had the maze beneath Roskide memorized in the same way other children had the passages of sacred texts memorialized in their mind. She had a chance.

Heavy thuds followed her down the tunnel, gaining on her. Caroline spun down a corridor, but the man whipped around just as fast behind her. A meaty hand smacked into the top of her head as he reached for her, trying to snatch a fist full of hair but coming up short, and she shrieked.

Caroline came upon a set of stairs descending to a lower level and she paced down them, taking two at a time until she came to a platform. She took off as soon as she hit the landing, keeping her hands in front so she wouldn't crash into a wall in the dark.

Her fist smashed into a corner, sending a jolt of pain up her arm, and a cry escaped before she could stifle it. The man chuckled from too close behind her.

Fingers grazed the back of her silver gown, and the next swing hit higher up, landing on the base of her neck. A strong hand gripped down hard, halting her course, and jerking her around to press her face first into a wall.

She was gasping from the running, or the fear, or both. The blood soaring in her ears echoed and drowned out all other sounds. Convulsions wracked her body. Wait, the rattling was coming from the man gripping her neck.

"Answer me!" he demanded, wrenching her away from the wall so he could shake her more thoroughly.

"I can't—" she eked out between shallow breaths.

"Where's your sister?" The man's voice was as gruff as his grip on Caroline, which tightened in emphasis. She was incapable of responding, so he dragged her down the passageway. As they made their way through the maze under Roskide, Caroline's panicked breathing evened, and clarity slowly cleared the mist of her fright clouded mind. She wouldn't make it easy for this man. *This assassin.*

He was going to kill her anyway, and if he had found them in the hidden tunnels, it meant the Ivanslohe's had uncovered Roskide's secrets or there was a traitor amongst them.

Caroline thrashed under the man's grip, swinging, and flailing her arms, connecting a few slaps against his solid flesh. He grunted as the back of her hand connected with what she assumed was his jaw.

"I see you've recovered," he said.

The assassin gripped the scruff atop Caroline's head, jerking back so hard a bolt of white-hot lightning shot down her neck. "Where is she?" he demanded again, breathing acrid air into her face. Caroline couldn't see him, but this assassin was a foul creature. "Show me her little hiding spot, bastard, and I may let you live."

"We separated," Caroline forced out, then gurgled a cry as the man's grip tightened on her hair, making fresh tears burst from her eyes. "I swear. She made me go this way."

Heavy breathing engulfed her as the man considered her answer. "Where did she run off to?" he growled, slamming her back into the wall and wrapping a hand around her throat before Caroline could suck in a breath.

She raked her claws down the assassin's arms, feeling skin and blood gather under her fingernails, but he didn't ease the vice-like grip he had on her throat. Her lungs burned, and she was becoming light-headed. He was going to kill her. That was the moment she understood her father was dead. Which meant the queen was dead too. She wasn't sure if the lack of air or the grief flooding through her would kill her first.

Her arms and legs slackened, and the assassin's meaty hand was the only thing keeping Caroline pinned to the wall.

King Thom should have been able to use the Gift to stop the assassins. That one of them was slowly suffocating her could only mean one thing. Emmy, her half-sister, who had shoved her out into the passageway as bait for their enemy, was now queen.

Upon the ruling Dallimore's death, the Gift, the ability to take another's will as your own—to compel, would pass to the succeeding ruler. It was the gift to the Dallimore's from the Gods, and the price they demanded was paid eagerly in exchange for such a power, though the king never shared with Caroline what the Gods demanded in return.

Surely Emmy would feel her new power and come save her. Caroline's eyes rolled back in her head, and she used the last bit of strength she had to reach up and tap her lips.

"Good girl," the man said, releasing her.

Caroline crumpled to the ground, gasping for breaths. *Time.* She had to buy herself some time, but her mind was a torrent of conflicting thoughts.

She pushed you into the hallway. She might as well have left you for dead.

No, Caroline, she chastised herself. If Emmy were queen, it would be Caroline's duty to sacrifice herself to save her sister.

But they could have stayed hidden in that alcove. They both could have lived, and the man towering above her would have eventually given up, or Emmy could have used her power against him. Even if he'd heard them, it was pitch black and sound reverberated in the tunnels, so it was a challenge to tell where the sounds originated from. He couldn't have known he was right above them.

The heel of his boot crashed into her side, making her cry out, interrupting the war raging inside her mind. "Talk, girl," he said. "I'm losing patience."

"She's gone to the treasury. It's the safest place."

"Take me there." Fabric ripped as he grabbed the bodice of her gown and yanked Caroline to her feet. "Move!"

Caroline's lip trembled as she stumbled to her feet. "I don't know the way," she lied. "I'm a bastard, remember?" She hoped he would find that plausible, though it would likely lead to her death. A Dallimore would live, though, and Everstal would have a ruler, even if it was her traitorous sister.

"I don't believe you. Take me to the treasury. Now!" he growled.

Metal scraped, the clang reverberating off the stones, seemingly a favorite scare tactic of his. The assassin tapped it twice when it didn't elicit the expected response and pressed a sharp point into Caroline's back. The stinging bite right below her shoulder blade caused an involuntary step forward.

Emmy could still come.

Something otherworldly crawled across Caroline's skin, and she gave a violent shiver, trying to shake the sensation off. She failed, and the hole bored into her core, and buried itself deep in the pit of her stomach where her deepest breath came from. It was an unfamiliar fullness that almost made her gag with its relentless churning. Was it some sort of twisted knowing that happened right before you died?

The assassin used the weapon to prod her along toward what he believed was Emmy's hiding spot. As she led him through the maze of Roskide, far away from the new queen, it occurred to Caroline that Emmy was not coming for her. The heaviness that inched up your throat right before you retched swirled upward from her gut. She didn't care if her sister would be queen. If the situation were reversed, she would have gone for Emmy. That's what sisters do.

Later, Caroline would look back on this moment and wonder if that was when her heart had turned black, or if it had been the second the heel of her sister's boot touched the small of her back. Caroline was on her own. There was no one coming to save her. Not her father, not Torac, commander of the guard, or her older sister who now carried the Gift, the Power of Kings—a gift to the Dallimore's from the Gods.

With a thought, Emmy could have forced her captor to impale himself on his own blade. Bitterness wrenched her insides as she took another turn through the labyrinth. Six more steps in the dark, then stairs. The thud of the assassin stubbing his foot against the first step sounded. He grunted in pain, momentarily letting his blade drop.

Caroline gritted her teeth. She could run. This was her chance while he was distracted. *Run.* Caroline flew up the stairs. The assassin didn't know the way through the tunnels. She would be faster this time. A streak of sunlight refracted around a corner ahead, one of the few places in the tunnels that snaked near the outside walls of Roskide, far away from the underground vault where the treasury of Everstal was hidden. Her captor would know she'd been leading him astray as soon as he saw the light.

There was a fork in the tunnel that laid ahead at the top of the stairs. The assassin's footsteps were falling behind as she chased up the narrow, winding staircase. She was small enough that she didn't need to duck, giving her an advantage over her assailant. Caroline's bare feet nimbly gripped the slick stones as she crested the last steps, taking two at a time.

A figure stepped out of the darkness, and she crashed into it, stumbling back, catching herself against a wall before she tumbled down the stairs.

"What do we have here?" a new voice slithered across her skin.

Caroline took in the second assassin, who stood before her in the reflected light. He was a narrow man, scars crisscrossing his neck and black paint covered his eyes, nose, and mouth, leaving the rest of his gaunt face in stark contrast. He wore a black tight-fitting one-piece which covered everything up to his neck. A black mask sat pulled up, resting on his forehead. The new assassin licked his lips and twirled a small dagger in his hand, and a shiver flittered up Caroline's neck.

"She's not for you, Servius. Hollis wants this one alive," the larger assassin, who wore the same black attire, huffed as he came up behind her, clamping down on the back of her neck once again.

He spun her around and pulled her toward him so they were eye to eye, and Caroline startled at the brilliant blue of his eyes. The royals from the northern kingdom of Veetula had vibrant blue eyes, like the clearest mountain lake, but up close, they almost glowed with their own innate light. She'd seen them from a distance, that defining characteristic, but she didn't realize even assassins might carry the trait, or a royal might be an assassin.

"You've been leading me in circles," he hissed.

Caroline clenched her jaw tightly, refusing to answer. They would not end her life after all, so why should she speak?

As if reading her thoughts, the first assassin said, "Just because I'm not going to kill you, doesn't mean I can't make you wish you were dead." A seedy grin crept across his blunt features, and any hope Caroline had melted away.

Grubby fingers dug into her skin, and he directed her toward the narrow window the light was filtering in through. She fought, kicking, flailing wildly as he picked her up and shoved her head-first through the opening. Screaming pain shot up her legs as her knees scraped over the exposed edges of the broken stones, and her stomach dropped as she free-fell over the edge.

At the last second, she jolted upward as the larger assassin's firm grip sealed around her ankles. Front-facing, she slammed into the rose-vine-covered wall. Dagger-like thorns of the historic rose bushes, a symbolic feature wrapping Roskide in a blanket of flowering vegetation year-round, dug into her flesh and her whole body sparked in agony.

Wind howled, whipping around over the turrets and across the rounded wall she dangled from. Her silver dress slipped down, bunching around her torso, and she had to grab the gown so it wouldn't slip entirely off her shapeless form.

"You will lead me to your sister. We will not leave this castle until we can deliver her lifeless body, along with that of King Thom and Queen Cerise, to our sovereign."

Tears streaked down Caroline's cheeks as fast as the hate filling her heart. The rage consumed her so fully she barely felt the tiny rivulets of blood trickling across her throbbing skin from the scratches inflicted upon her by the thorns. She peeled open her eyes and surveyed her options.

Directly beneath her, a crimson rose was splayed open in full bloom. She wrinkled her nose in disgust, the horrible flower causing the image of her sister and that hideous dress to flash through her mind. A single drop of her red blood dripped down onto its petals before sliding off to journey down the woody vines.

It was told the creeping vegetation was what kept the aging castle held together, but that was only a folktale. Still... Caroline reached out, grabbing ahold of a vine, testing it to see if it might hold her weight. If she could free her legs from the assassin's grip, she might be able to shimmy down the vines like a ladder and escape.

She squeezed her hands around the thick, crawling stalks, stifling a sob as the thorns pierced her palms. She yanked. They held firmly affixed to the wall. It was worth the risk, she assessed, so she began kicking anew, slapping her ankles together, hoping the man's knuckles would smack and he'd lose his grip.

"Haven't had enough?" he growled at her, shaking her up and down.

She couldn't repress the scream that ripped from her throat as fresh cuts and scrapes raked across her body. Then he was pulling her back up inside the window.

The first assassin planted her back on her feet, and she swayed, disoriented from hanging upside down for so long.

"If you don't cooperate, it will be Servius's turn." The larger guard, whose name she hadn't learned, patted his blade against the other assassin's chest.

Servius grinned, exposing a row of gleaming white teeth trimmed with metal brackets attaching somewhere in the shadowed cavern of his mouth, which added pointed edges to the six teeth across the top. The gesture was effective in its intent and Caroline could feel the color drain from her skin.

Servius tapped his foot anxiously as he waited for her to give him a reason to strike. His muddy eyes were hungry, though she wasn't sure for what. That prospective horror made her tremble, then step back. The assassin ran his palms down his black clad thighs, leaving a darkening trail of moisture behind them.

Caroline's heart seized up. She tried to move, but her body clung glued to the wall and her heavy, panic-filled limbs remained stationary. Opening her mouth, she tried to speak, tried to raise a hand to point. Hot shame battled with sticky dread. This was why she could never have been the heir. Her fear had frozen her.

Servius stepped forward, placing his hands on either side of Caroline, boxing her in. He leaned his head down and ran his nose across the exposed skin of her neck which the dress's tiny straps didn't cover, breathing her scent. With his next excruciatingly slow pass, hot metal grazed her skin and a wet tongue trailed it, tasting the sweat and blood dotting her flesh.

Caroline closed her eyes. If she could not escape, if she could not save herself, she would do so inside her mind. Lock herself away in her imagination. She would envision herself as the type of woman, powerful, like her father, who could have easily taken down these two assassins standing before her, well within the range of his power.

She imagined hurting them like they hurt her. Relished in the thought of exacting retribution on them. Caroline and Emmy had always giggled at the torments and pranks they inflicted on their attendants, the cooks and gardeners, their teachers, and tailors. They had never been truly cruel. Until now, Caroline wouldn't have understood what being truly cruel even meant.

Searing heat scored across her shoulder, bringing her out of her dream into the present. She gritted her teeth and squeezed her eyes tight, redoubling the effort. Caroline thought of that sharpened edge of the blade carried by the first assassin. How sweet it would feel to drag it across his throat and watch the warm blood flow out of his neck.

No. Her father would have compelled the other assassin to do the work for him. Then turn the blade against himself. Imagining their death might be the only way she'd survive this torture. The way the larger man would slip the blade out from its sheath, the sound the metal on metal would make—she could almost hear it.

So quietly, he would slip behind Servius while he was engrossed in marring her delicate skin. The assassin would wrap his hand across the other man's forehead, yank him backward, and run the weapon across Servius's exposed throat.

Hot liquid squirted across Caroline's face, and she opened her eyes to see the wide eyes of Servius clawing at the ruby gash on his neck. Caroline darted her gaze around the hallway, searching for her sister.

She had come. How had she known where to find her?

She almost started crying anew, relieved that she was no longer alone, but her sister was nowhere in sight. It was impossible. *Unless you had taken blood of the person you meant to command, your target must be within your line of sight.* It's how someone had thrown the rosenwood dagger which struck her father, from some carefully concealed location.

The first assassin took two startled steps back, trying to shake the blade free from his hand. Servius slumped to the floor, lifeless. Caroline gripped the wall for support, but weak knees buckled beneath her, and she slid down to rest in the blood pooling around the dead assassin.

She looked up and met the horrified gaze of her original captor.

It couldn't be. The man before her struggled to escape the force pinning him to the spot. She glanced down at the body in front of her, then back up at the man. And grinned.

Experimentally, she imagined him raising the weapon just a little. His jerky hand elevated. Caroline surveyed the cuts and scrapes across her tattered body, and reached a hand up, touching the torn skin at her neck. Her hand came away red.

The sour smell of piss brought her attention back to the first assassin. A dark stain covered the front of his pants, and he was visibly seething between bouts of shaking.

"If it makes you feel any better, I don't think either of us expected today to end this way." Caroline huffed a laugh, which grew in strength as she pushed herself up the wall and onto unsteady feet.

This time, when she imagined what she did with the knife, she did not close her eyes.

The assassin let out a forced breath as he pressed the blade deep into his belly. Caroline stepped out of the way, around the dead body to allow the man to climb up on the window ledge. He stole one last glance at her, fear blazing in his blue eyes, before he threw himself over.

Caroline reached a shaky hand down and picked up Servius's dagger, forcing her damaged palm around it. She clenched it to her breast as she made her way down the winding steps.

If this power had passed to her instead of Emmy, what did it mean? Was her sister still alive? Were there other assassins?

An emptiness, like hunger but far more corroding, pulsed at the space above her navel. Only a few steps taken, and she was out of breath. After she'd tripped for a third time, Caroline decided it would be safest to sit on the steps for a moment to make sense of what had happened and wait for her energy to renew. Just for a moment, she told herself.

CAROLINE THE CRUEL

CHAPTER 3

C aroline winced as she blinked her eyes open. Blinding white light shone down upon her, and she raised her hand to shield her eyes while they adjusted.

"The new heir," an ethereal voice whispered.

"Indeed," another answered.

Caroline dusted herself off as she scrambled to her feet, assessing her gore covered body. Her silver dress was soiled with dirt, blood, and little tears from the rose thorns. And she was still oozing in places, which opened as she moved.

Wrinkling her brow, she touched the wound at her neck, then glanced up to the five figures sitting on simple stone benches in a semicircle around her. Could there have been something on Servius's metal teeth, a poison? Was that why she'd gotten so tired after she'd killed them both?

Her eyes peeled back as realization struck and she stumbled a few steps away from them. She surveyed the Gods, for that was surely who was before her. "Am I dead?"

They were eerily similar in appearance and appeared neither male nor female. All clad in white draping robes, pale ivory hair pulled back from their alabaster faces. Gaunt cheeks, pale pink lips, and small straight noses. The strangest thing was their eyes. Five pairs of the palest platinum pupiless eyes stared back at her, the irises so faint they almost blended in with the whites. Long ivory eyelashes surrounded them and fluttered as they blinked.

The only apparent difference between them was the amulet that hung on the silver chain around each of their necks, though she wasn't near enough to get a glimpse of the symbols on each. She had learned enough about the Gods to understand that they must represent the five orders: Life, Death, Justice, Pain, and Love.

One by one, they cocked their heads to the side, then glanced between themselves as if they did not understand her.

"Am I dead?" she repeated, a little more firmly.

The first one huffed a laugh under its breath. Another mimicked the sound, then a cacophony of flittering laughter filled the nearly vacant, colorless space...

To continue the story, get your copy of Caroline the Cruel available on kindleunlimited, paperback, and special edition hardcover.

At fourteen she was left for dead. At fifteen she raised an army. At sixteen she took back her kingdom.

Ten years after the most unlikely fate, Caroline the Cruel rules with the Gift and her wits.

An enemy lurks right under her nose, ready to finish what his family set in motion. But Caroline won't be as easy to kill. She won't forgive and forget. There will be no peace celebrations between the two warring kingdoms. She won't be lulled to sleep like her father.

Caroline, the bastard princess turned queen, will do whatever it takes to keep Everstal from teetering into chaos. Even as a new guard is introduced into the rotation who makes her question her ways which are what has stood between her and total destruction.

Caroline the Cruel is an enemies to lovers fairytale romance about a morally grey queen and the man who loves her despite everything he's been taught. You can expect spice that builds throughout with a HEA payoff at the end.

The Joined Kingdoms Novels can be read as a series or as standalone fantasy romance books that feature a different couple in each. Perfect for fans of Danielle L. Jensen, Elise Kova and Tricia Levenseller.

ALSO BY JENNIFER M. WALDROP

Realm of the Skyborne

ACKNOWLEDGMENTS

Dear Reader, Thank you from the bottom of my heart for taking the time to read *THE RAT KING*. I hope you enjoyed Avery and Nighval's love story—I had a ton of fun writing it.

If you enjoyed the *The Rat King*, even a little, I would be honored if you went to Amazon, The Storygraph, or Goodreads and left a review. I know leaving a review can be time consuming, but it helps us indie authors more than you know and may help other readers become exposed to our work.

If you enjoyed my writing and like unique worlds or morally grey heroines, then you might be interested in my other work, Skyborne Series (*Realm of the Banished*, and *Realm of the Skyborne*), and *Caroline the Cruel* both available on kindle**unlimited**, paperback, and hardcover.

I want to say thank you to a few very special people whose support, insight and feedback was invaluable to me in the writing and publishing process.

First, I have a question. Have you ever worked with someone who you inspired you to think, *Man, that person really knows what they're doing*? Well, that is what working with editor and book coach Casey Harris-Parks of heart full of ink is like. I gave Casey *The Rat King* for developmental edits at 96,000 words, and through that round and the line edits, we added another 32,000 words to the project and I couldn't be happier with the result. It is such a breath of fresh air to work with someone who makes you feel like they are invested in the collaborative effort of the project, so **THANK YOU, Casey!** You rock and I look forward to working with you on many more novels in the future.

Finally, I am grateful to have worked proofreader Belle Manuel again for this fourth novel. She continues to deliver excellent results.

ABOUT THE AUTHOR

Jennifer is an artist, small business owner and author of new adult adventure fantasy and fantasy romance books. She holds a Bachelor of Fine Arts with a minor in Art History from the University of Central Oklahoma. Jennifer enjoys creating and paints with that same imaginative stroke throughout her writing.

When she's not writing, you might find her whipping together her favorite dark chocolate mousse, power walking a beach in a tropical destination, or lost in the minutia of one of her excel spreadsheets. Jennifer lives with her husband and two dog children in Oklahoma City.

Find me on:

Instagram @authorjmwaldrop

TikTok @authorjmwaldrop

www.jennifermwaldrop.com

CPSIA information can be obtained
at www.ICGtesting.com
Printed in the USA
BVHW071108121122
651766BV00004B/131